Also By
HEATHER BARTLESON

The Blue Series

Carolina Blue
Blue Blood

Coming Soon

Blue Moon

Ethereal Mutation Productions, LLC

Ethereal Mutation Productions, LLC

979-8-9898335-4-2 (Ebook)
979-8-9898335-5-9 (Paperback)
979-8-9898335-6-6 (Hardcover 5.5x8.5)

Book Cover by Ethereal Mutation Productions, LLC
Graphic Artist: Heather Bartleson

Published by Ethereal Mutation Productions, LLC
etherealmutation.com

First edition 2024

To Derek,

Yup, I decided to dedicate this book to you too,
Life is Short, Make it Sweet.

. . . and I still Love You More.

Chapter One

Time was a funny thing. It tended to move forward at the speed of light, leaving me wondering where it had gone. Yet, at any given second, it could stop on a dime. Sometimes, I blinked and wondered how I had gotten somewhere, having no idea of the steps I had taken. Other times, it was a moment so overpowering that my brain just seemed to move in slow motion...either that or I *wished* it would.

I was having one of those moments right now. One I would love to slow down and record so I could watch it again and again. Wait, this was the twenty-first century. Where the heck was my cell phone? I looked around wildly but didn't see it anywhere nearby.

With a grumble of annoyance, I peered out from behind the book I was pretending to read, gazing at the man bent over on the beach in front of me. He wore nothing but a pair of light running shorts that hugged every curve of his perfect backside. Moonlight glinted off the strong, sleek muscles of his back and massive arms, covered in a fine sheen of sweat. Practically salivating, I watched him drop to the sand and execute another series of pushups, sit-ups, and lunges.

I sighed.

I think I need a new hobby. Either that, or I need to get laid. Who am I kidding? I need both.

"You know, I can feel your eyes on me." I dipped my head behind my book, causing him to chuckle. "You could always join me."

I shuddered at the thought. As tempting as he was, exercise and I didn't see eye-to-eye. Though I engaged in it when I had to—which was way more often than I'd like—it was usually accompanied by a lot of whining and grumbling. He turned toward me, and my gaze traveled of its own volition over the sculpted lines of his chest and down over his tight abs before following that defined V to the edge of his low-riding shorts. I shuddered again, but this time for a different reason.

"Blue..." His voice had deepened, and it caressed my skin.

My gaze jerked back to his, my cheeks flushing. "Sorry. Um...I'm good. I've got my book here to keep me occupied." I held it up as if it were a barrier that could help me keep my hands to myself. "You just go on with..." My attention diverted to a drop of sweat weaving its way down his chest, sliding over each taut muscle. Shaking myself again, I sucked in a breath and pulled on my willpower. "Whatever it was you were doing."

He chuckled again while shaking his head and bounded up the steps. Dropping a quick kiss on the top of my head, he opened the back door. "I'm going to take a shower."

He eyed me suggestively, but I just nodded, refusing to look at him. I tried to force my brain away from the picture it immediately started to create of him standing in the shower with the water flowing over his naked body. He smirked, easily able to read my thoughts, then headed inside.

Dammit.

Why couldn't I figure out how to block him from my mind like I could with everyone else? Slamming my book onto my lap, I crossed my arms over my chest and stewed. Well, I pretended to anyway. I mean, really, who was I trying to kid? I wasn't actually angry. I didn't mind Keane being in my head ninety-nine percent of the time. I smiled ruefully. It was just that one percent I wished I could sometimes keep to myself.

Dropping my hands to my lap, I absently stared at my book, marveling at how much life had changed in such a short time. Not five months ago, I had been like everybody else. I had a job I loved, a core group of good friends, and a solid grasp on life.

Enter the Fae. A group of otherworldly beings with a myriad of mystical abilities who just happened to live alongside the human race without us even being aware of their existence. And as it turned out...I was one of them.

My introduction to the Fae world had not been easy, to say the least. I had been forced to participate in an archaic tradition called the Trials. A dangerous set of games with a weighty prize: becoming Queen of the Moon Tree Clan and the wife of Tristan, the King of the Fairies. I had only recently recovered from that *lovely* experience—at least physically. Mentally, I was still trying to come to terms with everything. Not only the fact that I wasn't human but also that I was an all-powerful Fairy with a side of godly powers.

Slouching in my lounge chair, I watched through half-closed eyes as the ocean waves crawled gently to the shore. My treacherous thoughts irrevocably led me back to Keane and the temptation to go and join him in the shower. I shook my head resolutely and picked up my book again, trying to concentrate on the words in front of me. After reading the same paragraph for the fifth time, I thumped the hardback shut and set it aside in frustration.

It was no use. I'd been having a hard time controlling my damn libido of late, and tonight was proving especially challenging. Though we had gotten close over the past few months—including sleeping in the same bed—I had yet to have sex with Keane.

When everything went down after the Trials, I needed weeks to recover. Keane had been patient and never forced the issue, though he never let an opportunity pass to tease me with glimpses of what I was missing. And it was slowly driving me insane, which I was positive was his plan. I wasn't exactly sure why I was still holding back—I wanted him as much as he wanted me.

Obviously.

But something about the Vaimpír society's view on our soulbond weighed on my mind. A soulbond was a sacred bond that usually only occurred between two Vaimpír who'd magically joined their souls. Considering I wasn't part of the seven Vaimpír houses—or even technically Vaimpír—it was unheard of for a bond to form between us.

Hence why Keane was seeking approval from within the Vaimpír society—specifically from his parents. I was worried that if we didn't get the okay, Keane would decide to release our bond. And if our relationship progressed further than it already had, I was afraid the rejection would tear me apart.

Keane stepped back onto the porch, smelling of clean, masculine soap and his unique dark scent. It reminded me of the ocean wind on moonlit summer nights when you could practically smell the electricity in the air from an impending storm. It was a dangerous combination. I groaned inwardly and ducked down further in my chair.

After running his fingers through his wet hair like some kind of *GQ* model at a photo shoot, he folded his large frame into the chair next to mine. I studiously avoided looking at the generous expanse of muscle encased in a tight, black T-shirt and snug jeans that hugged...well, everything.

Keane's lips tugged up at the corners of his mouth, but he didn't bother to comment on my thoughts. "I just talked to my father. We're going to have dinner with him and my mother on Friday."

I felt my heart skip a beat before it stuttered forward, tripping over itself a few times before finally evening out. To say I was nervous about meeting Keane's parents would be the understatement of the year. Not only were they the head of the most powerful family in the Fae world, but they also happened to be the King and Queen of the Vaimpír. I wasn't sure how they would react to the fact that their son—the Dark Prince—had formed a bond with me, a mere Fairy. However powerful I might be.

Keane reached over and squeezed my hand. "Relax, Blue, they'll love you. And you know as well as I do that you're not just a mere Fairy. If you were, this,"—he gestured between the two of us—"wouldn't even be possible."

"Do you think they know about our bond already?"

He shrugged a shoulder and settled back into his chair before closing his eyes. "Most likely. I'm sure Jasmine ran right to my mother and told her the minute the Moon Tree Clan released her."

"Why would your mother have anything to do with the woman who cheated on you right before your wedding?"

Keane let out a long-suffering sigh. "My mother, for whatever reason, still believes what Jasmine told her about being under a spell that night. I think it has more to do with the information Jasmine provides than anything else. Regardless, Mother refuses to believe Darrius that Jasmine had been pursuing him for months prior to it happening, so a spell is unlikely. Needless to say, my brother and mother aren't on the best of terms."

I shook my head. "To be expected, considering he's only your half-brother through your father."

Keane opened one eye to peer over at me with a grin. "True. It does, however, make for interesting family dinners." He wriggled his brows.

I held back a smile not wanting to encourage him. "Will Darrius be there on Friday?" I was still surprised at how much better Keane and Darrius's relationship had been of late. Due to the Jasmine incident, they hadn't spoken for years. Until recently.

Keane chuckled and closed his eye again. "No, he's currently on a mission for King Barracus."

"What about Sabrianna?" Darrius was Sabrianna's personal bodyguard, and I couldn't imagine him leaving her for any extended period.

"I believe she went with him."

I wondered how Sabrianna was doing. We had become quite close during the Trials, but I hadn't talked to her since they ended. I actually hadn't spoken with *any* of the Fae since that night—aside from Keane, of course. Not that they hadn't reached out. I had at least a dozen messages from Tristan sitting on my phone and another dozen from one of the Fae Elders, Kieran—who also happened to be my grandfather.

Keane looked my way, naturally reading my thoughts. "Speaking of your grandfather, he called again." He paused to make sure I was listening. "He said the Elder Council would summon you to come before them soon to discuss Larkin's disappearance."

I heaved a deep sigh. I still wasn't sure how I would handle the Council. I couldn't reveal what had actually happened to Larkin—the man responsible for enacting the Trials and the subsequent chaos that ensued. That would only expose me and the magnitude of my new powers. Being an all-powerful Fae was hard enough to bring into the mix. Being an all-powerful Fae who could take magic from others and use it for herself—as I had done to Larkin...well, that was something that could get me locked up for the rest of my life. Or worse.

"You don't think they'll make me submit to a mind-reading, do you?"

Keane shook his head. "They have no reason to believe anything occurred other than Larkin somehow escaping capture that night. I think they are more interested in learning about the spell you used that made Riona a corporeal ghost while somehow managing to release everyone from Larkin's control at the same time."

"But I still don't know what I did. I don't remember creating or using a spell."

"Perhaps you can attribute it to what you did for Tristan and Queen Astra." I tilted my head to the side in question and he continued. "How you were able to pass on your ability to see and feel Riona to Tristan, when she was just an incorporeal ghost. And then how you somehow unconsciously released Queen Astra from Larkin's control back at the Misty River Clan when he kidnapped you."

"I guess that could work, though that doesn't explain how everyone can now see and feel Riona—even those not present when my supposed spell went off. Or the fact that it seems I released people from under Larkin's control who weren't even there during the battle."

"That does cause a bit of speculation. We both know some of it was because you took Larkin's magic and absorbed it. Naturally, we can't tell them that, but perhaps we could reveal a little more about you that the Elders don't already know. Something to redirect their curiosity."

"And what should we tell them? I don't think revealing that my father is a god is such a good idea. Or the fact that I can travel incorporeally." I had learned, quite by accident, that one of my new powers was separating my soul from my body and traveling around that way. While I hadn't managed to do it since the first time it'd happened, it was something only someone of a god's bloodline could do.

"I was thinking more along the lines of your ability to use different forms of magic. During the Trials, you consistently demonstrated your elemental magic, and since they are aware of our bond, they know you can wield Vaimpír magic. But you never revealed your ability to use ley line magic."

"But Kieran already knows I can use it. As does Tristan. Not to mention, my magic doesn't work that way anymore. I don't pull on the different types like I used to. It's now a thing unto itself."

"True, but they don't know that."

"You don't think Tristan or Kieran would've revealed the Warlock influence to the Elder Council already?"

Keane lifted his shoulders as if about to shrug but then shook his head instead. "I don't think so. I think both have kept most of what you can do to themselves. Believe it or not, they each want to protect you as much as I do. Look at how Tristan used his healing ability on you not once, but twice now. You know what that costs him."

For Tristan to heal me, he'd had to give me a piece of his soul—essentially connecting himself to me forever. It was different than, say, a Vaimpír's healing ability, which came from their blood. While a Vaimpír's blood could heal basic injuries like cuts, bruises, and broken bones, Tristan's ability could bring someone back from the brink of death. As long as their soul was still connected to their body, their ailment didn't matter.

Thinking about his healing ability brought up another troubling thought. "You don't think Tristan saw anything in my mind when he was healing me from Larkin's death spell, do you? About who I am, or what I can do now?"

"I can't say for sure, but I don't think he can search or direct what he sees in a person's mind when healing them. From what I know, he should only get glimpses of incidents and emotions that have to do with him. Like when he healed you before, he saw why you used the secret of Riona's child to push him away."

A grimace crossed my face. That incident was still a bit of a sore spot. Maybe it was time I listened to Tristan's voice messages. My stomach flip-flopped at the thought. If he knew what I had done to Larkin or who Riona's child was, for that matter, things could get...complicated.

As if my thoughts had somehow conjured him, I looked up to see the unmistakable outline of Tristan coming toward us through the darkness on the beach. I groaned inwardly.

He casually mounted the back steps, his determined gaze locked onto me. "Beautiful evening, isn't it?"

Keane stood and stepped between us, clasping Tristan's forearm. "Your Majesty, it's good to see you. How have things been back at Dock Street?"

Momentarily distracted, Tristan turned to Keane. "As well as can be expected given recent events." His lips quirked. "You put me in a spot, leaving as suddenly as you did and taking all your men with you. I've had a hard time replacing you with another Vaimpír. You lot are quite territorial."

Keane smiled tolerantly at Tristan and dropped his arm. "Circumstances being what they are, Blue is my top priority. And you know my men go where I do."

I saw a flash of annoyance cross Tristan's features before he pushed it aside. "I suppose it's understandable, what with your *bond* to Blue and all." I could tell it pained him to say that. He still didn't want to accept the bond Keane and I had formed.

"Tell you what. When I see my father, I'll ask him if any Vaimpír are looking to take on a guardian position, seeing as I won't be returning."

Tristan nodded before hesitating. It seemed he had finally figured out that Keane was standing protectively between us. He cleared his throat. "Would it be okay if I spoke to Blue privately?"

With a sigh, I threw Keane a mental message to let Tristan by. It wasn't like I could avoid him forever.

Keane nodded slightly before stepping aside. "I'll make myself scarce." As he was walking by, he stopped and set his hand on my shoulder, looking briefly at Tristan in warning before heading into the house. I shook my head. This bond was making him much more territorial. I could hardly look at another man without him staking his claim anymore. I wondered why, as he hadn't been that way until these last few months. Perhaps completing the bond had awoken something in him.

Tristan took a seat on the lounger Keane had just vacated, dragging my attention back to him. "So...things are going well with you and Keane?" I cocked an eyebrow at him. "Right, right, stupid question."

He looked out toward the ocean before taking a deep breath and turning back to meet my eyes. "I've missed you, Blue. Things haven't been the same since you left."

When I didn't respond and just stared silently at him, he sighed and looked down. "Riona says hello. She's been worried about you. She was hoping you'd come to visit."

"Why are you here, Tristan?"

He flinched slightly at the edge in my voice. "You've been ignoring all my calls and texts. I didn't know what else to do."

"Tristan—"

He quickly interrupted me. "I know what happened...all of it was overwhelming. I know you needed time. But, Blue..." His gaze lifted to meet mine again. "It's been three months. Three *agonizing* months without a word from you."

I held his stare for a second before looking away from the hurt in it. "I'm sorry, Tristan. I wanted to reach out, I really did, but I just...couldn't. I needed time to process everything away from all outside Fae influences. To come to terms with what and who I am now. It hasn't been easy. To tell you the truth, I still don't know if I'm ready to face that world again."

"So, you're just going to pretend like it doesn't exist?"

I laughed slightly in amusement. "You know as well as I do that would be impossible."

"How much longer do you plan on staying away then? Is there anything I can do to convince you to come back to Dock Street?"

I shook my head slightly. "Tristan, while I'll return to the Fae, I want you to know that I won't be staying at Dock Street. I'll either stay here or at Keane's, where I can maintain a semi-normal life. I still want my photography business and to hang out with my friends while not involving them in the Fae world."

"You don't plan on telling your friends about the Fae?"

I shook my head. "I don't think I want them to know, to shatter their illusions of the world around us. Not to mention, put them in the kind of danger that seems to come with that knowledge."

Tristan nodded in understanding. "I'll make sure they are taken care of and under our protection—silently, of course. As I promised before, I won't let any of the world of the Fae touch them."

A small smile touched my lips. "Thank you, Tristan."

"Anything for you, Blue."

As his expression softened and he started to lean toward me, I quickly changed the subject. "Riona is doing well?"

Tristan cleared his throat and pulled back. "Ah, yes. She has smoothly integrated herself back into her role within the kingdom. It's almost like she never left."

"That's good to hear. A fitting end to the mockery of the Trials. How about the Elders? Are they still at Dock Street?"

A look of aggravation crossed Tristan's face. "Unfortunately. Even after three months, they still have yet to unravel everything Larkin has done. His influences went deeper than anyone ever imagined. All the clan leaders have come together to deal with the fallout and continue the search for him. I still can't fathom where he's hiding himself. We've searched every corner of every kingdom and still haven't found a trace of him."

I quickly guarded my expression and added an extra layer to the shield around my mind. "Perhaps he's no longer alive. He did have a lot of enemies. And with the fall of his empire..."

"No, he's still alive. We would know if someone had assassinated him. I'm beginning to wonder if perhaps his associates within the gods are hiding him."

Tristan didn't know how close to the truth he was. While Larkin's associates within the gods weren't hiding him to protect him, they *were* holding him prisoner. Sebastian, a guardian of sorts who worked for Poseidon, had taken Larkin before what I had done to him could be revealed. He had then turned Larkin over to a few powerful gods he had angered over the years.

Sebastian still popped up periodically—usually at the most inopportune times—with the excuse of letting me know how Larkin was fairing but I think he just enjoyed tormenting me. His main mission lately had been to try and convince me to finally meet my real father, Poseidon—another being I had studiously avoided these last three months.

Had he wanted to, I knew Poseidon could have forced the meeting, but it seemed he was giving me a chance to come to him on my terms. To which I was grateful. While Keane had explained to me that the gods weren't all-powerful deities, as the human race perceived them, but rather just another species that happened to be powerful and immortal, I still couldn't help but be in awe of them. My human upbringing made it difficult to convince my now-Fae brain otherwise.

Realizing I had wandered off into my thoughts again, I turned my attention back to Tristan. "Have you had any luck finding Larkin's cohorts who escaped that night? Celeste or Elder Avner?"

Tristan's mouth tipped down at the corners in frustration. "While we were able to track and capture Avner, who is now awaiting his trial, we haven't been able to locate Celeste. I have a feeling her father is using his position within the Vaimpír society to keep her hidden."

I nodded thoughtfully. "I'll have to talk to Keane about that. I'm sure his influence would hold a lot more sway when it comes to something like this. More than Celeste's father, at any rate."

"Just be careful, Blue. I don't trust her not to do something to you out of spite. Though not as powerful as Keane's, her family still holds a lot of sway in both the Fae and Vaimpír worlds."

"Don't worry about me, Tristan, I can handle myself."

Startling me, Tristan moved to the edge of his chair and grasped one of my hands with both of his. "Of that, I have no doubt, but you still have that pesky human moral compass." He smiled flirtatiously while rubbing his thumb back and forth over my palm. "Things the Fae are willing to do may extend far beyond what you would even consider."

"That's why she has me." Keane stepped back out onto the porch. He had been gone a lot longer than I figured he would be. He didn't leave me alone for long lately—especially while in the company of other men. Stepping between us, which forced Tristan to take his hands back, Keane slid me forward on my lounger so he could position himself behind me. I sighed in relief at the interruption before hiding a grin as he slipped his arms around my waist and pulled me back tightly against him in a possessive gesture.

I saw Tristan frown before hiding the look by rubbing his hand over his face. "I'm glad she has someone so strong to back her up. Did you hear what we were discussing about Celeste?"

Keane nodded as he regarded Tristan. "You know Vaimpír. As a rule, they rarely involve themselves in Fae politics, which is probably why you haven't been able to find anything. However, I'll have a quiet word with a few of the Barons for you while Blue and I are at my parents."

"I'd appreciate that. Are you planning on petitioning them to honor your bond with Blue while you're there?"

"Naturally. The Elder Council has approved it, but I'd also like to see it approved by the Vaimpír."

"I see." Tristan didn't sound pleased at all, but he didn't pursue it any further. "I should probably head out. Several matters still require my attention before I can retire for the night." I watched as he rubbed a hand along the back of his neck, his face showing his exhaustion. "This was a much-needed distraction, though. Thank you for seeing me."

"You're always welcome here, Tristan. You know that."

He gave me a lopsided grin. "Honestly, I wasn't so sure. For all I knew, Keane had orders to forcefully remove me if I showed up here unannounced."

I huffed a small laugh. "Hardly."

Tristan's smile slipped a little. "Blue, I want you to seriously consider coming back to Dock Street." He held up a hand as I moved to protest. "Not to live. I understand your need to keep yourself separate in some ways, but I think it will be essential for your mental healing process to see the clans outside of a time of strife with all that went on before, during, and even after the Trials. I also think the people need to see *you*. To know you're still out there. After all, you were their savior, and it was through you that Riona returned to them."

I sighed, knowing he was probably right. "I'll think about it, Tristan."

He nodded, then stood and waited expectantly. Keane's grip tightened around me briefly before he let me stand. I motioned for him to stay put. He grimaced but nodded as I walked Tristan down the steps to the beach.

"It was good seeing you, Blue." After a hesitant glance at Keane, Tristan moved closer and drew me into a tight embrace. We stood there for a minute before he leaned down to whisper in my ear. "I want you to know if you should ever decide to change your mind about us, I'm still waiting for you."

Before I could form a reply, he turned and walked down the beach, disappearing in a cloud of mist. As the haze dispersed, leaving nothing but empty sand, I shook my head and rolled my eyes.

Fairies...

Chapter Two

After putting the finishing touches on my makeup for the evening, I stepped back to view myself critically in the full-length mirror. I had dressed in one of my most expensive pieces: a couture gown I had brought back with me from Paris the last time I had been there with the fashion company. One of the many benefits of being a photographer for famous designers was the clothes they gifted you with. The dress was a one-of-a-kind Dior, which featured a daringly low-cut corseted top, sheer cap sleeves, and a flowing A-line skirt that reached the floor. The fabric, a dark-purple color, hugged my curves to the waist before flaring out in multi-layered chiffon. The corset and skirt were embroidered with swirls and flowers and adorned with pearls and soft feathers. After seeing my rather large breasts, which I had affectionately named Pinky and the Brain, the designer on set exclaimed that I needed the dress, as it was *made for me.* I had to admit, he was right. The girls did look amazing showcased behind the sheer panel that went from bust to waist in a deep V down the front.

Keane walked into the room and came to a dead stop, his eyes widening. I did a twirl for him. "Do you think it will suffice? I know you said your mother has expensive tastes, so I figured it was a good time to put this dress to use."

He shook his head, seeming speechless, and walked over to me. Encircling his arm around my waist, he simply stared down at me, his eyes quickly darkening to a deep red, his fangs lengthening.

I laughed and put my hands on his chest. "I'll take that as a yes."

"Blue, you look divine. I've never seen another woman as beautiful as you." I smiled and shook my head. Keane was always telling me how beautiful I was, though I didn't believe him. While I didn't think I was ugly, I'd always just considered myself average. I felt like I tended to blend with the crowd rather than stand out. Probably a byproduct of having gorgeous friends who were now supermodels. Reading my thoughts, Keane shook his head. "Mm, you're far more beautiful than any of your friends, Blue. I wish you could see yourself the way I do."

I just smiled. Rising on tiptoe, I placed a kiss on his lips. When I would've pulled back, he wrapped his hand around the back of my neck and held me still. Deepening the kiss, I moaned as his tongue slid past my lips to explore my mouth. I pressed tightly into him and slid my tongue along one of his fangs. He groaned when I pierced the tip and allowed a little of my blood to flow into his mouth.

He pulled back, his voice a deep growl. "Blue, you're killing me. How am I supposed to behave at my parents' with you doing that, not to mention with you on display like this?" He indicated my bare neck. "You do know that having a bare neck is like an aphrodisiac for a Vaimpír."

I eyed him with an amused smile. "*You're* the one who said to wear my hair up and not wear a necklace."

He groaned playfully. "It's almost more than I can bear, which is why…" He reached into the inside pocket of his tuxedo jacket and pulled out a long, thin box. "I brought you this."

I looked between him and the box. "What is it?"

"The perfect piece to complement such beauty."

I raised an eyebrow at him curiously as I took and opened the box. Inside lay the most beautiful antique lariat necklace I had ever seen. It was white gold and had three purple gemstones surrounded by diamonds in varying sizes dripping down its length. Keane pulled it from the bed of velvet and turned me to face the mirror. As he fastened it around my neck, I admired how it draped and lay snuggly between Pinky and the Brain.

"It's gorgeous, Keane."

He leaned down and placed a kiss on the curve of my shoulder before stepping back. "Only the best for you, Blue."

Turning around, I finally took him in. He wore a custom-tailored black tuxedo that would've put even James Bond to shame. It contoured his body perfectly, looking like he had been born wearing it. My eyes traced over the muscles of his arms and chest to his tapered waist before dipping farther and taking in how his pants molded to every part of him. I found my body heating up just looking.

"Keep looking at me that way, *ma moitié*, and we will not make it to my parents'."

I loved when he called me *ma moitié*. It was an endearment used by the Vaimpír for their soulbound partners, meaning: my other half. The way it slipped off his tongue was like a smooth caress across my skin, and I had to stop myself from stepping forward to press against him again. Shaking off the desire gripping me, I brought my eyes back to his suggestion-filled gaze. With a concentrated effort, I smiled saucily up at him. "And waste all the effort it took to get me into this getup?"

Keane let out a mock disappointed sigh while winking at me. "We had better get going, then. We'll be late as it is."

I followed him into one of the spare bedrooms he used to make his portals. "Where do your parents live?"

He looked at me for a moment with a mischievous grin before turning back to the wall. "You'll see."

Closing his eyes, he whispered the words that would bring up the portal using his Vaimpíric powers. Soon enough, a glowing blue line outlined a rectangular shape before solidifying into a door.

I *really* needed him to teach me how he did that.

Reading my thoughts before I could even voice them, Keane smiled. "Soon enough, *ma moitié*. Allow me to have at least one thing you can't do for a while."

I grinned as he opened the door and gestured for me to precede him. I stepped through and came out in an old cemetery. There were above-the-ground tombs of different types and styles among low-hanging branches. And while clean, you could see the passage of time on their surfaces. The moon shining brightly on us left highlights and shadows on their facades, giving an eerie yet beautiful feeling to the whole area.

Keane stepped up behind me, and I watched as he shut the door. It disappeared, leaving behind the entrance to an extremely large, ornate tomb. I looked at the name above it.

Rutherman.

"Do I even want to know why this tomb has your surname on it?"

He looked up at it and smiled. "Because it's our family vault. Every generation since the beginning of our line has been brought here to be laid to rest."

"I thought Vaimpír were immortal."

Keane shook his head. "No, that is another Hollywood myth the humans attribute to vampires. While Vaimpír do live extremely long lives—longer than most of the Fae—we are not immortal. As I said before, only the gods are."

"I wonder where I'll fall on that spectrum, being part Fae and part god."

Keane shrugged his shoulders and held out his arm. "Only time will tell. It all depends on which part of you is more dominant. Shall we?"

Taking his proffered arm, he carefully guided me among the tombs toward a large, wrought-iron gate that stood open under an arched entryway. As we passed under it, I turned to read the inscription on the arch above.

Lafayette Cemetery No. 1.

I started in surprise. "Are we in New Orleans?"

The smile on Keane's face widened, and he spread his free arm out. "Welcome to the realm of the Vaimpír, the Crescent City."

Of all the places I expected to end up, New Orleans had not been one of them. Though with the paranormal lore the city was steeped in, I shouldn't have been surprised. One thing I'd quickly learned while among the Fae was that every myth and legend had some truth to it.

"Why did we have to enter through the graveyard? Aren't you able to portal right to your parents' place?"

Keane flashed me his signature grin—a dimple peeking out on his cheek. "As their son, you'd think I'd be able to, wouldn't you?" He shook his head. "They have a magical dampening spell around their house to prevent anyone from portaling directly in. Being who they are, it's a necessary precaution."

"I guess that makes sense. Though had I known we'd need to walk, I'd have worn different shoes." I looked down at my strappy heels.

Keane pulled us to a stop as a long, black limo pulled up to the curb alongside us. I sighed in relief, causing Keane to chuckle. "Really, *ma moitié*, do you think me remiss in my duty to you?" He opened the door and helped me slide into the back seat. Once he was comfortably ensconced next to me, he signaled to the driver to go.

"Do your parents live here in the Garden District?"

Keane turned from the window and nodded. "It's only a short ride from here. We found the cemetery is the best place to enter. Less chance of coming face-to-face with a human by accident."

"But isn't the cemetery open to the public?"

"Only till late afternoon. Plus, the area around our tomb is protected by a type of magical barrier, though it only repels humans."

"Oh." I lapsed into silence as we rode through the beautiful, tree-covered streets. While I enjoyed the views, I was becoming more and more nervous.

Keane reached over and took my hand, bringing it to his lips. "Relax, Blue. There is nothing for you to worry about."

Easy for him to say. He wasn't meeting his parents for the first time. "What if they disapprove of me?"

"They won't."

"What if they reject our bond? What will we do then?"

"Though I doubt that will be the case, we'll deal with it if it happens—not worry about it beforehand."

"What if they demand you dissolve our bond? What if...?"

Keane silenced my tirade of doubts by leaning over and pressing his lips to mine. When I tried to pull back, he just followed me, cupping my face between his large hands. My resolve not to give in quickly crumbled as he pulled me onto his lap—hiking my dress up so I could straddle him. Pulling me tightly to him, he devoured my mouth like a starving man. His hand slipped between us so he could palm my breast through my dress, causing my nipples to stand erect. I whimpered into his mouth when I felt his erection harden between us, and an answering heat immediately flowed between my thighs.

"Keane..." I gasped for breath when he finally released my mouth to trail his lips down my neck to my pulse point. I moaned as he bit slightly, not breaking the skin. "Keane, we can't..."

He silenced me again with another hard kiss. I soon lost myself in the sensations arcing between us. Since I could feel his emotions and desires like they were mine, it ramped everything up to an almost unbearable level. I squirmed in his hold, rubbing myself back and forth across his erection.

"We're here, sir." The sound of the driver's voice caused me to freeze. My eyes flew open wide, and I turned my head toward the front of the car. I sagged in relief when I saw the driver had raised the black privacy glass between us.

I felt Keane chuckle before he pressed a button next to him. "Thank you, Nigel." With a gentle touch, he brought my face back to his and pressed one more kiss to my lips before drawing back. "Showtime, *ma moitié.*"

Picking me up, he set me next to him so I could adjust my clothes and touch up my makeup. After I had things back where they belonged, he opened the door and stepped out before reaching in and taking my hand to help me from the car. As I passed close to him, I whispered so only he would hear me. "That was cheating."

He chuckled and pulled me against his side. "That was the point."

Taking his arm, I walked with him toward the large, white house in front of us. Though calling it a *house* was like calling a diamond a rock. It was one of the most elegant mansions I had ever seen, even in the Garden District. A textbook example of southern antebellum architecture, it boasted Corinthian-fluted cypress columns, endless verandas, ornate cast-iron, and floor-to-ceiling windows. Walking up the front steps, I almost expected Louis or Lestat from *Interview with a Vampire* to come waltzing down them. Just as we got to the front door, it opened to reveal an aging man in a set of black tails. I blinked in surprise. Did people actually still have butlers?

"Good evening, Your Highness. Your parents have been expecting you." He bowed before showing us into a large, opulent foyer. More columns like those on the outside of the house adorned the inside around the circular, white room. A grand staircase rose in front of us, ascending toward a large window before sweeping elegantly left and right. Marble pedestals topped with enormous vases of flowers sat on either side of the staircase's entrance. Winking above us was a huge crystal chandelier, which rose to touch the top of the high, vaulted ceiling before sweeping down in many glittering layers.

I'd bet they were real crystals, too.

"Good evening, Reginald. How are you, my old friend?"

The older man cracked what I was sure was a smile reserved for very few. "As well as can be expected what with catering to your parents' whims, especially those of your mother."

Keane grinned and turned toward me. "Reginald has been the butler for our family for more years than I can count, though at this point, he's more like family than a servant."

Reginald cackled merrily. "Yes, indeed. Long, long before he was born. I can still remember the day he came barreling into this world. Gave his mother a run for her money, he did. Still does, for that matter. You should have seen how he handled her demands to take a wife—"

"Ah, let's not start with the embarrassing stories. You haven't even met her yet."

At Keane's interruption, I wondered—not for the first time—about his past. He had told me very little about his life before coming to the Moon Tree Clan, and even less about his childhood. Now that I thought about it, he always managed to avoid the subject.

Reginald smiled before reaching out and taking my hands. "You must be quite something to catch the interest of our boy here. We were beginning to despair that he would never find someone."

Keane grimaced. "You act as though I'm ancient. I still have many good years left, you know."

Reginald cackled again. "That you do, though you're well past the normal age for a Vaimpír to take a wife—especially one of the Royal Family. And now here you are, showing up on the doorstep, not with a Vaimpír wife but an *âme sœur liée* in tow. Your mother is going to have a conniption."

I looked at Reginald, a bit confused. "What is an *âme sœur liée*?"

"A bonded soulmate."

My eyes widened in surprise. "How did you know I was bonded to Keane?"

Reginald grinned. "I may be just a servant, but I still hear things. Plus, I can see it. What you have is strong and becoming stronger by the day, if I had to guess. It's not the usual Vaimpír bond either. There's something special about it. Something more…"

I nodded, a bit amazed at his insight.

Keane just rolled his eyes. "Reginald here is an Inntinn. He can see things others cannot."

"Like a psychic?"

Reginald chortled merrily. "Not exactly. More like I can read energy fields and auras. They *speak* to me, for lack of a better word."

I thought about it before looking at Keane. "Is it kind of like what I can do when judging what a Fae is? How I read their energy fields?"

Keane nodded. "Similar. Reginald's talent is a bit more in-depth. He can delve into a person's energy field and see exactly what makes them who they are. From their species to their abilities. Even who they are supposed to become and what their intentions are. It's very useful in a butler."

I looked at Reginald speculatively. I wondered if he knew what I was. If he could see who *I* was supposed to be. As a small smile spread across his face, I knew he was aware of much more than he was letting on.

Keane reached over and took my hands out of Reginald's. I hadn't even realized he was still holding them. "I probably should've warned you. A lot of Reginald's intuition is by touch." My eyes flew to Reginald's. He just smiled at me unabashedly. "Reginald, this is Blue, by the way."

"It's indeed a great pleasure to meet you, Miss Blue. I look forward to seeing what the future holds for you and Master Keane here."

I felt Keane tense just before a soft, feminine voice floated toward us. "Reginald, why are you just standing there in the foyer? Please bring our guests in."

"Yes, ma'am." As quickly as Keane had tensed, so had Reginald. He now held himself stiffly and formally with a scowl on his face. Turning, he gestured us forward to where a woman stood partially hidden in the shadows. My eyes started at the visible tips of her sky-high heels, traveling up a gorgeous, floor-length, gold-sequined gown that hugged every curve. The front of the dress was so open and dipped so low I was afraid we might be treated to a show of her assets if she moved the wrong way. Either that or she was sporting some serious cleavage tape.

As she stepped forward into the light, I sucked in an appreciative breath. She was gorgeous. I didn't think there was an imperfection to be found in any of her sharply defined features. Undeniably Vaimpír.

"Keane, my darling." She held out her hands toward him, and I couldn't help but feel a bit of jealousy at the familiarity in her voice.

Keane stepped forward and took the woman's outstretched hands, bowing over them before pressing an air kiss to both of her cheeks. "Isabela. To what do we owe this pleasure?" Though he sounded amiable, I felt he was less than pleased to see her. Which went a long way toward soothing the green-eyed monster threatening to pop out of me at any second.

She laughed, the sound grating on my nerves, and placed her hands on his chest. "Oh, Keane. This is the first time you've been home in so long. Did you think I'd miss the chance to see you? Haven't you missed me, my darling?" She stared up at him coyly. When he didn't answer her, she finally slid her gaze to me. "And who is this lovely little creature you've brought with you?"

Keane disentangled himself from Isabela's arms and stepped back to my side, taking my hand in his. It caused her to scowl just a bit. "Isabela, this is Carolina Blue of the family Grayson. Blue, this is Isabela, the chosen daughter of House Dalca."

I glanced sideways at him. The chosen daughter. Which meant this was one of the women who had been selected as a possible candidate to become Keane's wife. Each family within the seven Vaimpír houses had one chosen woman who was brought up and trained to be presented to the Royal Family when they came of age. Keane was supposed to have already chosen one of them to become his wife, but he hadn't yet.

Isabela looked me up and down. "And what business do you have with *my* Keane? Are you his feeder?"

I bristled at the possessiveness in her tone, not to mention her insulting question. Placing a condescending smile on my face, I wrapped my arm around Keane's waist and curled myself into his side while toying with the necklace at my throat. "Hardly. And as to the nature of our relationship, well...that really is none of your business, Miss Dalca."

A frown marred her face as she stared at the necklace I was playing with. I heard Reginald chuckle behind me before another voice came down the hall.

"Reginald? Is that Keane? Please bring him back to the salon, will you?"

"Yes, Your Majesty. Right away." Reginald pushed past Isabela and indicated for us to follow him.

Keane stepped just ahead of me and started talking quietly with Reginald, which left me with Isabela. As I went to move past her, she reached out and grabbed my arm, digging her sharp nails into the soft skin.

"I don't know what game you think you're playing, but know you cannot win. You're not of the seven houses, nor are you a pure-blooded Vaimpír. Which means you're nothing and not worthy of him. I will have him as mine, and I will become the next Queen of the Vaimpír."

I rolled my eyes, my anger starting to rise. "What is it with you Vaimpír women? All so dramatic. First of all, you're right, I'm not of the seven houses, nor am I a pure-blooded Vaimpír. However, what I am is something far beyond what you could ever hope to be." With a quick shot of magic, I used where she was touching me to push a fraction of my power across her skin. She shivered as it snaked over her, leaving her frozen in place. Pulling my arm away, I quickly used a feature-changing spell to make my eyes Vaimpír red and then manipulated the magic again to produce a pair of fangs. Leaning forward into her face, I growled at her. "Do not mess with me, Isabela, or I'll make sure you regret your entire existence." I felt my power spike and was pretty sure my eyes started to glow. Her pupils dilated in fear.

Stepping back, I smirked at her. Then, with a quick flick of my wrist in her direction, I released her before turning and walking the way Keane and Reginald had gone. After I rounded the corner, I let out a heavy breath and leaned against the wall, taking the time to retract my fangs and change my eyes back to their normal hazel color. It had taken every ounce of self-control I had not to lose my temper or control of my magic. I had to be very careful nowadays. The power within me always seemed to be brewing just beneath the surface, and any type of strong emotion could set it off—especially anger.

Once I was sure I was back under control, I straightened and looked at my arm where Isabela had grabbed me. There were small points of blood where her nails had dug in. With a grimace, I siphoned off some of Keane's healing magic and watched as the skin knit itself back together. Licking my thumb, I rubbed away the blood left behind. When I was sure I was presentable, I straightened my shoulders and caught up to Keane. He looked back at me oddly, but I just smiled in his direction.

"Where's Isabela?"

I shrugged nonchalantly. "She'll probably be along shortly."

He seemed about to say something more, but before he could, Reginald opened the doors in front of us and announced us to the room beyond. "Your Majesties, the Crown Prince Keane and his guest, Miss Carolina Blue."

As I walked past him, Reginald leaned over and whispered in my ear. "You're more worthy than any of those supposed chosen. Don't let them make you lose sight of who you are."

I smiled in his direction, glad I seemed to have at least one person in the Vaimpír world in my corner. Stepping forward, I took Keane's arm again as we headed for the two people in the room. The woman who had been seated in a chair in front of the lit fire stood and came toward us. Dressed in a body-hugging, dark-green velvet dress, she was tall and lithe like most of the Vaimpír. Her cool, ice-blue eyes watched me with curiosity before turning toward her son.

"Keane, my dear. It has been so long since you last visited me. Are you avoiding me or something?"

Keane leaned over so he could hug his mother and kiss her on the cheek. I wondered just how long it had been since he had last seen or spoken to his parents. "Of course not, Mother. I've just been very busy of late."

"Too busy for even your mother?"

"Oh, stop giving the boy a hard time, Camille. Keane, my son. How are you?" There was no doubt as to who the man moving forward was. Where Keane hardly resembled his mother, he was the spitting image of his father. "It is good to see you, son. You know your mother only misses you now that you have grown into your own." After shaking his hand, Keane's father brought him into a manly hug.

Keane smiled at his Father before stepping back and bringing me forward. "Mother, Father, I'd like you to meet Carolina Blue of the family Grayson."

Turquoise-blue eyes much like Keane's met mine before crinkling up at the corners. He reached out and took my hand before bringing it to his lips. "Carolina, it is indeed a pleasure to finally make your acquaintance. I have heard many rumors where you are concerned, and I am looking forward to finding out if they are true." He stepped back and wrapped his arm around his wife. "I am Malakai, and this is my wife, Camille."

"It's a pleasure to finally meet both of you. Keane has told me so much about you. And please, call me Blue. Everyone does."

Keane's Mother smiled, though it didn't quite reach her eyes. "Blue it is, then. I'd love to say I've heard about you, as well. But alas, Keane hasn't mentioned you at all." I saw Malakai's arm tighten around his wife's shoulders in what I assumed was a subtle warning. "I am, of course, looking forward to getting to know the first woman my Keane has brought home."

Though she continued to smile, I could tell she was only saying that to appease her husband. Something told me the reason Isabela was here was because of Keane's mother. As if on cue, Isabela walked into the room, immediately moving to Camille's side.

"Isabela, my dear. There you are." Camille put her hand on Isabela's shoulder. "Have you had a chance to meet Blue yet?"

Isabela smiled sweetly at Camille, though she refused to look at me. I smirked. "Yes, we met earlier in the foyer."

"Oh, did you go to greet Keane first? You naughty girl. You just couldn't wait to see him, could you? I'll bet he was over the moon to see you here."

Malakai seemed to note the displeased expression on Keane's face and moved toward the door, bringing Camille with him. "Now that introductions are over, why don't we adjourn to the dining room for dinner?"

We followed sedately behind Keane's parents and Isabela. Keane leaned down to whisper in my ear. "I'm sorry Isabela is here, *ma moitié*. I had no idea my mother would invite her. I've warned her many times not to interfere in my love life, but she doesn't listen. It's one of the many reasons I haven't been home in so long."

I squeezed his arm and smiled up at him. "Not to worry. Isabela and I already had a little chat. I think she's well-aware of my feelings on the matter."

Keane smirked, his eyes dancing in amusement. "That is what I'm worried about."

We were led into a large dining room that could easily seat dozens of people. I hoped they didn't follow tradition and sit on opposite ends of the table. Talk about awkward. To my relief, Malakai seated his wife to his left before taking the chair at the head of the table.

"Blue, dear, why don't you sit next to me?" Camille gestured to the chair beside her, but Keane shook his head and led me to the other side of the table. A look of annoyance crossed Camille's face, but she quickly covered it. After Keane had seated me, he took the chair next to mine, which left Isabela to sit beside Camille. She also didn't appear happy with the seating arrangements. The two of them had obviously been plotting for tonight's meal, and I wondered what else they had up their sleeves.

Malakai signaled to the waitstaff to start serving the food. As the first plates were set in front of us, he opened the conversation. "I have been in contact with the Elder Council about everything that happened at the Moon Tree Clan. It is hard to believe one man orchestrated and executed such a complex plan."

Keane nodded in agreement. "It seems he had quite an extensive network. I just spoke with Tristan the other night, and he said they were still trying to unravel everything Larkin put in place."

"The Council is very unsettled with what Larkin was able to accomplish under their noses. They have even invited your grandfather to sit in on recent meetings to get his insight." Malakai took a bite of food before continuing. "Speaking of the Moon Tree Clan, is it true that you and your men are no longer acting as guardians for Tristan?"

Keane easily met his father's probing stare. "I was hoping to speak with you about that while I was here. I want to send over a Vaimpír or two looking to take on a guardian position to take my place."

"You do not plan to return?"

Keane shook his head. "There are other things in play I need to devote myself to."

Malakai glanced in my direction. "I see. Would this have anything to do with your beautiful companion this evening?"

Keane looked over at me and smiled. "Yes, it does."

The animosity coming from the other side of the table was almost palpable. Neither woman was happy nor trying to hide it. Oblivious, or just ignoring the rancor coming from the two women, Malakai smiled in my direction.

"Tell me, Blue, are the rumors about you true? I have heard you are more powerful than any Fae our kind has ever seen. Even more powerful than your mother, Queen Iridia."

I wasn't sure I wanted to be classified as the most powerful Fae. That seemed like a bit of an overstatement, not to mention a dangerous title. I was also a little surprised that he knew who my mother was, but if he'd been in discussions with the Elders, I supposed they'd revealed that fact to him. "I'd hardly classify myself as the most powerful Fae of our kind. While I've shown the promise of a great many talents so far, we are still discovering all I can do."

"And have you discovered who your father is yet?"

I shook my head. "No. We're still working on that." I hated lying to him, as he seemed like he would be a trustworthy ally, but it was a necessary precaution.

"I see." He watched me for a moment before returning to his dinner.

"I heard he might be a Vaimpír." Camille pretended nonchalance, though I could tell she was fishing for more information. It seemed the Council had imparted what we had told them were our supposed suspicions, even if we knew it wasn't true.

I shrugged. "It's possible, considering my command of Vaimpír magic. But without my mother here to ask, I don't know."

"Is it true she abandoned you to be raised by her *human* half-sister?" Isabela's lips curled in disdain.

"Isabela." Malakai's rebuke caused her to immediately put her head down.

"Malakai, darling, she didn't mean any harm, she was merely curious. Weren't you, Isabela?" Camille looked over at Isabela, who nodded, though remained silent.

Clearly, these women—though they pretended otherwise—knew exactly who I was prior to me coming here. I smiled tolerantly in their direction. "I wouldn't say she abandoned me, but yes, I was raised by my Aunt Alannah."

Camille looked at me with fake sympathy. "It must have been hard being raised by a human, then being suddenly thrust into the Fae world."

"It has been an adjustment. If it weren't for your son, I'm not sure I would've been able to cope as well as I have."

Camille smiled. "My Keane has always been good at helping others. It's one of the things that will make him a great King when it's his time to rule. Though I had hoped he would have a wife by now to help ground him."

"Mother, please don't start."

"I'm serious, Keane. You're well past the age to select your wife. You need to think about your future and that of this kingdom. What does it say to the other houses that you haven't taken one of the chosen daughters as a wife yet? Look at Isabela here, wasting her best years waiting to see if you'll choose her."

"Mother, I'll not discuss this with you again."

"But, Keane…"

"Enough!" Keane slammed his hand on the table. "I will not discuss this further. This is why I never come home anymore, Mother."

Camille pursed her lips. "I'm only trying to help you do what is best for you, Keane."

"Well, stop. I don't want or need your assistance. As a matter of fact, that is the reason Blue and I came here tonight."

I tensed at his words. While I was sure his father would consider our bond, I now knew there was no way his mother would bless it.

Malakai looked between us. "Perhaps we should adjourn to my study for this discussion. If everyone is finished eating, that is."

Nodding, though we had all eaten very little, everyone stood and followed Malakai toward the back of the house. His study was a large room filled with all manner of papers, books, and relics. A large desk dominated the center of the space with several chairs placed in front of it, while a small sofa was situated off to the side. A huge, stone fireplace took up one wall, though there wasn't a fire lit in it. Placed prominently on the fireplace mantel was a bronze statue with two lions holding a shield beneath a crown—a royal crest. Embossed onto the shield's surface was a familiar raven seated on a Celtic crescent moon. Keane actually wore a necklace with the same design on it. This version had an added phrase around it. *Neither by Chance nor Fate.* I idly wondered if it was a family motto.

After looking around, I carefully sat in one of the empty chairs situated in front of the desk. I was relieved when Keane stood next to me, his arm resting on the back of the chair. Malakai leaned against the front of his desk while Camille and Isabela took the couch across from us. I wasn't sure why Isabela was still with us, as this had nothing to do with her. Keane seemed to come to the same conclusion.

"Isabela, why don't you run along to your room? This is a family matter."

Camille put a reassuring hand on Isabela's leg. "No need for that. She's as much family as any of us at this point."

Keane scowled at his mother. "She is not family and never will be. And you know it, Mother."

Camille just huffed. "We shall see."

Malakai seemed to sense an argument would break out again, so he cleared his throat. "My son. What is it you came here to discuss?"

"As I'm sure the Council has revealed to you, Blue and I have found ourselves in a very unique situation."

Malakai nodded, acknowledging he had heard something, though Camille appeared clueless. She narrowed her eyes at her husband.

"As you now know, Blue was raised by a human. What you may *not* know is that she had an enchantment put on her that locked down her powers so no one would know what she was. Even her."

Camille interrupted, looking annoyed. "Why would they do that?"

"Shush, Camille, let Keane continue. I am sure all your questions will be answered when he is done." Malakai indicated for Keane to continue.

"When Blue was unwittingly thrown into the Trials by Celeste, Blue's grandmother, Galene, stepped forward and admitted that her daughter Iridia had created the enchantment to protect Blue. It seems Blue, like her mother, holds a great deal of power." I could tell Keane was carefully picking his words about what to reveal.

"Her mother and grandmother were afraid if anyone were to discover the depth of her power, they would either kill Blue for the threat she posed or use her as a weapon. Instead, Iridia decided to bind Blue's magic in hopes that she could live out her life as a human, being none the wiser. Unfortunately, with the Trials, not having her powers would have meant her death. So, Galene released the enchantment. Once her magic was unrestricted, Blue soon found she was able to wield different forms of magic—one of them being Vaimpír. Upon the awakening of her Vaimpíric powers, Blue accidentally bound my soul to hers."

Isabella surged to her feet, her eyes darkening. "This can't be! How is it possible? Even if she can wield our magic, she's not Vaimpír. It shouldn't work."

Camille, who had remained seated, seemed especially shocked, which I found interesting. Apparently, Malakai hadn't told her everything the Council had revealed to him—nor had Jasmine come here. "You...you're bound to her? How? Can she release it? You haven't bound yourself to her in return, have you?"

Keane waited patiently while his mother continued her tirade. "Malakai, we cannot allow something like this to go on. This is blasphemous to our kind. Keane must wed and be bound to one of the seven houses. He cannot…"

"Camille, that is enough. I would like to hear what our son has to say."

"But, Malakai, surely you can see this…"

"Silence." Malakai's eyes had turned red, and I knew he had used his power of domination. Camille's mouth immediately shut, and she bowed her head in submission, as did Isabela, who immediately dropped back into her chair. While it didn't affect me, I could feel the residual pull of it. It was a power only a true Royal of the Vaimpír bloodline had, and only one person per generation. I wondered idly if Keane had inherited it.

Malakai eyed the two women before him, his expression stern. "If either of you interrupts again, you will be removed from the room and will not be allowed to be a part of this conversation, is that understood?" Camille and Isabela nodded meekly. "Good." Malakai turned back to Keane. "You were saying."

"After Blue accidentally bound me, I did not complete the binding." I heard Camille let out a sigh of relief. "Though the Elder Council blessed the union, Blue was still involved in the Trials, and I wasn't sure how it would affect her. However, during the final battle with Larkin, Blue intercepted the death spell he intended for the Elders and King Tristan. To save her life, I had to complete the bond."

Camille's eyes shot to me, her red gaze filled with fury. She practically vibrated with the anger running through her, but due to Malakai's ultimatum, she was unable to speak. Malakai, however, looked thoughtful. "You were able to complete the bond with someone who is not a Vaimpír?"

"Yes, and it's stronger than anything I've ever felt or even heard of. Even Reginald could detect it by merely touching Blue's hands."

"How curious." Malakai turned to me, his lips quirking into a smile. "Are you sure you are not a pure-blood Vaimpír?"

I smiled back in amusement. "I can show you my wings if you would like. I can't say for sure, but I think that might be a good indication that I'm not."

Malakai chuckled at my response. "You are quite right. Any decent Vaimpír worth his salt wouldn't have a set of wings. Unless they were bat wings." He raised his eyebrows, causing me to laugh at his intended vampire joke. He laughed, as well. "No? Well, it was worth a shot. I am, however, curious as to what makes you so different from other Fairies. I have a feeling you are not telling me everything."

I grimaced a bit before offering him a small smile. "Some things are better off not being said at this time." Malakai stared at me a bit intensely. I could tell he was trying to read my mind, but even a Vaimpír King wouldn't be able to pass through my blocks now.

"Father." Malakai turned from me to face his son. "We have come here to ask for the blessing of House Rutherman on our soulbond."

Malakai raised his eyebrows. "You wish to keep it?"

Keane nodded but didn't say anything.

"I see." His father's look turned introspective. "I will have to think on this. It is an unusual situation. Especially with you being the heir to my throne."

"I understand, Father."

"I would like for the pair of you to remain here for the time being. I may have more questions for you. Send Nigel to collect your things for a short stay."

Keane bowed to him. "Certainly, Father. We can stay as long as you wish." With a glance at his mother and Isabela, he turned back to me, took my hand, and placed it on his arm. "I think we would like to retire for now. I presume our rooms have already been made up?"

At Malakai's nod, Keane bowed again. "Mother, Father…Isabela. Good night."

I nodded my head in respect to both the King and Queen, completely ignoring Isabela before walking with Keane out the doors. As we shut them behind us, I heard raised voices and knew the battle had only begun.

Chapter Three

Reginald was waiting for us on the other side of the door. "Well, that went as well as could be expected."

I raised my eyebrows at him and smiled in amusement. "Reginald, were you eavesdropping at the door?"

He cackled lowly. "What good, self-respecting butler wouldn't? Now, let me show you to your rooms."

As we followed him up the stairs and through the halls, I noted all the paintings on the walls. They were obviously Keane's ancestors, as he looked like most of them. Talk about strong genetics. When Keane saw me looking wide-eyed at a particularly stunning gentleman dressed in...nothing, he chuckled.

"My uncle. Aléxandros. He had a unique sense of humor, to say the least. My mother has tried to remove the painting several times, but Aléxandros had a spell put on it, so it always returns."

I giggled at that. "He sounds like someone I'd like to meet."

Keane grinned, too. "I'm sure you will at some point. He's currently traveling somewhere in the tropics, but he does pop in now and again to say hi."

Reginald stopped in front of one of the many doors in the hall, a look of distaste on his face. "Your mother originally had a room in the back of the house next to the servants' quarters made up for Miss Blue, but I took the liberty of having the one down the hall from you prepared."

Keane sighed in exasperation. "Thank you, Reginald. But Blue will be staying in my suite."

"I was hoping you would say that. Your mother put Miss Isabela in the room next to you. Knowing her, she's bound to be up to all kinds of no good."

"Thanks for the heads-up."

We reached the end of the long hall. "I had everything readied for you, just as you like it." Reginald opened the double doors for us. "Have a good day's rest. I'll be by to bring you your breakfast at the usual time."

"Thank you, Reginald. Don't overwork yourself on my account. I know where the kitchen is."

Reginald smiled and nodded. "That you do. Be that as it may, I'll come by later."

With that, he moved back down the hall, humming to himself. I looked at Keane. "I like him."

Keane guided me into the room. "I'm glad. He plays a very important role in my life. He's like a second father to me."

I moved past Keane into the sitting area of his suite. Floor-to-ceiling windows covered the back wall, while another had a fireplace. A large TV hung over it, and a few framed pictures rested on the huge mantel. I went to look at them. There were several of Keane with his father and others I didn't know, though they all looked similar. I assumed they were his siblings, though he had yet to talk about them. There were also some with Ethereal Mutation—his bandmates and best friends. I smiled at the shenanigans in the pictures. Seemed time hadn't changed much.

Peeking through an open doorway, I saw a bedroom all done up in differing shades of gray and blue with a queen-size bed. Though it was neat and clean, it didn't have anything personal in it. Walking to the other side of the room, I saw it was another bedroom, larger than the first. This one looked to have been lived in with personal mementos spread throughout. A large, king-size bed in the same grays and blues as the other room dominated one wall, while a dresser, desk, and bookcase were on the others. Peeking in the other doorways, I saw a walk-in closet and an en suite bathroom. I moved over to the windows and saw that they looked out onto the balcony, the sculpted back lawn of the mansion beyond. Keane walked up behind me and kissed the back of my neck. I shivered in reaction. Chuckling, he rubbed the goose bumps that popped up on my arms.

"I called down to the kitchens to see if they could send up a food tray. I know you didn't eat much earlier and must be hungry."

Before I could reply, there was a knock on the door. Keane stepped away, his brows knitting. "That was fast."

I stayed where I was, staring out into the night. After a moment, I heard Keane talking to someone with a small, feminine voice. Curious, I moved to the door of the sitting area. I looked out while leaning casually against the doorframe.

"Come on, big brother, just let me meet her."

Keane shook his head. "You can wait until tomorrow, munchkin."

The young girl before Keane brought out the puppy-dog eyes and pouty lip. I couldn't help the laugh that slipped out, causing both heads to turn in my direction. The young girl managed to slip past Keane as he made to grab her and moved to stand before me. I looked down at her with interest. She was maybe seven or eight and wearing a long nightgown with red hearts.

"Are you really my brother's soulmate?"

"Amelia, get back here. You can talk to Blue tomorrow."

I smiled down at her. "Hi, Amelia. It's nice to meet you."

She ignored her brother and continued staring up at me with wide, probing blue eyes. "My mother says you're just an interloper."

"I'm sure your mother had a lot of interesting things to say about me."

"She says Isabela is going to marry my brother, not you."

"I honestly don't know who your brother will marry, Amelia. Only he can tell you that."

"I don't like Isabela."

"You know, I think I agree with you. I don't much like Isabela either."

"Do you really have wings?"

I nodded. "Yes. Large, white-and-purple ones."

"Can I see them?"

I smiled. "I'll be happy to show you tomorrow after I get out of this dress."

"How are you a Vaimpír if you have wings?"

"I don't know."

"Do you have fangs?"

I nodded.

"Can I see them?"

Keane walked up and took his sister by the shoulders. "Enough, Amelia. You can talk more with Blue tomorrow."

He started to move her toward the door. When she was almost to it, she turned back to me. "I don't care what my mother says about you. I think I'll like you."

"Thank you, Amelia. I think I'll like you, too."

With that, she skipped out the door, and Keane shut it behind her. "Sorry about that. She can be quite tenacious when she wants to be."

I smiled and shook my head. "You've never told me how many siblings you have."

"I'm the eldest of five full-blood siblings, plus Darrius, my half-brother. Amelia is the youngest."

"She's what, seven?"

Keane nodded.

"And that would make you?"

He hesitated, but another knock sounded on the door before he could answer. "Ah, that's probably the food."

I shook my head. "Still not going to tell me, are you?"

Keane opened the door, but instead of a servant with a food tray, Isabela was there, wearing a long, sheer nightgown and robe. I raised my eyebrows. She sure worked fast.

Keane frowned at her. "What do you want, Isabela?" I had to give him credit. He didn't even glance down at everything revealed by her negligee.

She gave him a seductive smile. "Keane." She practically purred his name. "Obviously, I'm here to be with you."

I leaned against the bedroom doorframe, crossing my arms over my chest, intent on watching the show, as she seemed oblivious to my presence.

"I thought I made myself perfectly clear downstairs, Isabela."

Her smile turned coy. "Oh, you mean that little act you put on for your parents?"

"It wasn't an act."

She let out a trilling laugh. "Oh, Keane…" She swayed forward, pressing herself against him. He grabbed her by the shoulders and tried to push her back, but she just clutched at the lapels of his jacket, holding on to him.

"Don't you want to kiss me, Keane?"

"No."

"Don't you find me desirable?"

"No."

She gave an exaggerated pout. "Why are you being so mean?"

Keane sighed heavily. "Isabela. Let go of me and go back to your rooms. It's late."

"But I want to stay here with you." She pushed. It seemed to catch him off guard, causing him to take a couple of steps into the room. She locked the door behind her as soon as she crossed the threshold. Still not realizing I was there, she stepped toward Keane and slipped the robe from her shoulders, letting it pool on the floor at her feet. "I've been waiting for a chance to get you alone."

"Isabela…"

"I know the kind of needs you have. I can take care of them—all of them." She began unlacing the front of her nightgown. "Your mother made sure I was versed in all forms of pleasure."

"Probably shouldn't mention one's mother when you're trying to seduce them." Keane leaned against the couch, his arms crossed defensively over his chest as he watched Isabela through narrowed eyes.

"She only has your best interests at heart. As do I."

The laces on her nightgown came free, and she pushed the fabric from her body, leaving her standing in only her underwear.

"And what interests are those?"

"Those of this kingdom and your family, of course."

"Ah, and I suppose you feel you would be the ideal wife. The consummate Queen."

"I've been trained my whole life for it." She raised her chin before her look turned sly. "And besides, I was handpicked by the Queen herself."

"Indeed. But I've already found my other half, as you heard tonight. And I plan to keep her."

A slight sneer crossed her lips before she could check it. "That Blue woman? Who is she, in truth? A nobody who happens to be related to a prominent Fae family. No Vaimpír would accept her as their Queen. I honestly don't get what you see in her anyway." She paused, tilting her head to the side in consideration. "But...I'd be willing to let you keep her as a pet if that is what you desire once we're married. You would, of course, have to break the bond with her. I think that's fair, don't you?"

"Hmm...what do you think, Blue?"

Isabela visibly started, her eyes going wide as I sauntered into view. "I'm afraid that's going to be a hard no for me."

Isabela quickly grabbed her nightgown off the floor to cover herself. "What are you doing here?"

"I could ask you the same thing."

"I belong here."

"Do you? 'Cause it seems to me that you were the uninvited one, not the other way around."

Isabela sputtered as I looked on in amusement. She turned angry eyes to Keane. "Are you going to let her talk to me that way?"

Keane stood in one smooth motion. "I believe Blue can talk to you however she sees fit. And she's correct, she's here at my invitation. You, however, are not."

Her face turned even redder. "Your mother will be hearing about this!"

"Excellent. Now, if you would be so kind as to return to your room as requested..."

Snatching up her robe from the floor, Isabela stomped out of the room. Just as she stepped through the doorway, she turned back and glared at me. "This isn't over. I *will* get rid of you, just you wait." She slammed the door on her parting words.

I turned and gave Keane an amused look. "I have to say, that was interesting."

Before he could say anything, there was another knock on the door. "For heaven's sake. Who else is going to bother us tonight?" Impatiently throwing open the door, Keane growled at the person standing there.

"Well, I never." A small, plump woman with winter-white hair and vivid green eyes stood on the other side dressed in a bright, floral blouse covered by a white apron. She had a large, covered tray in her hands, emitting drool-worthy smells. "Keane Aléxandros Rutherman. I know I taught you better manners than that."

Keane was immediately contrite, ducking his head like a scolded schoolboy. "I'm sorry, Esme. I didn't realize it was you."

"Oh, and that makes it better?"

I covered my mouth as a giggle bubbled to my lips. Keane gave me a cheeky grin over his shoulder before turning back to the woman. "Here, let me take that. It looks much too heavy for you."

"I've got it, you impertinent boy. I was carrying things much heavier than this long before you were born." She bustled past him and set the tray on the table in front of the couch. Dusting her hands on her apron, she turned back to Keane. "Now, let me look at you. Good lord, what are they feeding you over there at that Fairy clan? Muscle gainer three thousand?" She squeezed his biceps. "Must have an incredibly accomplished chef to keep you in such prime shape."

"No one's food compares to yours, Esme."

"Damn straight. Now, come give this old woman a hug."

Keane's grin widened as he stepped forward and scooped the little woman into his arms. "I've missed you, Maman Esme." Keane kissed the top of her head.

"I've missed you, too, my boy. It's just not the same around here without you getting into all kinds of mischief." She stepped back, discretely wiping at her eyes. "Now, introduce me to this pretty young lady of yours. I've been hearing all sorts of tales from Reggie, but I want to judge her for myself."

"Maman Esme, this is Blue. Blue this is Esme. She's been the chef for our family for centuries now. Though, she's so much more than that. She practically raised me while my mother was off doing whatever it is she does."

Esme swatted Keane. "Don't be showing no disrespect now. Your mother may have her issues, but she's still your mama." I straightened my shoulders as Esme turned to me and looked me up and down. "Could use some more meat on your bones. So skinny." She reached out and patted my cheek. "But don't you worry, ol' Maman Esme will take good care of you now that you're here. I'm right pleased to meet you, Blue."

"It's a pleasure to meet you, too, Esme."

"My Reggie tells me your path is a bright one and very closely entwined with Keane's."

"Reggie?"

"Esme is Reginald's wife." Keane wrapped an arm around Esme's shoulders.

"That I am. Five hundred blissful years." My mouth must've been hanging open a bit because Esme laughed. "It goes by in the blink of an eye."

"You've set a lofty goal. I'll have to endeavor to be worthy of such devotion in my life."

"Something tells me you already are." As she shared a look with Keane, I blushed and stood there awkwardly, not sure what to say. "Well, now, why don't we get you settled and see about getting something good to eat in you? I know you ate very little at dinner, and you, my dear, cannot afford to skip meals."

With half-closed eyes, I smiled at Keane and patted my full stomach. "Okay, that made everything else that went on this evening worth it. Do you think we could convince her to come live with us so she can cook for me all the time?"

Keane chuckled. "Don't tempt her." His smile faded a bit. "I'm sorry about my mother, Blue. Her actions tonight have been beyond disrespectful."

I shook my head. "Don't worry about it, Keane. Honestly, it wasn't unexpected. To think your parents would just welcome me with open arms was a fantasy. They are the King and Queen, after all, not just your parents. They have to weigh the political consequences of everything as much as their children's desires. It can't be easy on them."

"You're way too understanding for your own good. My mother—"

I reached over and put my fingers over his lips. "Enough about it for tonight. Right now, I just want to curl up in bed and sleep off this food coma."

Keane smiled against my fingers before brushing a kiss on them. "You can have your way for now, but we will discuss it later. Come on, let's get you to bed." Standing, he leaned over and scooped me up out of my chair.

"Put me down, Keane. I can walk." He just pulled me tighter against his chest and walked into the main bedroom before setting me on the bed. "Shouldn't I be sleeping in the other room?"

Keane growled. "You're not sleeping anywhere but with me."

I shook my head in bewilderment. "You're so territorial now. What has gotten into you? You were never this possessive before. Does it have something to do with the bond being complete?"

Keane opened his mouth as if to say something but then closed it and shook his head before moving to the closet. "Let me get you one of my old T-shirts to sleep in for now."

I sighed, a bit frustrated. There was, without a doubt, something more going on here than he was telling me, but I just couldn't figure it out. Standing, I stripped out of my dress, laid it over one of the chairs in the room, and went into the bathroom to take my makeup off. I only hoped he would feel confident enough to confide in me with time.

Chapter Four

Something had brought me out of a deep sleep. As I lay there with my eyes still closed, enjoying the warmth of Keane wrapped around me, I tried to figure out what it was. Keane breathed deeply, asleep for the first time in days. As a Vaimpír, he didn't need to sleep much, but lately, he had only been sleeping maybe once a week—and even that was only for a few hours. I was seriously starting to get worried about him. He wouldn't talk about what was bothering him, and I still couldn't read his mind through his blocks, so I had no idea what was going on.

Opening my eyes, I slowly looked around but didn't see anything out of the ordinary. Moonlight filtered through the curtains covering the large windows, spreading bright spots amid the dark room and creating strange shadows around the furniture. That meant I had only been asleep for an hour or so as the sun had yet to peek over the horizon.

Carefully easing myself out of bed so as not to disturb Keane, I walked over to the windows. Opening one of the curtains, I looked out across the lawn. Nothing seemed to be moving out there either. Shaking my head, I turned to go back to bed, but before the curtain dropped fully back into place, something caught my attention out of the corner of my eye, drawing me back to the window.

As I lifted the curtain again, a light out in the distance flashed briefly before going out. I waited a second before seeing it again—this time, closer.

Placing my hand on the window, I leaned forward to get a better look, trying to figure out what it was. Without warning, the glass pane I was leaning against disappeared, throwing me off balance. I sucked in a sharp breath as I fell forward. Stumbling over the windowsill, I managed to catch my upper body before I face-planted.

Grumbling about my clumsiness, I stood back up and turned to look at the window to see what had happened, but it was gone, as was the room beyond it. Turning in confusion, I looked out to where the lawn should be, but that was no longer there either. Instead, I was standing in a deep blackness surrounded by a gray mist that seemed to take on a life of its own. It swirled around me as if taking my measure before sliding over parts of my exposed skin in a light touch.

I tried to wave it away, but it just reformed and continued moving around me. Taking a few steps forward, I put my hands out in front of me so I didn't bump into anything. I couldn't tell if this place was in the dark or just made of darkness.

As I moved forward, the mist seemed to form into the shape of a man. He reached out, and his ghostly hands swirled around my fingertips, making them tingle. I went to pull back, but something tugged on me. Though the mist wasn't solid, I could feel it pulling me forward.

I decided to follow along for now. It wasn't like I had any other ideas for where to go. After a few minutes of walking in what I hoped was the right direction, I saw the small spot of light appear again, bobbing in the distance. The mist moved me toward it, and I followed, carefully putting one foot in front of the other. As we got closer, the light spot grew larger until it became a rectangle the size of a door.

Stopping before it, I hesitated, not sure if I should go through it or not. The mist urged me forward. Taking in a deep breath, I stepped into the light. Well, not *the light*—at least I hoped it wasn't. I really wasn't ready to end my existence on Earth just yet. Raising my hand to my face, I blocked the brightness from my eyes. Once I had moved through the doorway, the bright light went out. I blinked several times, trying to clear my eyes to see in the new darkness.

"Welcome, my dear Blue. I've been waiting for you."

I jerked my head toward the deep, male voice. I could just make out the outline of a man sitting in a high-backed chair before a roaring fire. I tried to take in his features in the darkness, but they kept changing as the firelight danced over them.

"This has been a long time coming. But, oh, it has been worth the wait." He stood and slowly started moving toward me, his movements smooth and graceful as if he were stalking me. "I see you're as beautiful as your mother, and by the feel of you..." He moved to stand behind me and leaned forward, taking in a deep breath before letting it out. "You're even more powerful than she is."

"Who...who are you? Where am I?"

He laughed lowly, the dark, masculine sound sending shivers down my spine before he eased from behind me to take my hand and bow over it. "How crass of me. Allow me to introduce myself. I'm Hades, God of the Underworld."

My eyes widened, and I felt my heart stumble over itself before it took off at a gallop. Did he just say, *God of the Underworld?* I took in a deep breath and let it out, trying to calm myself.

This was so not happening.

I attempted to convince myself that this had to be a dream of some sort, though it felt nothing like my previous jaunts into the world of dream walking. I searched my mind for another plausible explanation but couldn't come up with anything.

Meanwhile, Hades stood perfectly still before me, seeming to watch every thought and emotion as it crossed my face. Now that he was close, I could see his features clearly and found my gaze wandering over him. He was certainly a magnificent specimen of a man—well, *god*. He stood about five inches taller than me and had the most mesmerizing amber eyes I had ever seen. His midnight-black hair was cut short on the sides with the top a bit longer, and he had that sexy, disheveled, just-rolled-out-of-bed look.

A slight five o'clock shadow dusted his sculpted cheeks and highlighted his chiseled jaw. His black button-down shirt was open at the throat and rolled at the sleeves, showcasing his muscular forearms. It fit him like a second skin, showing hints of the muscles rippling beneath the surface before trailing down to a tapered waist encased in form-fitting black dress pants. He smelled of heat, leather, and something else. Something so deep and masculine I was hard-pressed not to lean in just to get closer to it. With effort, I brought my wandering gaze back to his.

His mouth quirked up into a devastating smile. "Like what you see?"

I opened and closed my mouth a few times but couldn't seem to find my voice.

"Hmm…" He practically purred the word before winking and moving back to the large, throne-like chair he had been sitting in when I first entered. "Come take a seat, Blue. I wish to talk to you." He indicated the chair across from him.

As I tentatively sat, I saw movement by his side. Freezing in place, I watched as an enormous, black animal stood and stretched its massive paws before leaning back on equally large haunches. Immense jaws opened on a yawn to reveal rows of razor-sharp teeth. I gaped at the creature. It would almost look like an oversized dog, except it didn't seem to have any fur, just large, ridged scales. Not to mention the glowing red eyes and the fact that it breathed smoke out of its nostrils. Noting the direction of my stare, Hades placed his hand on the creature's head.

"This is Scythe, one of my hellhounds."

I eyed the creature as it stood and came over to me, barely daring to move a muscle. He sniffed my legs and arms before looking me directly in the eyes. An intelligence far beyond any mere animal seemed to lay behind his gaze, and I blinked slowly. He blinked back before nodding his great black head and licking the back of my hand. To my amazement, he settled on the floor at my feet, seeming content with my presence.

"It seems he likes you."

I let out my pent-up breath and tried to calm my racing heart.

Hades nodded at the hound. "You should feel honored. Scythe gives his approval to very few."

"Where am I?" I asked the question he had neglected to answer earlier, though if the hellhound was any indication, I knew exactly where I was.

"In my castle in the Underworld—my realm."

"How am I here? Am I dream walking again?"

"Dream walking?" Hades chuckled and shook his head. "No, my dear, you've come to me the way only my people can. As a soul."

"Wait, what!?" I gripped the arms of the chair I was sitting in, causing Scythe to growl at my sudden movement. I carefully relaxed, not wanting to agitate the hellhound. "I'm not...dead, am I?"

Dammit, I knew I shouldn't have stepped into the light.

Hades eyed me in amusement, making me wonder if he could read my thoughts even through my block. "Of course, not. You've just traveled incorporeally as a soul."

I sat back in relief before looking down at my hands in confusion. Now that I looked closer, they *were* a bit wispy, as if I wasn't quite solid. "How did I do that? I haven't been able to become incorporeal since the first time it happened. And that was quite by accident."

"Because I summoned you here."

"Summoned me?"

Reaching for something on the floor, he lifted a very familiar-looking sculpture. It was the statue Brody had done of me when he started to have visions of me in the Trials.

"Where did you get that?"

Hades smiled, his lips tipping up at the corners to reveal perfectly white teeth. "Why, I stole it, of course."

"You...you stole it? But I thought Larkin's Nixies..." The statue was taken from my house back before the Trials started. We thought the Nixies had done it under Larkin's orders. It was funny, but the theft of that statue had been the catalyst that launched me fully into the Fae world. I wondered now if that had been its purpose.

Laughing, Hades set the statue on the table between us. "Naturally, I stole it from them."

"But why?"

"Haven't you figured it out yet, Blue? Riona, Iridia...every statue Brody creates from his visions traps a small piece of the person's soul within it, sealing the memory shown to Brody in the statue. To you, it was a connection that allowed the lost souls of those people to find you. To someone like me, it's a direct link to that person's soul, and I can use it to forcefully bring them to me. That is *if* they are dead or...have the gift."

"The gift?"

"The gift that comes with the blood of a god. I wasn't sure until now, but since you're here, I can see it's true. I have to wonder, though, which of my kin managed to conceive you without anyone knowing?"

"I have no idea what you're talking about."

Hades smirked. "You cannot lie to me, Blue. But it's no matter. That you're here is proof you're part god. And I'm so, so glad."

"What do you want?"

"Can't I just want to meet one of my own?"

I quirked my mouth to the side derisively. "You don't strike me as the sentimental type."

He let out a low, amused chuckle. "How right you are. But as to my reasons, now is not the time for me to share them with you. Come, there is something I want you to see."

Hades nodded his head toward Scythe, who stood and walked forward. As I watched, the hellhound opened a portal that led into a deeply wooded area. Hades stepped up to Scythe, placing his hand on his back before motioning for me to follow. I stood and hesitantly stepped through the opening. Looking around, I took in the peacefulness of the space we had just entered. The only sounds were the hum of insects and the rustle of leaves as the wind gently blew through the trees.

"Where are we?"

Hades smiled as he glanced back at me. "Nowhere of consequence."

He moved through the trees, leading me along a narrow path. I followed, not sure what else to do. Before long, we came upon a small cottage nestled among the trees and foliage. Hades didn't even knock, just strode forward and opened the door. As I looked inside, a familiar voice floated out to me.

"What do you want now, Hades?"

I stood frozen in place. "Mom?"

When she didn't respond, I looked at Hades, and he smirked. "Only I can see you right now."

"Why can you see me when I'm incorporeal if others can't?"

"Because all souls, whether solid or not, are real to me. I can see and touch you, no matter what state you're in." I wondered if I had the same talent, and that was why I had been able to see and touch Riona right from the start.

Turning back to my mother, I thought about what I had done the last time I was in this state to make it so Larkin could see me. Reaching out with my senses, I felt three different sets of energy vibrations. I could easily differentiate Hades, but I couldn't tell which of the other two was my mother's, so I matched them both.

My mother, who had been glaring at Hades, stopped in her tracks, her eyes widening. "Carolina?"

Guess it had worked.

I ran forward and hugged her, glad my arms didn't just go straight through her. "Mom, what are you doing here? How did you get here? You're not incorporeal, you're actually here."

Iridia hesitated, seeming reluctant to say anything with Hades standing there.

He smirked and moved toward the door. "I'll leave you for a few minutes to get reacquainted." He whistled for Scytho, but the hellhound refused to leave my side. Hades stared at him for a moment before shrugging and leaving the house, gently shutting the door behind him.

As soon as we were alone, Iridia turned worried eyes to me. "What are you doing here with Hades? It's too dangerous for you to be with him, even incorporeally."

"I don't know, Mom. I...I think Hades forced me to come to him. He has my statue, the one Brody made of me."

Her look quickly turned to one of alarm. "No... How did he get it?"

"Seems he stole it from Larkin."

She started pacing the room. "This is not good. Not good at all."

"Tell me about it. Knowing that Hades has a direct link to my soul is disturbing on so many levels, I can't even begin to tell you."

She ignored my flippancy and continued. "You have to get away from him. You need to find a way to block him from bringing you to him. This can't be happening, after everything we did to keep you out of his hands..."

My eyes narrowed on her. "What do you mean, after everything you did to keep me out of his hands? What is going on here, Mother?"

Her pacing faltered, and she looked at me fearfully. "I...I...didn't mean, I just..."

My gaze narrowed even more. "What aren't you telling me?"

"Hades wants to see if he can use you for your powers to overthrow his brother, Zeus. It's why your mother and I sent you away to live with your aunt."

I turned around in surprise at the new voice. Before me stood a man about my height with a blocky yet strong build. He had intelligent brown eyes behind wire-framed glasses and a slightly rounded face with a trimmed beard. His hair was cut short and parted neatly to the side. He looked exactly as you would expect a Warlock to look—minus the robes and pointy hat.

"Aiden?" I wondered how he was able to see me, but then realized he must have been the other energy vibration in the house I had matched to.

He nodded and smiled, showing slightly crooked teeth. "The one and only."

"Technically, there are a lot of Aidens out there, so you can't be the one and only." I laughed mentally to myself, thinking of the time I had told Keane that exact same thing.

Keane!

With a jolt, I realized I couldn't feel my connection to him. I had been so caught up in everything going on, I hadn't even realized it was gone. I felt a bit of panic welling up. The last time I had gone incorporeal, the only way I had gotten back into my body was through my connection to him. I took a deep breath to soothe my frayed nerves. It would be okay. Iridia did this all the time. She would know how to get me back into my body.

Unaware of my inner turmoil, Aiden went to stand beside Iridia and put an arm around her. "I see she has managed to take on your fondness for sarcasm—even without you being around."

Iridia glanced sideways at Aiden and gave him an innocent look. "Whatever do you mean?" He shook his head with a smile and lifted her chin, placing a light kiss on her lips.

My face softened as I watched them together. It was obvious they were very much in love.

"Your mother is right. You can't be here. Hades can't be allowed to get control of you."

I crossed my arms over my chest. "How does Hades even know about me?" My mother studiously avoided my gaze while Aiden's turned weary.

"Why don't we sit?" Aiden took my mother's hand and led her to the couch before indicating for me to sit next to her. When I merely perched on the arm of the chair, giving him my best deadpan stare, he sighed before meeting my gaze head-on. "Hades knows about you because you were born here, and he helped to raise you."

That took me back a step. Of all the things I'd expected him to say, that wasn't one of them. "Wait, what?" I seemed to be saying that a lot today.

"I know your mother has told you the story about how I was held captive, and she came to rescue me. What she didn't tell you was that I was being held by Hades."

I slid off the chair arm onto the seat. "Why?"

"As bait to get to your mother."

"Her magic…"

"Exactly. He was convinced she had this special *gift* he needed to overthrow Zeus. Once he captured her, though, he quickly discovered that your mother wasn't as powerful as he thought. He said her gift was too diluted. I'm still not exactly sure what he was talking about."

I nodded absently, my thoughts going in circles. I had a feeling I knew exactly what *gift* Hades was referring to. I pondered where in the family tree the blood of a god had entered. Iridia, obviously, wasn't a direct descendant if Hades said it was too diluted. I also wondered why only she seemed to have developed the powers that came with her heritage. Though if I thought about it, the Grayson family *had* always been known for having talents that were far more powerful than most. Maybe this was the reason.

Another thought made me pause. "Why hasn't Hades let you go or killed you if you're of no use to him?"

My mother finally met my gaze. "Because I'm the bait now." I sucked in a sharp breath. "You need to leave. Leave and never come back. Find a way to get your statue or block him, whatever you have to do. He can't be allowed to get his hands on you in your physical form. And under no circumstances can you come looking for us."

"Mom..."

"He kept me prisoner here after he realized I was pregnant. Threatened to kill your father if I didn't do what he wanted. I wasn't sure why until after you were born and your powers started to develop. Once he started seeing what you were capable of, he began asking questions, he started spending time with you." She paused and shook her head.

"I...I knew then there was something very special about you, and that whatever it was, Hades wanted it. Your father and I came to the decision that we had to send you away from here. We had to protect you at all costs. We put the enchantment on you, blocking your powers, and with a little...inside help, we were able to get you to your grandmother, who took you to your aunt, Alannah, to be raised." Iridia wiped at a stray tear that had fallen down her face.

"When Hades learned you were missing, he went ballistic. He began sending out all his best trackers to try to find you. To throw him off your trail, we told him we thought someone from Olympus had kidnapped you. With your powers sealed away, he was unable to find you. Until now."

"Why didn't you two ever try to escape?"

"We can't. We are bound by some strange god magic I don't understand. Until Hades releases us, we're trapped here. Now, you should go, you must return to your body and figure out how to stop him from finding you."

"But since I have my powers again, why is he still struggling to find me?"

She shook her head. "I don't know. Something must still be shielding you."

I looked between her and Aiden, wondering if I should tell them that Aiden wasn't my father as they thought. That my father was actually a god, and *that* was most likely why Hades wanted me. I questioned again how Poseidon had managed to impregnate my mother without her knowing. Perhaps it was time for that reunion. I had a few important questions for dear old dad.

Speaking of important questions. "Mom, how do you intentionally separate your soul from your body? And, more importantly, how do you return to it? The last time this happened to me, it was under extreme duress, and I almost died before I could return to my body."

She blanched and covered her mouth. "You almost died?"

I grimaced but nodded. "Long story short, I intercepted a death spell meant for King Tristan and the Elders. The pain of it pushed me from my body. But as you can see, I'm fine now. I just don't know how to do it when I want to. And it seems I need to learn."

Iridia moved to the edge of the couch and reached over to take my hands. "Close your eyes. Imagine seeing yourself floating above your body, looking down at it. Now, you have to move your soul to where you're imagining it."

Since I was already incorporeal, I obviously couldn't do what she was telling me, so she showed me. Using my senses, I delved into her essence so I could feel everything going on inside of her. She inhaled sharply when she felt me, her eyes opening wide, as she stared at me in wonder. "How are you doing that?"

I shrugged one shoulder. "Just something I picked up along the way."

"What? What is she doing?" Aiden, ever the scientific mind from what my mother had told me, wanted to know everything that was going on. Iridia explained to him how she could feel my presence inside her. He looked thoughtful. "I've never heard of such a thing. I wonder if it has something to do with how you were conceived."

He didn't know how right he was. I was pretty sure that little trick came from my godly half, as no other Fae seemed to be able to do it. I, of course, didn't say as much. I just couldn't seem to bring myself to dispel his notion that he was my father. At least, not yet. It would come out eventually, but for now, I didn't think I needed to roll out that little secret. They were under enough stress as it was.

Iridia continued showing me several times how she exited and entered her body. I noted that when she went incorporeal, her body went into a coma-like state. I wondered if my body was the same where it lay next to Keane. I *really* hoped he didn't wake up before I got back. In the state he'd been in over the past few months, it might be the one thing that sent him over the edge.

"One last question. You said before that Aiden could contact you when you were in this state in case of an emergency. How?"

"You need to find someone you trust implicitly. You'll be forming an exceptionally close bond with the person so when you're in stasis, they can enter your subconscious mind."

I nodded with a soft smile. "I think I can handle that."

Noting the look on my face, Aiden peered at me suspiciously. "Is there something—or rather, some*one*—you want to tell us about?"

His voice had taken on a fatherly scolding tone, causing my grin to widen. "His name is Keane. Mom has met him. He's a Vaimpír."

"Keane. Keane Rutherman? The Dark Prince?"

I eyed him with a slight frown. By his reaction, I didn't think he was too pleased about the revelation. "Yes."

"Are you sure you can trust him? You do know the rumors about him and his family, don't you?"

"Honestly, no. Nor do I care. I know the man, and there is no one I trust more."

Aiden's eyebrows drew together in a scowl. "This isn't a good idea. I don't trust that family. You need to pick someone else."

I heaved a huge sigh, barely resisting rolling my eyes, and slouched back in the chair I was sitting in. You would think I was sixteen years old the way he was acting, forbidding me to date the bad boy down the road. If he didn't like the idea of Keane being my partner for this, then he'd truly hate what I had to say next. "Keane and I are soulbound."

"What!?" Aiden jumped to his feet and roared. "Absolutely not. I forbid it!"

I just shook my head and smirked at his anger, looking to Iridia, who rolled her eyes. "Dear, sit down. You're acting as though she's some rebellious teenager."

"She might as well be." He seemed to calm a bit at her words but continued to grumble. "And I'm her father. Don't I get a say in this?"

Iridia shook her head and pulled him back onto the couch before looking at me. "Carolina…"

"Please, Mom. It's Blue now, remember?"

"Right. Sorry, I forgot." She gave Aiden a meaningful glance when he seemed as if he might interrupt before turning back to me. "How is it possible for you to be soulbound? You're not a Vaimpír. I thought a soulbond could only happen between two pure-blooded Vaimpír?"

I straightened and shrugged. "I'm not sure how it was possible, to tell you the truth. All I can tell you is that it happened. The Elders have blessed the union, and we have recently petitioned House Rutherman to recognize it, as well."

I didn't go into how badly that seemed to be going.

Aiden's face was slowly turning a bright shade of red the more I spoke, and I was afraid he'd give himself a heart attack or stroke if he didn't let off some steam. I shouldn't have worried, though, as a few seconds later, he exploded again.

"You plan to keep it!? Are you crazy? Evidently, we need to have a talk about the Vaimpír society and set some boundaries, young lady."

I shook my head. "Aiden..."

"Dad."

I shifted, a bit uncomfortable with the title, but conceded for now. "Dad, I know this may come as a bit of a shock, but I'm a grown woman now. *I tie my own sandals and everything.*" When he didn't seem to get the reference, I sighed. Didn't anyone watch Disney movies anymore? "Look, I've been making my own decisions since I was sixteen. This isn't something you can dictate or control. I'd appreciate it if you could trust my judgment on this one." I crossed my arms over my chest and gave him a stern look.

He seemed to deflate at the reminder. "I've missed so much. I missed your whole life until this point. I never thought I would have children, so I never considered what it would be like, what it would feel like. Then you came along and a whole new world opened up. But circumstances forced you away, and I was left with the feeling that I had let you down somehow." Iridia put a comforting arm around him.

I flinched internally, letting my arms fall to my lap. What did one say to something as heartfelt as that? "You didn't let me down. You did what you thought was best for me. No, you *did* what was best for me. While my upbringing may have been unconventional, I was safe, and for the most part, happy."

He smiled at me gratefully, his gaze a bit watery. I cleared my throat and quickly brought the subject back around to our original conversation before he started getting too emotional.

"So, what does Keane have to do to bring me back to myself if he needs to?"

"Normally he would need to use a form of dream walking to enter your mind, but with a soulbond, he should easily be able to do it through your connection. You'll have to practice, and he'll need to find his way past your conscious mind into your subconscious to alert you."

Before I could ask any more questions, the front door was thrown open, and Hades strolled in. "It would seem visiting hours are over."

"Please, Hades. Please leave Blue alone. You have me, why do you need my daughter? Her gift has to be even more diluted than mine." Iridia was practically on her knees begging him.

Hades laughed darkly before directing his amused gaze to me. "I see you haven't told them yet. Interesting."

Iridia looked at me, confused. "Told me what?"

I grimaced and looked down at the floor. "Mom—"

Hades stepped between us. "Unfortunately, that little revelation will have to hold for another time." Grabbing me by the waist, he practically dragged me from the house. Aiden made a last-minute grab for me, but Hades merely flicked his wrist and sent Aiden crashing back against the wall—his head making a sickening thud when it hit. He slumped to the floor, unconscious.

The last thing I saw as Hades closed the door, was my mother rushing to Aiden's side, crying his name. I only hoped the injury wasn't too severe.

I tried to yank myself out of Hades' grasp, but he just tightened his hold and pulled me closer. His touch was light, but I had a feeling it would become increasingly rougher if I struggled. Instead, I fumed next to him, not saying anything while going along obediently as he guided me through the portal.

Once back in his study, I pushed out of his grasp and turned on him. "Why won't you let my parents go if they are of no use to you? Do you just enjoy torturing people so much?"

Hades looked sideways at me, a small smile hovering on his lips. "I never said I wouldn't let them go."

I narrowed my eyes, knowing there was a catch. "So, why haven't you?"

He leaned over and ran a finger down the side of my face before tipping my chin up. "Perhaps I haven't had the right motivation yet."

I looked at him suspiciously. "What kind of motivation? What do you want to release them?"

"You." His amber eyes seemed to glow in the low light of the room. "I want you, Blue. All of you. Body, mind, and soul."

Adrenaline pumped through my veins at his predatory tone, causing my eyes to widen for a fraction of a second. Frowning at him, I took a few more steps away. "Is this about overthrowing your brother? You think to use me to get to him somehow? Do you honestly harbor that much animosity toward him?"

Hades shrugged nonchalantly, not seeming surprised that I knew. "I'm only interested in taking back what should have been rightfully mine."

"Why do you say that? Wasn't it your brother, Zeus, who gave your father that potion to make him regurgitate you and your siblings? Wasn't it Zeus who struck the killing blow with his lightning bolts and defeated your father, sending him to Tartarus? Didn't you draw lots for who would get what realm to keep it fair?"

Hades laughed bitterly, his face twisting in anger. "Oh, yes, the tales of the mighty Zeus. Written by philosophers on my brother's payroll. Contrary to the human accounts, our father didn't actually eat us. He just imprisoned us in the same depths of Tartarus where he now resides. I spent my childhood in that squalor of a prison while my brother was kept hidden away in the mortal realm with some Fairy, living in the lap of luxury—away from the horrors I faced and the starvation and beatings I endured day in and day out."

He dropped his gaze to the floor, a haunted look on his face. When he looked back up into my shocked gaze, his eyes were definitely glowing. "Who do you think planned our escape? Who do you think worked secretly with the Titans to create the weapons to defeat Kronos? Who do you think strategized and planned our attack on him? Who commanded the armies against him? And what did I get? Sentenced to rule the very place I was tortured while my *little brother* continued his life of decadence in the clouds. Funny how those *lots* were drawn, isn't it?"

I stared in surprise as he turned away from me and walked over to a sideboard containing bottles of liquor. I watched as he poured a glass of some dark liquid, downed it in one gulp, then poured another.

I wasn't sure if I believed him or not. He could just be trying to garner my sympathies. But somehow, I sensed that wasn't so. I felt like every word he spoke was the truth—one he hadn't necessarily wanted to reveal to me.

The room was still dark, only lit by the large fire, so I couldn't read the emotions moving across his face, but I could somehow feel them. Much like with Keane, they filtered in along with mine, and I wondered about it.

His deep, husky voice broke into my thoughts. "You're more powerful than I originally thought. I haven't told any of that to another living soul. And now you are feeling what I feel, aren't you?"

I nodded hesitantly, taking a step toward him.

"I can feel your emotions, as well. The turmoil, the uncertainty, the pity. I don't need your pity, Blue. I'm not a good person. You should know that I plan to find you so I can use you for my sordid revenge. And if I can't, I *will* make you come to me, using whatever means necessary. Even if that means killing those you hold most dear."

I stood stock-still, allowing his emotions to flow over me. He wasn't lying. I could feel his determination, his absolute certainty, and his driving need for vengeance. But I could also feel another emotion just below the surface. He was blocking it, pushing it down and trying to pretend it wasn't there. Sadness. I sensed a deep sadness in him. He narrowed his eyes at me, no doubt sensing my feelings, as well.

A growl escaped him as he stepped forward and grabbed me by the throat, pressing me against the wall. "Don't feel sorry for me, little one. I don't like it."

I stared into his gaze, oddly unafraid of him. "You can't stop me from feeling what I feel—even with brute force."

Hades let out an involuntary chuckle, and his hand on my throat loosened before finally dropping. "You're more god than I gave you credit for. We'll see how it sustains you in the coming months. Let the games begin." An evil smile graced his lips as he snapped his fingers.

"Scythe. Please take our guest through the void. We wouldn't want her getting lost before we even have a chance to start."

With that, he turned from me, and I felt myself being sucked through a portal. My last glimpse of Hades was of him grabbing one of the bottles of liquor from the sideboard and throwing it angrily into the fire, where it exploded. I shielded my eyes as the light flared, only to be replaced by utter darkness. I looked around and found I was back in the deep blackness I had come through earlier.

This was the void. The portal through which a soul could enter the Underworld. I was thankful for the help I had received the first time, as it was said you could get lost forever while slowly losing your sanity if you didn't have a guide. I had to wonder just who had guided me.

This time, I felt the heat of the hellhound next to me. He nudged me forward before moving to my side again. I placed my hand on his scaly hide to help guide me as I walked. Before long, we reached another bright doorway. Through it, I saw Keane's room just as I had left it, with the moonlight peeking through the curtains. Obviously, time flowed a lot differently in the Underworld. It was as if I hadn't been gone but a minute. Scythe huffed beside me and butted his head against me. I leaned down so I was level with him. Though I had been afraid of him in the beginning, I felt an odd connection to him now. I somehow knew he wouldn't harm me.

Running my hand over his head, I looked him in the eyes, hoping he could understand me. "Thank you, my friend."

"If you ever have need of me, I'll be by your side instantly, Mistress. You only have to call my name, and I'll be there."

I pulled back, astonished as the hellhound's thoughts ran through my head. He seemed to smile as he gazed at me before disappearing and leaving me alone. Turning, I walked through the portal and entered Keane's bedchamber. I saw myself curled up in his arms and smiled.

This is where I wanted to be. There was no way I would let Hades take this away from me. I would find a way to stop him from summoning me. I would learn how to get the upper hand so he couldn't use me or those I loved against me. I would find a way to rescue Iridia and Aiden, no matter the cost.

Chapter Five

Though I hadn't thought I'd be able to fall asleep again after everything that'd happened, it seemed I was wrong. When I finally pried my eyes open, it was to find a small elfin-like face pressed directly into mine, causing me to pull back in surprise.

"Are you still alive?"

I blinked rapidly, trying to clear my vision. "Um...I think so."

"Good. You need to get up so we can go rescue my big brother."

I finally brought Amelia, Keane's little sister, into focus. "And why do we need to do that?"

"Because, silly, you slept so long, Isabela now thinks this is her chance to spend time with my brother so she can steal him from you. She was thrilled when he came down by himself earlier and even more so when you didn't show up for midday meal. She's hoping you won't make it to supper either so she can have Keane all to herself tonight, but we'll sneak attack her." Amelia started jumping up and down on the bed in excitement. I rubbed my eyes as I tried to bring my brain into the present.

"What time is it?"

Amelia stopped jumping long enough to glance at the clock on the bedside table. "Just past two in the morning."

I groaned. I'd been asleep for twenty-plus hours. The last time I'd slept that long was right after the Trials when my body was trying to heal. I hoped traveling incorporeally didn't do this every time. I couldn't afford to lose days like this. Stretching out the kinks in my body, I slowly pulled the covers back and trudged to the bathroom. A glance in the mirror showed a woman in a too-large T-shirt with a pale face, wild hair, and sleep-encrusted eyes.

Not my best look.

After taking care of business, I started the shower and picked up my toothbrush. Sleeping for that long took morning breath to a whole new level.

A small head peeked around the bathroom door a few seconds later. "I picked out some clothes for you. They're on the bed." I raised my eyebrows at her. I wondered just what a seven-year-old thought was appropriate supper attire. "Oh, and here..." I made a startled grab as she tossed something at me before ducking back out, slamming the door behind her. I shook my head in amusement at her antics.

Juggling my toothbrush and the items in my arms, I glanced down at the fabric, my eyes widening in surprise. She'd just handed me a set of sexy black lace lingerie. A strapless, long-line corset bra and matching panties. What did they teach children around here?

Setting the items on the counter, I decided I'd better start getting ready before Amelia came back. Apparently, she was steering the ship this evening. I showered quickly and dried and styled my hair before applying minimal makeup. Thankfully, it seemed Nigel had picked up all the toiletries I'd need for my stay here while I was asleep.

Wearing just my undergarments, I made my way into the bedroom to see what Miss Amelia had chosen for me to wear. On the bed lay a little black dress. It was short, off the shoulder, and had a slit that seemed to take up half the dress. I wasn't sure how one was supposed to sit in such a thing and remain decent.

Amelia came racing back through the door, now dressed in a beautiful pink gown. "You're not dressed yet? Come on, it's almost time for supper."

"Amelia, where did you get this dress?"

She looked at me in amusement. "From your closet, silly. Oh! Wear the necklace you had on last night, that should really get her riled up."

"Why would my necklace bother her?"

"Because it belonged to Grandmama Mila."

I looked at her in surprise. "Are you sure?"

Ignoring me, she went zooming into the closet for who knew what else. I picked up the necklace in question, which I had set on the dresser. I couldn't believe Keane had given me something that belonged to his grandmother and hadn't said anything. I had thought it was just something he had picked up. I'd have to ask him about it later.

Clasping it carefully around my neck, I turned and eyed the dress still on the bed. I wasn't sure if I should trust Amelia's choice. The garment seemed a bit much for supper—at least in my opinion. But then again, who was I to say? Most of my suppers consisted of wearing a pair of soft cotton shorts and a tank top while eating food from a delivery bag. Shoring up my courage, I picked up the dress and stepped into it. Shimmying it over my hips, I slipped my arms into the arm holes and then attempted to zip up the back. It only got about halfway before it stopped—running into a tight spot due to my oversized chest. Doing some maneuvers that would've made a contortionist proud, I finally managed to get it all the way up. I stopped for a second to catch my breath. Who knew getting dressed could be such a workout? Amelia finally emerged from the closet, holding a pair of high heels, causing me to grimace. Elegant and poised, I was not, and these were much higher than the ones I usually wore.

"Amelia, where are you getting all these clothes and shoes? I don't think they're mine."

"Yes, they are."

"Are you sure?" While I didn't recognize them, that didn't mean anything. I did, after all, have a closet full of things given to me by designers over the years that I'd never worn or even paid attention to. I tended to gravitate toward the same things—shorts, T-shirts, and, most definitely, my Converse sneakers.

"Yup. Nigel brought it all yesterday while you were sleeping."

I wondered how Nigel had decided what to bring. If he had been the one selecting my underwear, things might get a little awkward the next time I saw him.

Sliding on the shoes she handed me, I turned and looked at myself in the full-length mirror. A small sound of surprise escaped my lips at what I saw. The woman staring back at me was not what I expected. She was sexy yet strangely sophisticated. The dress fit me like a second skin, hugging my curves in just the right places and revealing just enough without being too much. Drawing my shoulders back, I felt a bit of confidence flow over me. Maybe Amelia did know what she was doing after all.

Amelia clapped her hands behind me. "You look perfect. Isabela will spit nails when she sees you."

I laughed and turned to face Amelia, almost falling off the side of my shoe in the process. I really hoped I'd be able to walk in these things and not break something.

"Okay, I guess I'm as ready as I'll ever be. Do you know where Keane is?"

She nodded as she skipped to the door. "He's been in the study all night with Papa."

My heart skipped a beat. I wondered if Malakai had come to a decision about our bond. Shoring up my courage, I followed Amelia out the door and down the hall. Reginald met us just as we were descending the stairs—with me moving extra slowly to make sure I didn't trip over my feet and end up at the bottom much faster than I'd like.

"Good evening, Miss Blue. It's so good to see you up and about again. I must say, you're looking quite beautiful this evening. I trust you're feeling better?"

"Thank you, Reginald. Yes, I'm feeling much more refreshed now. And it's good to see you again. Anything of note happen while I was out of it?" I wobbled precariously and had to grab the banister to balance myself.

Reginald chuckled and took my hand, setting it on his sleeve so he could help me down the rest of the stairs. Thank goodness for old-world gentlemanly manners. It would've taken me a month of Sundays to make it down the rest of those stairs on my own.

"Thank you, Reginald. You're a godsend."

He guided me toward the dining room with Amelia still skipping happily in front of us. He leaned over so he could whisper in my ear. "There has been a lot of suspicious activity around here while you were absent. Miss Isabela is certainly plotting something where Master

Keane is concerned, as is his mother. I'd highly recommend you put those two in their places and soon."

"I'll do my best, though I'm not sure I can do much about his mother. She is, after all, the Queen."

"Don't let that intimidate you. Remember who you are. She holds no sway over you."

"But Keane..."

"Can hold his own against his mother, don't you worry about that. He's been doing it for a long time. Trust me, he's had plenty of practice."

I thought about asking Reginald just how old Keane was since Keane didn't seem to want to tell me, but then I reconsidered. The last time I learned something Keane wasn't ready to share with me, he was rather upset. Best to just let him tell me in his own time, no matter how curious I was.

As we approached the dining room doors, I felt my stomach flip. I wasn't looking forward to facing Keane's family again. Nervously smoothing my hand over my dress, I looked down at myself and hoped Amelia hadn't steered me wrong in my attire.

Reginald stopped just outside the doors while Amelia continued in. "You look exquisite, Miss Blue. You'll be sure to make Miss Isabela green with jealousy."

"Thank you, and thank you for escorting me down the stairs, Reginald. You truly are my hero tonight." I leaned over and gave him a peck on the cheek.

He winked and stepped back. "It has been my pleasure." Bowing, he moved off down the hall, leaving me to enter the room alone. I took a deep, steadying breath and stepped over the threshold.

As I entered, three sets of eyes turned my way, two of which instantly darkened with annoyance.

"Ah, Blue. It is so good to see you back up and about. I trust you slept well?" Malakai moved forward and took both of my hands in his. "And might I say, you look quite ravishing this evening. I can see why my son is so taken with you."

I blushed, not quite sure how to respond to his compliment. "Ah...thank you."

He placed my hand on his sleeve and escorted me toward the table—and the two unfriendly women. I looked around for Keane or Amelia but didn't see either one. Resigning myself, I plastered a smile on my face and greeted the two women. "Good Evening, Your Majesty. Isabela."

Malakai waved a hand in the air. "Oh, no need to be so formal, Blue. You must call us by our first names. Especially considering your relationship with our son." I smiled gratefully in his direction while watching Camille and Isabela exchange glances out of the corner of my eye.

"He's right, my dear. No need to stand on formalities." The smile Camille flashed me was even faker than mine, and I almost giggled at the absurdity of it all. "How are you feeling? Are you sure you're well enough to come to supper? We wouldn't hold it against you if you needed more time. I could always have the servants bring something to your room."

Isabela nodded enthusiastically. "Oh, yes, we wouldn't want you to overtax yourself. Since you didn't seem to bring along a maid, I could even lend you mine. She could draw you a lavender bath with some replenishing oils."

I shook my head while trying my darndest not to roll my eyes. Though they were making it very difficult. They could not have been any more obvious that they were trying to get rid of me.

"Thank you for your concern, but I'm feeling quite all right now."

"Oh. Well, if you're sure, my dear. How are your room accommodations? Are they to your liking? I know they are a bit far back, but I'm having several of the guest rooms overhauled and wanted to make sure you wouldn't be troubled by all the noise."

I looked at her strangely but realized she didn't know I was staying in Keane's suite. She still thought I was back by the servants' quarters, where she had initially asked Reginald to stash me. I cut a quick glance to Isabela, wondering just what she had told the woman about our last encounter. That was if she had even mentioned it to her. It had been an embarrassing failure on her part, after all.

"Oh, everything is quite satisfactory, thank you. You were so thoughtful for thinking about my comforts like that." Though my words were laced with sarcasm, I had a feeling it went right over her head.

"Excellent. If you have need of anything, please don't hesitate to ring the servants. They'll be sure to take good care of you."

Before I could reply, an arm encircled my waist, pulling me tightly against a hard, muscular body. I looked up into Keane's warm, blue gaze and breathed a sigh of relief. He turned me toward him before putting his finger under my chin and tilting my face up to him. His eyes searched mine before he leaned forward and pressed a light kiss on my lips. I heard a sharp intake of breath from next to us, but Keane just ignored everything and everyone but me. "*Ma moitié*, you should have sent for me the minute you woke." His voice was part admonishment and part relief.

I smiled. "I would have, except a certain young firebrand was hell-bent on getting me up, dressed, and out of the suite as quickly as possible. She seemed to think you were in dire need of rescuing. She even picked out my clothes—right down to my underwear—to make sure I was ready."

Keane stepped back while still holding my hands and looked me up and down. "And quite the job she did. You look stunning, Blue."

The aforementioned firebrand came bounding out of a dark corner of the room. Stepping between us, she put her arms around her brother's waist. He let go of my hands so he could wrap his arms around her and pick her up. "Just what mischief are you up to now, you little minx? And what do you think I need rescuing from?"

Amelia leaned over and whispered loudly in his ear—which naturally meant everyone could hear her. "Isabela, of course. *Sheee* thinks if she gets you all to herself tonight, she'll take you away from Blue. I heard her and Mama plotting." She eyed him very seriously.

I could see Keane struggle to keep a straight face. "Oh, really? And you don't like that idea?"

Amelia shook her head sharply while sticking her lip out. "Uh-uh. I don't like Isabela. She's mean to me."

Keane narrowed his eyes and threw a suspicious glance at Isabela. "Is she, now?" Isabela rolled her eyes while twisting her mouth to the side in annoyance. Meanwhile, Keane turned back to Amelia. "And how about Blue, do you like Blue?"

Amelia nodded enthusiastically, a smile blooming on her face. "Oh, yes. I like Blue very much. I think we should keep her."

A chuckle escaped Keane. "You know, I think I agree with you."

"Okay, that's quite enough." Camille clapped her hands to get everyone's attention. You could tell she wasn't happy with the way the conversation was going. "It's time for supper. Amelia, sit over here with me." She reached out for her, but Amelia just shrank back into Keane's arms and shook her head. Camille let out an exasperated sigh. "Amelia, come over here this instant."

She moved to grab her daughter, but Malakai stepped forward. "Camille, my dear, Amelia hasn't seen her brother in months. Let her be."

She turned her glare in Malakai's direction but then seemed to think twice about saying anything more. "Very well."

Once we were all seated, Camille cleared her throat. "I've decided to throw a ball tomorrow night in honor of Keane's return."

"Mother."

Camille raised a hand. "There is no use arguing, Keane. The invitations have already gone out to all seven houses, and they have all accepted."

Keane growled and wiped a frustrated hand over his face.

Malakai reached over and gripped his son's shoulder. "Son, allow your mother this one thing. You have not been active in Vaimpír society for quite some time. I think it will be good for them to see you."

There was a slight shift in his gaze toward me before it rested back on Keane. It was so subtle that I almost missed it, but Keane hadn't. "Of course, Father. If you think it best, I'll attend." He reached under the table and took my hand, squeezing it. I wasn't sure what introducing me to the seven houses would do, but if Malakai thought it was a good idea, I'd go along with it.

"I think it would be best if you kept your...relationship with Blue a secret for now." Keane's eyes snapped back to his mother, angry once again. "Hear me out before you argue, Keane. It's for her safety. How do you think the seven families will view an outsider who isn't even Vaimpír suddenly taking the place of one of their chosen? She would be eaten alive."

"Mother…"

"We'll introduce her as a friend of the family. Let everyone get to know her before anything about your bond is revealed."

While I didn't like it and knew that Camille had ulterior motives for doing it, what she said did have merit. The fact that this was the first bond to ever happen with someone who wasn't Vaimpír was sure to rock some of the elder generations' views on customs and traditions. Plus, as the heir to the throne, Keane would have to choose a wife eventually, regardless of his or my personal feelings on the matter. Better not to upset the other houses right now when he may need to make a political alliance later. I had to wonder if we would be able to hide the connection, though. If past experiences were any indication, the female Vaimpír seemed to be able to sense it. Though Camille and Isabela had both been blindsided when we told them, so maybe not all of them could.

While I was thinking, Keane had been arguing with his mother. "Keane, I think she's right."

Keane paused mid-sentence and looked at me askance. "You're agreeing with her?" The hurt in his emotions rippled over me while his mother's eyes flashed with triumph.

I put my hand on his arm and opened my mind further so he would see what I was thinking. "I'd like nothing more than to tell the world about our bond, Keane, you know that. But I think she's right in the fact that not all of Vaimpír society will handle the news well. I think it will come as a shock to a lot of the older generations, and they'll react much like your mother did at first, pitting them against you. Against us. Maybe if they get to know me first, they'll be more accepting when the time comes. Plus, it'll give you the political advantage."

Keane still didn't seem convinced, but I could tell he was thinking about it more rationally now. "We would only keep it a secret for a short time?"

Camille nodded enthusiastically. I was sure she was thinking whatever plans she had would come to fruition long before that happened.

"But after Blue is established, House Rutherman will give its blessing on our bond?"

Malakai nodded solemnly while Camille hesitated.

"Mother..."

"Fine. Yes. If *all* seven houses accept her, I'll give my blessing."

I frowned, noting her choice of words. I could already see the wheels turning in her head as she formulated a plan to make sure that didn't happen. I sighed, knowing we still had an uphill battle ahead of us.

———

After supper, Keane and his father went back to the study to continue doing whatever it was they had been doing all evening. Camille and Isabela disappeared together to discuss party plans and, I was sure, how to get rid of me. Which left me with Amelia.

"Looks like it's just you and me, kiddo. Unless you have other plans."

She smiled widely, stood, and took my hand. "I want you to meet someone."

Intrigued, I followed her out of the room. About halfway down the hall, I stopped and took off my shoes. No reason to torture myself any longer if I didn't have to keep up appearances. Amelia giggled and followed suit, sliding her flats off and holding them in her arm. She retook my hand and led me farther back into the house to a section I hadn't been to before. After moving past several doors, Amelia finally stopped in front of one, knocked softly, and waited.

After a moment, I heard a male voice on the other side. "Come on in."

She opened the door and let go of my hand, dropping her shoes, then bounded in with her usual enthusiasm. "Rhys! I brought someone for you to meet."

I watched as she jumped into the lap of a young man in a wheelchair. I studied him as I shut the door, setting my shoes on the floor next to Amelia's. He had the same hair and eye color as Keane, and if he were standing, he would probably be around the same height. Though he wasn't quite as muscular, you could tell he used his upper body a lot to maneuver himself around.

The corners of his eyes crinkled when he smiled, and you could tell he did it a lot. "Oh, you have, have you?" He reached down and tickled Amelia, who laughed and squirmed in his lap. I smiled at the sight. You could tell that there was a lot of affection between the two.

"Ssstop! Rhys!"

"Do you give up?"

"Yyyesss!" Amelia was laughing so hard tears were forming in her eyes. When he finally stopped tickling her, she sat up and wrapped her arm around his neck.

"Blue, this is my brother, Rhys. Rhys, this is Blue, Keane's *âme sœur liée*."

I shook my head at the title but moved forward with my hand outstretched anyway. "It's a pleasure to meet you, Rhys."

Rhys moved his chair forward and met me halfway. Taking my hand, he brought it to his lips. "The pleasure is definitely all mine. I've heard a lot about you from this little hellion here. I hoped she would bring you to see me. So, you're my brother's âme sœur liée."

I again ignored the title. "And you're Keane's younger brother."

He smiled, revealing an enchanting dimple in his left cheek—much like his brothers. "Yup. Number four of five."

"Did you just arrive?"

He shook his head with a bit of a sheepish look. "No, I live here. I apologize for not introducing myself before now."

I looked at him, feeling a bit confused. "If you live here, why haven't you been at meals?"

"I rarely leave my rooms. My mother finds it hard to accept my condition, being a Royal Vaimpír and all. I don't usually socialize with the family, especially when they have new guests."

I was taken aback. "She's ashamed of you? Because you're in a wheelchair?"

"Yup." He popped the p on the end. Turning his chair with Amelia still on his lap, he wheeled it over to the couch before indicating for me to sit. "And there you have it, one of the dirty little secrets of the infamous Rutherman family."

I laughed, enjoying his jovial attitude. He may have a physical disability, but he didn't seem to let it affect his outlook on life.

"Can I ask how you ended up in the chair? You don't have to answer if it's too invasive."

He shrugged his shoulders, still smiling. "It doesn't bother me to tell you. I've been this way since birth. Weird for a Vaimpír, I know, what with our healing abilities and all. I can heal everything about myself except my legs. Some weird quirk, I guess."

"Is it unusual for a Vaimpír to have disabilities?"

"Quite. They believe it's some recessive gene in the Vaimpír that shows up now and again. I've only met two others besides me in my lifetime."

"And just how old are you?"

He laughed and put a hand to his chest in mock hurt. "Seems I know far more about you than you do about me. I'm the same age as you. Twenty-eight."

"I'm sorry to say I don't know anything about you or your siblings as yet. Keane is rather secretive when it comes to himself and his life before I met him."

Rhys chuckled and rolled himself into the kitchen. "That doesn't surprise me. He's always been one to keep things to himself. You want a beer?"

"Sure. Are there any other relatives living here I should know about?"

"No, it's just Amelia and I here besides our parents."

"Why haven't you ever moved out?"

"And have the Rutherman name tarnished with constant proof of a defective Vaimpír?" He said this sarcastically before breaking out into a smile again. My heart broke for him. "Honestly, it's just easier. My parents provide me with whatever I need, and, in return, I stay out of the public eye."

"That's awful." I felt anger welling up in me at Camille Rutherman. Not only was she a manipulative bitch to Keane, but she was also the world's worst mother to her physically disabled son. I had to take a couple of breaths to push the anger back down so it didn't take over.

Rhys only shrugged as he came back into the living area and handed me a bottle while giving Amelia a juice box. "Don't feel too sorry for me. I do have a life outside this house, unbeknownst to my mother." He winked and gave me a devilish grin. "Not even the great Camille Rutherman can hold back all this from the world." He indicated himself with a flourish before taking a swig from his drink.

I smiled widely and toasted him. "Here's to showing Camille that she can't dictate everything in life, regardless of what she thinks."

He laughed, choking on his drink. "Not too fond of my mother, are you?"

"Let's just say I'm not her biggest fan. But the feeling is mutual, so no loss there. Camille and Isabela are probably planning the ball while simultaneously plotting how to dispose of my body even as we speak."

Rhys grunted and rolled his eyes. "The ball. You're right, I'm sure they're trying to find the best way to get rid of you so Keane will finally marry Isabela. Little do they know that even if they manage to get you to leave, he would never marry that woman."

"Not a fan of Isabela either?"

He shook his head fiercely. "Absolutely not. That woman is a terror. Cut from the same cloth as my mother, I'm afraid."

"Will you be attending the ball?"

He snorted and took another drink of his beer, not even bothering to say anything.

"I think you should come." I gave him a meaningful look.

"Oh, yeah. My mother would be over the moon with that idea."

"Who says you can't? Did she specifically tell you not to go?"

"My mother doesn't speak to me unless absolutely necessary. She just figures if she doesn't tell me what's going on, I won't know. Little does she realize that I hear everything. Being basically a shadow in your own home does have its advantages."

"Well...you can come as my escort."

He gave me a crooked grin. "And what about Keane?"

"Your mother thinks it would be in my best interests—for my safety—that I be introduced as a friend of the family before anything about my connection to Keane is brought up."

"Probably more so she can force Keane to marry one of the *chosen* bimbos."

I laughed, loving that he seemed to be on the same wavelength as I was. "My thoughts exactly. Though I do believe she's right about me being introduced before my bond to Keane is revealed."

"Really?"

"As much as I hate saying I agree with something she says..." I feigned a dramatic shudder of revulsion, causing Rhys to crack up. "I have a feeling the older Vaimpír won't take to these things easily. If I can work my way into their good graces first, maybe it will help when it comes out."

Rhys seemed to think about it. "You're right. It's going to shake up their view of how things work in our world. Considering there hasn't ever been a case of a non-Vaimpír bonding with a Vaimpír before. Speaking of, have you figured out how it was even possible?"

I shifted in my chair. I wanted to confide in Rhys about my godly bloodline and everything that appeared to go along with it, but I knew I couldn't.

"I..."

"You don't have to tell me yet. I know we just met, and that I have to earn your trust first."

I smiled my thanks. "When the time is right, I promise I'll tell you everything."

"That's a deal." We clinked our bottles together in solidarity.

Then I gave him a mischievous grin. "Now, about attending the ball..."

Chapter Six

Lying in bed, I stared up at the ceiling, unable to fall asleep. I was sure the twenty-hour snooze fest had something to do with my insomnia. Not to mention, I was a little afraid to fall asleep again since I still hadn't figured out how to block Hades from summoning me. I didn't think he would be able to do it as long as I was conscious, but once I went to sleep, my guard would be down, and I could be manipulated easily.

Keane came back just before sunrise. He got undressed, slid into bed, and pulled me against him. "I'm sorry for leaving you alone all evening, *ma moitié*. My father and I had much to discuss. I promise I'll be all yours tomorrow evening."

I let out a small laugh. "Now, that is a promise you can't keep."

"Why ever not?"

I turned over to face him. "Your mother's ball, remember? You have to play the part of the Dark Prince and everything it entails."

Keane groaned and closed his eyes. "You're right. I somehow managed to block that part of the evening out. I don't know how I'll get through it."

"Just smile and wave, boys, smile and wave."

He opened his eyes and grinned at me. "Stop stealing my lines."

"Never." He had said that to me once when we went out to eat, and his popularity as a member of the band Ethereal Mutation had caused a bit of a commotion. I still found it amusing that a big, bad Vaimpír watched cartoons.

He reached out a hand and tucked a stray curl behind my ear. "Mm, so tell me, what did you do for the rest of the evening to keep yourself entertained without me?"

"Amelia took me to meet someone."

"Oh?"

"Your brother, Rhys."

I felt Keane tense a bit before he relaxed when he saw the encounter in my mind. "I should've known better than to believe you would think less of him for his disability."

I smirked at him. "Yes, you should've. Do you suppose I'll meet the rest of your siblings tomorrow night?"

"Only if you're unlucky." I raised my eyebrows at that. "The last two you haven't met yet are the twins. Hayden and Hugo. And they are...unique, to put it mildly."

"Unique, how?"

"Uh-uh, I'm not going to tell you. I want to give you the opportunity to have an unbiased interaction. And don't go asking Amelia or Rhys, either." He wagged his finger at me before giving me an evil little smile.

"Ookay. I'm a little scared now."

Keane shook his head in amusement before his expression turned serious. Propping himself on an elbow, he looked down at me. "Are we going to discuss what the hell happened that caused you to go into a healing stasis again?"

"Funny you should mention Hell…"

I opened my mind so Keane could see everything that had happened the previous evening while I told him about it. When I finished, he looked thoughtful.

"Let me get this straight. Your father was kidnapped by Hades to use as bait to capture your mother. Once Hades had your mother, he found out she wasn't powerful enough to do what he wanted. Then, he found out she was pregnant and had some sixth sense that you might be what he needed. So, when you were born, Hades helped to raise you, but your parents feared his interest in you and secreted you away to live with your aunt in hopes it would mean Hades couldn't find you.

"Fast forward some years, and Brody creates a statue of you that contains a piece of your soul. Said statue gets stolen by Larkin, only to be later stolen by Hades. And now, Hades can use it to summon your soul to him at will because of your godly status, but he still can't find your physical form, which he needs to defeat his brother, Zeus. Does that about sum it up?"

I nodded when he paused.

"Tell me. What is it you can do that would be needed to defeat a god? And why your physical form? You've already proven you can do pretty much any magic, even when incorporeal."

I shrugged my shoulders. "I don't know. It's not like Hades was spilling his secrets to me."

"But he did tell you things he didn't want or expect to. Which means you have some sort of power over him. I wonder if you could pull even more information out of him if you saw him again."

"Or he could use my mother against me to make me tell him where I am."

Keane grimaced and shook his head. "There is that."

"We need to rescue my mother and Aiden, Keane."

"But wouldn't that be doing exactly what he wants?"

"Perhaps, but there has to be a way."

"Maybe we should consult Kieran. He has to know a thing or two about the gods, and maybe one of his books says how to block a summons from the likes of Hades."

I nodded slowly. "I don't want him to know about Iridia, though. Not until I can figure out how to rescue her."

"We. How *we* are going to rescue her."

"Are you sure you want to follow me into Hell and back?" I quirked a smile and raised an eyebrow at him.

Keane smiled back, but his tone was very serious when he answered. "*Ma moitié,* I would follow you to the ends of the Earth and beyond if you needed me to."

I stared into his turquoise-blue gaze, seeing the truth of his statement. He would indeed follow me anywhere. Lifting my hand, I ran it softly along his jaw. Taking it, he kissed the center of my palm before placing it against his chest. I squirmed a bit, knowing where his mind was going. Trying to lighten the mood, I gave him a mock-serious look.

"Now, it's your turn. What subject was so important to discuss with your father that could possibly excuse your leaving me all by my lonesome on my first evening here?"

"You."

"Me?" I lay back in surprise.

"You."

"What about me?"

"Everything."

"Everything?"

"Yup."

"You told your father everything about me?"

His lips stretched into a sideways grin. "From the instant our eyes connected across that busy bar till the moment I left you sound asleep in my bed."

"Um...did you...did you tell him about my powers? About my father?"

Keane reached out a hand and cupped my cheek, searching my gaze. "Do you trust me, Blue?"

"With my life."

"Good. Then you know I'd never reveal anything that could put you in danger."

I sagged in relief. Not that I didn't want his father to know about me. I had a feeling he was trustworthy and would keep my secrets. I was just hesitant about how I would deal with it all once it *did* come out. And speaking of coming out...

"Keane?"

He was lazily running his fingers along my shoulder and arm. "Hmm?"

"What should I expect at the ball tomorrow?"

"A lot of rich men strutting around trying to prove they are stronger and more powerful than each other as the women gossip behind each other's backs while smiling and hugging one another like long-lost friends."

I laughed and shook my head. "Doesn't sound much different than the parties my aunt used to throw."

"It's exhausting."

"What about all the chosen daughters? I assume they'll be there, vying for your attention."

Keane groaned. Rolling onto his back, he threw his arm over his face. "Don't remind me. I have to play nice with all of them for the sake of politics. But in reality, I can't stand but maybe two of them."

"Oh?"

Keane peeked at me from under his arm with a grin. "Jealous?"

"Not yet."

He chuckled and put his arm back down. "No need to be. Neither Audrey nor Leilani actually wants to be a chosen daughter. They are only doing it for the accolades it affords their families."

"What would they do if you had to choose one of them?"

"More than likely step down from their position. Audrey already has someone she's going to marry once she gets the nerve to break it to her family. And Leilani is married to her career. I'll have to introduce you to them so you'll have someone you can trust at the ball. Things can get pretty tricky with how you present yourself at functions such as these, as I'm sure you're aware."

"Yes. You can be assured I know exactly how to behave. My aunt drilled it into my head from a young age and would punish me severely if I disobeyed or embarrassed her."

Keane reached over with his other hand and interlaced his fingers with mine, squeezing them. "I'm sorry you had to grow up that way, *ma moitié*."

I shrugged one shoulder. "It made me who I am today. If life hadn't happened the way it did, who's to say who or where I'd be now." It had taken me a long time to come to that conclusion. To forgive Aunt Alannah for her shortcomings and abandoning me.

"I guess you're right. If you weren't who you are, you might never have walked into the bar that night, and I can't imagine never meeting you." Keane turned his head and looked at me, an emotion I wasn't ready to identify floating in the connection between us. He cleared his throat. "Now, it's time for you to sleep. I'll watch over you. If I sense anything trying to pull you away, have no doubt I'll find a way to stop it."

I smiled softly. Knowing Keane, he would indeed find a way to protect me, no matter the circumstances.

The night of the ball found me sitting on the floor in the closet, sifting through the dresses Nigel had brought for me. Thankfully, he had anticipated a few black-tie affairs and grabbed my cache of designer gowns.

My makeup and hair were already done, but I had yet to choose a dress. I originally planned to wear the one I had worn the first night we had dinner with Keane's parents but then thought better of it with Isabela attending. While I didn't care what anyone thought of me, I didn't want to give her gossip fodder to spread that could potentially embarrass Keane and his family. Especially since they were essentially sponsoring me within their society. While I knew his mother wanted me to fall flat on my face, she also had to do it in a way that didn't reflect on her.

I let out an exasperated breath and set aside yet another gown, deciding it was too conservative. I needed something that would make a statement but not be offensive to the older generations. Thinking back to my last contract with Versace, I dove farther into the closet. Finally, my hand closed around a solid black silk gown. It was a one-shouldered, long-sleeve mermaid-style gown. The sleeve was made of black lace with large flower appliques that morphed into shining black silk on the right shoulder. The silk crisscrossed over the chest in a sweetheart neckline, leaving the left shoulder bare before flowing down into the skirt. The surprise was at the left hip, which featured a sneaky cutout panel of the same see-through lace from the sleeve that also flowed into the silk. If you weren't paying attention, you wouldn't even realize it was there. It was elegant yet cheeky. It would also mean ditching my underwear. I frowned but then decided to throw caution to the wind. What the hell? I grabbed a simple pair of black heels, not so high I wouldn't be able to move around with ease all night but high enough to settle the dress at the correct length, leaving the small train to trail behind. I quickly slipped out of my panties and into the dress before walking out of the closet.

Keane was sitting on the bed in yet another custom-tailored tux. All black like the one before, but this time he had paired it with a black tux shirt. As the author from one of the books I had recently read said about her male lead character, he looked downright lickable. I'd never thought that phrase would work in the real world, but here we were.

I found myself wondering what would happen if I just climbed onto his lap and slipped his jacket from his broad shoulders... Shaking my head, I stopped myself. Nothing good would come of letting my thoughts go down that road.

Looking down at my dress, I noted that his shiny black vest and tie perfectly complemented me. Not that we were going as a couple, but it was still nice to show that we were connected in a subtle way. He stood as I walked in, giving a low whistle.

"*Ma moitié.* You're simply breathtaking."

"Do you think it will project the right image for your family?"

"I think the men will be unable to keep their eyes off you, and the women will be torn between jealousy and admiration." He stepped forward and helped me zip the back of the dress before dragging his lips along my bare shoulder. "It's going to be torture not being able to touch you as I want all night long."

I shivered as his breath floated across my skin. "The feeling will be mutual." I turned and smiled at him, running my hands under the lapels of his jacket. "What jewelry should I wear? I don't want to exude the wrong message, and I know necklaces are used as a sign of what you're trying to project in this world."

"Right, you are. However, I want you to leave your neck bare."

"But didn't you say that was like an aphrodisiac to the Vaimpír?"

He laughed softly. "It will drive them mad."

"Keane, is that really what we want to portray? I'm not sure I feel comfortable with that."

"Don't worry, *ma moitié.* I wouldn't throw you unarmed to the wolves." He pulled out a small square velvet box.

"Another of your grandmother's pieces?"

He looked at me in surprise. "How did you know the necklace I gave you belonged to my grandmother?"

"Amelia told me."

"Of course, she would know. No, these were not hers. I picked these out, especially for you." He opened the box and held it up for my inspection.

My mouth made a little *O* of surprise. Inside lay a pair of long, layered diamond earrings and a matching bracelet.

"These will give the message of: *Look but don't touch unless told to do so.* It shows you're available yet powerful enough to hold your own should someone try to take you without your permission."

"Are they real?"

Keane looked partially offended. "You don't think I'd be so thoughtless as to give you something fake, do you?"

"Keane, you know that I wouldn't care."

"You don't, but they do. If they were fake, they would be spotted from a mile away and diminish what we're trying to project. We want to convey the message of your wealth in both money and power."

"Power?"

"Power is key in the Vaimpír world, and you have it in spades. We just want to flaunt it a bit."

"What power do I have that would be coveted by the Vaimpír?"

"Your family is already well known for its magical powers. Also, because of the Trials and everything that happened afterward, you're being touted as the most powerful Fae our kind has ever seen. And finally, it seems a rumor has recently started circulating about your possible connection to the gods."

I frowned at that. "What do you mean? Someone knows about my father?"

Keane shook his head. "No, it's saying you can garner favors from the gods."

"But why would they think that?"

"Who knows? But we're going to use it to our advantage."

"How would I even begin to prove something like that?"

Keane smirked and rubbed my shoulders. "You don't need to. A few well-placed words in the right ears and it'll be all over the ballroom. All you have to do is play the part."

"And what part is that?"

"That of a supremely confident woman, well aware of her worth. Keep your answers short and vague, and your mystique will spread like wildfire. Trust me, the Barons will eat it up."

"So, I'll be like Aubrey Hepburn in *My Fair Lady* when she's presented at the embassy ball?"

Keane smiled at my excitement over the notion and nodded. "Exactly like that. Except I won't be the ass that Professor Higgins was afterward."

I laughed, loving that he had seen the movie and knew it well enough to make a comment like that. "Is there anyone I need to be wary of?"

Keane tilted his head as he thought about it. "The chosen daughters, certainly. They will be doing whatever they can to discredit you in front of their families. You remember what I told you about each of the houses?"

I quickly sifted through everything we'd talked about the past few months and nodded slowly.

"Good, use that knowledge to your advantage."

"Wait, Isabela knows about our connection, won't she tell everyone?"

"Isabela will keep her mouth shut because my father has deemed it so."

"What about Mariana? She was a chosen at one time. Will she be there?"

"Mariana is still sequestered away from Fae society, so she won't be in attendance."

"How about your ex, Jasmine? Will she be there? She also knows about our connection."

"Jasmine only surmises. She doesn't know for sure. She'll be there somewhere, but I highly doubt she'll start any trouble at this large of a gathering. After the scandal she caused, she fell out of favor with her house."

"She's not one of the chosen?"

"Not any longer. After everything that happened, she was stripped of her title, and her cousin, Isabela, took her place."

This surprised me. "Jasmine is part of House Dalca?"

Keane nodded, toying with a stray curl that had fallen onto my neck. "Yes, Isabela has only been a chosen for the past few years."

"Then why is your mother pushing so hard for you to marry her?"

Keane shrugged and, with a delicate hand, repinned my curl. "Who's to say why my mother does what she does?"

"This is going to be a long night, isn't it?"

Keane chuckled and pulled me into a tight embrace. "That it is, *ma moitié*. That it is. But for the chance to have you by my side and finally in my bed in every way..." He looked down at me and winked. "I would walk through the fires of Hell."

I looked up at him and smirked. "Oh, don't worry, you get to do that later."

He chuckled again and kissed the top of my head. Stepping back, he glanced at the watch on his wrist. "As much as I hate to say it, it's time."

"Where is the ball being held, here at your parents' house?"

It was Keane's turn to smirk. "Not exactly."

Taking my arm while refusing to tell me more, he led me down the stairs toward the salon. Upon entering, I saw Malakai standing with Camille by the fireplace. Isabela was nowhere to be seen, so I assumed she would be going to the ball with her family. Malakai was dressed much like Keane except with a traditional white shirt, while Camille wore yet another long-sleeved velvet gown. This one was red with a sweetheart neckline, squared-off shoulders, and a slit that traveled the entire length of her thigh, coming to rest on her hip, where the fabric twisted, creating a beautiful draping ruche.

"Ah, there you are, Keane. Blue, you look lovely this evening. If I may say so, that dress is the perfect choice for tonight."

"Thank you."

Camille eyed my attire critically. "Are you sure you should be going without a necklace on? That is a bit brazen, don't you think? Or do you even know the meaning of it in our society?" She was wearing a very wide choker covered in draping diamonds that swept to her collarbone.

I smiled at her serenely, not letting her barbs get to me. "I'm well aware of the meaning, and it's exactly what I want to convey to the seven houses."

Camille huffed but didn't say anything further.

"Excellent. Then, shall we?" Malakai reached over to the fireplace and pressed a small lever hidden in the scrollwork. I watched in amazement as the entire unit pulled away, revealing a long, winding staircase. "After you."

Keane placed his hand on the middle of my back and guided me forward. I was a bit nervous to go first, but I knew Keane would never put me in a position that could be dangerous. The stairs were well lit, and the steps wide, making descending them easy, even in heels. Everything in the stairwell was gray and unassuming, from the walls to the light fixtures, not giving even a hint as to where we were going. I wondered if this was a place like Dock Street that had been magically created for the Vaimpír.

Once we reached the bottom, Keane guided me to the large door that faced us. He stopped just before it and whispered in my ear.

"Before you can go through, you need one more thing." I instinctively put my hands up when something slipped over my face.

"A mask? It's a masked ball?"

Keane laughed lightly as he secured it behind my head. "Did you expect anything less of my mother?"

I turned and saw that he was already wearing a plain black silk mask over his face. It emphasized the blue of his eyes, drawing me into his gaze and putting naughty thoughts into my head yet again. I felt the sharp sting of desire pulse through my veins and head straight between my thighs as we stared at each other. I wanted nothing more than to pull Keane into a dark corner so I could pop the buttons of his shirt one by one and put my mouth on his skin to taste him. The urge was so strong my hands moved to his chest as if they had a will of their own.

Reading my thoughts, Keane groaned and pulled me in close, sliding his nose down my throat before brushing his lips over my pulse point. I shivered in response. "Blue..."

"Are you two ready? The people are expecting us."

Camille's voice brought me back to my senses, and I blinked away the lust-filled haze that surrounded my brain.

Keane sighed in regret, running a thumb over my bottom lip. "We'll continue this later, *ma moitié*." His voice was low and full of promise, causing my desire to spike even higher. I took in a couple of shaky breaths to try to calm myself. It would do me no good to walk into a room full of Vaimpír in a heightened state of arousal—not to mention that I currently wore no underwear.

Keane took my hand and placed it on his arm. "Of course, Mother. Lead the way."

She pursed her lips, looking between the two of us in warning. "Don't forget to pay your respects to each of the Barons as well as their daughters, Keane."

"I know how to carry out my duties, Mother."

She nodded, casting me one last hard glare before plastering a smile on her face and walking through the door that Malakai held open for her.

Taking a deep breath, I followed them and soon found myself walking into another world.

Chapter Seven

The Vaimpír ballroom was enormous. It seemed to stretch on infinitely in all directions. I shook my head in wonder, barely managing to keep my mouth from hanging open. I had thought the Moon Tree Clan's ballroom at Dock Street was massive, but this...this made that one look like a closet in comparison.

I felt Keane chuckle next to me and nudged him with my shoulder. *"Stop it."* I spoke to him mentally so we didn't draw the Queen's ire again.

"What? I didn't say anything."

"You didn't have to. You were thinking it."

"Oh? Can you read my thoughts now?"

"Well...no. But I know what you were thinking."

"Oh, ma moitié. You have no idea what is going through my mind right now." He gave me a quick, smoldering look that caused my breath to catch in my throat, and my pulse to skyrocket once again.

Oh, hell.

A small smirk tugged at the corner of his lips before he turned back to the crowd, his princely mask once more falling into place. I let out the breath I had been holding and tried to gather my wits.

One look.

That's all it had taken to unravel me. I really was pathetic. I took another cleansing breath before refocusing. If he could play his part, then so could I.

I laid a hand on the railing in front of me and looked down curiously. We had entered on a high terrace set above everything else, giving an uninterrupted view of the assemblage below. Beneath the balcony, I saw several additional tiered entrances with family names engraved on the arches above each one. I was sure they went according to house rank.

Shiny black marble walls, along with the architecture's smooth, clean lines, gave the ballroom an open, modern feel. The furnishings and fixtures placed around the room were done in varying shades of black and gray, with small pops of color thrown in. Mirrors lined the space, reflecting everything back on itself and making the room appear even larger.

The people moving about were a sea of color against the dark backdrop, dressed in lavish gowns and tuxes, all wearing various ornate masks. Entertainers doing acrobatics high above the crowd added to the fantasy of it all, making me think of the movie *Van Helsing* during the ball scene.

As the King and Queen came into view, the entire gathering below looked up and quieted. Malakai stepped to the railing with Camille on his arm. "Welcome! I am so pleased you were able to join us this evening on such short notice to celebrate the return of our son, the Crown Prince Keane." Applause broke out from the crowd, along with a few shouts and whistles. Malakai smiled and waved his hand for silence once again. "Yes, yes. We are just as excited to have him back in the fold as you are. Please, enjoy our hospitality and everything the night has to offer." With that, Malakai led Camille down the walkway to the grand staircase at the end.

I held back with Keane, trying not to draw too much attention, though I could already feel dozens of eyes looking our way. Keane turned his back to the crowd so they wouldn't see and raised my hand to his lips. "Are you ready, *ma moitié?*"

"Do I have a choice?"

He laughed softly and started moving us forward. "Certainly, you do. Everything in life is a choice, even if it's to do something you don't want to." He covered my hand on his arm with his and squeezed. "My mother may be forcing us to play a role in her little drama tonight, but that doesn't mean we can't have fun with it." He looked down at me mischievously and winked.

He was right. Tonight was all about perception. Tonight, I needed to do whatever I could to win over the houses. A grin crooked the corner of my mouth. I'd make sure it was a night they wouldn't soon forget.

By this time, we had reached the top of the grand staircase. I took in a deep breath and started carefully down the stairs. Keeping my chin held high, I toned down my grin to a serene smile and boldly looked back at the people staring up at us, meeting eye after eye. Some bowed their heads in a submissive nod, while others held my gaze. Some were curious, while others looked jealous—those mostly the ones I assumed were the chosen daughters. They all wore white gowns that resembled wedding dresses and were standing slightly apart from the rest of the groups.

Leaning over, I pulled Keane down to my level and whispered conspiratorially in his ear. "I believe your intendeds are waiting for you. Some of them are giving me quite the murderous glares."

Keane glanced through his lashes at the waiting crowd below and smirked. "I see a few covetous eyes being thrown your way, as well. I have a feeling they're all wondering just who you are."

I lifted my chin a notch. "Good, let them wonder."

"That's the spirit, Miss Doolittle."

I grinned as he straightened. By this point, we had reached the bottom of the stairs. My grin widened as a figure in a wheelchair rolled through the crowd toward me. He wore a simple, black silk mask along with a black tux that was almost a replica of Keane's and looked just as good.

"My lady." He bowed his head and took my hand in his, pressing his lips to the back of it. "Your radiant smile has made the hours apart worth every second."

I giggled quietly while Keane scowled. "Laying it on a bit thick aren't you, little brother?" Keane kept his voice low so he wouldn't be overheard.

"You're just jealous that Blue is mine tonight." At Keane's growl, he winked at me while turning his chair around. Taking my hand, he placed it on his shoulder. "Allow me to escort you, as well."

We moved forward together until we were beside Malakai and Camille. I could feel the watchful eyes around us taking in every move we made. Malakai turned toward us, the smile on his face widening as he spotted Rhys. "Rhys, my son, what a wonderful surprise. I didn't realize you would be in attendance tonight." Malakai leaned forward and shook Rhys's hand while patting him on the shoulder.

"Father. I could hardly stay away. Not only do I want to show my support for my older brother, but this beauty here needed an escort while he was away attending to his duties." He rested his hand over mine.

Malakai looked at him in surprise. "You know Blue already?"

"Of course."

Just then, Camille turned toward us from the conversation she was having, her smile faltering as she spotted Rhys. "Rhys, what are you...? I mean, it's so good to see you out and about. I didn't realize you were feeling well enough to attend. You should have told me." She leaned in and air kissed his cheeks, though I could tell it pained her to acknowledge him.

"Mother."

Camille looked at my hand still resting on Rhys's shoulder and frowned. "Are you planning on staying long?"

"I'm escorting Blue this evening."

Camille's eyes jerked to mine, flashing in anger before she quelled it. Instead, her look turned calculating. "Isn't that just perfect? You can take on the duties of introducing Blue around, leaving your brother free to dote on the chosen daughters as he should."

I felt Keane stiffen next to me. I squeezed his arm and spoke to him mentally. *"Relax. What happened to having a bit of fun? Tonight, you get to play the part of the charming, carefree bachelor returned to play within his kingdom."*

He grimaced slightly before relaxing his expression. *"I don't like the thought of you being introduced around without me."*

I slanted him a look and grinned. *"Don't worry, I can handle myself. Remember I was brought up in this type of society, plus Rhys will be right there*

*if I need him. Tonight, I'll be the mysterious socialite. Aloof, untouchable...
I'm thinking she might just be a bit of a bad girl, as well."*

Keane's shoulders loosened, and he smirked at me. *"I like bad girls."*

Malakai interrupted our silent conversation. "Blue, I wanted to
introduce you to a close friend of mine."

I turned to find a tall, dignified gentleman standing next to Malakai.
He was probably around the same age as Keane's father, though it was
hard to tell with the mask. His dark, nearly black eyes held a twinkle of
amusement as he watched me.

"Uncle Si! It has been a long time, has it not?" Keane reached over and
shook the man's hand, momentarily diverting his attention from me.

"Yes, it has. Sometimes, life has a funny way of putting unexpected
things in our paths that sidetrack us from our everyday routines."

Keane smiled and looked down at me. "That it does. Uncle Si, allow
me to introduce my companion, Miss Carolina Blue of the family
Grayson." Those intense eyes moved back to me, and I was struck with
a sense of familiarity, though I didn't know why. "Blue, this is Silas
Aegaeus. He's my father's best friend."

I reached out my hand, which he immediately took and raised to his
lips. As soon as our skin touched, a strange power skittered up my arm.
Judging his energy field, I couldn't seem to pinpoint exactly what he
was, though I could tell he was not Vaimpír. It was almost like he was
blocking his energy signature somehow. Every time I zeroed in on it,
it would simply slip through my senses, fragmenting into millions of
pieces and drifting off.

Weird.

"Blue, it is a pleasure to finally meet you. I have heard a great deal
about you and have been looking forward to this meeting for a while
now."

I smiled with a bit of mischievousness. "I hope I live up to everything you've been told."

"Oh, I am sure you will."

Malakai clapped a hand on Silas's shoulder. "Come, my friend, why don't we go somewhere quiet to catch up? There are a few things I would like to run by you."

Silas nodded to his friend before turning back to me. "Blue, I hope we will get a chance to speak again later. Perhaps you could save a dance for me?"

I nodded. "Of course."

With another lingering glance in my direction, he smoothly moved off to follow behind Malakai. I watched him curiously until he was out of sight. Turning to ask Keane more about him, Camille cut in before I could.

"Keane, why don't you go ask one of the chosen daughters to be your partner for the opening dance."

Keane bowed to his mother mockingly. "Your wish is my command, Your Majesty." She just rolled her eyes at him and turned to greet another group of Vaimpír who approached her. "Guess that means duty calls."

Rhys rolled his chair forward. "Don't worry, Keane. Nothing will happen to her as long as she's with me."

Keane placed his hand on Rhys's shoulder. "Brave words, little brother." He lowered his voice to a stage whisper while glancing at me. "Just so you know, she seems to attract trouble left and right. Best be ready for anything." I smiled and shook my head, not the least bit offended. He wasn't wrong. Keane put a finger under my chin. "I'll see you later. Do try to behave yourself." With that, he swaggered off into the crowd, leaving several women sighing.

I watched him walk away, appreciating the view myself before tearing my gaze away to look down at Rhys. "So, where, or should I say *who*, should we start with?"

Before Rhys could reply, a familiar voice floated toward me. "*Señorita* Blue!" I turned to find Alejandro Rodriguez making his way through the crowd toward us. Alejandro was a good friend of Keane's and now mine after a few incidents during the Trials. He was also the head of the Rodriguez family.

"Alejandro!" I stepped forward to take his outstretched hands.

"*Mi amiga*! Oh, it's so good to see you again. I swear you grow more beautiful with each passing day." After placing a kiss on each of my cheeks, he turned and acknowledged Rhys. "*Príncipe* Rhys. It's always a pleasure."

"Please, Alejandro, just Rhys."

Alejandro smiled and nodded. "Of course. And if I might introduce you to my beautiful *esposa*, Luciana. Luciana, this is the *especial* woman I was telling you about. Blue."

"*Buenas noches*, Señorita Blue. My Alejandro has told me so much about you. I feel as if I already know you."

I smiled widely, taking an instant liking to her. "I'm so glad to meet you."

"Thank you for all you've done for our family."

I looked at her in confusion. "But, Luciana, I haven't done anything."

She smiled serenely. "*Sí*, you have. You could have easily killed our *hija*, but you spared her life. For that, I'll be forever grateful." Their daughter, Mariana, was the chosen woman I had asked Keane about before coming to the ball. When she discovered the bond between Keane and me, she tried to kill me. During the scuffle, I took her magic and trapped it in her core so she couldn't touch it and hurt anyone.

When she threatened to do whatever she could to take everything from me, Keane had put his foot down and removed her from her position as one of the chosen. He had also banished her without her magic to somewhere outside the Fae community until she learned her lesson.

"Luciana..." I started to protest.

She shook her head. "No, Blue." She took both of my hands. "You'll forever have the loyalty of our house. If you ever have need of anything, no matter what it is, we'll be there for you."

I was humbled by their devotion. "I—"

"Isn't this just sweet?" I turned at the sarcastic male voice. "Already groveling to the new Rutherman pet, hoping to garner more favor with the family? Shameless."

I narrowed my eyes at the new stranger, about to give him a piece of my mind, when Rhys touched my hand. He shook his head slightly. Right, I had to make friends with these people, not antagonize them.

"Jealous, Petrov?" Alejandro didn't seem to be the least bit intimidated by him.

Petrov just sneered. "Hardly. It's going to be my daughter, Karina, who marries the Prince. So, in the end, it won't matter. I'll be the top-ranking house, and you'll be nothing."

Alejandro just laughed. "Even if your daughter married Príncipe Keane, which she won't, that wouldn't remove the years of service and loyalty our family has provided to House Rutherman."

"Oh, do you think your Mariana is a better choice? I've heard a few rumors where she's concerned..."

Rhys cleared his throat and insinuated himself between the two men. "Good evening, Ivan."

"Oh! Your Royal Highness." Ivan quickly bowed. "Good evening. I...I'm sorry, I didn't realize that was you."

"Think nothing of it. I know I don't usually attend events such as these anymore." I noticed that Rhys didn't invite any familiarity with him as he did with Alejandro.

"Still, forgive me, Your Highness."

Rhys waived him off, acting every bit the Royal. I almost giggled at the sight. It was in such contrast to his normal laid-back personality. "Ivan, since you're here, I'd like to introduce you to a good friend of my family." He reached out for my hand, and I stepped forward, smoothly taking it. "This is Miss Carolina Blue of the family Grayson. She's currently staying with us at the manor. Blue, this is Ivan Petrov, the head of the Petrov household."

I reached out a hand to Ivan, which he took almost reverently, mimicking Rhys's aloofness. "Mr. Petrov, it's so nice to make your acquaintance. I've heard a great deal about you from the Ruthermans." Keane had briefed me on each of the houses, so I knew that the Petrov house was ranked fourth, followed by Lavigne, Akana, and Cargill. The Rodriguez house was second, and the Dalca house third. It was said the Petrov house was considered the most unsavory of the seven houses. Their businesses were shady, and their associates even more so. They did, however, provide an indispensable service to the Crown as they were in charge of the cleanup crews. The people who had to go in and make sure the human world didn't know the Fae existed. Their crews covered up any exposure, including altering the minds of anyone who might have seen something they shouldn't have.

Ivan stared at me wide-eyed. "Carolina Blue? As in the Fairy who single-handedly took down Larkin and his forces when they attacked the Moon Tree Clan?"

I smiled tolerantly while rolling my eyes in my head. Is that what people thought? That I single-handedly took down Larkin and his forces? "You flatter me. I was hardly alone in that battle."

He appeared to be a bit flustered. "It's a great honor to meet you. I didn't realize you were connected to the Rutherman family, as well."

I smiled and put my hand on Rhys's shoulder. "We've become very close friends since I was introduced into Fae society. I don't know what I would've done without them." Rhys put his hand over mine and smiled up at me.

"If you have the time, I'd love to introduce you to my family, especially my daughter. I think you would get along well with her." I could practically see the calculating look in his eyes.

"Perhaps later tonight," Rhys interrupted smoothly. "For now, I have several people I'd like to introduce Blue to."

I smiled in Ivan Petrov's direction. "It was a pleasure meeting you, Mr. Petrov."

"Ivan, please."

I nodded my head in concession. "And you must, of course, call me Blue." I flashed him the practiced smile I had learned as a child. He returned it with a large one of his own before quickly moving off—I was sure to start spreading the rumors.

I looked down at Rhys. "That seemed to go well. I wasn't sure at first."

Rhys shook his head. "I figured he'd be a pushover. He's all about improving his house rank and status by any means necessary. You can be sure he's running to tell his cronies all about being the first to meet the infamous Carolina Blue."

"I had no idea people viewed the incident with Larkin the way they do."

"Oh, you have no idea the stories and rumors that have been flying around about you. I'm surprised Keane hasn't said anything."

I turned to follow Rhys and realized that Alejandro and Luciana were still standing nearby. I smiled at both of them. "We'll have to get together later, hopefully when Keane is available. I'd love to talk with you in private about what we are trying to accomplish here."

Alejandro looked at me knowingly. "I think I have the idea. You can count on our support, as well as my family's silence on certain other things." He winked at me before taking his wife's arm. "I'll do my part to make sure the appropriate rumors are circulating about you. Until later, mi amiga."

Rhys and I waved the couple off and started in the opposite direction. "I think we should seek out *the Baron* next. If he hears that you've met with other houses before him, he'll be quite put out."

I looked a Rhys quizzically. "The Baron?"

Rhys chuckled and started to move forward. "Yes, he likes to refer to himself by his title. His name is actually Gavril Dalca."

"Keane didn't tell me he went by *the Baron*."

"Probably because Keane doesn't acknowledge it. And since he's a Prince, Gavril has no say in the matter." Rhys smirked, looking exactly like his brother in that moment.

"Do you think he'll be against me being here since it's his daughter your mother is pushing so hard for?"

"That shouldn't be an issue since he doesn't know about your bond with Keane. However, he's all about his power. So, he's likely going to look down on you and will definitely test your patience."

"Sounds like fun."

Rhys grinned as he continued to move us smoothly through the crowd. I made sure to acknowledge people with a nod while keeping a pleasant look on my face. "Almost there," Rhys whispered to me.

I looked at the man we were approaching. He was heavyset with broad shoulders and a head of slicked-back, dark gray hair. The tux he wore had a white jacket with black lapels, which made him stand out in the sea of black surrounding him—something I was sure he intended. He had a deep, booming voice that seemed to carry around the room, and a loud, boisterous laugh. My steps slowed as I took notice of Isabela standing next to her father...on Keane's arm.

Rhys noticed my hesitation and looked at me. "You okay?"

"Isabela is with her father. As is Keane."

Rhys looked in their direction. "Hmm, well, I guess this will be a good test of your acting skills then." He grinned in my direction.

"Dude, just so you know, I suck at acting."

Rhys gave a hearty laugh. "Please, don't sugarcoat it, Blue."

At his mock sarcasm, my shoulders relaxed, and I laughed along with him, drawing the attention of the group we were walking toward. I met Keane's eyes as he stared appreciatively at me. Next to him, Isabela glared in my direction while tightening her hands around Keane's arm. I checked the jealousy that rose and pushed it down. There was no place for that tonight. Instead, I concentrated on Gavril Dalca. He watched me with a rather intense stare. I wondered what he was thinking.

The Baron was the first to speak up. "Rhys, my boy, it's good to see you out and about." He reached over and shook Rhys's hand. "And who is your lovely companion this evening? I don't think I've ever seen her at any of these gatherings before."

"Baron Dalca, always a pleasure. This is a good friend of our family, Miss Carolina Blue of the family Grayson. Blue, this is Baron Dalca, the head of his house. I believe you're already acquainted with his daughter, Isabela."

The Baron didn't reach out his hand toward me. Instead, he looked down his nose haughtily, and I had to wonder what his daughter had told him. I didn't have to wait long. "Ah, so you're the Fairy who competed in the Trials at the Moon Tree Clan that was supposedly *human-raised*."

From the derision in his voice, I could tell that Baron Dalca would be a hard one to win over. I gave him a patient smile. "I see you've heard the rumors. Yes, my Aunt Alannah raised me. Considering my *unique* gifts, my mother, Queen Iridia, thought it would be in my best interests to be raised as a human until I came of age."

The Baron, who had just lifted a drink to his lips, choked and sputtered on the liquid. "Q-Queen Iridia is y-your mother?"

"Oh, dear. I seem to have surprised you. I thought that little secret had already made its way around, as well. I do apologize." I patted him on the back, doing my best to appear concerned. "Are you quite all right?" Keane and I had discussed it earlier and agreed that letting it slip who my mother was could only benefit me within this society, considering her reputation.

"Fine, I'm fine. Thank you." While he was still looking down on me, I could tell that I had just risen considerably in his estimation. Keane was having a hard time covering his smirk. "I must say, that is a very interesting fact. So, that makes you royalty then."

I shrugged one shoulder. "I suppose it does."

"I guess that explains why someone of your upbringing was able to make it to the final five in the Trials. I wondered what made you so special."

"Oh, Father, you give her too much credit." Isabela had taken courage from her father's disdain and decided to join in. "Everyone knows her close association with King Tristan is what kept her in the Trials, not any real talent."

Annoyance washed through me, and I narrowed my eyes at her. "Really, Isabela. Are you ready for a demonstration of my powers again so soon?"

She visibly shrank back, causing her father to raise his brows. She glanced at him before straightening her shoulders, though I could still see the wariness in her eyes.

Keane looked down at Isabela dispassionately. "I can assure you, Isabela, Blue rightfully earned her place in those Trials through her talents alone. You would do well to curb your tongue and not insult a friend of our family so directly."

He started to disentangle himself from her, causing her to grab onto him tighter. "I'm sorry, Keane, you're right. Forgive me. I was putting too much stock in the rumors going around."

Keane merely shrugged off her hands. "If you'll excuse me, I have some other obligations to attend to." With that, he bowed his head in my direction before calmly walking away toward yet another chosen. It was an obvious slight toward Isabela that many were already whispering about behind their hands.

Isabela turned toward me, her eyes filled with vehemence. "You!" I merely raised an eyebrow.

"Isabela, enough." She turned surprised eyes toward her father. "Prince Rhys, Miss Blue, if you'll excuse us? It seems my daughter and I have a few things to discuss."

I bowed my head in his direction. "Of course, Baron. It has been a pleasure to make your acquaintance."

He hesitated, staring at me before inclining his head as well and moving off, dragging his daughter alongside him.

"Something tells me she's in big trouble with Daddy Dearest." I turned to Rhys, who was grinning up at me. "Do I even want to know what you did to her that caused that look of fear?"

Before I could respond, the orchestra queued up, and the crowd parted to reveal Keane and a tall, beautiful woman with shining auburn hair. They began waltzing around the room, looking every bit the perfect couple.

The first time I had seen the Fae dancing this way at Dock Street, I'd been surprised by it. I mean, who waltzed anymore? My grandfather, Kieran, had explained to me that due to their long lives, the Fae tended to see and experience time differently, so it was very common for old practices like these to still be in use when outside of human influence. Thankfully, my aunt had been a socialite herself and raised me as such. This had unquestionably included dance lessons.

"That's Audrey Lavigne. Daughter of Raphael and Annette, the heads of House Lavigne."

"Are all the chosen the daughters of the heads of each house?"

Rhys nodded while he continued watching the couple. "Yeah, that's what gave them their positions."

I noted how Rhys couldn't seem to take his eyes off Audrey and began to wonder about his interest in her. When the couple passed close to us and Audrey looked at Rhys, I was sure I was right. I gave Rhys a nonchalant glance. "Keane told me that Audrey has someone she wants to marry, she just has to work up the nerve to tell her parents."

Rhys started and turned surprised eyes toward me. "He told you that?"

I nodded, my grin widening as he took on a contemplative look. "So, how long have you two been together?"

"Hmm, four years..." His gaze remained distant and distracted before his eyes widened and shot to mine in realization. "I mean...um...shit! Blue, you can't breathe a word to anyone. If it were to get out..."

I leaned down and put a hand on his shoulder. "Your secret is safe with me."

He let out a long breath. "Thank you, Blue."

"Hey, what are friends for?"

⁓ ℓℓ ⁓

As the night continued, Rhys and I made our way around to meet the rest of the houses. All the while, I kept an eye on Keane as he smiled and wooed the chosen and their families. He truly was adept at this political thing. He made sure to spend the same amount of time with each family and danced the same number of dances with each of the chosen, never showing a preference. The only one he didn't approach again was Isabela—and I was sure she was fuming.

"He is quite the vision, isn't he?" I turned toward the self-assured, female voice. She was tall and curvy with luminescent light-brown skin, long, wavy black hair, and deep chocolate-brown eyes. She smiled widely and stuck out her hand. "I'm Leilani."

"Oh. Leilani. I'm so glad to finally meet you. Keane has told me all about you."

She smirked and wrapped an arm around my shoulders. "I'm sure he has. So, what's a nice girl like you doing in a place like this?"

"Killing time?"

She chuckled and turned to Rhys, giving him a fist bump. "Hey Rhysy Cup, how's it hanging?"

"A little to the left." They both laughed. "Good to see you here, Lei."

"Like I'd be allowed to miss it."

"Your father still believes you have a chance with Keane?"

"Delusional as always, but I still love him." She shook her head, still grinning. "I'm surprised to see you here, though."

Rhys grabbed my hand and pulled me away from her so he could snake his arm around my waist. "I'm here with Blue, so hands off."

She pouted for a second before laughing. "You'd better not let Audrey see you doing that."

"She's well aware of the situation. We all have our parts to play tonight."

"Touché." She chewed on her bottom lip, seeming to consider something before dismissing it. "Hey, are we all meeting up later to have the real party?"

"We'll be there."

"Okay, I'll see you two later, then. I think it's my turn to rescue Keane from the terrible trio." She winked and sauntered off, the silk of her white pantsuit shining in the low light.

"Wow, she's something else." I watched her in a bit of awe. To have that kind of self-confidence...

"That she is."

"What was she talking about, *the real party* later?"

Rhys dropped his hand from my waist. "It's a tradition. After one of these forced shindigs, we all sneak out and meet at the Dungeon."

"The Dungeon?"

"A Fae-friendly bar. The tourists all say it was opened as a place for vampires to secretly prey on humans." Rhys snorted and shook his head. "In truth, it was inspired by a wealthy Turk named Suleiman. He used to have these huge, lavish parties where anything went at the mansion over on Dauphine Street. Until one night, the place went silent. After a few weeks of seeing no one coming or going, the police were called to investigate. They found everyone in the house brutally murdered."

"That's pretty gruesome."

"I guess. Considering Suleiman was a Zannie and fed off the pain of others, it was hardly surprising that he finally lost it."

"Is he still around?"

"No, he was taken down by his brother for going rogue."

"His own brother killed him?"

Rhys shrugged his shoulders. "It happens. There was no love lost between the two. Suleiman was trying to usurp his brother's position as sultan at the time. He had actually been banished to New Orleans from some Middle Eastern country due to his many attempts on his brother's life."

"Damn."

"Yeah. Anyway, the Dungeon was opened about a hundred years later as some weird type of tribute to the excesses of Suleiman. Probably by someone hoping to capitalize on his reputation and the weird stories fed to the press about it. The bar now warns patrons they are *entering the Dungeon of the Prince*." Rhys rolled his eyes. "We have an area upstairs away from the tourists, though. It has a full-service bar, which includes Fae-friendly drinks and a dance floor."

"Sounds like fun."

Before Rhys could reply, a smooth, cultured voice interrupted. "Good evening again. Rhys. Miss Blue."

I turned to find Silas Aegaeus standing next to us. "Mr. Aegaeus. What a pleasant surprise to see you again."

"Uncle Si. Enjoying the party?" Rhys gestured around the room.

Silas appeared to consider the question. "Watching a bunch of overstuffed, pompous, power-hungry men set on outdoing and overthrowing each other? It's been...mildly entertaining."

Rhys and I laughed. "What brings you over here?"

"I've come to claim my dance with the lovely Miss Blue."

"By all means"—Rhys gestured—"just promise to return her to me when you're done."

Silas inclined his head with a smile. "But of course. Miss Blue?"

He reached out his hand and held it between us in invitation. I placed my palm in his with a smile. "I would be honored."

As he guided me toward the floor, I looked back at Rhys, who had moved farther into a darkened corner. It made me sad that he felt the need to hide.

"Your friendship will soon open many doors for him that were previously closed, do not worry."

I turned in surprise toward Silas. "What do you mean?"

He just smiled mysteriously and took me into his arms, smoothly moving us among the other dancers already gliding across the floor. I pondered what he could have meant by that statement. Did he somehow know about Keane and me?

"I know everything about you..." He leaned in closer to my ear. "Daughter."

My gaze jerked to his, my eyes widening. I almost stumbled over my feet, but he held me securely. "D-daughter?"

His grin widened. "Do you not recognize your own father? Did you not feel our connection as soon as we touched?"

I thought back to the strange power that had flowed from him when he took my hand earlier.

He nodded, a look of amusement on his face. "Yes, that."

"But you're Keane and Rhys's Uncle Si, Malakai's best friend, a longtime friend of the Rutherman family..."

"They don't know who I am, of course."

"But...how?" I was totally flabbergasted and having a hard time digesting this.

"I have never felt the need to reveal who I am. People tend to treat you differently once they discover you are a god. Especially people like the Vaimpír, who are only interested in power. While I don't think Malakai would be that way, I never wanted to take that chance. I enjoy our friendship too much." He shrugged his shoulders.

"How are you able to hide the fact that you're a god?"

"The same way you do."

I looked at him in confusion. "But I don't do anything."

He smiled and spun us around a few times before answering. "Maybe not consciously. But you do utilize a diffuser spell that hides the fact that you are mostly a god."

"Mostly a god?"

"Seems my genes were pretty dominant."

I pursed my lips and narrowed my eyes at him. "Speaking of genes, how is it that my mother doesn't know you're my father?"

Poseidon grimaced and moved us away from another couple so they wouldn't overhear our conversation. "She had me remove her memory of us."

"Why?"

"So that she couldn't accidentally reveal to Hades what you were."

"Wait, you know that Hades has her?"

Poseidon nodded with a sigh. "I met your mother just before she found out that Aiden was still alive. We had a short affair, which resulted in her getting pregnant. A complete surprise for both of us.

When she found out Hades was holding Aiden, she was determined to rescue him, much against my wishes. She had me remove her memory of our time together and the fact that she was pregnant just in case she was captured."

"Why haven't you tried to rescue her?"

"She would have no idea who I was, why would she trust me, another god?"

"But to just leave her there…"

"Have no fear, I keep an eye on her. I will not let my brother hurt her. I'm just biding my time."

"Biding your time for what?"

He just shook his head. "Now is not the time."

I opened my mouth to refute him but then stopped. While I was curious about his reasons, I had a lot of other questions that needed to be answered first. "Are you the one who helped secret me away when I was a child?"

"No, that was…someone else. But I did make sure they got you to Galene."

"Does Galene know you're my father?"

Poseidon shook his head. "No, I let them all continue to believe that Aiden was."

I mulled that over. I wondered what would happen when I finally told them, how it would affect Iridia and Aiden's relationship. I shook my head and moved on. "Did you know I would be here tonight before you decided to come?"

"Of course. I keep a close eye on you, as well, Blue. I wanted to be here to support you. I know that it is important to both you and Keane to have your bond recognized."

"You're okay with it?"

"Certainly. I couldn't have made a better match for you myself. Not only because he is the son of my best friend but also because of who he is."

"Who he is?"

Poseidon smiled slyly while shaking his head. "You will see in time."

I huffed out a breath. Everyone was always so cryptic when it came to my life. I was about to question him further when a deep power flowed through the room—one I was now familiar with. My eyes darted around in panic.

"What the hell is he doing here?" Poseidon growled, looking over my shoulder.

I glanced behind me. There, highlighted by the spotlights from the stage, stood Hades, his hand resting on Scythe's head.

Chapter Eight

People slowly backed away from Hades as they took in his presence. Though he was dressed like everyone else, in a formal tuxedo with a black mask tied around his face, it was obvious from the power emanating from him exactly what he was. That and the hound by his side.

Poseidon turned me back to look at him. "Blue, you need to hide. He cannot know you are here."

I opened my mouth to question him, but Poseidon shook his head. "There is no time, Blue. I will come to you later so we can talk. For now, you need to get somewhere safe."

I nodded and quickly made my way back over to Rhys.

As soon as I reached his side, Rhys took my arm and pulled me closer to him. "What's going on?"

"It's Hades."

"What on earth is he doing here?"

"I don't know, but I can't let him see me."

Rhys raised his brows at the urgency in my voice but didn't question me. "Follow me. I know where we can hide and still see what's going on."

Together, we made our way around the outside of the crowd until we reached a small hallway. Rhys turned into it and went straight toward a floor-to-ceiling glass display with an array of weapons. Opening the access door on the side of the case, he reached in and pulled on one of the swords. There was a click, and the case slid away from the wall. Motioning for me to precede him, I entered a small, empty room. Rhys followed me in and quickly pressed the lever that moved the display case back against the wall. Then he wheeled over to a set of silver doors and pressed his palm to a small box on the wall beside them. With the touch of his hand, the light turned green, and the doors opened to reveal an elevator.

We climbed in, and Rhys quickly pushed the buttons. As the elevator started to ascend, I let out a little sigh of relief. I quickly mind-linked with Keane.

"Keane!"

"Blue. Where are you?"

"Rhys is taking me to a safe room. Hades is here."

"I know. Stay hidden until we can figure out what he's up to and get rid of him."

"Please, be careful."

"I'll be fine, ma moitié. Just stay hidden."

The elevator doors in front of us opened, revealing a large, open room with couches, several TVs, and a bar along one wall. It reminded me of the sky boxes at sporting events. I hesitantly walked toward the floor-to-ceiling glass.

"Don't worry, it's one-way. We can see out, but no one can see in."

"Where are we?"

"It's a private room located at the top of the ballroom. It's used for clandestine meetings, and somewhere my father could go to sneak away from my mother's boring parties." He chuckled and wheeled himself over to the bar.

"Who else knows about it?"

"Only the immediate family has access. Want something to drink?"

I shook my head and walked toward the windows. Looking down, I could practically see the entire length of the ballroom, but my gaze was solely on the area by the orchestra stage. All activity below had stopped, and everyone was staring at Hades.

"My, my. What an auspicious occasion. Please, don't let me interrupt the festivities." His booming voice coated the room. Turning toward the orchestra, he smiled, his eyes glowing. "Play."

The musicians nervously took up their instruments and began playing again. Hades turned back to the crowd, his gaze sliding over the occupants. When it landed on Poseidon, he strode forward, the crowd parting as he moved past.

"Brother. It's been a while. Is this where you've been hiding yourself these days?" I was surprised I could hear them perfectly, even from this high up. "And why ever are you blocking yourself from these good people? Are you ashamed of who you are?"

A look of annoyance crossed Poseidon's face, but then he just sighed and shook his head. I felt it the minute he dropped his diffuser spell. His power rocketed through the entire room. There were several gasps of surprise, but none from Malakai or Keane. Though Poseidon hadn't thought so, I had a feeling the two men already knew just what Silas Aegeus was.

Rhys rolled up next to me, a drink in his hand. "I always knew he was something more than what he appeared to be."

I nodded but kept my eyes trained on the men below.

"There, brother. Now, doesn't that feel better? To finally have it all out in the open and not have to hide who you are?"

"What do you want, Hades?"

"Can't I just visit my brother without a reason?"

"At a party you were not invited to? Really, Hades?"

"Hmm, maybe if you hadn't been avoiding me for so long, I wouldn't have had to track you down here, would I?"

Poseidon sighed and clapped his hand on Hades' shoulder. "Let us take this somewhere more private. We do not need to trouble these people with our family issues."

Hades abruptly stiffened, his nose lifting into the air. His intense gaze shifted to his brother, his eyes starting to glow again. "Now *that* is an unexpected turn of events. Just what are you hiding, my dear brother?"

"What are you talking about now?"

"There is a certain person that I've been trying to find for the last several decades who's managed to evade my grasp. One you claim to have no knowledge of. Yet, here you are, with her scent positively all over you." Turning, Hades eyed Poseidon. "Where is she?"

"Where is who?"

"Don't play coy with me, my dear brother. You know exactly of whom I speak." Malakai started to step forward, but Poseidon put up a staying hand. Hades didn't even spare him a glance. "Don't make me use force. We wouldn't want to see anyone here get hurt now, would we?"

The people standing closest to the two brothers started slowly backing away. Probably a good idea, considering the power shimmering between the two men. They had squared off and were now facing each other.

"Give her to me."

Poseidon shook his head sadly. "I am afraid I cannot do that. She is far too precious to me."

A dawning understanding crossed Hades' face, and he looked at his brother in surprise. I had a feeling he had just figured out that Poseidon was my father.

Shaking his head, Hades seemed to become more determined. "You leave me no choice, then." Small flames sprang up along his outstretched arms, spreading until his entire body was covered. With a pulse of power, they burst from him, causing Vaimpír to dive out of the way. Soon, he was engulfed in huge, bright-blue flames. In answer, a torrent of water sprang up around Poseidon. I wasn't sure where it had come from until I saw the tendrils flowing from every wall and doorway. People let out small yelps of surprise as it moved past them.

Hades leaned over to Scythe. "Find her." The hellhound nodded his large head and, putting his nose to the ground, started to slip away. Before he got far, Keane was standing in his path.

"Going somewhere, my friend?"

I watched helplessly as things started spiraling out of control. Hades and Poseidon circled each other, water and flames meeting, creating steam hot enough to burn anything in its path. The Vaimpír had moved back to give them plenty of room and avoid being hit with either the flames or the steam.

Keane was in a standoff with Scythe, the hellhound now blanketed in small, red flames. I watched as the hellhound jumped on Keane, burning through his clothes in spots. Keane grunted in pain before gritting his teeth and clamping himself around the hellhound. As fast as his skin healed, the hellhound burned it again. I screamed and pounded on the glass, feeling his pain through our bond.

"Blue, stop! There's nothing you can do."

I barely registered Rhys as he tried to pull me back from the window.

Malakai moved to help his son, as did Alejandro and several others. They all surrounded the hellhound. Scythe snarled and lashed out, not liking being trapped. I reached out mentally to the hound.

"Scythe, please stop."

"Mistress. I cannot disobey my master. I'm sorry."

I felt anger spike through me at his refusal, and a burning rage started low in my belly. Who the hell did Hades think he was? Coming here, making demands, trying to hurt the people who meant something to me. I heard Rhys's quick intake of breath as he wheeled back a bit. "Blue..."

Out of the corner of my eye, I saw Scythe lunge toward Keane again, his razor-sharp teeth bared. A scream tore from my throat, cracking the glass in front of me. The crowd below, intent on the fight before them, all froze and slowly looked around for the source of the sound. I heard another sharp crack before splinters quickly spread in both directions, starting at the break I had created.

In seconds, the entire window exploded into thousands of tiny shards and rained down on the screaming crowd below. Power burst from my body, making it feel alive and weightless. My wings appeared, and before I could even second-guess it, I was out the window and flying toward Keane. I landed directly in front of him and put out my hand for Scythe. "Enough." My voice was a soft command that reverberated around the room, freezing everything in its place. Everything except Scythe. I gestured toward him.

"How are you still able to move?"

He sat back on his haunches and grinned a doggy smile at me. *"I was not created the same as those around us, so your powers of time don't affect me."*

I felt my anger drain away at his calm response. It was almost as if he had been waiting for me to intervene. I looked around me at the disarray. Glass, lights, and debris littered the area. People were frozen mid-scramble to get away from the two warring gods. I looked at them. Hades' face was a mask of concentration, his flames still burning about his body, while Poseidon looked angry, his torrents of water frozen right along with him. Each had lost their mask sometime during the fight.

I reached up and touched the one still on my face. I'd forgotten it was even there, and it suddenly felt foreign. Pulling on the ribbon that held it in place, I untied it and let it drop to the floor.

I turned back to Scythe. "I thought the gods were immune to Fae magic."

"They are."

"Then how did I freeze them along with everyone else?"

"That is your gift. Each god, much like each of the Fae, has a special gift unique to them. Hades' talent is his ability to call souls to him, while Poseidon can communicate with all manner of creatures."

"Are others immune to it like you?" I thought about how Sebastian hadn't seemed affected by my ability to freeze time either.

"Of course, but it depends on what form you're in. When doing magic in your incorporeal form, for instance, it's a lot less powerful. You wouldn't have been able to stop them." Scythe huffed toward the two gods.

"Is that why Hades wants me in my physical form? So he can use my power of time to trap and control Zeus?"

"Partly, but there is another skill that he wants, as well."

I tilted my head to the side. "And what is that?"

"*Your ability to take another's powers.*"

My mouth fell open. "He wants me to steal Zeus's powers? But why?"

Scythe shook his head. "*I don't know, Mistress.*"

I didn't understand. What good would it do for me to take Zeus's powers? It wasn't like I'd be able to control them. I couldn't even figure out how to use Larkin's, and he was just a mere Fae. I sighed and looked at the two men, completely in control of myself now. "Any idea how to break this up?"

A sound much like a laugh rumbled from Scythe. "*You genuinely have no idea what you are capable of, do you?*"

"Clearly not." I was a bit annoyed. It wasn't like this kind of thing came with an instruction booklet, and as I seemed to be different from everyone else, be it Fairy or god, no one could teach me.

"*I'd suggest sending Hades back to the Underworld and binding him there, though it will only be temporary. He's much too strong for you to hold for long.*"

"How would I do something like that?"

"You simply request it, of course."

I spun in surprise at the deep voice with the English accent. "Sebastian!"

He smiled devilishly and swaggered toward me, his long, white wings swaying behind him. "Miss me, my enigmatic little Fairy?" Taking my hand, he lifted it to his lips. "I see you're in a bit of a situation yet again. Seems every time I'm nearby, you're in need of my assistance. It's a good thing I decided to drop by and check on you." He grinned.

I grimaced and pulled my hand back. "It does seem that way, doesn't it? Can you really take Hades back to the Underworld?"

He nodded, crossing his arms over his chest. "With Scythe's help getting through the void, that will not be an issue."

I looked between him and Hades worriedly. "He won't know it was you, will he? I don't want him taking his wrath out on you."

"Of course, not. I'll just need you to hold your time freeze on him for a few minutes so I can deposit him back in his home, comfy as you please."

I nodded, looking thoughtful. "I think I can do that. What about the binding thing?"

"You know that Warlock spell used to bind people's magic so they can't tap into it?" At my affirmative nod, he continued. "You just need to change it a bit to bind his magic to a place instead of inside of him. In this case, the Underworld."

"I can do that to a god?"

Sebastian smirked and pointed a finger at me. "*You* can, yes."

I looked at him, confused. "But if Fae magic doesn't work on gods, why does it work when I use it on them?"

Sebastian moved to stand in front of Hades and Poseidon. "Because when *you* use Fae magic, it's combined with your god magic, turning it into something completely different. And..." He paused, his look turning contemplative. "Seemingly something more powerful. You need to stop thinking of your magic in separate terms. It's no longer Fairy, Warlock, or god magic. It's simply *your* magic."

"Okay." Walking over to Hades, I put my hand on his chest. His flames danced around my fingers as if playing with them. I watched them, mildly surprised they seemed to have no effect on me. Closing my eyes, I manipulated the gold ball of energy I always imagined was in my core. Pretty soon, I had what I needed for the binding spell. I just wasn't sure how to attach it to a place as large as the Underworld.

"Think smaller."

"Smaller? How about...his castle?"

Sebastian smiled and nodded, looking smug. I scowled. It still annoyed me a bit that he could read my mind, even through my blocks. Pushing those thoughts aside, I concentrated on my magic before pushing it into Hades. I hoped this worked, or things could get really complicated, really fast.

Sebastian leaned over my shoulder and placed his hand over mine, causing the flames to dance higher.

"Perfect. That should hold him, at least for a while."

I let out a sigh. "What do I owe you this time?"

Sebastian chuckled and stepped back. "Let's just leave it as an owed favor for some later date."

"They're starting to add up."

He leaned over and placed a kiss on my cheek. As he did, his hair shifted to black, as did his wings, and his eyes turned a dark red. "Mm...are you ready, my favorite little Fairy?" At my nod, he stepped over to Hades. "Keep things frozen for another ten minutes. That should give me enough time. Scythe?"

"*I just need to hear the words from my mistress.*"

I found it odd that Scythe referred to me as his mistress when I was anything but. "Scythe, could you please guide Sebastian and Hades through the void?"

Scythe bowed his head to me. "*Your wish is my command.*"

With that, they both disappeared, leaving me standing by myself amid the frozen crowd. I looked around at the chaos before glancing up at the broken window, stories above us, where I could just see Rhys at the edge, peering down.

I was sure Malakai would be quite upset about the damage. I just hoped it could all be fixed. I sighed. I had a feeling this little incident would put a damper on my entrance into Vaimpír society, considering they had all seen me lose it. And I was sure Camille would somehow spin it against me.

Wandering to Keane, I looked him over. He was braced, his muscles bulging, ready to meet Scythe's attack. Running my hands over him, I checked the burned spots to make sure they had healed. The damage was minimal, and I had a feeling Scythe had done his best to keep it that way. While he was forced to obey Hades, we seemed to have some sort of connection, as well. Perhaps something had happened between us when I was a child. Arms pulling me into a tight hug brought me abruptly out of my thoughts.

"Blue."

I looked around in a panic, thinking I had accidentally released time and put Sebastian in danger, but then I realized it was just Keane.

"Keane? How did you break free?"

"What do you mean?" He looked around him in awe, realizing we were the only two moving. "I know I've seen your memories of this before, but they are nothing like seeing it in the flesh." He looked back down at me. "Are you okay? You're not hurt, are you?" He ran his hands over me as if checking for injuries.

I smiled crookedly and looked up at him. "Shouldn't I be asking you that? You were, after all, the one taking on a hellhound." I placed my hand over one of the burned spots in his jacket.

"Shit! The hellhound." He swung around. "Wait, where is he? For that matter, where is Hades? What happened, Blue?"

"Well..." I opened my mind so he could see what had gone down after I froze time.

"Hell, Blue, you're just incredible." He hugged me tightly to him again before relaxing his grip. "So, Hades is bound to his castle?"

"At least for now. Scythe said it wouldn't last long, though." I looked around the room sadly. "I'm sorry about all of this. I know it will probably make getting the house's approval nearly impossible now."

"Are you kidding me? With what you just did? It was beyond anything I've ever seen or felt, Blue. Your power defies description. I could feel you, even over the two other gods in the room. After that little demonstration, I have a feeling everyone will accept you without question."

My brows furrowed, not quite believing him. Looking over at the clock, I realized that our ten minutes were up. Stepping out of his arms, I sighed and looked at him. "Ready to put our masks back on and play our parts again?"

Keane smirked. "No more masks, no more pretending. From now on, we present our real selves to the world, no matter what they think or say. Go ahead, Blue. It's time to set things straight."

Raising my hands, I took in a deep breath and pushed time back into motion.

Chapter Nine

As time slipped back into the present, I watched people slowly return to themselves, some looking around in confusion. I turned in a slow circle, seeing for the first time that all six Barons—the heads of each house—had come to the aid of their King and his son. It was good to know they would all band together when the situation called for it. Malakai brushed off their concern and came to check on Keane, who assured him he was fine.

Poseidon appeared by my side without a sound and leaned down to whisper in my ear. "I don't know how you did what you did, but we will, without a doubt, be discussing it later in private, oh daughter of mine." He stood again, possessively placing his hand on my shoulder as if to claim me.

I couldn't help the smirk that crossed my lips as the Barons' gazes turned as one to stare at us. I wasn't sure if it was Poseidon, me, or both that had them so awestruck. Keane walked past the staring men and took both my hands, pulling me against him. Looking down, he tilted up my chin, and his mouth brushed softly against mine.

"*Ma moitié*...you may want to tone it down just a bit." I pulled back and looked at him questioningly, causing him to chuckle. "Your aura, it's quite...powerful right now. Even your eyes are glowing."

I looked over at Poseidon a bit helplessly. I had no idea how to rein it in since I seemed to do it unconsciously. He smiled and showed me how to put the diffuser spell in place without a word, knowing I'd be able to delve in with my senses to feel how he'd done it. Closing my eyes, I did as he showed me. I felt the heaviness return to my body before I opened my eyes and looked up at Keane.

"Better?"

"Much...and now, your wings?"

I let out a little gasp. I'd forgotten they were even there. Keane chuckled again and, still holding my hand, turned toward the Barons as I made my wings disappear.

"Father, Barons, if you could spare me a few minutes of your time, I would greatly appreciate it. Given recent events, I believe there are a few things we need to discuss—including the business of the chosen. Shall we adjourn to somewhere a bit more private?"

They all looked up at the ruined skybox in unison. Still on the ledge, Rhys gave them a crooked smile and a wave.

Malakai stepped forward. "We'll use the conference room on the east side. Please, follow me."

"Thank you, Father." Turning back to me, Keane raised my hand to his lips. "I'll be but a moment, *ma moitié*. Do you think you can stay out of trouble for that long at least?"

As one of the nearby chosen gasped, probably at his use of the Vaimpír endearment, I grimaced. "I can't make any promises."

Keane grinned and, with a slight caress along my cheek, stepped back and turned to Poseidon. "Uncle Si, if you would join us, sir? I could assuredly use your support."

"Certainly."

A light arm encircled my shoulders as I watched the men walk off. "Damn, girl, you sure know how to make an impression." I turned my head to find Leilani and Audrey standing next to me.

"Shit, Lei, that's an understatement." Audrey looked at me with laughing eyes. "I sure hope I never get on your bad side." I smiled at both women, enjoying their comradery.

We stood together, watching the servants from the various houses make quick work of the mess I had made. Before long, Audrey spoke, breaking our companionable silence. "Do you think he'll really do it?" She started chewing on her thumbnail.

"Do what?" Leilani reached over and smacked Audrey's hand out of her mouth like she'd done it a dozen times before.

"Release the chosen."

"Oh. I hadn't thought of that." Leilani looked down at me speculatively. "I suppose it's not out of the question now."

Just then, Rhys came wheeling over with a huge grin. "Holy shit, Blue. That was amazing. I've never seen anything like it."

"I didn't hurt you, did I?" I looked him over to make sure there weren't any visible cuts or bruises.

"No. The window exploded outward. There was actually very little glass left upstairs." Rhys looked around expectantly. "Where's Keane?"

"He took your father and the Barons somewhere for a meeting."

"A meeting about what?"

Audrey, who was back to chewing on her thumbnail, stepped closer to him. "I think he's going to release the chosen."

Rhys's head jerked toward her, hope glimmering in his eyes. "Are you sure?"

"He called Blue *ma moitié*. That means he's chosen her already, doesn't it?" She glanced at me expectantly.

I looked around at the many interested ears and lowered my voice. "I honestly don't know what the outcome of this will be."

⁓

With Keane away, I spent time entertaining family after family who tried to marry me off to their male heirs. It was amazing what a little display of power could do. Earlier, most of the Vaimpír wouldn't have given me the time of day. Leilani, Audrey, and Rhys stuck close to my side the entire time, helping me fend off the would-be suitors.

Time seemed to crawl by, and I kept finding myself intently watching the doors the men had disappeared through.

"What do you think, Hayden? Is she worthy of our big brother?"

"I'm not sure yet, Hugo. She has proven she's something quite unique and special."

"True, and we like unique and special things."

I turned to find two men standing with their arms linked together, regarding me. Tall and lean, they were dressed exactly alike, right down to the silver feathers attached to the sides of their masks. I couldn't make out much about their features, other than their intense, ice-blue eyes—which were currently fixed on me.

"Stop being so weird, you two." Rhys wheeled over to my side. "Blue, these are my brothers. Hayden, and Hugo. My mother's pride and joy." I raised a brow at his tone, causing him to roll his eyes. "Because they're twins. A rarity among the Vaimpír."

"Wow, two anomalies in one family. First you, and now them." Rhys just shrugged at me.

"Technically, we were here first..." Hayden pointed out.

"...so, it would be us and then him." Hugo finished.

I looked at the twins in amusement. "Do you always finish each other's sentences like that?"

Rhys eyed them in annoyance. "Creepy, isn't it?"

They just ignored him and moved closer to me. "*You* are an anomaly, as well. Something about you..." Hayden circled me, eyeing me curiously, while Hugo leaned in close.

"...smells different."

This wasn't the first time I'd heard that. My friend, who happened to be a Wolf, had told me the same thing when he first met me. I couldn't explain it, so I just shrugged at the twins.

Hayden regarded me inquisitively. "Your future is also curiously..."

Hugo tilted his head to the side. "...blank. We'll need to study you more before..."

"...we make up our mind about you." Hayden finished. Okay, Rhys was right. The way they talked was a bit creepy. They shared a look before linking arms again and bowing to me. "We'll see you again very soon, Miss Blue." With that, they melted back into the crowd, disappearing as quickly and silently as they had appeared.

"*That* wasn't weird at all." I looked at Leilani, who had moved to stand beside me.

She shivered dramatically. "Those two give me the willies. I don't know how you can stand to be related to them, Rhys."

Rhys just laughed and shrugged. "I'd say you get used to them, but honestly, you don't."

An hour later, I finally saw Keane striding toward me through the crowd. He had taken some of his time away to clean up and change into a new tux jacket and shirt. I sighed at the sight of him. People tried to stop him as he strode along, but he just moved toward me with a single-minded focus.

Reaching my side, he grabbed me around the waist and lifted me off the ground before laying a toe-curling kiss on my lips. Sliding me suggestively down his body, he buried his fingers in my hair, which had come loose from its confines earlier. Tilting my head to give him better access, he took advantage and deepened the kiss. I felt his fangs descend and groaned, pressing closer to him, loving his show of dominance.

"Whoa, whoa now. Keep it PG, you two!" Leilani laughed beside us.

I pulled back from Keane, breathing heavily. "I take it things went well with the Barons?"

Rhys moved to his brother's side, his hand gripping Keane's jacket. "Did you actually do it? Did you release the chosen?"

Setting me back from him, Keane took my hand and laced his fingers with mine. "You're about to find out." Pulling me toward the grand staircase, he mounted the steps, moving until he was about halfway up. Turning, he faced the crowd. I started to pull my hand back, but he held on to it tightly.

"Ladies and gentlemen. If I could have your attention please." As Keane's deep voice flowed over the crowd, they all turned toward us and quieted. I felt a sense of curiosity and anticipation wafting off them. "It has long been the tradition of our people to find the strongest, most beautiful, most powerful women from each family to be brought before the Royals to become one of the chosen. They provide a position of power to their family, helping to increase political advantage and forge alliances. Their position elevates them to an elite status few get to experience. Seldom does a Royal look outside of such perfection." He paused.

"However, there are rare occurrences when a woman comes along who is an even greater prize—whose power and beauty far surpass those before her." Keane looked over at me and squeezed my hand before turning back to the crowd.

"After conferring with my father and the Barons, I have decided... To release the chosen." Two shrieks of outrage rent the silence of the room, coming from the women in white, and I watched as yet another slid to the floor in what appeared to be a faint. Keane waited until the uproar settled down before speaking again.

"The Barons and I have reached an accord. While the chosen are no longer beholden to me and are free to do as they choose, their families will maintain their current status until such time as a new set of chosen is needed, as per tradition. That leaves the matter of my soul-bound partner."

Keane pulled me in close to his body, wrapping an arm around my waist. "I wish to introduce to you, Miss Carolina Blue of the family Grayson. Daughter of Queen Iridia of the Fernsong Clan, granddaughter of Kieran, the Elder of the Moon Tree Clan, and as demonstrated to you tonight, one of the most powerful Fae of our time—"

"But she isn't Vaimpír." A cutting, feminine voice interrupted him. I watched as Isabela, Karina, and Rosaline pushed to the front of the crowd, their eyes a deep red and their fangs fully out.

"On the contrary, she is." Keane slipped off his jacket and started unbuttoning his shirt. Pulling the collar away, he revealed to the assemblage the marks on his neck that I had left when I first fed from him as a Vaimpír. He had told me that as long as our bond was in place, the marks would be there. "These marks are proof that not only is she Vaimpír, she is also worthy of the soulbond." I heard a few whispers moving through the room.

Keeping my head high, I removed the spell that hid my marks, as well. Keane reached over and lovingly ran his fingers over them. "And as you can see, she also bears my mark. Hers to mine."

"Mine to his."

"The bond is complete." Keane lifted my chin and ran his thumb over my lip, causing me to smile.

"I will not accept this! She's not a pure-blooded Vaimpír. She's not of the seven houses." Isabela's voice was shrill, and she stamped her foot like a petulant child.

"I'm with Isabela. Our families will fight this." Karina stood next to Isabela, her arms crossed over her chest.

"This is not right. We have been raised our entire lives to be your Queen, not this imposter." Rosaline added her two cents.

Keane turned to the three women. "Your families will *not* fight this. Nor will you. If any of you raises a hand to interfere or poses a threat to Blue or anyone she holds dear, you'll not only forfeit your family's position, but you'll also become enemies of House Rutherman." Keane pulled himself to his full height, his eyes turning red and his fangs lengthening.

"Keane, please listen to reason. You can't want someone like her with no pedigree. She's not worthy of your greatness, not like I am. Even your mother wants me." Isabela's voice had taken on a cajoling tone.

"Enough!" This time, I felt the power rush out of Keane. It rolled in waves around the room, causing men and women alike to bow their heads in submission—some being driven to their knees by the force of it.

Keane had not only inherited the power of domination, but his talent was ten times more powerful than his father's. Letting go of my hand, he walked down the steps to stand in front of the three women.

"You will not disparage Blue. You'll show her the respect she deserves, not only as my other half but as a Royal. You'll cease your whining. Even if I hadn't chosen Blue, I wouldn't have picked any of you. *You're* the ones unworthy of *me*." Keane stood towering over the three women, his domination forcing them farther to the ground.

"One more word, and I'll bring down the wrath of House Rutherman on your families. Do you understand?"

"Please, Your Highness. We beg your forgiveness for our daughters' foolishness." Gavril Dalca, Ivan Petrov, and Raymond Cargill came running forward, all bowing before Keane as they shakily pulled their daughters behind them.

Ivan spoke for the three men. "You will not be troubled by them again, we promise." He looked toward the other two men, who nodded solemnly. "And as a show of our goodwill and loyalty, we offer you a token. The woman, Celeste Beaumont, whom you were inquiring after. We know her whereabouts, and we will gladly bring her to you."

I came down the stairs and laid a hand on Keane's shoulder. I felt him immediately relax at my touch, his domination lessoning. "Very well, gentlemen. I accept your token. Please turn Celeste over to my father's guardians by tomorrow." They all nodded and slowly backed away, towing their daughters along with them.

Keane turned his gaze to the surrounding crowd as if daring anyone else to protest. As I watched, the people before us slowly dropped to one knee. Within minutes, the entire ballroom was down and bowing their heads. Turning, Keane picked up his jacket before wrapping his arm around my waist and leading me up the grand staircase. When we reached the railing at the Rutherman balcony, he raised a hand. "I bid you all goodnight." He then opened the door and led me into the hidden stairwell that would take us back to his family home. As soon as the door shut, I let out the breath I had been holding.

Keane reached over and tipped my chin up before gently cradling my face in his hand. "It's done, *ma moitié*. You've officially been accepted by all the Vaimpír houses. And thus, our bond has the blessing of House Rutherman. We no longer have to hide our relationship."

I smiled widely and leaned into his touch. "Can we go home now?"

He smiled back at me and, with a final caress, dropped his hand. "Soon, *ma moitié*. I promise."

We ascended the stairs and entered the salon from behind the fireplace. As we came through, Camille was there waiting for us.

"What have you done, Keane?" She practically shrieked at him. "How could you do this to me? Do you have any idea what I went through to get rid of Jasmine so Isabela could be the chosen instead? And now you're just going to throw all my hard work away?"

"What do you mean, what you did to get rid of Jasmine, Mother?"

Camille gave a short laugh. "That stupid little cow. She didn't deserve to be one of the chosen. The only reason she was even put in the position was because her father bribed most of the family to do so. He didn't want to lose his seat as the head of the house. She was much too headstrong to be a chosen. Didn't want to do what she was told. We needed someone more malleable. Someone we could sculpt and shape to be what we wanted. Someone to become the perfect wife."

"*What* did you do, Mother?"

Camille waved off-handedly. "I simply had an old friend put a spell on her—one that made her lust after that worthless half-brother of yours. I knew he would be just as much of a hedonist as his mother and wouldn't let the opportunity to sleep with her pass. It was a simple matter of making sure you walked in on it."

"So, Jasmine actually was under a spell." Keane sounded thoughtful yet surprisingly calm.

"Yes, but I did it for your own good. She was unworthy of taking the Rutherman name. That and that worthless father of hers. Can you believe he actually thought I'd want to sleep with the likes of him?" She turned and rolled her eyes.

"And yet you're pushing someone from the same family. Why would you want me to marry someone from House Dalca if you hold such disdain for them?"

"I would be interested in hearing the same thing." I turned in surprise to find Malakai nonchalantly standing behind us. As he moved to my side, I wondered how long he had been there. "Well, my dear?"

Camille stood stock-still, her mouth opening and closing. "I, well...Isabela, she's already like a daughter to me. You know that..."

"It seems to me that you have had a slight preoccupation with the Dalca family of late. Especially Gavril Dalca and his daughter." Camille's face lost a bit of its color. "And while I usually turn a blind eye to your *dalliances*, you know my feelings toward Gavril."

Her voice dropped to a coaxing tone. "Malakai, my darling, you know that—"

Malakai held up his hand to silence her. "We will continue this discussion in private. For now, as to the matter of our son and his soulbond, your blessing is required."

She shook her head. "No. Keane must marry a pure-blooded Vaimpír. If not Isabela, then someone else. Not this imposter." She looked at me in disgust.

Keane narrowed his eyes. "You gave your word, Mother. If Blue was accepted by the seven houses, you would give your blessing."

She gritted her teeth. "I've changed my mind. I'll never give my blessing to this atrocity. She's of mixed blood. We must keep our line pure."

"You're hardly one to talk about mixed blood, Mother."

Her eyes widened in surprise, though she tried to hide her reaction. "What on earth are you talking about?"

"After you managed to birth the twins, I became very curious. While twins are almost unheard of in Vaimpír society, they are very common in other Fae. Demons, for instance..." Camille's frightened eyes moved to Malakai before going back to Keane. "I have to wonder if that is also what caused Rhys's disability."

"I...I'm the daughter of Jasper and Lucy Cargill. Everyone knows that."

"Yes, you are, for all intents and purposes. However, no one even knew you existed until around the age of five. That is when you were quietly adopted by the Cargill family, isn't it, Mother? So they could sponsor you as a chosen and reap the benefits. With your beauty, who would ever think to question your bloodline? I always wondered why you and Father were not soulbound. Perhaps it's because you're not a pureblood?"

My eyebrows drew together in confusion. If his mother wasn't a pureblood, then that meant Keane wasn't either. What did that mean for our soulbond? How could it have come to be?

"Keane, this is all nonsense. I'm obviously a Vaimpír."

"Yes, you are. However, that only means *one* of your parents had to be a Vaimpír. The other could have been anything."

"I'm not entertaining this foolishness anymore. We are not talking about me but you. You must go back to the Barons and tell them you've changed your mind. That, in the excitement of everything going on, you lost sight of your family obligations."

"That isn't going to happen. I've made my decision, Mother, and it's final. Now, your blessing?"

She pursed her lips and seemed like she might refuse again.

Malakai cleared his throat. "Your word is your bond, Camille." He didn't use his domination on her, but I could see that his authority was more than enough to have her second-guessing her argument.

"Fine. You have my blessing on your soulbond. However, know that I'll not stop trying to change your mind about who you marry. If I have anything to say about it, your heirs will be pure-blooded Vaimpír."

"Thankfully, you don't." Keane turned away from her, ignoring her angry huffs. "Father, we'll be leaving at sunset tomorrow. Can you please have Celeste readied for transport?"

Malakai nodded and followed us from the room, leaving Camille stewing in anger. "I will have two of the guardians go with you as escorts."

"No need. My men will be here tomorrow. We'll be going straight to the Moon Tree Clan."

I looked at Keane in surprise. "We are?"

"Yes, Blue. Now that Hades knows where you are, you're in grave danger. He'll come for you once he can free himself. My father and I discussed this with Uncle Si, and he feels the same way. We think that going to Dock Street with the Moon Tree Clan is the safest place for you right now."

"But why would it be safer there?"

"Because of the Fairy wards. There are protective spells set around Dock Street to block almost everything from detection. Between your diffuser spell and their wards, Hades shouldn't be able to find you. It's probably what has kept you hidden for so long. We can use the time there to talk with Kieran and Uncle Si and come up with a plan against Hades."

I was feeling a bit overwhelmed with everything that had happened with the Vaimpír and the thought of having to go back to Dock Street. Thankfully, we had reached Keane's rooms.

Malakai turned to me, taking my hands in his. "Blue, it is truly a pleasure to welcome you to our family. I cannot tell you how happy I am that Keane found you. Know that I will do whatever I can to protect you as one of my own. Whatever you need, no matter what it is, it will be done."

I was both surprised and touched. "Malakai, I don't know what to say. Thank you for accepting me, even with all the craziness that seems to follow me. I started this journey with no one, and now, I seem to have acquired not one but two entire families."

Malakai pulled me into a brief hug. "No matter what happens, you will always have a place here."

With that, Malakai bid us goodnight and went back down the hall. I absently wondered how things would pan out between him and Camille.

Keane opened his door. "Don't worry about my parents. They'll figure things out. They always do. They've been together for centuries. Honestly, I think he already knew about my mother's bloodline. He just never cared enough to say anything."

"Speaking of knowing things and not saying anything. Did you know your Uncle Si was actually Poseidon?"

Keane sat on the back edge of the couch. "No. I knew he was more than what he presented himself as, and I was pretty sure he was a god, but I didn't know he was Poseidon. It explains a lot of things."

"How about your father?"

"I'm not positive, but I have a feeling he knew. He has always just had a way of knowing stuff like that."

"Does Malakai know Poseidon's my father?"

Keane nodded and, reaching over, pulled me between his thighs and into his arms. "After we met with the Barons, my father, Uncle Si, and I had a little meeting of our own. I thought it would be important to have everyone on the same page when it came to us and your safety. Was that okay?"

I nodded against his chest. "Yes. I was going to tell you we needed to tell him if you hadn't already."

"Good. I'm glad we're in agreement." Keane's voice tapered off as he tilted my face toward his. "Now, it seems that I finally have you all to myself..."

A shiver worked its way down my spine at his tone, and my heart rate picked up speed. Without the barrier of the bond acceptance hanging over our heads, nothing was stopping me from giving myself to Keane fully, and he knew it.

I sucked in a breath as I watched his gaze turn a dark red and his fangs lengthen. He leaned forward and ran his lips across my bare shoulder, scraping his fangs along my pulse point. "*Ma moitié...*"

I bit my lip, holding in the moan that threatened to slip free. Keane's hands splayed across my back before he found the zipper of my dress and slowly dragged it down, inch by inch. It stopped just as it hit my hips. Leaning back and looking me in the eyes, Keane slowly pushed the dress from my shoulder. It easily slid down to bunch up at my waist. He sucked in a breath as he took in Pinky and the Brain showcased behind the longline, black lace bra.

"I need to thank whoever talked you into buying all this sexy lingerie." His voice came out as a deep growl.

I giggled a bit breathlessly. "That would be Brianna."

"Next time I see her, she's getting whatever her heart desires."

Keane reached forward and cupped my breasts through the lace, running his thumbs over the nipples hidden beneath the fabric. "This is almost torture."

He groaned as he continued to run his hands down to my waist and the fabric gathered there. With a little push, the dress slid the rest of the way over my hips and pooled on the floor at my feet. Keane's hands followed, running over my hips and rear. His eyes widened and shot to mine when he realized I wasn't wearing any panties.

I shrugged and gave a small laugh. "They would've shown, so I just took them off."

Keane let out a low groan and, pulling me forward, pressed me tightly to his body so I could feel his hard arousal pulsing against my stomach. "I want to go slow. I want to savor this, but you're making it extremely difficult."

I brought my hands to his chest, where his shirt was still partially unbuttoned, and started slipping the rest of them open. "Maybe I don't want you to go slow." I ran my hands under his shirt, feeling the muscles flex at my touch before pushing it over his shoulders and trapping his arms. "Maybe I want you to go hard and fast. To dominate me. To show me that I'm yours and yours alone."

Keane growled, his eyes flashing. And with a roll of his shoulders, he ripped off his shirt. With one hand, he pulled me tightly against him while his other dove into my hair, wrapping around the back of my neck. He held my head still as his tongue plundered my mouth. I sighed with pleasure and pressed myself into him more, my hand slipping between us to stroke his length through his pants. Keane released my lips with a groan and ground himself against my hand, his eyes closed.

Lifting his lids, he watched me intently as his hand slipped from my waist and traveled down past the edge of my bra. I started panting a bit as his hand hovered over where I wanted him to touch—the anticipation almost killing me. Finally giving in, he slipped one of his fingers inside me. We both moaned.

"You're so wet. So ready for me."

I whimpered and threw my head back, my hands moving to grip his shoulders as he began stroking his finger in and out of my wet heat. Moaning, I pushed myself harder against his hand.

"Mmm, *ma moitié*. You have no idea what this is doing to me." He moved my hand back to his hard length, stroking it back and forth under his fingers. "I think we need to move this to the bedroom."

Just as he moved to pick me up, there was a knock on the door. We both froze, my gaze going from Keane to the door and back.

"Just ignore it," Keane whispered and again started to pick me up.

"I know you two are in there! I hope you're getting changed 'cause it's time to head out to the Dungeon. Leilani and Audrey are already on their way there." Keane leaned into my neck and groaned as Rhys jiggled the door handle. "Don't make me come in there!"

"All right, all right! We'll be right out." Keane lifted his head and looked at me, his eyes still full of desire. "Why is it that my brothers are always showing up just when I get you into this position?"

I laughed at his reminder of when Darrius had done the same thing to us. "We could always tell them no."

Keane chuckled and shook his head. "You don't know this group. If we don't show up, they'll just bring the party here."

I leaned forward and ran my tongue along his bottom lip and fangs before stepping back. "Okay, I'll go get changed then." As I turned my back to him, I unclipped the hooks from my bra and dropped it to the floor. I heard his groan as I walked away in just my heels.

"I'm going to kill Rhys when I see him."

Chapter Ten

I lifted my face to the breeze that blew across the yard and took in a deep breath. It felt good to be outside in the fresh air after being cooped up inside for so long. The only thing that would make it better was if the air contained the salty tang of the ocean.

We had snuck out by way of the balcony and were now making our way across the backyard toward the side street. A couple of blocks over, we would be able to pick up the streetcar that would take us into the French Quarter where the Dungeon was located.

Rhys met us at the gate. "Took you guys long enough." Keane scowled at him, but Rhys only laughed.

"My brothers seem to have this impeccable timing when it comes to interrupting me...at the worst possible moments."

Rhys smirked and glanced at Keane. "We do try to keep you on your toes."

A smile that promised retribution crossed Keane's lips. "Be careful, little brother. You know what they say. What goes around, comes around...when you least expect it."

They continued to quietly bicker as we made our way across the neighborhood under the cover of darkness. There wasn't a soul about, and the stillness was a bit unnerving. Even the moon seemed to find its way behind the clouds as if hiding from something. A feeling of trepidation worked its way down my spine, causing me to shiver a bit, and I looked around to make sure we weren't being followed. Not seeing anything, I pushed the sensation aside, chalking it up as a byproduct of the crazy events of the evening.

We jumped the St. Charles streetcar and rode it to the Canal and Bourbon Street stop before exiting and making our way down Bourbon. Here, life was in full swing. People were everywhere, drinks in hand, in various states of drunkenness. The bright lights from the bars lining either side of the street highlighted the revelry. Strains of jazz and other beats coalesced into a continuous pulse that carried us along as we wove in and out of the crowd.

By the time we got to Toulouse Street, the agitation I had been feeling had dissipated, replaced by a sense of excitement. It had been months since I had been able to let loose and enjoy myself. I shimmied my hips to the beat of the band playing at the Funky 544 bar on the corner, causing Keane to laugh. He grabbed me by the waist and spun me around before pulling me down the street toward a narrow, prison-like door made of black wood, sandwiched between two buildings. If you didn't know it was there, you might just walk right by it. Rhys opened the door, and I saw a narrow alleyway beyond. We moved in single file down the alley until we exited into a small courtyard bathed in red light. A large, black axe hung on the wall with the words *The Dungeon* splayed across it in red.

A few other people were entering the bar, and we followed. I looked around as we entered, noting the skulls and bones adorning the shelves behind the bar, along with all manner of graphic art, before my eyes landed on the mountain of a man standing next to us. I could tell that he was Fae—a shifter of some sort. As soon as he saw Rhys and Keane, he bowed in their direction.

"Good evening, Andre. It's good to see you." Keane reached out and shook his hand.

"Your Highness. It's always a pleasure."

"No need to be so formal, Andre, I thought we were well past that. Please, call me Keane."

Andre smiled a bit shyly, which was endearing on such a large man. "Of course...Keane."

"Andre, I'd like to introduce you to Blue. Blue, this is Andre, he acts as the enforcer for the Dungeon."

"Enforcer?"

"Kind of like a human bouncer but able to take on any Fae who decides to...misbehave."

Andre nodded his head toward me, not meeting my eyes. "Miss Blue. Welcome to the Dungeon. If you need anything, anything at all, you merely have to ask, and I'll take care of it."

"Thank you, Andre."

"I believe the others are already upstairs waiting for you." He led us to a narrow set of stairs in the back of the building.

I looked between the stairs and Rhys. "There is no way you're making it up those."

He laughed and looked at me challengingly. "Want to make a bet?"

I watched skeptically as he moved to the bottom of the staircase, putting the front wheels of his chair up on the first step. He grinned back at me. "Ready?"

Before I could nod, Andre moved past me and picked Rhys up—chair and all—easily carrying him up the stairs. I burst out laughing. "That's cheating!"

He laughed along with me. "You didn't say I had to make it up by myself. It pays to have a shifter on staff, especially when said shifter is a bear."

Rhys turned to Andre. "Thank you, Andre. I'm grateful for your assistance." He lowered his voice to a stage-whisper. "Especially when you make me look good in front of the ladies."

Andre looked down and met my eyes briefly before blushing and looking away. I was instantly charmed.

"Should I be jealous, *ma moitié?*" Keane had moved to stand close behind me, his breath tickling my ear, causing goosebumps to spring up along my skin. My breath hitched as he nipped the lobe, my nipples immediately hardening. Having felt my reaction, he chuckled softly against my skin.

"Behave yourself." I quickly went up the steps before Keane could try anything else.

The upstairs had yet another bar and cages with benches in them to sit in instead of tables. Andre led us past a dance floor full of people rocking out to the music blaring through the speakers to a door at the back of the room.

After knocking in several long and short raps, a small panel near the middle of the door slid back to reveal a pair of dark eyes. They surveyed Andre, then us, before the panel closed and the door opened. Andre blocked the view as we slid through, staying outside.

The person on the other side of the door turned out to be a young woman with long, black hair and strange, dark-purple eyes. She nodded politely in our direction but otherwise ignored us. Keane came up and took my elbow, guiding me around yet another dance floor—this one full of Fae. I saw Leilani and Audrey leaning against the bar, each with a drink in hand. They had taken the time to change before they left and were dressed much like me in distressed jeans and low-cut T-shirts, though they both still sported high heels while I had opted for my Converse sneakers.

"Hey, guys! About time you got here!" Leilani reached over and hugged first Rhys and then Keane, before draping an arm around my shoulders.

I watched as Rhys went over, took Audrey's hand, and pulled her down into his lap before kissing her fully on the mouth.

"Rhys!" Audrey tried to pull out of his arms. "What if someone sees us?"

Rhys laughed and tightened his hold on her. "It no longer matters. You're free to be with whomever you want."

She froze as the realization washed over her before a huge smile bloomed on her face. Looking at Keane, she jumped up and threw her arms around him. "Thank you. Oh, thank you, Keane!" She managed to place several kisses on his face before Rhys grabbed her and pulled her back into his lap.

"Hey, save those for me."

We all laughed, welcoming the release after everything that had happened that evening. Keane came over and pulled me away from Leilani, giving her a mock glare. "Hands off."

She just rolled her eyes at him and grinned. "Can't blame a girl for trying." She then turned and waved to one of the bartenders. "Kaleigh!"

A tall, curvy woman with shiny, jet-black hair and a tight black-and-red corset sashayed her way down the length of the bar before leaning casually against the scarred wood in front of us. She smiled, her dark red lips parting to reveal a row of sharp teeth. "Long time no see, Lei. Huginn here was starting to think you didn't like us anymore."

I assumed Huginn was the raven that sat perched on her shoulder. I tilted my head at him, and he did the same back while continuing to watch me with intense, black eyes. I blinked, and he blinked. I had a feeling this was no mere raven. As I watched, he leaned into Kaleigh and let out a few soft croaks. She tilted her head in his direction and nodded, seeming to understand him.

As if feeling my stare, she glanced at me and winked before turning back to her conversation with Leilani. As she tilted her head to the side, I thought I saw a few slits behind her ear. Curious, I checked her energy signature. It seemed that Kaleigh was a Siren.

"What can I get you and your friends to drink?"

"How about five shots of Fairy Dust?"

"You got it, darling." I watched as she poured out glasses of a liquid that glowed iridescent and seemed to have some type of sparkles floating in it. When she was done, Leilani passed the shots around. "To Keane and Blue. The ones who finally freed us from the oppressive obligations heaped on us by our parents."

We tapped our glasses together before tipping our drinks back. As the liquid slid down my throat, I was surprised by how smooth it was. I couldn't quite place the taste, though. "What was that?"

Leilani signaled to Kaleigh for another round. "A special Fae drink. It contains what equates to Fairy moonshine along with trace amounts of a spell made to release your inhibitions. I figured it was appropriate, considering what you are."

Audrey gave me a warning glance. "Careful, Blue, it's strong for someone not used to it."

I took the second shot from Leilani and, after clinking glasses, downed that one, as well. My whole body seemed to relax, my mind letting go of the worries from before. It was very freeing. "Wow, you weren't kidding."

Leilani grinned knowingly. "One more?"

I hesitated but then decided...what the hell? We downed our third shots, and I swayed a bit. "Okay, this stuff is dangerous."

Both girls laughed and dragged me onto the dance floor. Normally, I wasn't one to just go out and shake it for all to see, but the drinks had undeniably loosened me up. Soon, I found myself swaying and gyrating along with Audrey and Leilani, laughing and enjoying myself.

Before long, I felt a pair of strong hands gripping my hips before sliding to my waist and pulling me against a hard, male body. I smiled as Keane started moving in rhythm with me. Reaching back, I wrapped my fingers around his neck and closed my eyes. His hands skirted up my rib cage, stopping just shy of Pinky and the Brain before sliding back down and over my hips.

I pressed back and rubbed against him, feeling the effects of the drinks on my inhibitions. His hand slid to my stomach to press me back harder while leaning down and nuzzling my neck. I groaned softly and gripped the back of his head, burying my fingers in his hair. His lips continued their path up so he could whisper in my ear. "You're such a tease."

I smiled and slowly opened my eyes. I was about to turn toward him when an odd movement at the side of the room caught my attention. Focusing through the dim, red light, I saw the unmistakable outline of a hellhound. He wasn't corporeal—his form shifting within the shadows. My eyebrows drew together in confusion, my brain having a hard time processing what I was seeing.

"I'm sorry about this, Mistress."

Before I could even register what he meant, he leaped forward and grabbed me by the arm, spinning me around. Fear coursed down my spine when I saw Keane standing there holding my unconscious body, knowing what it meant.

"No. Keane!"

His head jerked up as if he'd heard me, his gaze shifting from panic to anger. As darkness surrounded me, I heard his roar of rage before Scythe pulled me fully into the void.

"Scythe, please stop. Don't do this." He just continued to pull me forward as I stumbled behind him, trying to dislodge his mouth from my arm.

Without warning, there was a bright flash of light, and I found myself stumbling across a stone floor, trying to regain my balance. Before I could orient myself, I was pushed hard against the wall, a hand wrapped around my throat.

"Hello, my dear little... Niece." I stared fearfully into Hades' enraged, glowing amber eyes.

"Ha-Hades."

"Surprised to see me, little one? Did you really think by trapping me here, you could hide from me?" He laughed darkly before tightening his grip around my throat. "While my powers don't work beyond this castle right now, I still have my hellhounds. Their abilities are not bound by my powers. All I have to do is command them to bring your soul to me, and they will."

I pushed my fear down, wishing that the effects of the alcohol had carried over to my spirit form to numb my emotions. Alas, no such luck. "What do you want, Hades?"

"Release me from your bond."

"No."

"Don't toy with me, Blue. You will not like the consequences."

"You...you won't hurt me. You need me."

His look turned malicious. "You're right. I'd never hurt you." He ran a finger reverently down my cheek. "Others, however..." With a snap of his fingers, my mother appeared in the room.

"Blue!"

"Mom!" I looked at her in panic.

"Now, release me."

I shook my head, causing him to sigh and cluck his tongue. "So headstrong."

With another snap of his fingers, a ring of blue flames surrounded Iridia. "I said, release me." As I watched, the fire inched closer and closer to her, singeing the edges of the dress she wore. I kept my mouth stubbornly shut.

"Do you think I won't hurt her?" I flinched when I heard her cry out, but I kept my determined gaze on his, calling his bluff. Hades narrowed his eyes at me and waited. When I didn't look away, he let out an angry growl before releasing my throat and pacing away like a caged animal.

For the first time, I took note of his appearance. His hair was in disarray, standing on end in places, and his clothes were wrinkled and askew. Far from the polished, suave gentleman I had seen earlier. Obviously, Hades didn't like being trapped here. Though he could still use the hellhounds to travel the void, he would have no powers if he were to leave his castle. He walked over to Iridia, who was still standing in the burned-out circle on the floor, clutching her arm where the fire had burned her.

"Too bad I can't bring that Vaimpír of yours here." I felt my anger spike at the mention of Keane but held my tongue. "Mmm, that bothers you, does it? Good to know. Perhaps I'll send my hellhounds after him."

"Go ahead. He'll just tear them apart. And then where will you be?"

"That confident in him, are you?"

"Yes."

"I'll admit, he does have a strange aura for a Vaimpír. Even I'm not sure what to make of it." Hades reached over and smoothed his hand down my mother's hair, causing her to flinch away from him. "It seems we are at an impasse then. I will not release you until you release me."

I crossed my arms over my chest, my anger fueling my confidence. "Why would I release you? You would just go after my physical body and trap me here yet again. Isn't that what this is really about?"

"True. You *could* save us both the trouble and give yourself to me. You know I'll eventually figure out how to break this bond. I'd even be willing to make an exchange." His look turned calculating. "Come to me of your own free will, and I...will release your mother." His glowing eyes met mine in a challenge. "I'll even throw in that Warlock of hers as a bonus."

"Blue, no. Don't listen..." Hades looked at her in annoyance and, with a final snap of his fingers, she disappeared.

I shook my head at him. "This is all starting to feel like a certain *Disney* cartoon. Are you waiting for the planets to align so you can release the Titans to help you conquer Olympus?" Hades glared at me, not seeming to appreciate my humor. Or perhaps he hadn't seen *Hercules*. Which would be a shame, it was a good one.

Stalking over to the fire that always seemed to burn in the hearth, Hades rested his hand on Scythe's head, tension evident in every part of his body. "Why would I need the Titans when I have you? With your abilities, the possibilities are endless."

"But you don't have me, do you? And with you stuck here, it kind of looks like you're not going to."

Hades snarled, turned angrily, picked up the large, potted plant sitting next to the fireplace, and hurled it in my direction. I ducked to the side and covered my face just as it smashed against the wall, shards and dirt flying everywhere. When I looked back up, Hades was once again standing in front of me, his face a mask of rage. Grabbing me roughly by the arms, he pulled me in close to him.

"I will have you. It's just a matter of time. I'll find a way to break this bond, Blue, and when I do, there will be no hiding from me. You'll come to me, and you'll help me take down my brother and punish him. Once he's buried in the deepest, darkest depths of Tartarus and made to feel and experience everything I did, made to suffer as I have, only then will I be happy. Only then will Alexandra finally be avenged." His emotions—hatred, pain, despair, and loneliness—swelled over me, causing me to take a deep breath as they pressed in.

"Who is Alexandra?" I breathed out, trying to dig myself out of his emotions.

Hades pulled back, looking at me in shock, pain etched across his face. He abruptly turned and dragged me from the room, Scythe following on our heels. I tried to jerk out of his grasp, but his hold was unrelenting. He led me to a large bedchamber before pushing me roughly through the door. I fell to the floor and looked back at him.

"You will stay here until I decide what to do with you." He turned to Scythe. "Watch her." Then, he left and slammed the door behind him.

I sat there in shock, staring at the closed door. Who was Alexandra? And why did she evoke so much pain and despair in Hades?

Scythe padded into the room and sat at my feet, looking forlorn. *"I'm very sorry, Mistress. He commanded that I bring you here, and I have to obey him."*

I sat up carefully, dusted off my hands, and crossed my legs under me as I shook my head. "Why do you have to obey him, Scythe?"

"He's my master. He commands all those he creates in the fires. We are bonded to him."

"Then why do you help me? And why do you call me Mistress?"

"Because I'm also bonded to you."

"Why would you be bonded to me?"

"You helped the master create me. Your blood runs in my veins. It's the reason your powers don't affect me."

I sat up straight and stared at him. "Is that what you meant when you said you weren't created the same way?" Scythe nodded, and I shook my head in bewilderment. "How old was I?"

"Four. I used to be your full-time protector."

"I wish I could remember."

"I could show you if you wish it."

I looked at him in surprise. "How?"

"I'll show you some of my memories. Do you wish to see?"

I nodded slowly. Reaching up, I placed my hands on either side of his head and closed my eyes as he instructed. Like falling down a rabbit hole, we tumbled into Scythe's memories.

As Scythe's eyes opened, he looked through the flames that surrounded him and saw a small creature. He didn't know why, but he felt an immediate connection to it, like he had been created for it.

Another creature, much like the small one only much larger, stood over him. "Do you know who I am, hellhound?"

Scythe shook his head.

"I'm Hades, your lord and master. You have been forged in the fires of Hell from the soul of a Demon and brought forth to serve me as one of my guardians. You shall henceforth be called Scythe. Bound by my blood, you will obey my every command."

Scythe bowed his head, not knowing why but knowing it was what he should do. "Your wish is my command, Master."

The little creature stepped forward and held out its hand, flames dancing across its skin but not burning it. "I'm Carolina, your lady and mistress. Bound by my blood, as well, you will obey my every command."

Scythe bowed his head again. "Your wish is my command, Mistress."

"There, little one. Once I've finished training him, you'll have your very own guardian. He'll never let any harm come to you while you're under his watch."

"Thank you, Uncle Hades. He's perfect."

"I'm amazed at how much your powers grow every day, little one. The magic used to create a hellhound is something only the strongest and oldest of gods can accomplish. I have the distinct feeling that Aiden wasn't truly your father, after all." The last part he said more to himself, as the small creature had moved over to the fires again.

She reached through the flames, ran her fingers over his head, and scratched behind his ears. Scythe felt a rumble go through his chest and his scales vibrated, making a chattering sound. The little creature giggled, causing the heart in his chest to give a loud thump, then another. He didn't know why, but he never wanted to be separated from this little creature.

"Come, little one, it's time for us to continue your other lessons."

The memory faded, and another took shape. It was just Scythe and the little girl, sitting before a large picture window in what appeared to be a bedroom that overlooked a wooded area. All manner of creatures just beyond the window sat frozen in time.

"Did you see me, Scythe? I stopped the forest."

"Very good, Mistress. You're becoming very powerful. Even more so than Hades."

Carolina's mother came rushing into the room. "Carolina, dear, release time this minute. What have I told you about doing that?" She picked his mistress up before looking at Scythe. "Please, don't mention this to Hades, Scythe."

"I will not say anything unless he specifically asks about it."

Iridia looked extremely concerned, and Scythe had to wonder why. She didn't like it when Hades learned about his mistress's new powers. Scythe didn't think Hades would ever harm the little girl. He treated her like his own daughter. It was curious.

The memory faded yet again, another taking its place.

His little mistress was on her bed, crying, causing Scythe to become agitated. He didn't know the reason for her distress.

"What is the matter, Mistress?"

She looked at him with tear-filled eyes. "They took my magic away, Scythe. I can't do it anymore." She held out her hands as if trying, but nothing happened.

Scythe got angry. "Who took it, Mistress? I'll bring them to you and make them give it back."

"It was Mommy and Daddy. They said it was safer for me to be this way. That they had to protect me from Uncle Hades."

Scythe tilted his head to the side. "Why would you need to be protected from Hades? Has he done something to harm you?"

His mistress sniffled. "No. They said he was a bad man. That he wants to use my magic and they can't let that happen. I...I think they are going to send me away, Scythe. Away from here, away from you." She began crying again.

"I will not let that happen, Mistress. You're mine to protect. Where you go, I go." No sooner had he said this, than something sharp pierced his thick scales. His body felt heavy, and he swayed on his feet before dropping to the floor.

"Scythe!"

"Hush, Carolina, he's fine. He's just going to take a little nap. It's okay."

"No, Mommy! Scythe! Scythe!" His mistress squirmed in her mother's arms, trying to get to him.

Scythe watched helplessly through half-closed eyes as Iridia ran her hand over her daughter's head, easily putting her into a deep sleep. He tried to get up, but his muscles refused to work—it took everything he had to remain conscious.

Iridia looked sadly down at her daughter. "I know this is the right thing to do, but I don't want to send my baby away."

Aiden laid a hand on Iridia's shoulder. "We have to, dearest. We've already gone over and over this. We can't allow Hades to use Carolina to start a war with his brother. He has already been grooming her magic to do what he wants. If he were to discover her extra abilities, there is no doubt he would take her."

"I know." Scythe growled low in his throat as they wrapped his mistress in a blanket and lifted her up. Iridia looked down at him in apology. "I'm sorry about this, Scythe. If Hades didn't have so much control over you, I'd gladly send you with her." With that, they left the room, and Scythe fell into a deep sleep.

As soon as his memory faded, I came back to myself. Dropping my hands to my lap, I sat staring at Scythe, thinking through everything he had shown me. An ironic smile quirked the corner of my mouth as I realized I had called Hades' *"uncle"* as a child without knowing that he truly *was* my uncle.

It was hard to believe that not only had I spent the first four years of my life with all my powers, but I had also trained with Hades. *And he had treated me as much more than just a prisoner.* Though I still couldn't remember the time, I could feel the emotions when I saw Scythe's memories—what I had been feeling. I had to wonder if those memories were still there, hidden somewhere deep down.

I looked at Scythe. "With our bond, can you track me like the Vaimpír do?"

"No, it doesn't work the same way. The bond makes me obey you. Even if I wanted to, I couldn't tell you or Hades no for something you asked of me."

"Is there a way to break the bond?"

"You wish to break our bond, Mistress?"

"No, I wish to break your bond to Hades."

"I don't know if that's possible. I've never heard of a bond being broken between Hades and one of his creations."

I sighed, wishing there was an easy answer. Perhaps that was something else Kieran could help me with. Not knowing what else to do—and needing time to think about things—I stood and walked over to the bed before lying down on it. I patted the spot next to me, and Scythe jumped up, lying at my feet. He was like a scaly, oversized dog. I must have drifted off because, the next thing I knew, I was being awoken by a deep, familiar voice.

"Blue?"

I sat up straight in the bed looking around the room. "Keane?"

"Blue, thank heavens." It took me a minute, but I finally realized that he was talking to me mentally, not here in the room. *"Are you okay? That bastard didn't hurt you, did he?"* I could hear the anger in his voice.

"No, I'm okay. How did you figure out how to contact me?"

"Your mother is here. She taught me."

"My mother? Is she okay? Hades didn't hurt her any more, did he?"

"She's fine, a bit shaken up, but Aiden took care of her." I sighed in relief. *"Blue, can you find a way through the void to get back?"*

I shook my head, even though he couldn't see me. *"It wouldn't matter anyway. Hades would just send his hounds again."*

"We're at Dock Street. We came straight here after I realized what had happened. Once you're here, he won't be able to find you again. I'll even have Tristan set extra wards for the hellhounds, just in case."

I looked over at Scythe. While I knew he would take me through the void, I knew he wouldn't be able to deny Hades if he commanded him to come after me. I needed to find somewhere for him to take me that Hades wouldn't be able to trace back to Dock Street. *"Can you portal back to the Dungeon and meet me there?"*

"I'll go there now." He seemed to understand my concern right away.

"Scythe?" The hellhound lifted his head and looked at me. "Can you take me back to the bar where you took me from?"

He tilted his head to the side. *"I can take you wherever you wish, Mistress."*

"Will Hades punish you if you do?"

"Perhaps, but he knows that I cannot disobey your command."

I was quickly becoming weary. Why would Hades leave Scythe to guard me if he knew the hellhound would have to obey any command I gave him? Was he testing me? Or trying to have me lead him straight to my body?

"Don't worry about me, Mistress, I'll be fine."

I nodded, still unsure but realizing this was the only way. I'd have to figure out how to deal with Hades later—once I found my mother and Aiden and rescued them.

"Okay, Scythe, please take me to the Dungeon bar in New Orleans."

He jumped off the bed and bowed to me. *"Your wish is my command."*

Just as I stepped through the portal into the void, the door to the bedroom slammed against the wall, and Hades stepped in. "No!"

I turned in alarm at the sound of his angry bellow, my heart rate skyrocketing. He lunged for me, but the portal closed just before he reached me. My pulse continued to beat out a heavy tattoo in my chest, knowing he would send more hellhounds after me any second now.

"Hurry, Scythe."

"Yes, Mistress."

The portal opened in the same room where Scythe had taken me from. Thankfully, it was empty now except for Keane and Andre. They stood by the bar, talking. Neither could see me as I was incorporeal, but Keane knew the minute I stepped through the portal.

"Blue?"

I closed my eyes and quickly matched their energy vibrations so they could see me. Both men took up a defensive position when they spotted Scythe by my side, but I just waved them away and ran into Keane's arms. "We need to go. Now." He hugged me close before stepping back with a nod. Turning to the empty wall, he started his portal spell. Before he completed it, I heard a low rumble, then several growls. I turned in fear. Twelve hellhounds poured into the room from another portal. "Scythe!"

"I'll keep them at bay, Mistress."

"Andre, you'd better come with us." I reached out a hand toward the large man, but he shook his head.

"No, I'll stay here and keep them busy so you can get to safety."

"Andre. They're hellhounds."

He just grinned at me in excitement. "Finally, a bit of a challenge. Don't fear for me, Miss Blue, please just take care of yourself."

"I'll make sure no harm comes to the bear, Mistress."

Andre huffed in annoyance. "Like I need your help, mutt."

Before I could say another word, Keane pulled me through the portal. The last glimpse I had was of Andre being jumped by five hellhounds.

As soon as my feet landed on the soft, tan carpet, I turned to Keane. "We have to go back and help him. We can't just leave him to the hounds."

Keane chuckled and pulled me into a tight embrace. "Trust me, it's the hellhounds you need to worry about. Andre can hold his own."

I'd have argued more, but Keane leaned down and brought his lips to mine, all his worry and relief pouring into his kiss. Still on an adrenaline high, a fire sparked low in my belly, quickly igniting my desires. I moaned as he pulled me in closer, pressing his lower half against me, his erection pushing against my stomach while his mouth ravished mine.

Rising on tiptoe, I wrapped one of my legs around his to bring us closer. Keane growled and ran his lips from my neck to my shoulder while one of his hands slid down to squeeze my breast through the thin fabric of my shirt. I arched into him, wanting to feel his skin against mine.

"Keane, you're back. Was your mission successful?" The voice jolted me back to reality, and I turned my head to find Tristan standing in the doorway at the end of the hall.

I almost laughed. Since Tristan couldn't see me, I had to wonder what Keane looked like making out with air.

Keane grimaced at the interruption, not even bothering to acknowledge Tristan.

"Let's get you back into your body."

Chapter Eleven

As soon as I reconnected with my body, I opened my eyes to find three anxious gazes staring down at me. I blinked several times, trying to bring them into focus. Before I had a chance to react, though, I was pulled bodily out of the bed and into three sets of arms.

"Blue. Thank the stars you're safe."

I smiled up into the faces of Mckile, Cullen, and Ronan—also known as the band Ethereal Mutation. "Hi, guys."

"Why does it seem like every time you're out of our sight, you get into trouble?" Mckile leaned in and kissed the top of my head.

I giggled a bit at all the attention. "Keane swears I attract it."

"That you do, sweetheart." Cullen chucked me under the chin.

"See if we let you go anywhere alone from now on." Ronan pecked a kiss on the tip of my nose.

"Okay, you three, break it up." Keane pushed them laughing from the room, but before he could shut the door again, another figure stood there. It was Riona. Keane bowed to her. "Your Majesty."

Riona waved him away. "Since when have you ever adhered to formalities? Blue, it's so good to see you up and moving again."

"Thanks, Riona. It's good to see you, too."

Tristan followed her through the door, his eyes running over me anxiously. "Blue. I'm relieved you're finally awake. Your continued state of unconsciousness was a bit unnerving."

I turned to Keane and raised my brows in question before communicating with him mentally. *"You didn't tell them why I was unconscious?"*

"No, I thought you'd like to do that yourself."

I turned back to Tristan and Riona with a grimace. "I think it's about time we talk about a few things I've kept to myself."

It was Tristan's turn to raise his brows. "Why don't we go out into the living area?"

"Is Kieran here at Dock Street by any chance?"

"Of course."

"Can you send for him? I'd rather do this all at once."

Tristan nodded, looking a bit concerned by my serious tone, before turning and walking from the room. We followed him into the living area, where I flopped onto the enormous, wrap-around blue couch situated in front of the slate fireplace. Keane sat next to me, laying an arm over the back of the sofa behind me. He toyed with my hair—which was probably standing up in a hundred different directions right now, but that was the least of my concerns. I looked over to where Mckile, Cullen, and Ronan were battling it out against each other on some shoot-'em-up game at the game station hooked up across the room. I smiled, thinking about how many times I had seen them just like that.

"How did things go with the Vaimpír?" I turned back as Tristan sat down next to Riona, who had moved to sit catty-corner to us.

I smiled and placed my hand on Keane's thigh. "Our bond has been officially accepted by all of the Vaimpír houses and blessed by the King and Queen."

"That was fast." I could see the disappointment on Tristan's face, though he tried to hide it.

Keane laughed softly and covered my hand with his. "Some *extenuating* circumstances helped to accelerate the process."

Before Tristan could ask further questions, the elevator doors opened to reveal my grandfather. I stood and went toward him.

"Grandfather."

"Blue, my girl, why have you not been answering any of my calls?" He pulled me into a hug before stepping back and giving me a stern look. "Three months without so much as a callback? Do you know how worried I have been? Thank goodness for that Vaimpír of yours, keeping me in the loop."

I grimaced and looked down at the floor for a moment before eyeing him from under my lashes in apology. "I'm sorry. Things were a little unsettled after everything that happened. It took me a while to get back to myself. I promise I won't ignore your calls from now on."

He gave a gruff huff. "See that you don't." I stepped back with a small smile, knowing he had forgiven me, and led him over to everyone else.

Keane stood and reached out his hand. "Kieran, sir. It's good to see you again."

Kieran shook his hand while patting him on the arm. "Keane, my boy. I hear from your grandfather that congratulations are in order." He looked between the two of us.

"Thank you, sir."

Kieran sat on the couch next to Keane while I remained standing. I took in a deep breath and then let it out, trying to calm myself. "I wanted to bring you all together so I could tell you a few things and ask for your help."

"Blue, whatever it is, you know we'll do whatever we can to help you." I smiled in Tristan's direction, knowing he might change his mind after I revealed all the secrets I had been keeping from him.

"What I have to say cannot leave this room for now, though I've a feeling it won't remain a secret for long." After everyone had nodded, I continued. "It turns out my father is not Aiden as we originally thought. My father is actually...Poseidon, God of the Seas."

Kieran looked thoughtful, while Triston sat up in shock. "So, all the things you can do... The reason you have so many different gifts..."

"Is because the blood of a god runs through my veins."

"Have you met your father yet?" Kieran seemed very intrigued with the revelation.

I nodded and turned to him. "He visited me while I was with the Vaimpír. This leads me to the next thing... Hades visited me, as well. Because of my powers, which it seems are unique, even to the gods, it appears Hades has taken quite an interest in me." I left out the fact that he had been searching for me since I was a kid. "He seems to think he can use me and what I can do to overthrow his brother, Zeus. But he needs me in my physical form to do it. And until recently, he has been unable to find me."

"Why couldn't he find you before now?" Tristan wrinkled his brow in confusion.

"Keane surmises that while the enchantment was on me, I appeared as only human, so Hades wasn't able to track any magical signature. He could have stood right next to me and not have known who I was. After my powers were unlocked, Keane believes I remained hidden because I spent most of my time here at Dock Street."

Keane leaned forward, placing his elbows on his knees. "We believe the Fairy wards keep her hidden from him."

Kieran nodded thoughtfully. "That would make sense. Not much can be detected within them."

"Exactly. That's why I decided to bring her here again. After our run-in with Hades, which resulted in him taking her soul for a bit, I figured this was the safest place for her."

"He took her soul?" Tristan moved to the edge of the couch in apparent agitation.

I nodded. "It seems Hades stole the statue Brody made of me from Larkin. Contained within that statue—much like Riona's—is a piece of my soul. With it, Hades can call me to him whenever he wants. Or whenever my guard is down—usually when I'm sleeping." I decided not to mention the fact that a hellhound had dragged me back this last time. Some things were better left unsaid.

Keane leaned back on the couch, stretching his long legs out. "We're hoping the wards will also stop Hades from being able to take her soul."

Tristan rubbed his hand over his face and sat back. "This is a lot to take in."

Riona, who had remained silent the entire time, finally spoke up. "What is it that you need our help with?"

I glanced toward Kieran almost apologetically. I didn't want to tell him this but didn't see a way around it. "Before I can have it out with Hades, I need help removing a bit of collateral he has over me."

"Collateral?"

"It seems that Hades has been holding my...mother captive."

Kieran sat up in surprise. "Iridia?"

I nodded with a slight grimace. "It seems Hades kidnapped Aiden all those years ago as bait to get his hands on Iridia. He seemed to think she had the gift he needed to help him defeat his brother."

Kieran looked confused. "What gift?"

"The gift of the blood of a god."

"But she isn't the daughter of a god."

"No, but it showed up somewhere in our family line. I have a feeling that's why the Grayson family is so powerful and has so many unique gifts."

"Interesting. I will have to go back and trace our family tree to see where it might have entered." He looked thoughtful before refocusing on me. "So, even though Iridia has some of a god's bloodline, she didn't have whatever Hades needs?"

"No. He said her bloodline was too diluted."

"And she's still being held prisoner there?"

I nodded sadly. "Hades is keeping her there as bait for me."

"Why? What power do you possess that he wants?"

I took a deep breath and then let it out. "I can stop time."

"You can what?" Tristan looked at me in astonishment. "When did you discover that?"

"I...well...I've known about it for...some time now." I hesitated, not wanting to let on how I'd discovered it when I used it against Larkin. "I haven't had control over it. It just happens sometimes."

"And now Hades seeks to use it." Tristan stood and started pacing, his brow furrowed. "If Hades is using Iridia as bait, wouldn't going after her be falling right into his hands? It's obviously a trap."

I shrugged. "Obviously, but I can't run from Hades for the rest of my life, and I can't face off with him while he's holding Iridia over my head.

He's already proven he's willing to do anything to get to me. I have to find her and rescue her."

"Do you have any idea where he's keeping her?"

"The first time he summoned my soul to him..."

"Wait, he's taken you more than once?"

I ignored Tristan's interruption. "He took me to see her. She was in a small cottage in a heavily wooded area."

Kieran sat forward in his seat. "Did anything unique stand out to you? Were there any animals, sounds, or smells that didn't seem to fit?"

I closed my eyes and concentrated, trying to pick anything from my memory that might help. "The trees were tall, not quite like the ones in the Misty River Clan territory, but close. And it smelled of earthy moss and pine. I'm pretty sure I could hear water running nearby, maybe a creek of some sort... Wait...there was something. A little bird. A woodpecker. Black-and-white-spotted with just a touch of red on its face. I thought it odd since it was pecking in a live pine tree, not a dead one."

Riona looked at me in surprise. "A red-cockaded woodpecker. They are the only species of woodpecker that uses live pine trees instead of dead ones. They are extremely rare and only found in a few places." We all looked at Riona. "Hades must be hiding her somewhere near the Fernsong Clan."

"So close," Kieran breathed. "She has been that close this whole time, and we didn't know it?"

I looked at him sympathetically. This couldn't be easy for him. Tristan did, too. "I'll call Brokk immediately so we can send out some search parties."

"Wait. We have to do this quietly. We can't just go stomping around and give away what we know to Hades."

Tristan flashed me a crooked grin. "Have no fear, Blue. I know how to conduct a clandestine investigation. Have faith in me."

I nodded, accepting his word. "We also have to figure out what is holding them there."

"What do you mean?" Kieran turned back to me.

"Iridia said they were being held by some type of god magic. That's why they haven't escaped before now. Is there anything in the Elder library that might help with knowledge of the gods? Like what type of magic could hold someone like that?"

"Perhaps. There is a rather extensive section on the gods, though I cannot say I have delved into more than just the basics."

"I am sure I can be of help with that."

We all turned in surprise to see a man standing in the middle of the living area. Ethereal Mutation immediately moved to surround him, but he just held up his hands in surrender.

"Father." I stood and went over to him, waving the guys away. "What are you doing here?"

"And how did you get in, for that matter?" Tristan grumbled in annoyance. "Where the hell are my guards?"

Poseidon chuckled and walked with me to the couch. "Keane invited me. And, honestly, there isn't much that would keep a god out."

Keane dipped his head in acknowledgment before addressing Tristan. "Which is why I've had your rune specialists modify your wards to specifically keep Hades and his hellhounds out should he discover where Blue is."

I sent a surprised look toward Keane. "You can do that?"

"If you have someone who knows the god's specific energy signature, then yes." He winked at me before continuing. "I invited Uncle Si, thinking he could give us the most insight on Hades and his magic."

"I will gladly tell you all what I know, though not even I can help you with some aspects of Hades' magic."

"What about the spell he's using to hold Iridia and Aiden prisoner?"

"It is most likely the *deorum sanguinem vinculum.*"

Flopping down onto the couch, I groaned. "Oh, no. I know that word, sanguinem. This has something to do with blood again, doesn't it?"

Poseidon chuckled and patted me on the head. "The gods' blood bond, to be exact. It is very old god magic. Honestly, not many can use it anymore. It ties a person or creature to the god. While under its constraints, they would have to obey everything the god demanded and would not be able to leave them."

I looked at Poseidon in surprise. "Like what Hades uses on the hellhounds."

Poseidon looked at me curiously. "I am not sure. I have never seen how Hades creates his hounds."

"Hmm...how do we break it?"

Poseidon scratched his chin. "That is the tricky part."

My eyes narrowed. "I'm not going to like this, am I?"

"Probably not. You are going to need Hades' blood."

"Ugh. Somehow, I knew you were going to say that. Why does it always have to be about blood?"

Poseidon laughed lightly and lifted his shoulders. "Like I said, it is old magic. All old magic utilized blood in some form or another. It is a powerful binder."

I grunted and laid my head on Keane's lap, where he proceeded to run his fingers through my hair while looking around the room. "If anyone knows how we can get our hands on some of Hades' blood, now would be the time to speak up."

Chapter Twelve

Unsurprisingly, after the events of the past few days, I was exhausted and more than ready for bed. While the others had just gotten up, I was still running on the Vaimpír's night schedule, so it was well past my bedtime. We decided to postpone our discussions until after I had gotten some sleep so I could at least function semi-normally. Keane lay beside me on the bed, ready to protect me should the wards fail and Hades try to take my soul again.

"Don't worry, *ma moitié*. I'll watch over you as you sleep. I won't leave your side." I smiled tiredly as he kissed my forehead, then snuggled into his warmth.

As I fell into a deep sleep, I vaguely felt something pulse through my bond with Keane. Not long after the darkness consumed me, images began taking shape in my mind, invading my dreams. I looked around in confusion. I was back at the Rutherman house in New Orleans—in Keane's bedchamber, to be exact.

A young man sat on a trunk situated under one of the windows in the main bedroom. He had one long leg drawn up to him with his chin resting on his knee. With a start, I realized it was Keane.

What was happening? How was I seeing this?

I moved forward, wondering if he could see me, but it didn't appear so. It just didn't make sense. Was Keane thinking about this memory? Had I somehow connected to him and fell into it?

Shaking my head, I turned back to the young Keane, studying him with fascination. His youthful face showed the promise of the rugged, handsome man he would become once fully grown. He wore a pair of high-waisted trousers and a tailed jacket with long, tight sleeves and a wide collar cut in a deep v to show off the waistcoat beneath it. I wasn't exactly sure, but I'd guess the fashion was from sometime in the mid-1800s, near the beginning of the Victorian era.

My thoughts tripped over themselves when I realized that meant Keane was well over two hundred years old. As I stood there in shock, a younger version of Reginald entered the room.

"Master Keane, there you are. Your mother has been looking all over for you, my boy."

Keane turned his head toward Reginald, his expression angry. "Well, she can keep looking. I don't want to see her."

"Now, Master Keane. You know better than that. She's your mother. You must respect her."

Keane snorted. "Do you know what she told me at breakfast, Reginald?"

"I can't even begin to imagine."

"That I must prepare myself to marry soon for the sake of the family line, and she has already chosen several girls for me to pick from."

"It's tradition, Master Keane."

"It's ridiculous! Here I am, barely out of short trousers, and my mother is trying to marry me off! What do I want with a wife?"

Reginald cackled merrily and moved to sit by Keane.

"Give me your hands, my boy."

Keane eyed him suspiciously. "Why would I do that? What are you trying to find out?"

"Just give me your hands."

Keane hesitantly placed his hands in Reginald's, though he still looked suspicious. Reginald closed his eyes while Keane and I both watched him expectantly.

"Mm. Mm-hmm, very interesting."

Keane sat up straight. "What? What is it?"

Reginald opened his eyes and looked at Keane. "As you know, I cannot see the future, only the paths that will lead you to who you are supposed to become."

"And who am I supposed to become?"

"Someone of great power, Master Keane. Someone who will inspire thousands and lead those around you to greatness."

Keane took his hands back and rolled his eyes. "Reginald. I'm to be King. What else would you see?"

Reginald chuckled and shook his head. "It's not your Royal standing I'm talking about. You'll accomplish these things long before you become King. What I see before you is something so rare it's almost unheard of within Vaimpír society."

"What do you mean?"

"Not only will you be gifted with a soul-bound partner, but she'll be your soulmate. A woman more powerful than anyone the Fae have ever seen before. She's the light to your dark, her soul perfectly in tune with yours. If you decide to fully bond with her, it will awaken that which is buried deep inside you. Eventually, it will bring you to your true power."

Keane looked at him, seemingly unconvinced. "I thought you couldn't see the future."

"I can't. Just the paths to be set before you until you become who you're truly meant to be."

"What power are you talking about? Isn't our family already one of the most powerful in Vaimpír society?"

"I'm not talking about political power. This is something completely different."

"I don't understand."

Reginald sighed and thought about it. "You know how your father has the power of domination?"

"Yes. I hope I'll inherit it once I come into my talents."

"Think about his power but multiply it many times over."

"How would that even be possible?"

Reginald just smiled. "You'll have to wait and see."

"But it'll be because of this woman?"

"Yes."

Keane turned from Reginald and appeared deep in thought until he spoke up again. "How will I know her?"

Reginald grinned and stood. "When you see her, you'll know. You'll feel the connection. And it will only grow stronger as time goes on until you fully accept it and unlock your true self."

"But what if my mother forces me to marry someone else?"

"Then I suppose it might be in your best interests to figure out how to avoid getting married."

"Hmph." Keane gave an involuntary smile.

"Now then, Master Keane. Your mother would like you down for supper. I suggest you clean yourself up and get down there...on time for once."

As Reginald left the room, I noticed the contemplative look on Keane's face before he turned and placed his hand on the window. Staring out into the night, his look turned deep and possessive. "If she's out there, I'll make her mine."

The memory faded, and I felt myself withdraw from Keane's mind. I started to slip into unconsciousness—my brain shutting down—and wondered what had sparked that memory. Was this what had been bothering Keane so much of late? And just how had I seen it?

❦

Stretching lazily, I reached out a hand to the other side of the bed, coming into contact with a warm body. A smile spread across my face as a large male hand enveloped mine and brought it to their lips. Slowly opening my eyes, I was startled when it wasn't the expected turquoise-blue eyes staring back into mine. I blinked several times to clear my vision.

"S...Sebastian?"

A grin spread across his lips. "Hello again, my little enigmatic Fairy."

"What are you doing here? Where's Keane?"

He put a hand to his chest. "You wound me. Aren't you happy to see me?"

I slanted a grin at him. "I'm always happy to see you, Bast. I just wasn't expecting it."

"Oh, throwing in a cute little nickname to try and charm me, are you? Well, lucky for you, I'm easily distracted."

I shook my head and sat up, throwing my legs over the side of the bed. Standing, I turned to him. "What brings you to Dock Street?"

"You, of course."

I chuckled and moved to the end of the bed, my eyes roaming over him, noting that his wings were missing. "Do the others know you're here, or is this a secret meeting?"

"Mm. Your father requested my presence. He seems to think there might be something I can do to help you. As that is my life's mission, here I am."

I leaned against the bedpost. "Helping me is your life's mission? What are you, my personal guardian Angel?"

His grin widened. "Of a sort. Your father has requested that I be your guardian for the time being. He seems to think you need the extra protection. Even your Vaimpír agreed with him."

Annoyance filled me. I turned and headed toward the door, intent on finding my overprotective father and suspiciously absent Vaimpír. I was seriously tired of their underhanded management of my life. You'd think Keane would've learned from the first time he tried to force his protection on me. "Just because I ended up in a few...sticky situations doesn't mean I need a full-time babysitter."

Sebastian laughed and, getting up, followed me. "Something tells me you're going to be unable to convince them otherwise. Either way, I wouldn't miss this for the world."

I found Poseidon and Keane in the living area, bent over a table full of books and maps. It hadn't been there before my nap, so I figured the men had been busy while I slept. I marched up to them and put my hands on my hips.

Poseidon was the first to look up, but I knew Keane had felt me the minute I approached. "Ah, Blue, you are awake. Did you sleep well?"

I arched an eyebrow at him and crossed my arms over my chest. "You want to tell me why you've taken it upon yourself to shackle me with your miscreant of an Angel as a keeper?"

Sebastian dramatically fell into one of the lounge chairs while crossing his arms over his chest. "Ouch, love. And here I thought we were friends." My lips threatened to tip up at his theatrics, but I held my glare.

Faced with my glower, Poseidon eyed me a bit nervously. "With everything going on with my brother, I thought, well, *we* thought,"—he gestured between him and Keane, who eyed me with amusement—"that it would be in your best interests to have another set of eyes to watch your back. Particularly one familiar with the gods. And while some of his methods might be…unorthodox, Sebastian is the best at what he does." He trailed off before giving me a persuasive smile. "You have to admit that you seem to consistently end up in the most outlandish situations."

I opened my mouth to retort, but then sighed, my anger deflating as fast as it had come. It wasn't like he was wrong. "Still, you could have talked to me about it first. I'd like to have a say in how my life is run."

Poseidon nodded quickly, a look of relief crossing his face. "I do apologize, daughter. I am not used to such strong and independent female offspring."

"Speaking of offspring, I never asked you… Are there any half-brothers or sisters I should know about?"

Poseidon started to squirm where he stood. "Erm…" I heard Sebastian start laughing behind me. "Triton is my only son within the pantheon. As for others, well, they have lived out their mortal lives already."

I just shook my head. "I guess that's to be expected when you're immortal." I finally turned to Keane. "Can I speak with you privately, Keane?" I heard Sebastian groan in disappointment.

Keane's eyes traced heatedly over my body, causing goose bumps to spring up along my arms. "Of course, *ma moitié*." His deep voice was like a caress across my skin, and I had to shake myself and steel my resolve. We needed to talk.

I hesitated but decided to go into the pool area instead of back to the bedroom. Keane smirked and gestured for me to lead the way. Out of the corner of my eye, I saw Tristan enter the living area. He gave Keane a dark look as he watched us walk away. Ignoring him, Keane shut the door behind us and twisted the lock. As the tumbler slid into place, it clicked loudly, echoing down the hallway. I swung around in surprise, and Keane grinned devilishly at me before slowly backing me against the wall and pressing his body into mine.

"Keane, we need to talk." I put my hands on his chest to try to push him away, but he didn't budge.

"Mm, okay. So, talk. I'm not stopping you." His head dipped down, and he ran his lips along my neck, then over my shoulder, bared by my tank top. He bit down lightly, causing me to shudder before sucking on the same spot.

"Keane..."

His mouth tracked a path back up to mine. "Hmm?"

I was having a hard time keeping my thoughts in order as he kissed the outside of my mouth before running his tongue over my bottom lip.

"Keane, we need to talk about—"

His tongue darted out and slipped between my lips. I couldn't help the moan that escaped. He took advantage and deepened the kiss, pulling my body tightly against his, stopping anything I might have been about to say. My hands involuntarily rose and buried themselves in his hair as I lost myself to the sensation of his hard body moving against me, of his mouth taking mine as if staking his claim.

I was a breathless, quivering mess when he finally released my lips. He chuckled lightly, his breath whispering across my skin as he once again dipped his head toward my neck. He sucked on the spot where his mark was, and I moaned again.

Upon hearing the sound, he reached down and picked me up. I wrapped my legs around his waist and my arms around his neck. I could feel his hard arousal pressing into me and I arched my back, rubbing myself against him. He groaned into my neck and took advantage of my position by trailing his lips down to my chest, sucking and licking as he went. When his mouth latched onto my nipple through my shirt, I cried out. He bit down, lightly scraping one of his fangs along the taut peak through the fabric.

"Mmm, you're so responsive. I can smell your arousal, and it's driving me mad." He brought his lips back to mine while grinding his hips into me. "I want to bury myself deep inside of you right now, feel you wrapped around every inch of me."

I panted against his mouth, his words evoking erotic images of us together, taking my arousal up yet another notch. I ran my tongue across one of his fangs, causing him to shudder against me, and I knew his control was nearing the edge. Just as I was about to give in, the handle jiggled on the main door, and we both froze. There was a pause and then a knock.

"Blue? Keane?" Tristan's muffled voice came through the wood. "We need you in the living area when you're done. We have things to discuss." I had a feeling he had interrupted us intentionally and sighed.

"We'll be there in a minute, Tristan." Keane practically growled before his eyes latched onto mine. "You need to put him in his place. Or I will."

Without warning, he leaned over my neck and bit down, his fangs sliding in, drawing a ragged gasp from my mouth. As the feeling of his bite flowed over me, I sagged in his arms, his strong embrace the only thing keeping me from falling to the floor. A Vaimpír's bite contained an enzyme that promoted sheer pleasure, similar to the natural hormone humans released when they had an orgasm. Even though I was used to his bites, it still turned me to liquid jelly when he did it.

He took his time, drawing out the sensations flowing through me. When he was done, he pulled back with a wicked smile on his face and slowly ran his tongue across his teeth, cleaning the blood that still clung to them before leaning forward and taking my bottom lip into his mouth to suckle. I whimpered when he pulled back.

"You're *mine*, and don't you forget it." Pricking his finger on his fang, he quickly wiped the blood over the holes in my neck, healing them before leaning forward and licking my skin clean.

As he pulled back and stared into my eyes possessively, I was reminded of the look from his memory and what I'd wanted to talk to him about before he distracted me. I searched his gaze. "Has your power increased since we've been bonded?"

Keane's expression turned weary. "Why do you ask that?"

"Just before I fell asleep, I had a dream...or rather, I think it might have been a memory you were reliving that I was drawn into."

He stiffened. "You saw that?" At my nod, Keane slowly lowered me to the floor. Once I could support myself again, he stepped back and ran his hand through his hair. "Blue, the memory you saw..." He sighed and shook his head. "I had honestly forgotten about that conversation until recently."

"What made you think of it?"

Keane shrugged and reached down to grab my hand. "I suppose this—us. I feel a connection to you that is far beyond our soulbond. It drives me to distraction. Blue... When I used my domination at the ball and quelled the entire ballroom? That has never happened before. It has always been powerful, to be sure, but to do that to hundreds..." He shook his head. "It's like your powers connected with mine and raised them to unbelievable levels."

"Isn't that part of the soulbond?"

"No. A soulbond only allows partners to share their magical gifts. It doesn't enhance them." Keane laced his fingers with mine. "I don't know what to call this. It's unlike anything I've felt before. It feels like I've always known you. Like yesterday and forever rolled into one. Like I've found a piece of myself I didn't even know was missing. I don't want to share you when you're with me, and when you're not, I feel out of control."

"Is that why you've been so agitated, so possessive?"

He nodded hesitantly. "I fought against it when it started happening, but then I remembered what Reginald said. You have to be the woman he was talking about, Blue. My soulmate."

I tried to stave off the feeling of giddiness that word gave me. Soulmate. It didn't have to mean romantically, but how else would you describe how our relationship was going? It would also explain why I had felt so comfortable with him so fast when we first met—something I had often questioned.

I looked at him quizzically. "I wonder why you're the only one who's experiencing the sensations. If it's because of our connection, shouldn't we both feel it?"

"I don't know. I do know it has been getting stronger and stronger by the day. I can actually feel some of your power flowing through me all the time now, not just when I pull on it."

I shook my head in confusion. "I wonder if it has something to do with what Reginald said about you fully accepting the connection."

Keane's look turned guilty. Letting go of me, he stepped away, running his hand over the back of his neck while looking down.

I raised an eyebrow at his reaction. "Oh?"

He avoided my gaze, and I felt a flicker of annoyance and anger filtering through our bond. I watched Keane, waiting for him to explain, but he remained silent, not looking in my direction.

I felt a bit of dread pool in my stomach but quelled it—closing off my emotions to Keane so he wouldn't feel it. Maybe things *weren't* going in the direction I thought. Had I been wrong about the relationship between Keane and me this entire time? What if it meant something completely different to him than it did to me? What if he just saw us as partners, and I had just been projecting my feelings onto him. Maybe the fact that we were soulmates wasn't something he wanted. I shook my head, breaking the spiral my mind was starting to go down—no good would come of it. When he still didn't look up, I stepped awkwardly toward the door. "I-I guess we'll talk later. Tristan and the others are waiting for us."

"Blue, wait..." He reached out for me, but I opened the door with a half-hearted smile in his direction and quickly escaped into the living area.

Chapter Thirteen

I spent the next few hours making plans with everyone while trying to ignore the intense stares Keane was giving me. Tristan had looked between us and tried to catch my gaze with questioning glances several times, but I just ignored him, too.

He had contacted Brokk, the King of the Fernsong Clan, and arranged for us to travel to his kingdom to begin our search for Iridia. Brokk had been quite emotional when he learned that Iridia was still alive and had been held captive somewhere nearby, just under our noses. In preparation for our arrival, he assured Tristan he would have the wards around his territory modified the same way the ones at Dock Street were, and said his trackers would be at the ready.

With that out of the way, we laid out a search plan using the maps Kieran had brought from the Elder library and Riona's knowledge of the territory. We narrowed things down to a few regions based on what Riona could match my descriptions to—though it seemed very little to go on. I hoped it would be enough.

Tristan planned to bring trackers of his own, one of which would be Cedric. I was a bit nervous about seeing him again, considering where our relationship had been when we last saw each other—not to mention that I still held the secret of who his parents were. But I knew he would be an asset to the team.

We finally broke apart to prepare for our departure, which would be the following evening. While traveling at night wasn't ideal, it was necessary for the Vaimpír. Thankfully, Nigel had come through and delivered our bags from Keane's parents' place. As they were still packed, I didn't have much to do.

Before I could sneak away, I felt Keane come up behind me. I looked around in panic for Sebastian, but he was nowhere to be seen—traitor.

"Are you hungry, *ma moitié?*"

I looked at him hesitantly, remembering his emotions from earlier, and wondered if this was what he really wanted. I felt Keane sigh and take my elbow, leading me toward the elevator.

"Obviously, there are some things we need to discuss. Come."

I stayed silent, avoiding his gaze as we rode up in the elevator. He didn't say anything either, just continued to watch me with his penetrating stare while leaning against the wall. As soon as the lift stopped and the doors opened, he took my hand and led me down the hall toward a brightly colored door—my favorite in all of Dock Street. It was Señor Alejandro's restaurant. As soon as Keane opened the door, I inhaled the spicy scents of Mexican food and the salty tang of the ocean. I sighed in contentment, the tension from moments ago flowing away.

I felt Keane chuckle. "I figured you wouldn't say no to Alejandro's."

I shook my head, my smile widening as Alejandro came over to greet us. He took both my hands in his.

"Blue. Truly a pleasure to see you again. Might I also offer my congratulations on the acceptance of your *vínculo* with Príncipe Keane?"

"Thank you, Alejandro. For both the felicitations and your help that night. You were an invaluable ally for us."

"It was my pleasure. Come, your favorite seat is always open for you."

We followed Alejandro past the brightly colored walls covered in photos and mementos of the Rodriguezes to our favorite table next to the open wall that faced the ocean. As we passed, I greeted several Rodriguez family members seated throughout the restaurant. They all bowed their heads in respect to both Keane and me. As I took my seat, I glanced down at the scorch marks that still marred the floor next to the table. This was where Alejandro's daughter, Mariana, and I had fought—her deadly spell leaving its mark on the hardwood floor.

"How is Mariana doing, Alejandro?"

Alejandro smiled widely as he pushed my chair in. "Very well, mi amiga. Thank you so much for caring about her even after what she tried to do."

"Regardless of her faults, she's still your daughter. I look forward to the day I can release the bond on her magic, and she can rejoin your family."

"So kind, *Princesa.* You'll make a wonderful *Reina* someday."

I laughed and shook my head. "I'm hardly a Princess, but thank you, Alejandro."

He looked at me in amusement. "Ah, but you *are* a Princesa. Not only your relationship with Príncipe Keane, but you're also Queen Iridia's daughter. You might as well get used to it."

I was a little taken aback realizing he was right. That would definitely take some getting used to.

"Now, I'd normally give you a choice, but tonight, I have something very special cooking that you must have." With a bow, Alejandro bustled off toward the kitchens.

"Blue." I tensed at Keane's tone, slowly raising my eyes to meet his. "About what happened earlier..." I opened my mouth to tell him not to worry about it, but he held up his hand. "It does matter, Blue. I want you to know exactly what is going on in my head. I know you, and I'm sure your mind has already come up with all the worst-case scenarios." I smiled slightly. He did know me well.

"The emotions I was feeling, the guilt, the annoyance, the anger? That was directed at me, not you." He took a deep breath before letting it out slowly. "With everything that has been going on, I've been out of my depth, and I don't like not being in control. It makes me angry. The fact that Hades was able to pull you, and I couldn't stop it, and not knowing if I'll be strong enough to protect you when the time comes to face off with him, not to mention the thought of you being hurt or taken..." He closed his eyes briefly before opening them and looking at me, his gaze glittering with determination. "I'll do whatever I can to protect you, Blue, even if that means giving my life for yours."

It felt like a weight had been lifted off my shoulders at his confession, and I raised my hand to his face. "We all have our insecurities, Keane. It's our ability to open ourselves and reveal them to others that shows our true character. Something I know I'm not good at either. I'm sorry for shutting you out."

He smiled and took my hand from his face, kissing the palm. "While you're extremely hard on yourself, you always manage to see others in the best light."

"Not always. I mean, look at Celeste. We were at odds from day one."

"Speaking of Celeste. She has been fully transferred to the Moon Tree Clan. The guardians that came with her left while you were sleeping."

"How is our dear friend?"

Keane smirked and sat back in his chair. "Angry, vowing revenge on you and everyone you love."

"Now, where have I heard that before?" We both laughed, breaking the final barrier the misunderstanding earlier had created.

"Tristan made Cedric her guard to ensure she can't bribe or coerce any of the others into freeing her. Though since he'll be coming with us to the Fernsong territory, we'll need to find a suitable replacement."

"Really? Cedric is her guard? When did he become one of Tristan's sentinels? I thought he was a tracker?"

"He is, but he requested to be assigned to her."

"I wonder why."

"I'm not sure. But since we can put her with very few, Tristan granted his request."

"Mmm. Maybe I'll check in on him and Celeste before we leave."

"We can go after we're done eating if you would like. I need to check on arrangements for his replacement anyway."

I grimaced as I caught a glimpse of my reflection in a nearby mirror. "First, I think I need a shower." I patted at my hair, which was definitely flowing in a hundred different directions. "Why didn't you tell me I had bedhead?"

Keane chuckled and leaned forward, his head tilting at a flirtatious angle. "Because I find it sexy as hell when you look like that."

I just rolled my eyes at him as Alejandro brought out our dinner.

Whether Keane found me attractive this way or not, I absolutely needed a shower. Keane had been detained by Alejandro to discuss some Vaimpír business after dinner, so I decided to take the opportunity to head back to Tristan's quarters to wash up.

As I neared the bathroom provided for the guest bedrooms, I thought longingly of the one between Tristan and Riona's room. It had a tub that could accommodate at least four people, with a magicked view of a gorgeous waterfall in a wooded area. With everything that had gone on the last time I was at Dock Street, I'd never gotten the opportunity to use the tub and longed to sneak in and finally try it out.

Finding the guest bathroom locked, I leaned against the wall next to it before glancing around. On my way in, Cullen had told me that Tristan and Riona were currently holding court and would be gone for the next few hours.

That meant no one else was down here except for the guys from Ethereal Mutation. With a mischievous grin, I crept down the hallway before pausing in front of Tristan's bedroom door. With a glance back to make sure no one was paying attention, I slipped through and quietly closed the door behind me. The lights were off in his bedroom, but the soft lighting hidden in the recesses all around the room flickered, giving the illusion of candlelight while lighting the way. I unerringly made my way across the room to the door that led to the bathroom. Opening it slowly, I peeked in and saw that it was empty.

With a giggle of anticipation, I went in and locked the door to Tristan's room and the other connecting door to Riona's. Dumping my stuff onto the counter cut into one of the rock walls, I absently noted that Tristan had repaired the sink bowl that had broken during my fight with Fiorian—Larkin's bounty hunter.

I walked over to the cliff's edge where a beautiful waterfall flowed in torrents and glanced down, remembering the fall from its rim with a bit of a shudder. That was an experience I had no desire to repeat.

Turning away, I ran my hand along the edge of the enormous tub situated so you could relax and enjoy the view while taking your bath. I turned on the water and adjusted the temperature before removing my clothes and pulling my hair into a messy bun. The tub filled quickly, and I slid into its warm depths when it reached about halfway. A pillow was already attached to one end, and I moved over to it and rested my head against it.

Closing my eyes, I luxuriated in the feel of the warm water slowly covering my body. When it was nearly full, I used my foot to turn off the tap before lying back down. Now this was heaven. The warmth of the water and the sound of the waterfall seeped into my senses, and I relaxed, letting my mind wander.

It was unsurprising that it went straight to Keane. I touched my lips, remembering his last kiss. I felt my blood heat as my mind drifted to what had happened in his room in New Orleans. I groaned and shifted in the tub, causing some of the water to slosh over the edge. Almost unconsciously, I ran my hands over my breasts, feeling my nipples immediately harden. Skimming one of my hands down, I slid it between my legs and stroked softly, pulling a gasp from my lips as I imagined it was Keane's fingers instead of mine.

I was so caught up in my fantasy that I didn't realize I wasn't alone until a masculine moan joined my soft, feminine one. My eyes flew open, and I saw Keane standing beside the tub, his hand stroking his erection in time with my fingers.

"*Ma moitié...*" His eyes were deep red and burning with desire. I looked between him and the door, seeing that it was still closed. "Fae don't tend to need keys."

I laughed softly at his reference to the first time we'd met. Come to think of it, I had been in just as compromising a situation then as I was now. But this time, I wanted him to join me. I stood slowly, letting the water cascade over my naked body, never taking my eyes off him.

Keane's gaze moved hungrily over my curves as I ran my hands over them, inviting him to touch me. With a growl, he quickly pulled his shirt over his head before kicking off his shoes and dropping his pants. Stepping forward, he drew me against him and immediately lowered his mouth to mine. I whimpered against his lips at the feeling of his naked chest pressed against my heated skin, causing shivers to quake through my body.

Not breaking our lips apart, he stepped into the tub and ran his hands down my back, pulling me tightly against him. My pulse skyrocketed at the contact, my senses already in overdrive from the mere taste of his lips. Coming up for air, he turned me around, then pulled us both down into the heated water, my back to his front. Reaching around, he fondled my breasts, his long fingers pinching their taut peaks, causing me to gasp.

"Was this what you were imagining, *ma moitié?* Were you thinking about my hands on your body, touching you, pleasing you?" I nodded, unable to speak as his hand dipped between my legs. He kissed the spot behind my ear before running his lips to my shoulder.

As his fingers stroked in and out of me, I couldn't stop the little mewling sounds that fell unbidden from my lips. "Keane..." I squirmed in his arms, feeling myself getting closer and closer to the brink but wanting to hold back.

"Mmm…let go, *ma moitié*. Cum for me." He crooked his finger just a bit, hitting the perfect spot and sending me over the edge. I moaned, riding the tide of pleasure as he continued to stroke his fingers in and out. "Good girl." His voice was a soft purr against my ear. "But we're not through just yet."

Sliding his fingers out, he turned me to straddle his lap. I gasped at the feeling of his hard erection pressed to the sensitive flesh between my thighs. Wrapping one arm around my back, he released my hair from its confines before tangling his fingers in it at the nape of my neck. Pressing his other hand to my lower back and lifting his hips, he slowly rubbed himself back and forth, prompting more tremors to pulse through my body.

Leaning forward, he took one of my nipples into his mouth and suckled, swirling his tongue around the sensitive tip before tugging it with his teeth. I sucked in a breath and pressed down, grinding myself against him and feeling the ripples of pleasure starting to build in intensity again.

Bending over, I licked the water droplets that had landed on his shoulder. His hand tightened in my hair, tugging, and I bit down, not breaking the skin but causing him to growl. He pulled me back and sucked on the other nipple. I buried my hands in his hair and held him to me as what felt like electric shocks traveled from my nipple straight to my groin, stoking the fires.

Pulling his head up, I leaned down and thrust my tongue into his mouth, flicking it against one of his fangs. He groaned and sucked on it. I reached down between our bodies, cupped his hard length against me, and slid myself back and forth over it, pausing to run my thumb over his tip.

He let out a shuddering breath into my mouth, his hips jerking up. "I want to be inside you, Blue."

I pulled back to stare into his lust-filled gaze. He seemed to be asking for my permission. I didn't even have to think about it. I wanted to be connected to him in every way possible, and this was the last tie. Lifting myself, I positioned him at my entrance. He sucked in a breath when his tip pushed past my opening, and I paused, prolonging the anticipation. With infinite slowness, I lowered myself onto him until he was fully seated inside me, filling every inch. We both moaned.

"God, Blue, you feel so damn good."

Without warning, I was in his head, and he was in mine. The connection was so perfectly balanced it was like we were one person. I could feel and see everything he did. The pleasure that pulsed through his body with each movement—no matter how small—our powers combining and rolling back and forth between us, pushing the intensity of everything to new levels. The way he saw me, how beautiful and desirable I was in his eyes. Above all that, was an unnamed emotion. One he didn't know what to do with. It was something he had never felt before, like there was nothing else in this world that meant more to him than me. I was humbled by the strength of what he felt, and I knew in that moment that I was lost to him. I belonged to him and him alone. There would never be anyone else.

Keane began moving beneath me, bringing me back to myself. Gripping my hips, he shifted until just the tip of him was still sheathed before slowly sinking back in. I let out a guttural moan, throwing my head back in ecstasy as he filled me again and again with slow, torturous thrusts. Water splashed over the tub rim, but neither of us paid it any mind. The only thing that mattered was the feeling of our bodies coming together.

Keane gritted his teeth. "I need to feel you beneath me, *ma moitié*." Standing, he lifted me out of the tub and laid me on one of the large, plush bath mats on the floor before lowering himself over me. Taking both my hands into one of his, he raised them over my head while his other hand traced my breasts before slipping between our bodies to run his fingers through my wet heat once again. My hips lifted in response, my breath coming out in little pants. He leaned down and nibbled on my lips before his tongue slid in, stroking mine in time with his hand. I tugged on my wrists, wanting to touch him, but he held tight, continuing to tease my body with his fingers until I was writhing beneath him.

"Keane, please..."

He raised himself onto his elbow, still pinning my wrists above my head, and with one quick thrust, he buried himself deeply inside me. He let out a throaty moan, his head dipping to my shoulder. I bit my lip as he eased himself out and then back in again, drawing out the pleasure with each meticulous stroke. The fire burning inside me intensified. I began lifting my hips to meet him, trying to get him to go faster, but he held me down with one large hand on my hip.

Driving himself into me, he slowly picked up the pace. I felt myself quickly approaching a second orgasm and twisted my hips, trying to find it. He pulled back every time I came close to the edge, teasing me with the slight sting of pleasure that racked my body each time. I growled, wrenching my hands from his grasp. This time, he let me.

Running my fingers down his back, I felt the muscles dip and flow as my nails raked over them, leaving little marks in their wake. Reaching his steely backside, I dug my fingers in and pulled him as deep as I could while wrapping my legs tightly around his thighs. He leveraged himself and drove even deeper, causing me to cry out from the pleasure of it.

With a low groan, seemingly unable to help himself, he thrust quickly, in and out, taking the waves of pleasure radiating through my body to unimaginable heights. Just when I thought I couldn't take any more, he thrust in deeply and bit my neck at the same time. I cried out his name as white-hot lights exploded in front of my eyes, and wave after wave of pleasure so sharp it bordered on pain rippled through me. I felt him stiffen as he released my neck, throwing his head back and growling my name. As he climaxed, and the pleasure of it rushed through our connection, I felt another orgasm push through, leaving me shuddering and panting.

Once our heartbeats started to slow and return to normal, Keane turned us onto our sides so he wasn't crushing me. Placing his head in his hand, he propped himself up on his elbow, grinning down at me.

"What?" I squirmed a bit self-consciously under his steady gaze.

"You're amazing."

I smirked and rolled my eyes. "I bet you say that to all the girls."

"Not even once."

I rolled closer to him, curling into his chest as he ran his fingertips over my shoulder and back. "Tell me it wasn't only me that felt the connection?"

Keane's fingertips paused before he reached down and tipped my chin up so he could look into my eyes. "Blue, I've never felt that with anyone. It was like we were one person. I was in your head, and you were in mine. Our emotions, our pleasure...it was indescribable."

I smiled and snuggled up to his chest. "We're going to need to take another bath."

Keane laughed and looked over at the tub. It seemed half the water was now on the floor. "I'm thinking we should opt for a shower instead.

And we should probably clean up this mess before Tristan comes in here to use his bathroom."

I lifted my head and, with minimal effort, used my magic to push all the excess water over the cliff.

"Nice." Keane untangled himself and stood. Reaching down, he lifted me from the floor. "Shower time, *ma moitié*."

As our naked bodies rubbed against each other, sparking desire between us again, I grinned suggestively up at him, causing him to laugh.

Chapter Fourteen

After finally managing to shower *and* get clean, we headed back into the main living area to find Poseidon and Sebastian whispering conspiratorially in the corner. When they saw us, they quickly broke apart.

I raised an eyebrow. "Well, that wasn't suspicious at all."

Sebastian looked at me, seemed to weigh something, then disappeared with a grin and a wink. I hated when he did that. I hadn't figured out dematerialization, and it irked me that so many others around me could do it.

Before I could question Poseidon, Kieran, and Tristan stepped off the elevator. Tristan's eyes immediately sought mine before he moved purposefully toward me. I glanced at Kieran, who looked merely intrigued, before moving my gaze back to Tristan. "Blue, we've been talking and think we might have come up with a way to discover where Iridia is." I raised my brows curiously but didn't say anything. "When you worked with the Aisling during your training before the Trials, did she happen to teach you how to initiate dream walking?"

"Um, sort of. We kind of glossed over it. Honestly, I've never tried to put it into practice though." I'd always wanted to try it out on Keane as he said Vaimpír didn't dream but had never taken the opportunity.

"We think you should try initiating dream walking with Hades. See if you can direct it to where he's keeping Iridia."

My mouth dropped open. "You want me to go into Hades' dreams? Isn't that a bit risky?"

Kieran shook his head. "Not if you are the one controlling it. As long as he is asleep when you enter, it will give you control. Plus, Poseidon assured us he is still tied to his castle by your magic and should be in a resting state about this time."

I glanced at Poseidon, who nodded. I wondered if that was what Sebastian had been reporting to him when we walked in. I looked between each of the men before my gaze landed on Keane. He hesitated but then nodded, as well. I took a deep breath. I wasn't sure I wanted to do this. So many things could go wrong. Not to mention, I wasn't sure I'd be able to reach Hades in the Underworld. I could only hope he was keeping my statue nearby so I could use that as a conductor.

"Okay, I guess we can give it a try." My voice trembled a bit with my nervousness.

Keane placed his hands on my shoulders and squeezed. "I won't let anything happen to you, *ma moitié*."

I nodded and moved to sit in one of the lounge chairs in the reading area of the room. Keane straddled the ottoman in front of me and held my hand. Reclining the chair, I closed my eyes and concentrated. Before I started, I prepped the spell I'd need to initiate Hades' dreams—if he wasn't already in that state.

Reaching out, I searched for Hades' energy signature. At first, I couldn't find anything, so I pushed farther and farther until I finally felt a faint pulse. A golden string lit up in my mind. It seemed to be linked to me and then ran along the ground, leading off into the distance. Mentally picking it up, I followed it through the blackness of my mind, letting it slide through my fingers. Instead of it getting longer, I just seemed to absorb it like I was the reel. I anchored myself to Keane with his touch, just to make sure I hadn't gone incorporeal.

"I've got you, Blue."

Going back into my mind, I followed the string through the nothingness until the darkness finally resolved into a strange bedroom. As I looked around in confusion, my eyes were drawn to the statue sitting on the bedside table. It was my statue. Looking down, I saw that the gold string connected us. I must be seeing how my soul was tethered to it.

Upon hearing a soft exhale, I jumped and spun around. Hades lay on the bed, his breathing soft and rhythmic. I walked over and looked down at him. He actually looked peaceful in sleep. Reaching out, I gently probed his mind but found no blocks. Taking a deep breath, I slipped past his barriers.

He was in a deep stasis, his mind perfectly blank. With a quick thought, I pushed out the spell I had prepped that would initiate the dream state in his mind. Hades shifted onto his back, seeming to fight it at first before relaxing again. I tried to create a dream around his capture of Iridia, but images began forming around me before I could.

Soon enough, I found myself standing in what appeared to be a large room facing a thick wooden door. It was so poorly lit I could barely see a few feet in front of me. The room appeared to have been cut out of rock and was hotter than anywhere I'd ever been. Even in my dream state, sweat formed and trickled down my back. My nose wrinkled as the smell of rotten food, unwashed bodies, and excrement hit it. Turning, I found the other side of the room was full of bars—prison bars.

As I moved closer, I saw that what I had initially thought were piles of shredded blankets were living, breathing things lying in locked cells. Moving carefully down the row, I saw that they contained all manner of creatures—some of which I didn't even recognize. Thankfully, as this was a memory, they couldn't see me. I was just observing something that had happened in the past. I found it odd that even though it was a memory, it wasn't from Hades' viewpoint. It was more like a movie—like I was an outsider.

Perhaps because I was initiating the dream?

As I came to one particular cell, I found a bare-chested man sitting on the dirt-encrusted ground with his back to the stone wall, his head leaning against it with his eyes closed. He had short, black hair that looked like it hadn't been washed in months, and a strong, muscular build. Wounds crisscrossed his chest, some old, some new and still bleeding. It looked like he had been whipped repeatedly. His face—devoid of any facial hair—was a filthy mass of dirt, bruises, and cuts, yet he was still incredibly handsome.

After staring at him for a moment, I realized it was a younger Hades. I looked around in shock. Was this the prison in Tartarus he had talked about? Where he had grown up? I shuddered in revulsion. He spoke just as I was about to see if I could direct his memories elsewhere.

"Don't just stand there and pity me, do what it is you came to do and leave."

At first, I thought he was talking to me, but then I realized a young woman was standing not too far away in the shadows. She timidly took a few steps into the light, and I saw that she had a tray of food in one hand and a pitcher and towels in the other. A burly man stepped out from behind her—obviously, a guard of some sort. He brusquely unlocked the cell and gestured the woman forward with impatient motions. She shuffled nervously inside and carefully set the food tray on the floor before moving to Hades' side.

Slowly sinking to her knees, she poured whatever was in the pitcher onto a towel and started cleaning Hades' chest. The rags came away full of dirt and blood. Though I was sure it hurt, Hades never moved the entire time she was cleaning his wounds. The only indication of his discomfort was a slight tick in his jaw when he clenched his teeth together.

When the woman finished, she started to stand, but Hades grabbed her arm, stopping her. She let out a frightened squeak but didn't pull away. Hades slowly opened his eyes, and I saw they were glowing amber. He stared at the woman for a second before letting go of her.

"Thank you."

She nodded slowly and turned to leave. Just as she was about to exit the cell, Hades spoke up again. "What's your name?"

She didn't seem like she would answer at first, but then, with a quick glance back at Hades, she whispered, "Alexandra."

My eyes widened. Alexandra? As in the woman Hades wanted to get revenge on Zeus for? I watched the young woman scurrying out the heavy, wooden door and wondered just who she was. Hades' memory faded, and another began. This time, he was strapped to a pole, his back a mass of blood and bruises from a recent beating. He was on his knees, his hands chained above his head. I could hear his labored breaths as he fought to stay conscious. Yet again, Alexandra appeared out of the shadows. She looked around as if fearing someone would see her but then resolutely moved forward. Pulling a key from the pocket of her apron, she unlocked Hades' shackles and lowered him to the ground on his stomach. With quick but careful motions, she cleaned his back, putting some type of ointment on the wounds when she was finished. Hades lay still after her ministrations, and I thought he had passed out.

"Why do you keep helping me?" His voice was gruff and a bit strained.

Alexandra bit her lip. "I don't know. I just...want to."

Hades leveraged himself up off the floor, his muscles quivering as he tried to support himself. He turned his intense gaze to her. "Who do you belong to?"

"A Demon named Eligor. My mother was made a slave when she was pregnant, and I was born while she was in his service. I suppose he inherited me when she died."

Hades stared at her unblinkingly before nodding and turning away. "You should go before they discover you've helped me. Don't come back."

The memory faded again, reforming into a barren landscape. Hades stood on the edge of a cliff, looking out into the distance. He still had iron bands around his wrists and ankles, but there didn't appear to be anyone guarding him. After a moment, Alexandra appeared and rushed into his arms. They kissed passionately, holding each other almost desperately.

Hades finally pulled back, cupping Alexandra's small face between his large hands. "I've struck a deal with the Titans and have already freed my brethren from this squalid prison. We are going to amass an army to fight my father."

"Hades..."

"Don't worry, my love. When this is all done, I'll return and take you to my new realm where we can live together."

"But Eligor..."

"I'll do whatever I have to in order to release you. Even if it means killing him." They kissed once more before Hades disappeared, leaving Alexandra standing by herself.

The memories were coming faster now. As another began, I hoped it didn't mean Hades was waking up. I knew I needed to find out where he was keeping Iridia, but my curiosity was too great. Who was Alexandra, and what had happened between Hades and Zeus that'd caused the rift between them?

I soon found myself standing in the same room I'd frequented in Hades' castle. Hades stood with another man I didn't recognize, though he appeared to be another god.

"I must beg your forgiveness, dear brother, as I've done something terrible." The unknown god hung his head in shame.

"My dear Zeus, you know there is nothing you could do that wouldn't warrant my forgiveness. You're my brother, after all."

"But alas, I think there is. I...I've fallen prey to a seductress."

Hades snorted and slapped Zeus on the shoulder. "That's hardly something new, dear brother. When it comes to the ladies, whether they be god, Fae, or human, you're always falling for them."

"But this one...well..."

"Just come out with it, brother."

"It was Alexandra."

Hades stepped back as if he'd been slapped, his face contorting in rage. "You slept with *my* Alexandra!?"

"It was not my fault, dear brother!" Zeus held up his hands in defense. "She came on to me, and no matter how many times I turned her down, she kept coming back. She would sneak into my bed at night after you fell asleep. She would wait to catch me alone every day. I...I'm ashamed that I finally gave in." Zeus broke down crying in the face of his brother's wrath.

Hades took deep breaths, his eyes wild. He started pacing in front of the burning fire, his hands clasping and unclasping into fists. "Why? Why would my Alexandra seek you out?"

"She said she wanted to be in the heavens, that she was tired of being trapped here in this dark, desolate place. She wanted to be where the sun shone, where she could grow things. She begged me to take her and make her my Queen."

"No. No! I don't believe it. I won't. She loves me. She said she didn't care where we were as long as we were together."

"I'm sorry, brother, but I can prove it." Zeus held out his fist, slowly opening it. On his palm lay a small, gold bracelet.

Hades stopped his pacing, his expression turning stricken. He held out a shaking hand and took the bracelet. Turning it over and over, he stared at it. Then, without another word, he stormed out of the room. With a suspicious glance at the smirk now curving Zeus's lips, I quickly followed Hades. He went straight to his bedchambers and threw open the doors. Alexandra was lying on the bed, waiting for him.

"My love."

"Did you sleep with my brother?" Hades' voice was deep and menacing.

"What are you talking about?" She looked completely taken aback.

"Did you seduce my brother Zeus? Did you tell him that you wanted to be his Queen in the heavens where you could be in the sun and not have to live in this dark, desolate place?" Hades was practically yelling, causing Alexandra to cower on the bed.

"No. Hades, I'd never sleep with your brother. It's you I love!"

The anger vibrating off him was palpable. "Then how do you explain this?" Hades pulled out the bracelet and threw it at her.

Alexandra's face paled as she caught it, her eyes going to the wrist she normally wore it on. "I...I don't know, Hades. I swear to you. I'd never, ever betray you. I love you. It's you and only you I want."

"Then how did Zeus come by your mother's bracelet? The one you swore to never remove."

"He must have stolen it somehow. Hades, you have to believe me."

Hades' eyes glowed brighter. "Alexandra Onasis Polydegmon, I henceforth banish you to the human realm."

"Hades, stop...you have to listen..." Alexandra dove off the bed to get on her hands and knees in front of Hades, tears flowing down her face.

"You will never again set foot in the Underworld. Get out of my sight." Hades slammed from the room, leaving Alexandra sobbing uncontrollably on the floor.

I stood shocked and more than a little bit confused as things changed yet again. This time, I was in what appeared to be a throne room. Hades sat on a large, ornate chair, looking bored as a woman who vaguely resembled him stood before him.

"I'm telling you the truth, brother. Zeus lied to you. He has lied to us all. He has been using and manipulating us to get what he wants. Do you think it a coincidence that he ended up with Olympus?"

"Sister, dear. Why would Zeus do that?"

"Because he didn't want to end up with the Underworld. He wanted to continue his life of decadence in the clouds. Do you know where he was while we were locked up in the prisons of Tartarus?"

"Being hidden from our father."

"Yes, in the lap of luxury with a Fairy Princess! And when he heard you had escaped and were planning a coup on our father, he wanted to make sure that he got the biggest and best piece of the pie."

"Demeter—"

"Don't you *Demeter* me."

Hades gave an exasperated sigh. "How do you know all of this?"

"Because I heard him gloating, and he admitted it when I confronted him. He told me how he had tricked all of us so he could be the King of the skies. How he forced you to take the very place you'd been trapped in your whole life, and even how he stole your one true love by seducing her while looking like you." She looked down at her nails for a second before side-eyeing him. "I always thought it a shame that you banished Alexandra to the mortal realm. I had quite an affinity for her. I found she had a great talent for growing things. Did you know that? I always wanted to take her under my wing and make her a true goddess—like the Goddess of Spring or something. What do you think?"

"What did you just say?" Hades' whole body had frozen, his tone going eerily quiet.

"That I wanted to take her and make her a true goddess?"

"Before that. What did my brother do to her?"

Demeter blew out an irritated breath. "Why don't I just show you?"

Demeter opened her mind to Hades so he could see all she had seen and heard. When she was done, Hades sat immobile, staring straight ahead.

"Do you see now? We have to do something about him."

"Thank you for telling me, Demeter. Please, don't concern yourself. I'll take care of our *little brother*." Though he didn't appear angry to Demeter, his very stillness said otherwise.

After Demeter left, Hades remained seated on his throne, his fingers steepled in front of his face and murder in his eyes. He stood abruptly and whistled. A pair of hellhounds appeared almost immediately.

"To Earth. To the home of Alexandra."

The hounds huffed in response, and all entered the void. I followed, stepping into a field that must have once been full of life.

It was now a desolate plane burned to the bare earth. Tall trees that should have been a vibrant green stood scorched and naked, their branches crackling in the breeze. Ash floated down like lightly falling snow, landing on Hades' head and shoulders. I turned slowly, feeling horror at the devastation, until I spotted the burned-out husk of a house standing on the edge of the woods, smoke still rising from its remains. Hades stood staring at the house, his face a blank mask. When one of the hounds howled, he seemed to come back to himself and took off in the direction it'd come from. I followed, not sure I wanted to see what the hound had found. As I cleared the side of the burned-out building, I sucked in a breath and came to a stop. For there, lying on the ground, were the burnt remains of a woman.

Tears pricked my eyes as Hades slowly lowered himself next to it, disbelief written all over his face. "No, Alexandra, my love..." He reached out a shaking hand to touch her, but as his fingers caressed her face, she crumbled to dust. The wind picked up the small pieces, slowly sweeping them away until the only thing remaining was a small gold bracelet. Hades picked it up and stared at it for a long moment before throwing his head back and letting loose a bellow. The hounds lifted their heads and joined him, their howls full of sorrow and pain. I closed my eyes against the heartbreaking scene.

When I opened them again, I was left sitting in the blackness of Hades' mind. No more memories surfaced. I couldn't believe what I'd just seen. No wonder Hades hated his brother so much.

Looking around, I realized I wasn't alone. Hades sat across from me, his leg drawn up to his chest. He looked as he had the last time I'd seen him, disheveled and angry.

"Come to taunt me, little one?" I shook my head, and he sighed deeply, his gaze tracing lazily over my face. "You haunt me in my waking moments, knowing you are the key to achieving what I desire most. Yet you remain just out of reach. And now here you are in my dreams, as well." He laughed bitterly before lying his head back and closing his eyes. "I guess I shouldn't be surprised."

I didn't know what to say, so I remained silent, allowing his feelings of sadness and loneliness to flow over me. When he spoke again, it was much quieter. "You were like a daughter to me, you know. Someone I could love and teach. And then they took you away, made you something you're not, and yet...I still see glimpses of the little girl you were in there."

I realized then that he didn't know I was dream walking. He thought this was still a part of his dream. I decided to try and use that to my advantage.

"Uncle Hades?"

"Hmm?"

"Where is my mom?"

"What do you mean, little one?"

"I can't find her, Uncle Hades. I need to find my mom."

"You don't remember? You used to know the area inside and out. Always sneaking away." He laughed lightly before his lips turned down at the corners. "To be expected. It seems that Iridia and Aiden took it all away from you. All your childhood memories, everything I taught you, everything I was to you.”

“Can you tell me where I can find her?”

“She is...”

His voice tapered off, and his brow furrowed. Slowly opening his eyes, he blinked owlishly at me. I realized with dismay that he was starting to wake up. Sleepiness in a dream indicated wakefulness on the other side. I felt his barriers starting to move into place in his mind.

“Can you tell me where my mom is, Uncle Hades?” I prompted again.

“Blue? Wait, what are you doing here?” He sat up a bit straighter and looked around. “You’re not just a dream, are you?” I staggered back as he tried to grab me. “You’re dream walking.” I gasped as his fingers locked around my wrist. I felt his power move through me, and my eyelids grew heavy. No! I couldn’t let him take control. I struggled to pull out of his grasp. “Come to me, Blue. Or stay here with me. Stop fighting me, little one.”

I shook my head, trying to maintain control, but he was quickly wrestling it from me. Just when I thought he had won, I felt a tug on my consciousness and a hand in mine. Keane. I struggled through the lethargy that gripped my body and found my connection to him. With the last of my strength, I pulled my wrist from Hades and barreled back to my mind. As I came to, I sucked in a lungful of air, then another, and another quickly starting to hyperventilate.

“Relax, Blue, I’ve got you. Just breathe, *ma moitié*. Slowly. In and out.” Keane sat me forward in the chair and rubbed my back.

“What happened?” I heard Poseidon’s concerned voice.

“I don’t know. It almost seemed like she was losing control. Like Hades was taking it from her.”

Finally getting my breathing under control, I sat back in the chair, my head pounding.

"Are you okay, *ma moitié?*"

"I think so."

"Did you get it? Did he tell you where to find Iridia?" Kieran moved to my side.

I grimaced and shook my head. "He realized I was dream walking before he told me and then tried to take control."

"You were in there so long…"

I turned away, a bit ashamed that I had let my curiosity consume me. I had wasted our only opportunity to find out where he was holding Iridia.

Tristan sighed and started pacing in front of the couch. "Can you go back in again?"

I shook my head vehemently. "Now that he knows I can initiate dream walking, he'll be on guard. It'll be too dangerous to attempt it again." I tapped my fist against my forehead. "If only I could remember. Hades told me that I knew where they were being held."

Kieran moved into my line of sight. "If that is the case, perhaps there is something we can do. But we will need the help of the Elder Council."

I looked up at him. "What can they do?"

"I think it is time we try to unlock your memories."

Chapter Fifteen

Since time was of the essence, Kieran left to see if he could call the Council together for an emergency meeting. I was a bit nervous since it meant I would have to reveal my parentage to them. For something that had remained a secret for so long, it was all coming out very quickly now. I knew the Council would have a lot of questions, and I wasn't sure how much I should reveal, especially about my gifts. Though if they went into my memories, it may not be up to me.

"Are you ready for this, Blue?" Poseidon sat on the couch I paced in front of. Everyone else had left to take care of various other tasks.

"Yes...no...I don't know."

"Relax, Blue. They aren't going to do anything to you for being part god. There is no law against it."

"It's not the being-part-god bit I'm worried about."

Poseidon watched me tolerantly. "Then what is it?"

I huffed out a breath before plopping onto the couch next to him. Guess it was time to fess up.

"It's one of my gifts."

"Oh?"

"It seems I have the ability to take powers from others and absorb them into myself."

"Ah, that."

I leaned back in shock. "You knew?"

"Of course. I have been keeping tabs on you since the day you were born. If I recall correctly, you often did it to Aiden when you were little."

My brows furrowed. "Wait. I did it more than once? How?"

Poseidon smiled patiently. "Naturally, you can return the gifts you take."

"I can?" This shone a whole new light on things. "What if I accidentally give them to the wrong person?"

"I don't know."

That was an unsettling thought. I had a feeling I knew why Hades wanted to use that power—to take his brother's abilities for himself. I reclined on the couch and stared at the ceiling, my stomach in knots. Shaking myself from those disturbing thoughts, I considered something else. "If I could give Larkin his powers back, then maybe I could tell the Council where he is."

"Perhaps, but I wouldn't recommend it right now."

"But how can I stop the Council from seeing everything if they get into my memories?"

"They will perform what is called a *memoria revelare*. While it requires them to combine all their skills, only one can see into your memories. We will just make sure that person is Kieran."

I turned my head to him. "How do you know so much about the Fae?"

Poseidon chuckled as he stood. "Because I have been around a lot longer than they have. Now, I have a few things I need to take care of.

Contact me right away if they call you before I get back. I want to be here."

I nodded absently as he walked away, still thinking about Larkin's powers and what to do with them. After staring up at the ceiling for a few minutes and getting nowhere, I decided I needed a distraction. Since Keane hadn't taken me to see Cedric yet, I figured now was as good a time as any to go find him.

I couldn't help the smirk that crossed my lips as I thought about *why* Keane hadn't taken me earlier.

"Ma moitié..."

I jerked out of my salacious thoughts as Keane's voice flooded my mind. *"Sorry...I was just, ah..."*

Keane chuckled. *"You were just, what?"*

I blushed, thanking the stars I was alone. *"Nothing."*

"Oh, no. I want to know. Why don't you tell me exactly what you were doing, ma moitié?"

I frowned at the amusement in his voice. *"You know, what? Mind your own business. Over and out."*

Keane's laughter filled my thoughts before I cut our connection.

Arrogant bastard.

I felt the smile creep back on my face.

As he had every right to be.

Shaking my head, I reached out with my senses to locate Cedric's energy signature. He appeared to be on a lower level of Dock Street. I hadn't realized there was anything beneath Tristan's quarters. Hopping onto the elevator, I looked around until I found a small black down-arrow I hadn't noticed before. It required a passcode, so I punched in Keane's, figuring he would have access to any level. Sure enough, the elevator began to descend.

As it moved farther and farther down, I started to feel strange—the connection to my magic becoming harder and harder to sense. By the time the doors opened, I felt almost like I had while under the enchantment that had kept me human for most of my life. Rolling my shoulders back, I tried to alleviate the sensation as I stepped out into a brightly lit hallway made of some type of metal. A guard stood near the entrance.

"State your name and business."

"Carolina Blue. I'm here to see Cedric."

He froze for a second, surprise flashing in his eyes, then he nodded. Speaking softly into a mic strapped to his ear, he watched me out of the corner of his eye as he waited for a response. After nodding a few times, he looked back at me.

"You've been granted access, Miss Blue."

"Please, just call me Blue."

He blushed and fumbled for his keycard before turning to open the door behind him. "Just follow the hall to the end and make a left. Jackson, another guardsman, will be there waiting to let you through the next checkpoint."

"Thanks...ah, I don't believe I caught your name."

"Arwyn, but most of the guys just call me Wyn."

"Thanks, Wyn." I smiled and moved past him.

"What you did for the Moon Tree Clan was amazing." I turned back to him, surprised by his sudden outburst. "The way you risked your life to save everyone from Larkin. I...I just wanted to tell you that I"—he swallowed—"I admire you."

I gave him a crooked smile and winked, causing him to blush again. "Thanks."

Moving down the long hallway, I peeked into the other doors along the way but didn't see anything but more passageways and empty rooms. When I finally reached the end of the hall, I made a left and came face-to-face with another guard—this one easily twice the size of Wyn. He seemed to fill the entire hallway.

"Jackson, I presume?"

He grunted and stepped forward. "I need to search you before you can go farther."

"Why didn't Wyn need to do that?"

"This is a higher security area."

Nodding, I turned and placed my hands on the wall like he indicated so he could pat me down. I felt like I was on an episode of *NCIS*, except this guy definitely wasn't Gibbs or DiNozzo. When his hand lingered as it drifted over my rear, I turned my head and quirked an eyebrow at him. He just grinned roguishly before stepping back. "All clear."

He turned and opened the door behind him, then shifted to the side. I eyed the hallway, knowing there was no way I'd get past him without rubbing up against him. With a sigh, I slid by, keeping as close to the wall as I could. Even then, I had to rub my body along his.

Cedric was waiting on the other side with a frown on his face. "Really, Jackson? You do know she's with Keane, right?"

Jackson blanched and quickly turned away. I muffled my laughter and stepped into a large room with big, shiny doors evenly spaced along one long wall. Each door had an extensive electronic monitoring and magical system on it. Though I was still having trouble fully accessing my magic, I felt the tendrils flowing from the doors. I looked around me, impressed. This seemed like a pretty high-tech setup.

"So, this is where you've been hanging out these days. Nice digs. Personally, I would've gone with a little less stark-modern and maybe added some homey touches."

Cedric burst out laughing. "Glad to see you haven't lost your sense of humor."

"Ha! Like that would ever happen." I paused and eyed him up and down as if considering something. "So, a tracker *and* a guardsman, huh?"

Cedric shrugged and leaned against the wall, crossing his arms. "Yeah, I wanted to do something useful, and this seemed like a good first step."

"Right back to the woman you were trying so hard to avoid? Kind of seems like one step forward and two steps back to me."

"Maybe I like the cha-cha." He put his hand on his chest and the other in the air like he was holding an invisible partner and danced around the room.

It was my turn to laugh. "You *are* a pretty good dancer." For a moment, it felt like our friendship before Cedric ruined it by trying to take things to the next level.

"I've missed you, Blue. It's good to hear your laughter. After everything that happened, I wasn't sure if you would ever want to talk to me again."

"Mmm, the past is the past. Let bygones be bygones."

Cedric nodded and took my arm, leading me down the length of the room—which seemed to go on forever.

"What is this place?"

"It's the Dungeons of Duck Street, for all intents and purposes."

"Now that has a ring to it. Pretty fancy for a dungeon."

"Nothing but the latest and greatest for the Moon Tree Clan. Top-of-the-line electronic surveillance system, DNA-encrypted weapons monitoring each prisoner should they decide to escape..."

"Wait. DNA-encrypted weapons? Like the ones Captain Gantu tried to hold Stitch with? That didn't work out too well for him..." Cedric shook his head, obviously having no clue what I was talking about.

"Remind me to have a *Disney* cartoon marathon one night for you."

Cedric chuckled a bit and shook his head. "I'll do that." We walked a little farther in silence before he turned his head toward me. "What was up with your whole disappearing act these past three months?"

I grimaced a bit. "Just trying to adjust to my new life." I quickly changed the subject when it seemed he wanted to question me further. "How is our dear friend Celeste making out?"

"As well as can be expected. Wanna see her?"

I nodded, and he led me to one of the cells near the end of the long room. "Due to Celeste's abilities, we must be very careful about what measures we take to hold her."

I placed my hand on the door, intent on looking into the slotted peephole, but jumped back when an electric current shot through my fingertips and down my spine.

"Careful! Her cell has an electrical field around it to prevent anyone from getting too close. It also dampens magic."

I took in a breath before letting it out slowly. "This whole place feels heavy and dampening when it comes to magic."

Cedric nodded while taking my hand to make sure it was okay. "Yeah, there are spells that prevent anyone who's not authorized from doing magic within its confines."

"Any magic?"

"Yup."

I shook my head. I didn't want to tell him that while I couldn't feel much, I *could* still feel whisps of my magic flowing in and out through my senses. Perhaps it was my connection to Keane. Maybe I was using him like a conductor or a familiar like witches did. I snickered at the thought.

Cedric turned and placed his hand on the scanner next to the door, then leaned down so his retina could be scanned. Finally, he took a puck off a clip on his belt and seated it into a slot next to the scanner. A blue light went around in a circle on the puck's surface before it lit up bright green and beeped. As soon as it did, the wall slid away to reveal an eight-by-eight room behind some type of thick, clear material.

There wasn't much inside, just a bed, toilet, and a few personal items. Celeste was stretched out on the bed, reading a book. She looked up, seeming unconcerned as the wall slid open until she spotted me. Her whole body went rigid, and her eyes flashed angrily. I just smiled in the face of her wrath and gave her a little finger wave.

"Hiya, Celeste. Cozy accommodations you have here. They even provided you with a personal attendant. How nice."

She gritted her teeth, obviously trying hard to hold back from saying anything. Her temper finally won out. "You! I'll make you pay for this. You think you're so high and mighty, but I'll show you in the end. I won't be here for much longer. Just you wait."

"Oh? Do you think someone will come to your rescue?"

"Larkin will find a way to get me out of here. And then we'll kill all of you."

I laughed and shook my head. "Sorry to break it to you, but Larkin is in no position to help anyone, especially himself."

"I don't believe you. He escaped. No one knows where he is. I'm sure he's plotting how to get his followers out even now."

"You just keep thinking that, sweetheart."

Cedric looked at me sideways. "You know where Larkin is?"

I just shrugged noncommittally.

Celeste huffed and rolled her eyes. "Why couldn't you have died during the Trials like you were supposed to? Larkin deserves to rule all the clans. You ruined everything."

"You know, you're as much to blame for Larkin's downfall as I am."

She looked taken aback. "What do you mean by that?"

"Honestly, if you hadn't so obligingly entered me into the Trials, my grandmother never would've removed the enchantment on me, thus giving my powers back. And I never would've been there to thwart Larkin in the first place."

"I...it wasn't...that's not..."

I laughed as she floundered angrily. "I guess you finally got what you wanted in the end, though."

She crossed her arms over her chest and glared at me. "And what is that?"

"Cedric's undivided attention."

Cedric snorted a laugh beside me. "Okay, enough antagonizing." He put a hand to the middle of my back and guided me across the hall.

I could feel Celeste's furious gaze on me as we walked away. "Don't get too comfortable, Blue. When I get out of here, I will find you, and I *will* kill you."

I have a very particular set of skills. Skills that make me a nightmare for people like you. I couldn't help the quote from *Taken* that popped into my mind. I turned my head and smirked over my shoulder at her, blowing her a kiss. "Good luck." Thankfully, in this case, I was the person with the particular set of skills. She didn't stand a chance.

Cedric led me to another door, which turned out to be a studio apartment of sorts. It had a small kitchen in one corner with a table and chairs propped against one wall, while a bed was set up on the other side.

"Oh, man, do you have to stay down here all the time?"

Cedric shrugged. "Not all the time. Jackson and Wyn switch out periodically to give me some time to go topside if needed. And it's not like it's forever. Celeste's trial is set to start in another two weeks."

I looked at the bed for a second but then opted for one of the kitchen chairs.

"Do you want something to drink or eat?"

I shook my head. "I'd rather not have anything in my stomach. I have to go before the Council shortly."

"Oh, I didn't realize they had called a meeting. I know they have many unanswered questions from the night of the final Trial."

"I'm not sure I can tell them more than they already know. I'm just as confused about some of the events as they are."

"Do you really know where Larkin is?"

I grimaced. I regretted letting that tidbit slip. "The less you know, the better, Cedric."

"You know I'll hold whatever you say to me in the strictest of confidence. I'd never betray you, Blue." He sat forward in his chair and took one of my hands.

I gave him a half smile. "It's not that I don't trust you, Cedric. It's just...safer for everyone involved if the secrets stay secret for now. You understand, right?"

He looked a bit frustrated but nodded. I tugged on his hand. "Soo, I hear you're going to be part of my tracking team for this next mission."

Cedric's eyes lit up. "Absolutely. I can't wait to get out there and try some new techniques I've learned. I've been working with Talib and Olwen on my tracking skills."

"Oh? Weren't those the two Wolves who came to my house when it was ransacked?"

Cedric nodded. "The best of the best."

"I'd say you're now ranked with them."

"I guess you could say that." He gave me a shy smile before his look turned contemplative. "Blue, there's something I've wanted to ask you."

I pushed back in my chair, leaning it on two legs, and folded my arms over my chest. "Hmm?"

"How is it that you and Keane have a soulbond?"

In my surprise, my chair plopped back down, and a small frown tugged at my lips. "How do you know that Keane and I are bonded?"

He gave me a one-shoulder shrug. "I heard the guardians who delivered Celeste talking about it. They said you're the first non-Vaimpír to ever create the bond and that it has even been approved by the King and Queen of the Vaimpír."

Apparently, this secret was coming out a lot faster than I'd thought. "This is all just between us, right?" He nodded emphatically. "I'm actually part god. My father is Poseidon."

Cedric sat before me with his mouth hanging open in shock, much like a cartoon character. "What...how...?"

"Well, when a male and a female are attracted to each other—"

"Blue." He gave me a deadpan stare, causing me to laugh.

I considered before I answered, unsure if I should tell him the whole truth. While he had tried to force our relationship to a place I didn't want it to go, he had also proven himself loyal time and time again.

With a sigh, I decided to trust him. "Between my mother's powers and my father's heritage, the combination somehow made it so I have all the powers of the Fae. I can utilize all types of magic, one of which is the Vaimpír's. It seems my control is enough that Keane and I were able to create a soulbond."

"That's...wow. I take it the Council isn't aware of your bloodline yet."

"No. And to say the least, I'm extremely nervous for all of this to come out."

"Are you afraid people will look at you differently?"

I looked at him archly. "Of course, they will. You see how people react whenever you mention the gods." I leaned over and put my head in my hands, the very thought of everything coming out making me feel sick.

"Blue, it won't make a difference to the people who matter to you, trust me. You're still you." Cedric gently laid his hand on my shoulder.

I looked up at him and smiled slightly. "Thanks, Cedric."

"Do you need me to come with you to the Council meeting? For support? I can have Jackson cover for me."

I shook my head. "No. But thank you."

"Okay, but if you need me, just send for me and I'll be there."

Looking into his bright-green eyes, I was suddenly pulled into a very different gaze. Cedric's face morphed into Larkin's, and I was struck by how very much Cedric resembled him. It was amazing that no one had made the connection before. At the thought of Larkin, I felt his powers surface. This time, it was his Wolf. It pressed against my consciousness, wanting to shift, wanting to break free, wanting to run. I felt myself slipping further into the Wolf's mind. Without my normal magic surrounding me, it seemed to be taking over. I could feel the wind on its face, smell the scent of the forest as it flew through the trees, and sense the absolute freedom it felt. I wanted to experience it for myself.

I felt my body start to shift. As a growl of pleasure escaped my lips, I was jolted back to myself, stopping just in time. I covered my mouth with my hands, my eyes going wide.

"Blue, are you okay? What was that?"

I shook my head in fear.

"Your entire scent just changed. It was strangely familiar, and your eyes...they transformed into a shimmering gold, almost like a Wolf's."

I stood abruptly, knocking the chair I was sitting in over. "I-I have to go. It was good seeing you, Cedric." I patted him on the shoulder and practically ran from the room, passing a surprised Celeste still lying on her bed in her cell.

"Blue!" Cedric's voice carried after me, but I just ran faster.

When I got to the exit door, I pounded on it. "Jackson? It's Blue. Can you open the door? I'm ready to go."

I didn't think he heard me at first, but then a loud beep sounded, and the door swung in. He blocked the doorway with his weapon at the ready, but when he saw it was only me, he stepped back. I must have looked as upset as I felt as his eyebrows drew together in concern. "Are you okay? Where's Cedric?"

"Umm...sorry, I just...I just need to go." I pushed past him and ran down the hall. Just as I made the turn, I heard Jackson confront Cedric.

"What the hell, man? What did you do to her?"

I ran all the way to the last door. After knocking, Wyn opened it. I nodded to him in acknowledgment and thanked him before going to the elevator and repeatedly pushing the button. "Come on, come on..."

I jumped when I heard a knock on the inner prison door and Cedric's voice requesting Wyn to open it. My heartbeat picked up speed, and I began cursing the elevator under my breath. Finally, the doors opened, and I dove inside, hitting the close button just as Cedric entered the room.

"Blue, wait!" The doors slid closed just as he reached them, and I leaned back against the wall, breathing heavily. Oh, god. What just happened? Larkin's Wolf had almost taken over. And Cedric said my scent changed. That it was familiar. Did he know it was Larkin's? I felt a bit of a panic attack starting and closed my eyes. It would be okay. He didn't know. How could he? When the doors opened on Tristan's floor, I found Keane blocking the exit.

"Blue. Are you all right, what happened? I felt your panic. What's going on?"

I fell into his embrace and started sobbing, not really sure why. He scooped me into his arms and strode across the room. Tristan, who had been sitting nearby, stood. "Blue?"

"Not now, Tristan." With a few quick instructions to his men, Keane took me to our bedroom and sat on the bed, still cradling me to his chest. He scooted up until he was sitting against the headboard.

"Shh, it's okay, *ma moitié*. Whatever it is, we'll figure it out together." He kissed the top of my head and rocked me back and forth, not asking any questions, just lending me his strength and comfort—which I appreciated more than he would ever know.

Sometime later, after I finally got my emotions under control and my magic firmly in place, I shared with Keane everything I had talked to Poseidon about and what had happened with Cedric.

"After we resolve this issue with Hades, I think we need to have a talk with your friend Sebastian. It may be time for us to pay Larkin a little visit and see about giving him his powers back."

I chewed on my bottom lip out of habit. "Do you think that's a good idea? Giving him his powers back?"

"To tell you the truth, I don't know. But we need to get them out of you. I wish you had told me it was getting this bad."

"I didn't want to worry you."

"Blue, we're partners. I'm worried about what you're worried about, and vice versa."

I slanted him a look. "So says the man who wouldn't tell me what was bothering him for the last three months."

"Touché."

"Do you think Cedric will figure it out?"

"I can't say. Would you like me to remove his memories?"

"You can do that?"

"Of course, I can. What kind of Vaimpír do you take me for?"

I smiled but continued to worry my lip in thought. Keane reached out with his thumb and slowly pried it from between my teeth before leaning in and sucking on it. "If anyone is going to chew on this, it's going to be me."

Picking me up, he turned me so I was straddling his lap, facing him. He kissed me softly on each corner of my mouth before he started to nibble on my lips again, teasing but not kissing me. Growling, I took his face in my hands and forced his mouth fully on mine. I felt his chest rumble against me in amusement at my impatience. Taking charge, I slowly explored his mouth while his hands slipped under my T-shirt to run up the muscles of my back before sliding down to my hips and pulling me tightly against him. Just as things started to heat up, there was a knock on the door.

I groaned and leaned my forehead against Keane's. "Every time."

He chuckled and pecked a kiss on the tip of my nose. "Come in."

Tristan's head poked around the corner, causing Keane to scowl. "I hope I'm not interrupting anything."

"And if you are?"

I pinched Keane's side, causing him to grunt. I turned to look over my shoulder at Tristan. "What's up?"

"Ahem. Well, I wanted to check to make sure you were okay. You were quite upset earlier."

"I was just feeling a bit overwhelmed, but Keane knows how to take care of me. Don't worry."

Tristan flinched a bit while Keane smirked. "Good. Well, I'm glad to hear it. Um, Kieran stopped by earlier. The Council will be meeting at eleven o'clock in the ballroom."

I glanced at my watch. It was already a quarter of eleven. "Oh, I guess I'd better get changed then. Thanks, Tristan. We'll see you there?"

He hesitated but then nodded. "Sure. I'll be there." With one last lingering look at me, he ducked back out and shut the door behind him.

Keane growled a bit. "I don't like the way he looks at you."

I smiled softly and put my hands on his face, forcing him to look at me. "He had his chance, remember? He chose his people, as he should have. And I chose you."

Keane growled possessively again and wrapped his hand in the hair at my nape, pulling my neck taut before running his lips over my pulse point. I sucked in a breath as he bit down, not breaking the skin. "You'd better not forget it either."

"Not likely." My voice was a bit breathless.

"Mmm, how I wish we had more time."

"Me, too."

He released me with a sigh, and I climbed from his lap. Walking over to the closet, I pulled out a fresh pair of jeans and a T-shirt that proclaimed, *Of course I talk to myself. Sometimes I need expert advice.* Keane chuckled and shook his head but didn't comment. I just shrugged and went in search of my Converse, which Keane had taken off me earlier. Across the room, Keane slipped his shirt from his shoulders, causing me to pause in my search. I watched the muscles of his back ripple with his movements. Turning with a new T-shirt in hand, I couldn't stop my gaze from wandering over his tight abs to the deep, hollowed grooves of his hips that dipped below the waistband of his jeans. A sudden uncontrollable heat coiled in my center and dipped lower.

"*Ma moitié...*" I glanced up and saw that his eyes had changed to deep red. I blinked several times before taking in a deep breath to try to quell my rising lust.

"S-sorry."

His lip quirked up at the corner. "Never be sorry for your desires, *ma moitié.* I love that just looking at me brings you to such a state." Avoiding Keane's hungry gaze, I quickly turned my back and stripped off my T-shirt, throwing the new one over my head. Shimmying my pants over my hips, I changed into my jeans. I finally located my shoes and slipped them on before reaching up and securing my hair into a quick ponytail. Keane came up behind me and wrapped his arms around me, nuzzling my neck. "As looking at you puts me in a state." I felt the evidence of his statement pressed against me and sighed. We were quite the pair.

My watch vibrated with a message, and I knew we were out of time. A quick glance showed a text from Tristan saying the Council was ready. I turned in Keane's arms and wrapped mine around his neck, bringing his head down for one last kiss. "Show time, *mon vilain homme.*"

He grinned, a slip of fang showing. "Your naughty man, huh?" As I turned to walk out the door, he slapped me on the butt. "And stop stealing my lines."

Chapter Sixteen

I felt a bit of trepidation as I stepped onto the ballroom's second-floor balcony. This was the first time I had been back since the chaotic ending to the Trials.

Everything in the room had been cleaned and put back to rights as if nothing had happened. I glanced down over the railing and saw the dais still set up along one wall, with the Elders' seven large, ornamental chairs on it, seeming to lord over the room. Instead of the platforms and raised stadium seating that had once been spread throughout the space, a lone table with multiple chairs was now on the floor in front of the dais. I rolled my eyes at the obvious power play.

Just as we started down the stairs, almost as if it had been staged, a door on the far side of the room opened, and the Elders trailed out in a single file line, wearing their ornate, black cloaks. I stopped midway down the stairs to watch them. Once they were all seated, one chair noticeably empty, I started back down, moving purposefully toward them. Keane followed a step behind, and as we approached, Poseidon appeared and mirrored his position. When we stood before the six men, I bowed my head in respect.

"Blue, it is good to see you back here at Moon Tree Hall. Your presence has been sorely missed these last few months." I wasn't surprised that it was Elder Demirtas who spoke. He always seemed to be the mouthpiece for the Elders. "Why don't you have a seat?" He indicated the table and chairs at my back. I glanced over my shoulder with a grimace. While I respected the Elders, I wasn't about to let them intimidate me. Lifting myself onto the table's surface, I sat on the edge with my legs swinging in front of me. Keane and Poseidon remained standing, flanking me on either side.

I saw Elder Demirtas' eyebrows draw together in annoyance before he wiped his expression clean and turned toward Keane. "Prince Keane, a pleasure to see you as always. I hope your father is well?"

"Yes, thank you, sir."

"Please send him my regards."

Keane inclined his head formally. "I will."

Elder Demirtas then turned to Poseidon. "I don't believe we have had the pleasure of your acquaintance yet."

Poseidon smiled amicably. "Gentlemen." With a nod, he released his diffuser spell. I watched as shock flowed over the faces of most of the men before us. "I am Poseidon, God of the Seas...and Blue's father."

Silence rang through the room after his statement. It was so quiet I was sure you could've heard a pin drop.

It was rather amusing to watch, actually.

The men before us seemed to go through a range of emotions until they finally gathered themselves.

"Well...ah...welcome. It is indeed a pleasure to have you here."

"The pleasure is all mine. I daresay I have been looking forward to a time when I could finally reunite with my daughter."

"Ah. Yes, yes. Well…" Elder Demirtas was floundering, having difficulty figuring out what to say. Tristan saved him by walking into the room with Riona on his arm. "Ah. King Tristan and Queen Riona. Welcome, Your Majesties."

"Thank you, Elder Demirtas. I hope we're not late."

"No, no. We were just getting to know Blue's companion here."

Tristan looked toward Poseidon. "Good to see you again, Poseidon."

"You, as well, Tristan."

Their brief exchange of pleasantries only seemed to confound the Elders further. Tristan turned his attention back to them. "Gentlemen, if we might begin?"

"Yes, yes. Of course. But first, a moment please?" Elder Demirtas stepped back, and the other Elders all gathered close together. They must've put up a protection bubble as I couldn't make out anything they said, but you could tell they were arguing vehemently. Keane, Poseidon, Tristan, and I all looked at each other in bewilderment. What was going on? Before we could comment, Elder Demirtas stepped forward again. "Before we get to your grandfather's request, we hoped you could answer a few questions for us."

"Questions about…?" I pretended as if I didn't know what they were referring to.

"To start, do you know where Larkin is at this moment?"

"No." I wouldn't elaborate. My best bet here was to keep my answers short and to the point. Elder Albrecht sat forward and scrutinized me, hard. One of his talents was his ability to taste a lie. Thankfully, I wasn't lying. At this moment, I didn't know where Larkin was. As long as they didn't ask specific questions, I'd be able to get around his talent. I looked directly at him. "Is there a problem, Elder Albrecht?"

"No, no. Of course, not." He nodded to Elder Demirtas before sitting back. I had obviously passed his lie-detector test.

"Blue, were you in league with Larkin?"

I started in surprise at the accusation while both Keane and Poseidon stiffened at my sides. Even my grandfather looked affronted. Anger quickly flooded me. "Excuse me?"

"You have to admit it looks suspicious. He showed up just as you took the floor to dance, and he was clearly besotted with you. Then, when everything started to unravel, he managed to escape, and you were somehow able to release all the people under his control, saving everyone."

I gritted my teeth to keep from lashing out. "Frankly, I'm not sure what I did to release the people under Larkin's control or if it was even me. Since they were all under his influence due to his charm talent, he could have simply lost control when he went insane and tried to kill everyone."

"Then how is it that you survived the death spell Larkin meant for us?"

"That would be thanks to my father's blood."

"What do you mean?"

"When Larkin's death spell hit me, my spirit separated from my body. I became incorporeal." Now that they knew Poseidon was my father, there was no need to hide the truth from them. "In doing so, I was able to prolong my life so Tristan had time to heal me."

"Did you know prior to entering the Trials that you were a god?"

I cocked my head to the side, narrowing my eyes at the abrupt change in the direction of his questions. "First off, I didn't enter the Trials.

Celeste tricked the bloodstone with some of my blood, forcing me into them. Second, I'm not a god. Only part god." I wouldn't mention the fact that I seemed to be more god than Fairy. Who knew where they were going with this? "And third, no, I didn't know. Not until my soul left my body."

"I believe that absolves her of any wrongdoing." Kieran spoke up forcefully while several others nodded their heads.

"Wait, did I miss something? Am *I* on trial here? First, you insinuate I'm in league with Larkin, and now you seem to have a problem with my parentage?"

I felt Poseidon's power spike as he fixed his steely gaze on the Elder. "Tread very carefully, Elf."

"A god may not enter the Trials. It is forbidden." Elder Demirtas spoke succinctly but I saw him sweating.

My brows drew together in confusion at his answer. "I thought anyone could enter the Trials. If it was against the rules, why would the bloodstone accept me?"

"We don't know. Perhaps because Celeste did the contracting? The circle should have kept you out."

I rolled my eyes and muttered to Keane. "Guess the fact that I saved all their hides and prevented some maniac from taking over the clans means nothing, huh?" The corner of his mouth twitched but he managed to keep a straight face.

"Blue, we are just upholding the laws of the Fae. We can't make exceptions."

"And yet you allowed Larkin to gain unprecedented power to utilize his gifts to control and manipulate people, including you. To the point where he almost killed all of you and took over the clans. If it weren't for me, you'd all be dead. You do remember that, right?" I felt my agitation rising, and Keane laid a comforting hand on my shoulder.

"We do owe you our lives, but..."

I gave a frustrated huff and held up my hand. "Look, it's all over and done with. I wasn't cheating to try to win the crown. You can lay that crime at Celeste's feet. I didn't even want to be Queen. All I was trying to do was stay alive. And it all turned out as it should have. You reinstated Riona as Queen."

The Elders all looked at each other before finally nodding in agreement. I released the breath I had been holding, allowing my temper to cool.

"Blue, we also wanted to talk to you about Queen Riona." Riona tensed a bit at the mention of her name. Noting her reaction, Elder Demirtas turned toward her. "If it is all right with you, Your Majesty."

"Certainly. Why wouldn't it be?" Riona waved him away regally, though I noticed the apprehension had yet to leave her shoulders.

"Thank you, Your Majesty." He turned back to me. "There is no easy way to ask this, so I will just come out and say it. What did you do that made Queen Riona corporeal again?"

I shrugged my shoulders. "No idea."

"What do you mean you have no idea?"

"Exactly what I said. I. Have. No. Idea." I punctuated each word.

"But how can you not know?"

Poseidon laid a hand on my other shoulder to keep me seated as my anger started to rise. "If I might interject." The Elders turned toward him, and Elder Demirtas nodded. "Not having been there myself, I can only surmise, but I believe Blue performed the *anima ortu*."

I looked at him in surprise. "What is that?"

He smiled patiently. "It is the soul rising. A talent of my brother, Hades."

I sat back in surprise. "But if it's Hades' talent, how can I do it?"

"He must have taught it to you. And with your ability to learn any magic..."

I turned to the Elders. "I think now would be a good time for you to return my memories."

My grandfather stood and faced Elder Demirtas. "You all already agreed. There is no reason to put it off any longer."

Elder Demirtas sighed and nodded. "You are right. I apologize. I will take the lead—"

"No." They all turned to me in surprise. "Only my grandfather is allowed in my head. He'll take the lead."

"My dear, this is a very powerful spell. We each have our strengths..."

"It is okay, Balin. I can handle it. If this is what my granddaughter wants, it is a small request in the grand scheme of things."

Elder Demirtas seemed as if he might argue but then looked around the room, seeing that he was outnumbered. "Very well."

Kieran nodded and turned toward me. "Blue, if you would stand over top of that rune."

"What rune?" My eyes widened in surprise as a symbol etched onto the floor lit up and turned a bright blue. It was a seven-point star with a swirling circle in the center. I slowly made my way over and, after walking around the rune, stepped onto it. As I did, I felt the power of it flow over me. I shivered. "How did you create a rune? I thought runes were only used in god magic?"

Kieran smirked at me knowingly. "A latent talent I have always possessed." Elder Demirtas looked at him sharply with a bit of suspicion, but Kieran just ignored him. "It merely helps to amplify our powers."

The Elders stood and formed a circle around me—each person taking a point of the star. I again noticed the empty spot, the one where Elder Avner would've been. "Will you be able to do this without the seventh person?"

"It will be more difficult, but with the addition of the rune, it should be enough."

"I'll be your seventh."

I looked toward Tristan in shock. "Tristan?"

"Your Majesty, while we appreciate the offer, we could not put you in such a position. We cannot take the chance that you could be harmed during it."

Tristan laughed lightly. "Don't worry. I'm well equipped to handle the *memoria revelare*. I've been practicing this magic since I was a boy."

Tristan took his position at the seventh point. As soon as he did, I felt the magic click into place. The seven men placed their hands in the circle, fingers spread. Closing their eyes, they started chanting. I turned toward my grandfather, who stood at the top point.

"Close your eyes, Blue. I want you to think about the very first memory you have. As far back as you can go."

I looked over the Elders' heads toward Keane and Poseidon. Both men nodded their encouragement. Taking a deep breath, I closed my eyes and let it out slowly. I carefully sifted through my childhood memories until I found the very first one I could remember clearly. It wasn't much, but for some reason, it had stuck with me over the years.

I'd been about five years old. My mother had sent me with my current nanny to one of the nearby parks to play. I remember it being exceptionally hot that day. I was playing by myself in the sandbox when a stranger walked up. He bent down to my level.

"What are you building there, little one?"

I looked up at him. I knew I wasn't supposed to talk to strangers, but for some reason, it felt like I knew him. My nanny moved to my side.

"A sandcastle…" No, that wasn't right. I shook my head to try and clear it. The image seemed to flicker like it had been interrupted, blurring before coming back into focus. When it did, I froze. I was no longer in a city park. I was now in a wooded valley surrounded by lush vegetation and tall pine trees. I looked down at the sand in my hands, but instead of sand, it was dirt and rocks. I had piled everything up to form a rune of some sort. My eyes shot to the man in front of me, his glowing amber eyes seeming to look into my soul. At my side was the familiar heat of my hellhound, Scythe.

I blinked, and everything went back to what it was—a city park in a sandbox, the strange man in front of me, and my nanny at my side. I shook my head again as a static sound filled it. Pressure started behind my eyes, and I put the heels of my hands against them to try to relieve the pain. As the pressure built, so did the agony. It became almost unbearable, and I cried out, dropping to my knees. A small trickle of blood flowed from my nose.

"Don't fight it, Blue. You have to let go. You need to let us in." I felt Tristan's soothing words flow over me as tears leaked out of my closed lids. I felt his presence in the back of my mind, softly probing. "Kieran, let me take the lead."

"But, Your Majesty—" Elder Demirtas started to argue.

"Enough, Balin. If he wants to take the lead, let him. He would not do so without a reason."

I heard their conversation as if I were standing at the end of a tunnel. As soon as Kieran released control to Tristan, I felt the pressure let up. "Attagirl. Easy now. Allow our connection to flow again."

I felt Keane start through our bond as he felt Tristan within me. "It's not possible..."

I opened my eyes to stare into Tristan's. His had that green glow, a mirror of it now in my eyes. "That's right, my *âme miroir*, open yourself to me." The Elders started to chant softly again around me, and I opened myself further. I felt my head clear, the static slowly dissipating until all was quiet. "Now, close your eyes. Keane, connect to her soul, blanket her essence with yours." I felt Keane's soul moving within me, wrapping mine in a warm embrace.

"What are you doing, Tristan?" Kieran asked curiously.

"Helping to open her pathways that are naturally resisting the intrusion. Keane is her soulmate, and I'm her soul's twin flame. Our connections to her run deep, and with them, we can ease the way past the blocks that were put in place. Okay, Blue. Concentrate on your memory again."

I tried, but it kept slipping through the cracks of my mind. "It keeps shifting."

Tristan nodded and spread his hands again. "It appears that whoever did this overlayed different memories on top of your current ones. And whatever they used was powerful. It will take me a bit to unravel them, but I know I can. Hang in there, Blue."

As Tristan worked, I felt the pressure begin to build again. Every time it did, Keane stepped in and siphoned some of it off. I didn't want him to take the pain—that wasn't fair.

"It's nothing, *ma moitié*. Allow me to help you."

Finally, the memory stopped flickering. It paused while I was staring into Hades' eyes before everything came flooding back like a tidal wave. I held my head in my hands as it all washed over me. I watched as I grew up in the wooded Glen. How Hades had taken me under his wing, how he'd trained me. Not just for nefarious reasons, but also because he felt a connection to me. He really had looked at me as one of his own. Considering he couldn't have children, I supposed I was the closest thing he had.

I watched as we created Scythe and bonded to him. I watched as he taught me about the Underworld and the creatures and other gods that lived there—even about the gods on Olympus. The knowledge that Hades had gifted me with was immense. It was hard to believe that a child as young as I'd been could've retained it all.

Slowly opening my eyes, I tried to stand but stumbled, my head spinning as new memories continued flooding in. Tristan caught me. "Easy now. It's going to take some time for everything to come back."

"Blue, we have more questions for you—"

Tristan held up a hand to stop Elder Demirtas. "That is enough for today. She needs to rest. Thank you all for your help." Keane stepped forward and scooped me up into his arms before Elder Demirtas could protest further, then walked toward the stairs, Poseidon and Tristan following closely behind.

Keane took me straight to our room after getting to Tristan's quarters and laid me down. When he went to pull away, I held on to him. He smiled and kissed the top of my head. "I'll be right back, *ma moitié*. I promise." I reluctantly let him go.

Tristan sat on the edge of my bed. "You knew we were twin flames, didn't you?" I nodded slowly. "How long?"

My voice was barely above a whisper. "The last night of the Trials."

"You blocked our connection." It was part statement and part accusation.

I shrugged and looked away. "Part of me thought it would be better for you. Give you time to settle back into life with Riona without the burden of our connection. While another part was quite selfish. I just wasn't ready to deal with it."

Reaching out, he brought my face back toward him. "Please, don't block me out again. It was like a piece of me was missing. And now that I know what it is, what you mean to me..."

I placed my hand over his. "I won't."

"This also means that when you face off with Hades, I'll be there."

"Tristan, it's too dangerous. You have to remember you're the King. Your people depend on you."

"I pushed you away once for that reason. Never again."

Tristan stood as Keane came back into the room. They nodded to each other with new understanding as they passed. I smiled slightly and shook my head. At least that feud was over.

Taking the spot Tristan had vacated, Keane helped me sit and brought a glass to my lips. "A special draught from Galene. She said it will help relieve the lingering effects of the *memoria revelare*."

I nodded and drank the potion, immediately feeling better. Lying back down, I waited until Keane was settled, then curled into his side before falling asleep.

Chapter Seventeen

I groggily pried my eyes open as I came to consciousness, wincing as my head started to spin. Ugh. Instead of the *memoria revelare*, they should have called it the brain twister.

I tried to turn over, but it felt like someone had added a hundred-pound weighted blanket to my chest. I groaned and rubbed a hand over my face. I considered just going back to sleep, but my bladder insisted it needed attention.

Sucking in a breath, I pushed with all my might and managed to get to my side before rolling out from under the fluffy comforter covering me. When my feet finally hit the floor, I paused with my face on the mattress to catch my breath. I felt worse than I had when I had let my three best friends talk me into drinking and partying all night with that Dublin Gaelic football team. Now, *that* was a night to remember.

"You look like crap."

My head shot up at the sound of the deep voice, the sudden movement causing me to groan and squeeze my temples. Peering through half-open lids, I could just make out the silhouette of Sebastian sitting on the end of my bed.

"What are you doing here?"

He tilted his head and grinned at me. "If I didn't know better, I'd think you weren't happy to see me."

I just ignored him and looked around. "Where's Keane?"

"Taking care of some last-minute business before we leave."

"Mmm, what time is it?"

"Just past three."

"In the afternoon?"

"Yup."

"Ugh. I feel like I got run over by a truck."

"You look it."

I gave him the stink-eye. "Why are you here again?"

"Because your father made me your full-time guardian."

"Shouldn't you be more, you know…supportive?"

"Mmm… No. I feel honesty is the best policy."

I harrumphed and steadied my feet beneath me. With a Herculean effort, I pushed myself off the bed and stumbled toward the bathroom. Sebastian followed. Opening the door, I gave an annoyed huff when I realized it was the closet door, not the bedroom. As I began listing to the side, I grabbed the first thing I could to stop myself from falling—which happened to be Sebastian.

I felt him sigh. "Let me help you."

"I've got it."

"Sure, you do."

After he had helped me maneuver into the bathroom across the hall, he continued to stand there with his hands on his hips. I waved him away. "I've got it from here, Sebastian. Thank you."

He tilted his head to the side and grinned. "Are you sure? I could always stay and help scrub your back. Be more *supportive* and whatnot."

"Out." I pushed him out the door, shutting it in his grinning face.

"If you're sure."

"Sebastian."

I could hear him laughing as he walked away. "I'll be in the living area if you need anything."

After a long, hot shower, I felt much more like myself. While my head was still killing me, at least it didn't feel like I had an elephant sitting on my chest anymore. The memories were still crowding around, trying to push through, but I kept shoving them back and filing them away for later dissection. The only one I concentrated on was where Iridia was. I was pretty sure I'd recognize it as soon as I saw it, but I still couldn't identify exactly where it was.

Since I hadn't brought any clothes into the bathroom, I made sure Sebastian was nowhere to be seen before creeping back to my room, wrapped in a towel. Digging through my suitcase, I pulled out an outfit I hadn't expected to wear again so soon. My fighting gear. During the Trials, Keane had the pants and boots commissioned for me, modeled after the gear the Vaimpír guardians wore. The black pants were outfitted with many hidden pockets for weaponry and had enough give to fight in any type of situation without tearing. The boots were also black, had nonskid rubber bottoms, and were extremely light weight. I sat on the bed and laced them up before securing the set of leather straps that wound around them and buckled on the outside, covering the laces.

Standing, I threw on the specially made long-sleeve black shirt with holes in the back for my wings, should I need to use them. One could never be too prepared. I then pulled on a wide cargo belt and strapped it tightly around my waist before loading up my pockets with all manner of weapons and ammo. Lastly, I secured my 9mm pistol, which I might or might not have named Hiccup, into his holster.

I quickly braided and coiled my hair on top of my head before doing one last check in the mirror.

Yup, still a badass.

I smirked and winked at my reflection before finding my way to the living area. There, I found Poseidon, Kieran, and Sebastian talking quietly among themselves while Keane and Tristan stood off to the side, having what appeared to be a heated conversation. The guys from Ethereal Mutation were unsurprisingly sitting in front of the gaming TV.

"Look what the cat dragged in."

I stuck my tongue out at Cullen, causing him to laugh, before moving over to my father and grandfather.

"Ah, Blue. It is good to see you up and about. How are you feeling?" Poseidon was the first to look up at me.

"Like I got run over by a truck, which then backed over me before running me over again."

He chuckled and glanced at Kieran. "Messing with one's brain can be a bit tricky. Especially one that has already been tampered with."

Keane looked over at that comment, a frown creasing his brow at whatever Tristan said. He glanced back at Tristan before shaking his head with what seemed to be a final *no* before approaching me.

"*Ma moitié.* Your head is still aching?"

I nodded but waved him off. "Nothing I can't handle. Are we ready to head out?"

"We just need to throw the suitcases in the trucks."

I looked at him in surprise. "We're not portaling?"

"No, we decided it would be too dangerous. It would make it much too easy for Hades to track you."

"Really? Easier than tracking a vehicle?"

"If Hades is monitoring the area, he could pick up on the magical signature a portal leaves behind no matter how long it has been since it was used. A vehicle is subjective when tracking. Especially if you have two sets of the same vehicles going in different directions at the same time. We'll do this the old-fashioned way."

"Sounds like fun."

After Cedric and the other trackers showed up, we all moved to the underground garage where six of the same black SUVs were parked. Those going to the Fernsong Clan split into three of the units, while some of Tristan's guards took three dummy vehicles. I ended up with Keane, Tristan, and Sebastian. Cedric tried to come with us, but Keane put a stop to it. I was sure Cedric wanted to talk about what had happened in the dungeon, but I *really* didn't want to get into it. Thank goodness Keane understood that.

I waved out the window to Poseidon and Kieran, who were staying behind to continue researching, before I closed the opaque glass and sat back in my seat. Keane and Tristan rode in the front while Sebastian and I were in the back.

"Should we play a few travel games?" I looked askance at Sebastian. "What? We're going to be in this car together for ten hours. We might as well make the most of it."

Thankfully, I talked him out of the travel games and distracted him with TikTok instead. It was worth giving up my phone and headphones for. We drove straight through the night, only stopping for short breaks to stretch our legs or switch drivers. By the time we arrived at the

Fernsong Clan territory, I was exhausted and more than ready to be out of the car.

Much like the Moon Tree Clan, the Fernsong Clan was located beneath a theater—the historic Saenger Theatre in Mobile, Alabama, to be exact. The Fae were very good at the performing arts, and Fairies seemed especially drawn to it.

Pulling up to the front of the large brick building, I looked up at the unique architecture. It had been designed in a French Renaissance style inspired by Greek mythology and coastal ornamentation. I was amused to see Poseidon's image cast above the entrance.

How fitting.

After exiting the vehicles, some of Brokk's men led us into the empty theater and up onto the stage. I noted that the theater itself was quite grand, and like Dock Street, had been recently renovated as well as given a few upgrades in the technology department if the new lighting system was any indication.

I didn't have much time to look around before we were taken through the thick, red-velvet curtain and into a back area. From there, our escort directed us down a long hallway to a magically sealed room—much like the upper doors at Dock Street were.

I watched as the Fae first placed his palm on the shiny wooden surface with his fingers splayed. Then, pulling his hand so just his fingertips touched the wood, he moved them drawing a clockwise circle, followed by a series of what appeared to be random swirling patterns he sketched with his pointer finger. Finally, he reached down and turned the knob. Opening the door, he stepped aside and indicated for us to precede him.

A vestibule with an elevator were on the other side of the door. Upon pressing the call button, the elevator doors opened immediately as if they had been waiting for us. As the lift was rather small, we split into groups with Keane, Tristan, Sebastian, and me going first. I was a bit nervous to meet King Brokk. He was, after all, my mother's husband—if in name only. I had to wonder what he thought of me considering...things.

Feeling my nerves, Keane reached out and wrapped an arm around my waist, pulling me into his side before leaning down close to my ear, his breath causing tingles to run down my spine. "Relax, *ma moitié*, he'll love you."

"That's what you said about your parents." Keane laughed softly at my sarcasm, but instead of commenting, he kissed the top of my head and stood back up.

Sebastian took the opportunity and leaned in. "Do you think you can manage to stay out of trouble for a little while?" I stuck out my tongue at him, causing him to chuckle. "I'm going to go do a bit of reconnaissance." Glancing at Keane, he gave him a sly grin and, leaning over, placed a quick kiss on my lips. Keane growled while Sebastian laughed and disappeared.

"That Angel had better watch himself. I don't care if he works for your father or not."

By this time, we had reached King Brokk's floor, and the doors slid open. We stepped into a large, opulent room that, much like the theater above, featured French Renaissance décor. The walls were white paneling with gold-filigree accents and molding throughout. Large, ornately framed paintings of flowers and elegantly dressed men and women graced the walls, some so large they were almost life-size. A huge chandelier hung in the center of the room, drawing your eyes to the assortment of paintings done on the ceiling. A variety of couches, chairs, and settees were placed throughout the living area, inviting visitors to sit and get comfortable. All in all, it was a lot to take in.

A man wearing a pair of black slacks and a white button-down shirt stood in the middle of the room. I sighed in relief. I half-expected him to be wearing pantaloons and a powdered wig. He was on the shorter side—probably not much taller than me—with cropped, dark-brown hair and large, expressive, brown eyes. He had a square-shaped face with a wide masculine jaw and a cleft chin. He wasn't exactly what you would call classically handsome, but there was something about him that drew the eye.

Tristan strode forward, his hand outstretched. "Brokk, it's so good to see you again, my friend."

Brokk shook Tristan's hand while covering their clasped hands with his other. "Tristan. I'm s-so very glad you were able to come. It has been much too long."

"It has, indeed."

Brokk seemed to have a slight stutter, which I found adorable. It just added to his appeal. Keane stepped forward to greet him. "Your Majesty."

"Oh, pish posh. Call me Brokk. We've known each other far too long to s-stand on formalities." He then turned toward me. "And who is this ravishing young lady you have with you?"

Keane grinned, his dimple peeking out. "This is Miss Carolina Blue of the family Grayson."

I stuck my hand out toward him. "You can just call me Blue."

He took my hand in both of his and stepped closer. "Finally. My dear, Blue, I've been waiting s-so long to meet you." His eyes got a bit teary. "When I found out you were the daughter of my dear Iridia, I just couldn't believe it."

I gave him a crooked smile. "I hope this isn't too awkward."

"Awkward? Why would it be awkward?"

"Being that you're married to my mother, but my father is...someone else." I wasn't sure if Tristan had filled him in on just who my father actually was.

Brokk chuckled and shook his head. "You're well aware of the nature of my relationship with your mother, are you not?" At my nod, he continued. "I've always wanted her to find happiness in matters of the heart, and even encouraged her when she would've given up on Aiden. Your father..."

I held up a hand. "Before you continue, I think I need to clear up the matter of my father."

"Oh?" Brokk tilted his head to the side and regarded me.

I took a deep breath. "My father isn't Aiden as everyone believes. It's actually Poseidon, God of the Seas."

Brokk blinked several times without saying anything before his mouth opened, closed, then opened again.

"I know it's a lot to take in."

"S-so Aiden isn't your father?" I shook my head. "You're s-sure of that?"

I laughed lightly. "Trust me when I tell you, I am one hundred percent sure."

He shook his head in bewilderment. "Wow. S-so, Iridia and Poseidon..."

I gave him a crooked grin. "Yup."

He took what seemed to be a fortifying breath. "Okay, if Poseidon is your father, is that why Hades is holding Iridia captive?"

I grimaced a bit. "Not exactly."

Before he could ask further questions, another man walked into the room from one of the back areas of Brokk's quarters. He was tall and lean with curly auburn hair and beautiful, golden-brown eyes. He was also drop-dead gorgeous—and completely human. My brows drew together. He looked quite familiar, but I couldn't place from where. I wondered if maybe he had been a model at some point in his life.

He walked up to Brokk and put his hands on his shoulders, not even glancing my way. "Why didn't you tell me we had guests?"

Brokk looked over his shoulder at the man with adoration. "They just arrived. I was about to call you." He turned back to me with a smile on his face. "Blue, might I introduce my partner, Nicholas Crofton. Nicholas, this is my wife's daughter, Carolina Blue. Though she likes to go by Blue."

I sucked in a shocked breath as the name registered, and I realized where I knew him from. He seemed to recognize me at the same time, his wide eyes locking with mine.

I had dated one Gerard Crofton back in high school. One of the popular guys at our school, I'd been surprised when he asked me out instead of one of my three gorgeous best friends. I should've known better.

During a huge house party Gerard had thrown while his parents were away, I found out his true intentions. It turned out that he had bet his friends he could seduce me and take my virginity before the end of the school year. Hurt, angry, and drunk off my ass, I decided to ruin his bet. In retaliation, I slept with the one person he looked up to instead. His older brother: Nicholas Crofton.

I stared at Nicholas. And I thought things were awkward before.

"Uh, hi Blue. It's, uh, good to see you again."

"Nick. It's been a long time."

Brokk looked between us in surprise. "You two know each other?"

Nick glanced at me and then back at Brokk. "Yeah. Ha. Blue here went to high school with my little brother. They even dated for a short time. Small world, huh?" He laughed nervously.

"Oh, how wonderful! You guys will have a chance to catch up on old times while s-she's here." We looked at each other uncomfortably. There weren't any old times. Our one and only interaction was that night. He went back to college the next day, and I went back to ignoring people like Gerard and Nicholas Crofton.

Thankfully, the elevator opened again to reveal Cullen, Mckile, and Ronan, preventing any further awkward conversation. Brokk and Nick moved over to greet them enthusiastically.

I flopped onto one of the couches and laid my head back, closing my eyes. I felt the couch dip as Keane sat next to me. "Well, that was enlightening." He had, of course, read my mind.

"Shut up." Keane laughed but didn't say anything else.

After Cedric and the other two trackers made it down, and introductions were made, we all gathered on a few of the larger couches.

"S-so, tell me what is going on. How did Iridia end up in Hades' hands?"

Tristan, who was seated next to me, sighed and sat forward. I settled back into the couch as he explained to Brokk how Hades had used Aiden to get to Iridia.

When he finished, Brokk looked confused. "But I don't understand. Why would Hades s-still be holding her prisoner? If she doesn't possess what he needs, why wouldn't he have either let her go or..." He paused, taking in a slight gulp of air. "Killed her?"

I opened my eyes to look at him. "Because he needs her as bait."

"For what?"

"Me."

Tristan pursed his lips as though he hadn't wanted to reveal that to Brokk.

Brokk's eyes widened. "Why would he want you?"

"Because, unlike Iridia, I *do* have what he wants. And at this point, he'll do anything to get it, which is why we need to rescue Iridia as soon as possible."

Brokk nodded. "My men are at your disposal. Anything you need, it's yours."

"Thank you."

Due to our long drive, we decided to reconvene after we got some rest—a few of us anyway. Keane and his men went out to scout the area before the sun rose. I had just changed into a tank top and shorts and was getting ready to climb into bed when a knock interrupted me. Expecting it to be Tristan, I threw open the door while rolling my eyes. "Do you always have to wait until Keane... Oh!" Standing outside my room was not the expected Tristan, but Nick. "I'm sorry, I thought you were someone else."

Nick was nervously rocking from foot to foot. "Sorry to bother you, Blue, but I was hoping I could talk to you for a minute. Privately."

Nodding, I stepped out of the entryway and gestured for him to come in before I shut the door behind him. He looked around nervously before perching on the edge of the bed. I came in and sat next to him.

"I...I wanted to talk to you about what happened between us in the past."

"Nick, that was eons ago. What is there to say?"

"I never apologized for what happened. I feel like I took advantage of you."

I smiled and shook my head. "If anything, it was the other way around. I was angry with your brother and looking for a way to get back at him."

"Yeah, but you weren't in your right mind. You were quite drunk."

"As were you, if I recall."

"All the more reason to apologize."

I shook my head again. "Please, don't. To tell you the truth, I'm kind of glad it was you. The guys I've slept with since then haven't been anything to write home about—well, except my current, but he's the exception."

"He is one hunk of a man."

I laughed and winked. "That he is."

"Can I ask you a favor?"

"Sure."

"Can you not say anything to Brokk about the nature of our past relationship? I think it would be exceptionally awkward if he knew that I had slept with his stepdaughter. Even if it was when we were kids."

"Oh, I hadn't thought of that." I wrinkled my nose and gave a soft laugh. "You can be sure I have no plans to *ever* tell him."

Nick slumped in relief, the tension leaving his shoulders. "Thank you. I'll leave you to get some rest then."

I stood and walked him to the door. Before he opened it, he turned toward me again. "Do you think you'll be able to find Iridia and bring her home?"

"Yes. I won't rest until she's free of Hades."

He looked down at the floor. "Do you think she'll have a problem with me being here? Being with Brokk?"

"Absolutely not. She loves Brokk like a brother, nothing more. She wants to see him as happy as he wants to see her."

Nick nodded and opened the door, hesitating again before stepping back and wrapping his long arms around me in a tight hug. He stood there for a moment before he leaned down to my ear. "I'm glad you were my first, too." He left, leaving me staring wide-eyed in surprise after him. I hadn't known that.

I went to close the door, only then noticing Tristan standing in the doorway of his room. He was watching me with his arms crossed over his chest and a hooded stare. I gave him a small wave before entering the room and shutting the door behind me.

Chapter Eighteen

I awoke early the next evening, feeling Keane's warmth beside me. I hadn't even felt him crawl into bed. Smiling, I rolled toward him. He was perfectly still, his body in sleep stasis, having been up for more than four days again.

Vaimpír didn't sleep like ordinary people. They only needed to rest once every four days or so, depending on their physical state—like if they had any injuries they needed to heal from. It was also more of a suspended state rather than actual sleeping.

His face was gentle when he was like this, all the lines smooth and the tension gone. I reached up and gently ran a finger along his cheek and jaw, knowing it wouldn't bother him. Not much would disturb him until he was ready to wake up.

I had a feeling this was the last time I'd get a moment like this. Once we found Iridia, things would move quickly forward, and the standoff between Hades and I would come to a head. I would do everything I could to keep Keane out of it, though I knew he would fight me tooth and nail. They all would, but this wasn't their fight. It was mine.

Sighing, I rolled over and started to slide out of bed.

"And just where do you think you're going?"

I turned in surprise to find Keane's intense gaze boring into mine. "You were asleep..."

A grin tilted the corner of his mouth. "I was."

He reached out and pulled me back toward him. I resisted at first—not that it did any good—but then relented and let him pull me into his embrace. "Don't you need to get a few more hours of sleep?"

"Mmm, I have a much better use for the time."

I squeaked when he moved swiftly, pulling me until I was lying on top of him, my legs straddling his hips. Desire coiled tight in my belly at the feel of him beneath me, and I flexed my hips in response. He moaned, his hands on my waist tightening before one came up to tangle in my hair and pull my mouth to his.

I kissed him hungrily before sitting up and pulling my tank top over my head. Keane's breath hissed between his teeth as his large hands came up to cup my breasts. I moaned and threw my head back as his fingers roved over my skin, sliding myself slowly back and forth over his hard length.

Keane's hands slipped down to grip my hips, guiding my motions and pushing himself against me. He allowed me to have control for a bit before flipping me onto my back with a growl. "We need to get rid of these..." He hooked his fingers into the waistband of my shorts and quickly slid them down and out of the way while I did the same to his.

Lying next to me, he raised himself onto his elbow and placed his head in his hand. Then he slid his other hand down along my stomach before running his fingers lightly across my opening, teasing me. I sucked in a breath and squirmed, wanting him to touch me harder, deeper. He chuckled and slowly slipped a finger in, causing my hips to lift. He used his palm to press me onto the bed while he lowered his mouth to mine, nipping at my lips. "Easy, *ma moitié*. I want to pleasure you."

I lay back, panting as he slipped his finger back in and out before slowly circling it around my sensitive clit. I bit my lip to hold back my sounds of pleasure, unsure how thin the walls were here. My hands fisted in the sheets as he continued to torture me with slow, languid strokes. Keane leaned forward to suck on one of my nipples, driving the sensations running through me higher. His thumb stroked my clit harder while his finger slid smoothly in and out, rubbing against that sensitive spot inside. I squirmed as my control slipped, and I tried to hold back. But it was impossible. My orgasm came rushing forward, overtaking me.

As I fell over the edge, Keane took my lips in a searing kiss, taking my cries of pleasure into his mouth. I shook as the orgasm tore through me and held on to the bed tightly as Keane continued to stroke and caress me, dragging out the pleasure. When he finally stopped, I lay panting, my body covered in a fine sheen of sweat.

"Mmm." Keane pulled his finger out and put it to his lips, tasting me. "Never have I tasted anything so sweet." Turning me so my back was pressed against him, he lifted my leg slightly and slid his erection against my wet heat. I sucked in a breath as it slid over the sensitive flesh. "Now, it's my turn."

My back arched as he thrust inside me, filling every inch. One of his arms snaked around my waist while the other wrapped around my shoulders, holding me tightly against him. He turned my head back toward him, his fingers slipping lightly around my throat as he started to move in and out. His lips hovered at my ear, his deep voice urging me on with dark, erotic words.

The fire in my center quickly ignited again as he drove into me. I pressed back as he thrust forward, drawing him deeper and deeper inside. I felt another orgasm quickly approaching and clutched at the arms holding me tightly. He seemed to sense that I was near and picked up his pace. Our harsh breaths mingled, our bodies moving against one another, drawing the pleasure higher and higher, until it finally crested and crashed over the both of us.

I bit my lip hard to keep from crying out, drawing blood while he buried his head in my neck, his cries muffled against my skin. We both quaked from the force of it as we rode it out together. When the intense feelings finally ebbed, we lay pressed together, our sweat-slick bodies cooling in the breeze created by the overhead fan.

I sighed and looked over my shoulder at him. "You're right. That was a better use of our time."

Keane opened his eyes, a smile creasing the corners. "I told you so." He lifted himself, pushed my hair aside, and nuzzled my neck before placing small kisses down my shoulder.

I shuddered and quickly slipped out of his arms and off the bed before he could start things all over again. "It's time to get showered and find something to eat."

He grinned wolfishly at me. "Can I help you shower?"

I wagged a finger at him. "You behave yourself. I'm sure the others are already waiting for us." As he dove across the bed to no doubt grab me again, I ran into the en suite bathroom and shut the door, locking it.

I heard him laugh on the other side. "When has a lock ever stopped me?"

After *finally* getting showered and dressed, we made our way into the living area, where one corner had been cleared and a dining room table set up. A wide server sat next to the table, loaded with all kinds of breakfast foods. My stomach gave a loud growl.

Keane laughed behind me. "Better feed that thing before it eats someone." I swatted at him playfully as we walked up to join the others. I greeted everyone, noting we were the last to arrive.

"'Bout time you two got out of bed. I was about to send the search and rescue party." Sebastian had, obviously, made it back and was sitting at the far end of the long table, three full plates in front of him. I stared at the sheer amount of food. He just grinned.

Brokk stood and pulled out a chair for me. I thanked him as I sat. "Blue, I hope you don't mind, but s-someone has been most anxious to make your acquaintance. I invited her to dine with us."

I raised my brows but said nothing. Who here knew me? Just then, the elevator doors opened to reveal a short, petite woman with long, wavy blond hair and bright-blue eyes. She looked familiar in an I-know-you-but-don't kind of way. As soon as she entered the room, our eyes connected, hers flashing with anger.

Uh-oh.

"Ah, Cora! Welcome. Come on in." Brokk waved her forward.

Marching right up to the table, she stood next to my chair. "Are you Carolina?"

I nodded uncertainly, feeling the animosity practically pouring off her. Without saying another word, she reached out and slapped me hard across the face.

"Cora!" Brokk jumped to his feet.

I raised a hand to my cheek, more surprised than anything else, though it did sting a little. Keane had jumped to his feet the second she raised her hand and now had her bent over the table, arms pinned behind her back as he bared his teeth at her. She merely glowered.

"What the hell, Cora?" Her head jerked in Tristan's direction.

"Tristan? What are *you* doing here?"

I felt an odd stirring in my bond with Tristan and looked at him curiously.

He studiously avoided my gaze, instead focusing on Cora. "We're all here to help rescue your sister."

I turned surprised eyes on the woman. "You're Iridia's sister?" No wonder she looked so familiar.

Her fury-filled eyes snapped back to me. "Yes, not that it should matter to you." A deep hatred flowed from her to me, and I just shook my head in bewilderment. What had I ever done to this woman? I didn't even know her.

"Cora, this is disgraceful." Brokk tsk'd and shook his head. "I don't understand this behavior. Now, I'll allow Keane to let you up if you promise to conduct yourself more appropriately."

After a moment, she nodded, and Keane slowly let go of her, moving to stand between us. She still glared in my direction but didn't make another move toward me.

Brokk pulled out a chair for her, and she sat in it with a huff of annoyance. "What's going on here, Cora? Why are you acting this way?"

"Please tell me you lot don't believe she's who she says she is." When she didn't get a response, she looked around the table incredulously. "Are you all mad? How can this woman possibly be my sister's child?"

Instead of answering her question, Tristan asked one of his own. "What makes you think she isn't?"

Cora's gaze swung to him. "How can she be? We all know Brokk didn't impregnate her, and being that Aiden is a Warlock, he couldn't have. This girl just shows up out of nowhere, pretending she doesn't know who she is, claiming to be a part of the Grayson family, and *you* just believe her?"

Tristan smirked. "And *you* don't think there is any other way Iridia could have gotten pregnant?"

Cora rolled her eyes. "Unlike you, my sister doesn't sleep with every Tom, Dick, and Harry when the mood strikes and then drop them for the first pretty thing that walks by when she gets tired of them."

I looked between Cora and Tristan with renewed interest. The air practically vibrated from the tension flowing between them, and I wondered what the story was.

Tristan crossed his arms over his chest, ignoring her jab. "Your father is the one who verified Blue's parentage. There was even a DNA test done." Not to mention, I had already talked to my mother, but she didn't need to know that.

"My father has always believed his precious Iridia was off living some happily ever after somewhere with that worthless Warlock, Aiden. Obviously, he would believe whatever story she fed to him."

Tristan shook his head. "Why so doubtful? What has Blue ever done to you?"

"Everyone sings her praises. Says she's the greatest Grayson to ever live. Ha! If she was half as powerful as they claim, she would've already brought Iridia back." She turned her scorn-filled eyes toward me. "You think you have everyone fooled. But not me. I'll show the world who you truly are."

Keane spoke up for the first time, his gaze a dark red, belaying his calm exterior. "I have a feeling the reason you hate Blue so much has nothing to do with your sister or your disbelief in who Blue is and everything to do with the notoriety you managed to attain when Iridia disappeared. You were finally noticed, out from under your little sister's shadow, and seen for your abilities. But then Blue came along, and people stopped talking about the oldest Grayson daughter once again. There was a new Grayson on the rise, one more powerful than anyone they had ever seen before—or probably will after."

"Nonsense." Her voice wavered a bit in the face of Keane's penetrating stare. "She's nothing but an imposter, and I'll prove it." She quickly got to her feet and, with one last glare in my direction, stomped back to the elevator. It opened as soon as she called it, and she disappeared into its depths.

At first, no one spoke, but then Brokk sighed heavily. "I'm s-sorry about that, Blue. Had I known her intentions, I never would've let her come here."

I waved him off. "It's not your fault. Cora obviously has some issues she needs to deal with. Once we have Iridia here, she'll have to face the truth."

After eating, we cleared the table and used it to lay out our maps and graphs. We showed Brokk what we had come up with and what Riona had pointed out for us so far. I also told him what I could remember about the area from when I was a child.

"My gut is telling me it's somewhere here on the outskirts of the Blackwater River State Forest." I pointed to a spot on the map.

Brokk seemed to consider. "It's possible. That's a very remote area. There aren't any trails or anything that run through that section. But there's also the De Soto National Forest, and the Talladega National Forest nearby. They all contain some of the same things you're describing."

I let out a frustrated breath. That was a lot of area to cover. "Do you still have anything of Iridia's that might contain her scent for the trackers? I know it's been a long time..."

Brokk nodded and turned, taking Nick's hand. "Yes, we've kept her things preserved magically and have sent out trackers periodically over the years in an attempt to locate her. I never gave up hope that she was still out there and alive."

I couldn't figure out the relationship between Brokk and Iridia. I knew it was a political match, but listening to him talk, it seemed like more. Iridia hadn't seemed quite as attached, but love came in all forms. While the men continued to talk, I noticed Sebastian sitting in the corner by himself, sipping on a glass of something. I went over and sat next to him.

"Any luck on the reconnaissance front?"

"Perhaps. Something feels...off about certain areas. I think your instincts about the Blackwater River State Forest are correct."

I nodded as we watched Brokk and Nick hand out items for the trackers to use. After a moment, I turned to Sebastian.

"Bast..."

"Uh-oh, the nickname is out. Should I be concerned?"

I laughed softly while shaking my head. "Do you think I stand a chance against Hades?"

"In what capacity?"

I shrugged. "After we rescue Iridia and Aiden, I'll have to stand up to him. It's inevitable."

"My little enigmatic Fairy. I believe you can overcome anything you set your mind to. You just need to have confidence in yourself. I've told you that before."

I laughed shortly. "I remember. When we infiltrated Poseidon's castle to rescue Allison. And look how that turned out—with my getting my ass handed to me and then almost dying."

"You accomplished what you set out to do, didn't you?"

"With a few setbacks."

"Nobody's perfect. Except me, perhaps." I arched an eyebrow at him, and he laughed, his hair turning black and his eyes taking on a red glow. "Practically perfect anyway."

"Okay, Mary Poppins."

"Cheeky."

We both grinned at each other before I stood to join the other group. Sebastian reached out a hand to stop me as I was stepping away. "Blue, be careful, won't you? I have a feeling Hades knows you're close. If it weren't for him being tied to his castle, he would probably be waiting for you the minute you stepped foot outside the Fairy wards."

"That's what I have you for, isn't it?" I grinned down at him. "You coming?"

He shook his head. "I have another lead I need to follow up on."

I stared at him, my smile slipping a bit. "Don't do anything stupid, okay?"

He smiled, flashing his exceptionally white teeth. "Aww, is that concern I hear in your voice?"

I rolled my eyes and turned away, his laughter trailing after me. I joined the others just as they were splitting up the areas they wanted to search tonight. Keane took the lead and issued orders.

"We're going to stick close to the territory at first. No reason to let on exactly what we're doing in case Hades is watching. Keep alert for any type of magical activity—no matter how small it might seem. I'm sure Hades has some type of wards or a cloaking spell on the area where he's hiding Iridia. Everyone imprinted on the scent?" At their nods, Keane clapped his hand on Cedric's shoulder. "I want you to stick with us."

Cedric glanced at me. "You got it."

With that, the teams broke up and headed toward the elevator to get started. Brokk and Nick would stay behind to keep communication lines open for each team to report in. They had tacked a large map to one wall with areas indicated in different colors so they could mark them off as we went.

I double-checked my gear, making sure my gun was loaded and my daggers were secure. I watched Keane do the same. Then I turned to Cedric. Unlike us, Cedric had no weapons on him and was only wearing a pair of sweatpants and a plain T-shirt. I winked at him. "Ready to wolf out?"

"You've been dying to say that, haven't you." He grinned and handed me a small backpack. "For my clothes and some supplies." I nodded and quickly strapped the bag around my shoulders. I looked for Tristan. He was standing near the elevator, seeming deep in thought. I wondered if it had anything to do with Cora. He'd been exceedingly distracted since the woman's appearance earlier. I was about to head toward him when I felt a hand on my shoulder. I turned to find Nick there.

"Good luck, Blue. I hope you find her."

I smiled. "Thanks. I do, too." I patted his hand before stepping away. As I looked up, I caught Tristan's hard glare at Nick and almost laughed. I had a feeling him seeing Nick coming out of my room the morning after we got here might have put the wrong idea into his mind. I shook my head with a smile and followed Keane to the elevator.

Chapter Nineteen

Keane opened a portal as soon as we exited the theater and took us to our first location in the Blackwater River State Forest. Once the quiet of the woods surrounded us, Cedric went behind a tree and stripped out of his clothes, quickly shifting into his Wolf form.

Just as I had once surmised, his Wolf was a white blond, the same as his hair color in his human form. Picking up his clothes in his mouth, he brought them over to me, and I stuffed them into the backpack before straightening.

"All right, Wolf boy. You're up. Time to put that sniffer to good use."

He chuffed at me, almost like he was laughing, but took the lead. As we followed, I idly wondered what it would be like to shift into a Wolf. Would it be as freeing as that one glimpse Larkin's Wolf had shown me? Shaking off my thoughts, I focused back on the area around me. None of it looked or felt familiar.

"This isn't it." I stopped and put my hands on my hips.

Tristan looked at me in surprise, but not without a little bit of doubt. "Are you sure? We haven't even gone far."

I knew that differentiating one forest from another might seem impossible to some, but I was pretty sure I'd be able to tell when we got to the right place. "Yes. This isn't it."

Not even questioning it, Keane opened a new portal amid Tristan's protests, and we moved to the next area. It was the same: not right. Tristan, still not believing I'd be able to tell so fast, had Cedric sweep the area this time before we moved on.

"Seriously, Blue, what if he purposefully changed the area you were in with magic so you wouldn't be able to identify it later? We need to be thorough."

I rolled my eyes, hating the waste of time, and plopped down on a log to wait. His lack of faith in me was annoying, and as strong as the emotion was, I had a feeling he could sense it. I knew Keane certainly could, given the smirk on his face. I managed to sit still for all of five minutes before I was back up and pacing the area, the persistent itch I felt between my shoulder blades telling me we needed to move on. I knew we weren't anywhere near where we needed to be—it was all wrong.

Tristan watched me pace for a minute before grunting in annoyance. "Blue, sit down. It should only take Cedric a few more minutes to circle the whole area. You're wearing me out just watching you." I gave him the side-eye and continued pacing. He really didn't know me well if he thought I could sit quietly for any length of time.

Keane leaned casually against one of the trees with his arms crossed over his chest. "What's the deal with you and Cora?"

Now, *that* piqued my interest. I turned just as Tristan tensed, glancing at me. He cleared his throat. "It's nothing of consequence."

"I wouldn't call the way you two were going at each other nothing. There is obviously some deep-seated history there."

Tristan grimaced. "We do share a past, but it's just that, something that happened in the past and is over with. Cora went her way, and I went mine."

I pursed my lips and glanced at Keane. "I believe he doth protest a bit too much."

Keane chuckled and nodded. "That he does."

"It's nothing, I tell you." He let out a frustrated breath at my disbelieving stare. "Fine. Cora and I were in a relationship when we were young—before Riona—but things ended on a sour note."

"Did she dump you, or did you dump her?"

Tristan's brow drew down in a frown. It didn't seem like he would answer, but then he let his breath out in a rush. "She dumped me."

"And from the commentary earlier, it was because of...cheating?"

"I did *not* cheat on her."

"I didn't say you did." I pulled my bottom lip between my teeth in thought, snagging his attention. Keane reached over and used his thumb to pull it out. Tristan looked away at the intimacy.

"She believed otherwise. She thought—obviously still thinks—that I cheated on her with Riona." He seemed to withdraw into his memories, and I felt the regret coming off him. Before he could say anything further, Cedric came trotting up. Clearing his throat, Tristan looked at Cedric. "Find anything?" Cedric shook his head.

"Are you satisfied now?" I looked at Tristan, and he nodded.

"Good, let's move on."

We spent the rest of the evening hopping from one area to the next. Each time, I could tell right away that it wasn't right, but Tristan insisted I wait while Cedric did a sweep. My patience was wearing thin, and Cedric was starting to drag by the time we finished covering the areas marked out on the map.

"I think we should call it a day," Tristan announced when Cedric returned from his last sweep.

You could see the exhaustion in Cedric's eyes, and I patted the spot next to me on the ground. He came over and lay down, his tongue lolling. "Want some water?" He nodded his shaggy head. I dug around in the backpack he'd given me and found a bottle and a collapsible bowl. Pouring the water into the bowl, I set it in front of him. He drank thirstily—and messily.

Shaking my head with a smile, I got to my feet. The itch I had felt before flared up between my shoulder blades again. I rolled my shoulders, trying to work it out. We were missing something. I just knew it. Closing my eyes, I retraced my memories as a child. I examined every tree, leaf, and mound of dirt I could, hoping there would be a landmark or something we could go by. It felt like I was forgetting something, like a memory that hadn't come back to me. Warm hands started massaging my shoulders, and I opened my eyes to look up at Keane.

"Don't force it, *ma moitié*. We'll find it."

My shoulders sagged, and I nodded. "I know. It's just frustrating."

He leaned over and kissed my temple. "Are you ready to head back?"

I looked over at Cedric, whose eyes were closed. He appeared to be sleeping. "Yeah. I suppose we should. I'm sure everyone could use a bite to eat and a good day's rest."

After Cedric had changed back into his human form and gotten dressed, Keane opened the portal back to the alleyway by the theater. I was curious why we couldn't just portal in and out of the building like we did at Dock Street, but I was sure there was a perfectly good explanation.

Keane looked over and winked at me. "I just haven't had time to establish a path through Brokk's wards."

When we got back to Brokk's living quarters, we found all the teams back. Looking at the map on the wall, I saw that no one had managed to find anything. I shook my head in frustration and went over to the sideboard to grab a plate of food.

Nick came up beside me. "Rough day?"

I looked over at him. "Just frustrating."

He reached over and smoothed the frown lines between my brows. "Hey, it was only the first day. You'll find it."

I smiled appreciatively.

Suddenly, a body moved between us, forcing Nick to step back. It was Tristan. "Excuse me." He grabbed one of the rolls from the tray in front of us before walking off to the table.

Nick stared after him. "I don't think he likes me too much."

I laughed shortly. "I think he just has the wrong idea about our relationship."

Nick's eyebrows rose. "What?"

I sighed. "He saw you coming out of my bedroom the other day and has been acting weird ever since."

"Are you two...together, too?"

I shook my head with a smile. "Not like that. He's actually my twin flame. So, we're connected, but not in a romantic sense."

"What's a twin flame?

"Essentially, twin flames are two halves of one soul."

"That has to be a close bond. You're very lucky to have found him, but...how does that work with Keane?"

"Keane is my soulmate."

"Wait. What's the difference between a twin flame and a soulmate?"

"While twin flames are part of one soul, soulmates are two separate, linked souls."

"That sounds...complicated."

"Heh, that's putting it mildly. It's all pretty new, too. So, we haven't really had time to work out all the specifics yet."

"While on the one hand, I'm jealous, on the other, I don't think I envy you trying to navigate that mess."

I barked out a laugh and gave him a light punch on the shoulder. "Thanks, Nick."

He grinned, and we both took our plates back to the table. Nick sat next to Brokk while I sat next to Keane. Tristan looked suspiciously between us, and I sighed. I really needed to pull him aside before he said or did something stupid.

⁓ e l e ⁓

The next evening, we were in another part of the forest, going through the same steps as before and still finding nothing. The itch between my shoulders had finally subsided but I was still feeling on edge, so while Cedric was doing his final sweep, I decided to take a little walk by myself.

"I'll be right back. I'm just going to walk around a bit while we wait."

Keane nodded in understanding while Tristan frowned in my direction. "Do you think that's wise, considering who's looking for you?"

I just shook my head and moved off into the forest, not bothering to answer him. As I did, I heard Keane stop Tristan. "Leave her be. I'll know if she's in trouble."

"I can feel her through our bond, too, you know."

"Yes. I'm quite aware, but your connection is different from mine. I feel everything she feels."

"Fat lot of good it did you in the past."

I heard Keane grumble, causing a smile to slide across my lips. Moving deeper into the forest, their voices became nothing but a low hum until, finally, I couldn't even hear that anymore. Taking a deep breath, I let it out slowly, trying to relieve some of the tension building in my core. I'd thought this would be the easy part of freeing Iridia, but it was proving much more difficult than I imagined.

I continued to walk as if something was drawing me forward until I heard the tinkling sound of water. Emerging from the tree line, I found the small stream we had come across earlier. I sat by its edge, leaning back on my elbows and stretching my legs out in front of me. Dropping my head back, I felt myself relaxing as a breeze started to blow, and the peacefulness of the forest seeped into my soul. The only sound was the burbling of the water and the soft scrape of the leaves in the trees as they moved against each other.

As I lay there, I unexpectedly felt another presence in my consciousness. It seemed to be peering out through my eyes—Larkin's Wolf. Instead of pushing him down, I allowed him to move in closer. I had to admit that I was curious. I had never tried to shapeshift into an animal before and wondered if I would even be able to.

I could feel the beast's excitement as I considered letting him out. He pushed against my consciousness as if encouraging me. I knew if something went wrong, Keane would come. With a bit of trepidation, I allowed the Wolf to move to the front of my mind. Slowly, I felt the change start. I gasped as the pain of it began sliding through my body—bones breaking and shifting, rearranging themselves. My face elongated, and my jaw snapped and moved.

The pain ripped a scream from my throat, but it quickly turned into a howl. I started shaking. It felt like the change went on for hours, but it was actually over in a matter of minutes. Opening my eyes, I blinked, everything appearing in monochrome. My senses were in overdrive: I could see things more sharply and smell a thousand more things than before. Looking around, I realized Keane and Tristan were now standing a few feet from me. Keane appeared amused while Tristan was awestruck, watching as I slowly gained my feet—or paws, in this case.

"Did she just shapeshift into a Wolf? How is that even possible? Shifters aren't the same as Fairies or Vaimpír. Their animal forms don't come from magic. They're a separate spirit that joins with theirs."

Keane looked down at Tristan. "There are some things you aren't yet ready to learn. Just go with it."

Larkin's Wolf—who I now knew was named Gareth—urged me to run. *"Come, Fairy, let me show you the freedom of being a Wolf."*

I looked toward Keane, who nodded in understanding. It seemed he could read Gareth's thoughts, as well. I let out a yip and allowed Gareth to take over our body. He immediately took off into the forest, leaving Tristan's shout of dismay behind. We ran hard and fast, deftly dodging between the foliage and over fallen trees. I sensed Cedric nearby a few times, but Gareth easily avoided him—almost like we were playing hide and seek. After an hour, Gareth finally began to slow, and we started to make our way back to the others.

"You may want to shift back before we get to the others if you don't want Cedric to see us."

Just as I was about to answer, a familiar scent floated toward us. I stopped and inhaled deeply, my eyes widening. I knew that smell. It was what I remembered from my childhood. I charged forward, finding

Cedric in his human form—his very naked human form—talking adamantly with Keane and Tristan.

"I'm telling you guys, I know that animal's scent. I've smelled it before. I just can't seem to place it."

Before either man could answer, I skidded to a halt next to them, causing Cedric to jump back with a yelp. "What the hell!?"

"What is it, Blue?"

"Blue?" Cedric looked in shock, glancing between me and Keane, but we both ignored him.

"I smelled it, Keane! The scent from my childhood memories. What I associated with my home."

"Where?"

"I'm not sure exactly, somewhere along the water. Gareth said he will help."

Keane nodded and turned to the other two men. I idly wondered if Cedric realized he was still naked. My eyes naturally wandered down, and I had to say...I was impressed.

"Oy, that's my pup you're ogling."

I laughed mentally. *"Sorry, couldn't help myself. Curiosity killed the cat, you know."*

"I guess it's a good thing you're a Wolf, then." He continued to grumble, but I heard the amusement in his thoughts. It was so weird having another spirit within my body—one with his own thoughts and feelings. *"Think how I feel being you're a woman."*

With another laugh, I focused back on the men. Cedric had shifted back into his Wolf form while Keane leaned down and ran his hand through my fur. "Lead the way, *ma moitié.*"

I nodded and turned to follow the water. The scent had been carried on the wind from upstream somewhere, so that meant the glen had to be magically shielded, just like Keane and Tristan predicted.

We followed along the water's edge for another hour before I picked up the scent again. Stopping, I lifted my nose. Pacing back and forth, I tried to figure out the direction it was coming from but couldn't seem to find it.

"It's here somewhere."

Keane turned to Tristan. "Looks like you're up, Your Majesty. Blue said the scent is coming from somewhere close, but she can't pinpoint its exact location."

Tristan nodded and closed his eyes. His lips began moving in some type of incantation or spell, and he raised his arms out to his sides. I felt the energy flowing off him in waves. It was like a pulse pushing against the air. Nothing happened at first, but then an area across the river seemed to shiver. Like his energy bursts were hitting something solid. We all looked at that spot, and Tristan turned so he could concentrate on it.

The more energy he pushed toward it, the harder the ripple. I felt it before it happened. The air seemed to freeze, almost like time had stopped, but only for a few seconds before a loud explosion tore through the forest, throwing us all back. The power that reverberated through the air caused me to shift back, and while not as painful as the first time, it was still no walk in the park. I lay panting on the ground beneath Keane, where he had thrown himself over me.

"Are you all right, *ma moitié?*" He looked down at me urgently, his hands roving over my body, which thankfully was still fully clothed. I wondered why I could maintain my clothes when I shifted while Cedric couldn't. Speaking of Cedric, he had shifted back, too. I grabbed the backpack from where Keane had dropped it and threw it at him.

"I'm fine. What happened?" I looked around but couldn't see past the smoke and debris littering the area around us.

"Tristan broke through the barrier that was shielding the place where Hades is keeping Iridia and Aiden."

"Tristan!" I realized that I didn't see him. "Where is he?" I scrambled from under Keane and ran to where I had last seen him. He lay on the ground, unmoving. "Tristan!" I carefully turned him over and saw blood covering his chest. "Keane!"

Keane knelt beside Tristan, placing his hand over his chest. "He has quite a bit of internal damage. The barrier Hades put on the glen must have ricocheted back and poured into him." Keane quickly bit his wrist and put it to Tristan's lips. He didn't stir. "Tilt his head so the blood runs down his throat." I did as he asked, my heart in my throat. When Keane seemed satisfied, he turned and opened a portal before reaching down and lifting Tristan off the ground. "We need to get him back to the theater. He's going to need several doses of blood to heal."

With one last glance back at the opening Tristan had created, I followed Keane and Cedric through the portal. I hoped it would still be there when we got back. I didn't want Tristan to have to break through it again.

Chapter Twenty

Tristan lay unconscious for the next two days.

Brokk had put a rotation of guards in place at the entrance to Hades' hidden land so no unsuspecting persons could accidentally wander into it. I knew that we needed to move forward with our plans as soon as possible before Hades realized we were there, but I couldn't seem to bring myself to go while Tristan still hadn't woken up.

I was sitting next to his bed, his still hand in mine, when the door to his room opened and Cora of all people walked in. She came up short when she saw me, and I raised my eyebrows. "What are you doing here?"

She tossed her head and glared at me. "I'm a talented healer. Brokk thought I might be able to help bring Tristan out of his coma."

I narrowed my eyes at her. "And why should we trust you? You could be hell-bent on doing him more harm for revenge."

Cora rolled her eyes. "I'd never hurt him."

"Why should I believe anything you say after your little performance the other night?"

Cora took a deep breath and stepped farther into the room. "Look, I may not like you, and I may be mad at him, but I'm a healer first and foremost. I would never use my powers to harm someone."

I stared at her distrustfully but finally relented when I took in her open expression. "Fine, but any sign of funny business and what I do to you will be worse than death."

She seemed about to issue a retort but then shook her head. "Fine." Walking over to Tristan's other side, she pulled the sheet down and laid her hands on his bare chest. Her lips moved as she whispered the words of her spell, causing a soft, blue light to emanate from her hands. It seemed to encompass Tristan's entire body before winking out of existence. She stumbled back a bit, her hand going to her head. I started to stand, but she waved me away. "I'm okay." Slowly, she sank back into the chair situated behind her.

I opened my mouth to say something but then heard Tristan groan. I was on my feet instantly. "Tristan?"

His eyes fluttered before finally opening. "Bl...Blue?" His voice was hoarse, and I reached for the glass of water on his bedside table. Lifting his head, I helped him drink some. He coughed a bit but then settled back. "Wha...what happened?"

I glanced at Cora before looking back at him. "You broke Hades' barrier. Keane seems to think it ricocheted into you."

"How long have I been out?"

"Two days."

A grimace crossed his face. "I take it the bloodsucker fed me his blood?"

A slow grin split my face. "How'd you guess?"

"Mmm...I seem to have this sudden desire to be near him."

I laughed lightly and shook my head. "He'll be by later. You can thank him then."

Tristan groaned, a hand going to his head. "I feel like I just got stampeded by a herd of bulls in Pamplona."

"That's oddly specific. Have some personal experience with that, do you?"

"Mmph."

"He tried running with the bulls one time. It didn't end well." At the sound of her voice, Tristan's eyes jerked toward Cora.

"What are you doing here?"

He tried to sit, and I pushed him back. "Shh, she's just here to help."

"I don't want her here."

I saw Cora's expression flash with hurt before she hid it behind a cold smile. "Don't worry, I was just on my way out, Your Majesty." She gave a low, mocking bow and left the room, slamming the door behind her.

"That went well."

"Why ever did you let her in here?"

I just shook my head, refusing to argue with him. "Time for you to get some rest."

"Why do I need more rest if I've been unconscious for two days?" He started to push the covers back.

"Ah, ah, ah. You're staying in bed if I have to spell you to it. Keane said you need to be here for at least another few days to continue healing properly."

Tristan glowered at me. "You're not going in to get Iridia without me, are you?"

Just then, the door opened, and Brokk walked in, saving me from having to answer. "Ah, Tristan! You're finally awake. Excellent." He moved to the chair Cora had vacated.

I leaned over and kissed Tristan on the forehead. "I'll be back later to check on you. Stay put."

"Blue...Blue!"

I ignored him and slipped out the door with a smile. Men, they could be so stubborn.

"Are you in love with him?"

I looked over to see Cora leaning against the far wall. I gave her a faint smile. "Not that it's any of your business, but yes, I love him..." Her shoulders seemed to deflate. "However, I'm not *in* love with him." I walked away without saying anything else. Let her chew on that.

I moved quietly down the hall and entered the living area. The lights were low as the others had gone to bed. I went over to what I was sure was a magical sideboard and lifted the lid on one of the trays. Sure enough, a plate containing a cheeseburger and fries sat underneath. My stomach grumbled. Just what the doctor ordered. I hadn't eaten much since we'd brought Tristan back. Now that he was awake, my appetite seemed to have returned.

"I hope you're going to share that." I almost dropped the plate in surprise. Squinting, I finally made out the figure of Sebastian sitting at the far end of the table in a darkened corner.

"Bast. You scared the hell out of me. What are you doing skulking around out here?"

I moved toward him with the plate in my hand, not sure if I would share or not. I mean, Sebastian usually ate enough to feed a small army. He'd probably eat the whole thing if I offered him a bite. As I got closer, I could finally make out his features and almost dropped the plate again.

"What happened to you?" Sebastian was a mass of bruises and cuts from his face to his bare chest and arms. Some of them looked like claw marks. "Bast?" My voice trembled a bit.

He grunted and pulled himself out of the shadows. "Nothing to worry about. Just got into a bit of a scuffle."

"A scuffle? Bast—"

He held up his hand, and I pressed my lips together to stop the tide of words. "Hades knows you're here. He sent a few of his hounds out to see if they could get to you. As your protector, I couldn't let that happen."

I sucked in a breath. "This happened because of me?"

Sebastian reached over, picked up my burger, and took a huge bite. "Not my first choice, but it could be worse."

"Oh, Bast..."

"Uh-uh. That's my job, remember? But it also means you guys need to get a move on with whatever it is you plan to do. I think I scared them off for a while, but there is no doubt they'll be back." He reached over and picked up some of the fries. "Mmm. Okay, I take back what I said. This is exactly what I needed."

"I'll call Keane, he can heal you..."

"No thanks. The last thing I need is more of that kind of blood running through my veins. I have a hard enough time with that side of me as it is. Don't worry. Some food and a good day's rest, and I'll be right as rain, love." I watched as he polished off the rest of the burger and fries, not saying a word. I'd lost my appetite. Once he was done eating, he stood and put a hand on my shoulder. "None of this is your fault, Blue. It's Hades'. Remember that." He limped toward the bedrooms while I remained at the table. That was two people who had been severely injured because of me. Contrary to what Sebastian said, it was my fault. This needed to end. Now.

Looking toward the bedroom, I listened carefully to make sure no one was up and about before slipping quietly into the elevator. Thankfully, due to Keane using so much blood to heal Tristan, he was in a sleep stasis again, so he wouldn't feel me slipping away. I just had to hope Ethereal Mutation was still on patrol, or this would be a short trip.

I checked for the weapons hidden in my gear, glad I hadn't changed out of it yet. Once I reached the top floor, I quickly used an invisibility spell to slip past the guards Brokk had stationed around the building. While that little trick didn't make me physically invisible, it did make me undetectable to others—more like a shadow.

I quickly made my way to the back alley where Keane created his portals, making sure no one else was nearby. I hadn't tried to open a portal yet, but I was pretty sure I could. I'd watched Keane do it more than enough times at this point.

Closing my eyes, I visualized where I wanted to go before saying the words Keane used. I felt the power race down my arm. When I opened my eyes, the blue outline of a door stood before me. Reaching out, I opened it and let out a sigh of relief. Beyond was the forest, the opening to Hades' land not far away. Stepping through, I closed the door behind me.

"Who goes there?" I jumped a bit at the voice. Dammit. I had forgotten about Brokk's guards. Maintaining my invisibility spell, I crept up behind the two men. Reaching into my core, I quickly manipulated my magic and created a sleeping spell. The last thing I needed was for these two to raise the alarm. Blowing on my hand like something was on it, I watched as a pink mist coated the two guards. They blinked heavily before slowly crumpling to the ground. That should keep them out for a while. At least long enough for me to do what I came to do.

Turning, I slowly walked into the glen I had grown up in. I gazed around, taking it all in. It looked just like it had in my memories. Like not even a day had gone by. The trees, the mounds of dirt, and the smell—that wet moss and pine scent. I breathed it in, taking a moment to prepare myself for what was to come.

On one final exhale, I summoned him. "Scythe."

Almost immediately, a portal opened, and he appeared before me. *"You called, Mistress?"*

"Scythe, is Hades still powerless here?"

"Yes, Mistress."

"Good. Can you bring him to me? I want to make a deal."

"As you wish, Mistress."

He disappeared into a new portal, and I sat on an old log to wait. I didn't know how long it would be or if Hades would even come. Though I had a feeling he couldn't resist.

As I waited, the sun slowly rose over the treetops, casting brilliant yellow and orange across the landscape. It had been a while since I'd watched a sunrise due to shifting to the Vaimpír's night schedule.

"A beautiful sight, isn't it?"

I turned my head to see Hades lounging against one of the nearby trees. He was dressed impeccably in another black suit, his hair perfectly slicked back, and his features composed, not giving anything away. A much different vision than the last time I had seen him.

"It is, indeed." I stood and faced him while he took the few steps that brought us toe-to-toe.

"I see you managed to find your way home, little one. Not that I had any doubt. To what do I owe this joyous little reunion?"

"I'm ready to accept your deal."

"And what deal is that?"

"If I come to you of my own free will, you'll release Iridia and Aiden."

"Really?" He eyed me shrewdly. "What changed your mind?"

"It doesn't matter. Take it or leave it."

"Mmm, I'd be a fool not to take it." He looked toward Scythe. "Go and bring my *guests*, won't you?"

"*Yes, Master.*"

I watched as Scythe disappeared yet again. "You surprise me, Blue."

"Why is that?"

"I figured you would find a way around this—giving yourself up and all. I expected a bit more of a fight from you."

"I guess I'm just full of surprises."

"Indeed."

He watched me carefully until Scythe returned through the portal, Iridia and Aiden in tow.

"Blue! What are you doing?" My mother quickly moved to stand between Hades and me. Turning toward Hades she pointed her finger at him. "If you harm so much as one hair—"

Hades held up a hand. "Silence." My mother was immediately rendered mute.

I frowned but didn't argue. "Our bargain?"

Hades looked at Iridia and Aiden and spread his arms wide. "Good news! You're free to go." He indicated the two sleeping guards. "I'm sure if you wake those two up, they'll be happy to escort you home."

He started to push them toward the guards when I cleared my throat. His eyes swung to mine in inquiry. "The god's blood bond? You need to release it first."

A sly grin spread over his face. "Ah, yes. Know about that, do you?" I arched a brow. "Of course, of course. Umm, since I don't seem to have any powers on this side of things, you'll have to do the honors." His look turned calculating. "That is if you know how."

I nodded with a sigh. Thankfully, I'd had Poseidon show me how it worked and how to release it—just in case. Being that we didn't have anywhere I could draw the rune I needed, I burned a circle in the grass in front of us and then found a stick. I quickly sketched the rune, which turned out to be the same one I had created as a child in my first memory.

Spreading my hands, I reached down into my center to the gold ball of magic there. I manipulated it until I had what I needed. As I pushed the magic out, the rune seemed to etch itself into the ground before it glowed a pulsing red.

"Mom, you first." She shook her head vehemently, but Aiden just pushed her into the circle. This earned him a glare, to which he just shrugged. "Give me your hand, please." When she finally placed her hand in mine, I took one of the small daggers from my side and sliced a thin cut in the center of her palm. She flinched but stayed silent.

I made a small cut on my finger with the tip of the dagger, massaging a few drops of blood onto her open palm to mix with hers. I then reached out for Hades' hand. He initially pulled back, but after a glare from me, followed by a smirk from him, gave it to me. I sliced a cut into his palm, placing it over hers. "By the blood of a god, from the blood of a god, I release you from your bond." Heat blossomed between their clasped hands before Hades dropped his. Iridia slumped a bit as if a weight had been lifted from her shoulders.

She looked at me wide-eyed. "You did it."

"Yay." Hades sarcastically twirled his finger in the air.

I just ignored him and indicated for Aiden to step onto the rune. I followed the same steps, and soon, he was released from the god's blood bond, too.

"Well...now that all theatrics are over, it's time for you two to leave."

"Not without our daughter." Aiden tried to step toward Hades, but Iridia held him back.

"Oh, I'm sorry, but she made a deal. Her for you. I rather think I got the better end of this. Don't worry, I'll take good care of her." He wrapped his arm around my shoulders, pulling me back against him.

Before I could react, Aiden leapt forward with one of my knives in his hand. He stabbed it into the arm Hades held me with. Hades immediately dropped me with a curse, and Aiden pushed me toward my mother.

"Go. Get out of here." He raised his hands, a green glow in each of them. I sensed the spells were deadly, though I had no idea if they would have any effect on a god.

"Are you sure you want to do this, Warlock?" Hades eyed him in anger before pulling the knife from his arm and dropping it to the ground. I watched as his skin knit back together.

"I won't let you have my daughter. I will fight you for her."

"So be it." A creature appeared next to him. It was enormous, and while humanoid in shape, covered in thick scales with claws instead of fingers and a long tail with deadly-looking spikes. It growled an inhuman sound, saliva dripping from its mouth as it unhinged its jaw to reveal rows of shark-like teeth. I took an involuntary step back. It was a Cythraul. One of Hades' deadliest warriors. "Defeat my best warrior, and you can take your daughter and go."

"Stop!" I tried to step in front of Aiden, but he just pushed me back. I snarled from behind him. "We made a deal, Hades."

Hades looked at me dispassionately. "He tried to kill me. That nullifies any agreement we made for his life." His gaze moved from me back to Aiden. "What do you say, Warlock? Do you agree to my deal?"

I tugged on Aiden's arm. "Don't. You have no idea what you're up against."

Aiden ignored me. "I do."

"Excellent."

"Mom, we have to do something." I glanced over at her before my gaze returned to the two men. Well, man and creature.

"Don't worry, your father may look like a scholar, but he's a trained warrior. He was once one of the best in our legion."

Without preamble, the creature manifested a long spear. Twirling it around from hand to hand and around its body, it took a step forward. Aiden, in turn, manifested a deadly-looking sword. I watched, horrified, as they charged each other. Sparks flew from where their weapons collided. The Cythraul swiped its tail around, and Aiden jumped, narrowly avoiding the spikes. He spun back and thrust his sword, the tip piercing the leather armor the Cythraul wore.

The creature released a howl of rage and raised its spear, cracking Aiden across the ribs. Aiden grunted and fell back, his breath knocked from him. The Cythraul quickly followed with another flick of its tail, which caught Aiden in the knees, swiping his feet out from under him. Aiden went down hard with the Cythraul's spear coming straight for his heart. Aiden rolled to the side in a lightning-quick move, narrowly missing the sharpened tip. He quickly gained his feet and threw out a momentum spell, knocking the weapon from the Cythraul's clawed fists.

The spear flew through the air, landing on the ground a few feet away. Instead of going for it, the Cythraul ran straight for Aiden, dodging the spells that Aiden threw his way. I had a feeling that magic would do little good against this creature.

When the Cythraul was close, he swiped out with his claws, catching Aiden across the chest. Aiden cried out in pain but didn't back off. Turning in a quick circle, he kicked out, catching the Cythraul in the shoulder and throwing him off balance. Aiden immediately thrust his blade out, catching the Cythraul deep in the thigh. The creature shrieked as blood poured from the wound before it twisted sharply away, the move pulling the sword from Aiden's grip and flinging it.

Aiden dove onto the Cythraul, pulling a dagger from somewhere on his person. He attempted to thrust it through the creature's heart, but it managed to get its feet between them and kicked Aiden across the forest floor. Aiden landed, rolling over several times.

As luck would have it, he landed right next to his sword. He picked it up and charged the Cythraul, who had also recovered his weapon. They continued to dance and weave around each other, the clanging of metal ringing through the forest as their weapons connected, blow after blow. Aiden managed to land several hits on the Cythraul, his blade slicing easily through the creature's thick scales.

I had to wonder if his sword was magically enhanced.

They were both covered in blood, and I could tell they were weakening. As their weapons collided once again, the Cythraul took advantage of Aiden's uneven footing and hooked its leg around the back of Aiden's, causing him to crash to the ground. Aiden grabbed the Cythraul's ankle and pulled it down with him. Swinging himself over, he straddled the creature.

The Cythraul fought with all its strength as they rolled over and over in the dirt. It was hard to see what was happening, but at one point, Aiden screamed in pain. When they finally stopped, Aiden had the upper hand. Before the creature could get loose, he raised his sword high above his head and brought it down, impaling the Cythraul through the heart. The creature froze, its eyes going wide before its body went limp.

He had done it! Aiden had defeated the Cythraul. I couldn't believe it. I watched as Aiden rose unsteadily to his feet, and the Cythraul burst into flames, leaving nothing but ash behind.

Aiden turned to Hades. "Our bargain?" he rasped out.

"That was an unexpected turn of events, to be sure." Hades paused, seeming thoughtful before continuing. "But I'm a man of my word." He turned to me with a smile on his face. "Your freedom has been won, little one. But I wonder if the cost will be worth it?" His smile turned cruel, and my brows furrowed. What had he done? "I'll see you again very soon, make no mistake. This is but a temporary reprieve."

With that, he turned with his hellhounds and stepped through the portal they opened, disappearing into the darkness before it, too, disappeared. I stood there, staring at the spot he had left, before I heard Iridia cry out.

Turning quickly, I saw that Aiden had collapsed to the ground. I ran over to her, cursing. "He's lost a lot of blood. We need to get him back quickly." Closing my eyes, I opened a portal that would take us back to the theater. As soon as I did, I saw Keane standing on the other side—a very angry Keane. I grimaced, knowing I was in for a severe talking-to later, but now was not the time to worry about it. "Keane! Help. Aiden lost a lot of blood."

Keane came running through the portal and quickly surveyed the area. "Where's Hades?"

"Gone."

He nodded and scooped Aiden up, carrying him to the theater. As soon as Iridia came into sight, all the guards scurried in surprise, bowing low. "Yo-Your Majesty!"

She waved them away. "Take us to my husband immediately."

"Yes, Your Majesty."

Our small group quickly made our way to Brokk's living quarters. Aiden was still alive, but his breathing was getting shallower and shallower. I didn't think he had much time left. Keane walked straight to one of the bedrooms and laid him on the bed. Iridia gave orders to get supplies to clean and bind Aiden's wounds and inform Brokk that she had arrived.

I set out to cut Aiden's clothes from him so we could see the extent of his wounds. Keane bit his wrist and placed it to Aiden's lips. As soon as the blood went down his throat, Aiden started to seize, foam seeping out of his mouth.

"What's happening?" Iridia cried, grabbing a cloth and wiping at Aiden's mouth while Keane raised his head so he wouldn't choke.

"Shit." Keane turned to me. "What did you say he fought?"

"A Cythraul."

"Did it bite him?"

"I don't think so..." I trailed off as I looked at his shoulder. Within the mass of blood, there was a row of teeth marks.

My eyes widened in panic, and I looked at Keane helplessly, but he just shook his head. "My blood will only poison him further."

"Tristan..."

"Under a heavy sleeping draught. When he found out you had left without us knowing, he tried to follow. We can try to wake him, but I don't think it will be in time."

"No... Cora! Where's Cora?"

Iridia looked up, tears streaming down her face. "My sister is still here?"

I nodded and ran out the door toward Tristan's room, where I knew she would be. I burst inside. "Cora!" The woman in question sat by Tristan's bedside, holding his hand. "Cora, we need your help." Hearing the urgency in my voice, she stood. I looked briefly at Tristan. "Someone was bitten by a Cythraul, and the poison is making it impossible for the Vaimpír to heal him."

"Tristan won't wake up, Blue. What we gave him will keep him under until at least tomorrow. Plus, you know he'll only use his ability for those he loves." The last part was said with a bit of disdain.

"I need you then. You said you were a talented healer."

She looked at me with a bit of distrust. "I don't know if I'll be of any help—"

"Will you please just try?"

She finally nodded and followed me as I quickly made my way back to the room Aiden was in. I probably should've warned Cora that her sister was there, but I honestly forgot. Throwing open the door, I rushed in. Cora halted at the threshold. "I-Iridia?" She started to shake, her eyes filling with tears at the sight of her sister.

"Cora! Please help." Cora shook herself out of her surprise and looked at the man on the bed. Walking over, she inspected the wounds but didn't ask any questions. Placing her hands over Aiden's chest, she called up her magic. A soft, blue light emanated from her fingers as she chanted.

After a few minutes, she shook her head. "It's...it's not working." Cora squeezed her eyes shut and poured more magic into Aiden. Before long, she started to sway and pulled back. "I'm so sorry, Iridia. There's nothing more I can do."

Tears started to fall from Cora's eyes as Iridia broke down in sobs. She leaned over and took her sister in her arms.

Aiden started to cough, and his eyes opened weakly, immediately finding mine. I leaned down to his side. "Aiden."

"Dad." His voice was a gruff admonishment that caused him to cough, blood leaking through his lips.

"Dad." My eyes filled with tears, guilt weighing heavily on my shoulders. "I'm so sorry, Dad. If I didn't...if you hadn't..."

"Carolina, it's okay." Aiden laid a bloodied hand on my cheek. "You're safe, your mother is safe. That's all that matters." Another round of coughing racked his body, and he gasped for breath. "I love you, Carolina. You were the b-best thing that ever happened to me. You and your mother. I'll be waiting for you both o-on the other side."

Tears fell from my eyes as his hand slowly slid from my face, and his eyes dulled. Iridia broke down in heaving sobs, still clasping his hand to her chest while her sister held her. I gently reached over, closed his eyes, and bowed my head, anger burgeoning in my heart. Though he hadn't been my real father, his death had been unnecessary, and Hades would pay for it.

After a while, Iridia leaned over and kissed Aiden's forehead, her tears falling unchecked. "Goodbye, my love. I will see you again." With that, she started to sing. It was a haunting melody in a language I didn't understand, but I knew it was a sendoff for Aiden's soul. Cora and several of the men who had come to help joined in. I saw Brokk rush into the room, only to realize what had happened. His sorrowful voice soon joined the rest.

As I watched, small, golden balls of light began floating up around Aiden. They danced over his body, covering the entire thing until they started lifting into the air one by one. As they did, Aiden started to disappear until there was nothing left.

I stared in shock at where his body had been. Keane wrapped an arm around my shoulders and kissed the top of my head. "A proper sendoff for a Fairy. Though he wasn't one in body, he was one in spirit." I turned into his arms, seeking his warmth and comfort as my thoughts circled, equal parts guilt and anger flooding me.

Chapter Twenty-One

As I lay in Keane's arms, his chin resting on my head, I wondered how I was going to deal with Hades. There didn't seem to be any easy solution. There was no way I could outpower him. He was a full-fledged god, while I was only part god. And I didn't see him reconciling with his brother anytime soon. Some things were unforgivable. I heaved a deep sigh. I didn't want anyone else I loved or cared about to be hurt because of me.

"If you're thinking about running off again to solve this on your own, you might as well get it out of your head. From now on, you go nowhere without me."

I smiled into his chest, both loving and hating his ferocious protectiveness. I pulled back and looked up at him. "I just don't know what to do, Keane."

He curved a finger under my chin, his expression serious. "We'll figure it out, Blue. But we have to do this together. One person alone can't fix it." I nodded and his gaze softened. "Now, get some sleep, *ma moitié*, you need it."

Wrapped securely in his warm embrace, it wasn't long before I drifted off into a restless sleep—my dreams filled with images of my past. At first, they started slowly: glimpses of my childhood with Iridia and Aiden, then my time growing up with Alannah. They picked up speed through my young adult life, until they were almost a blur while passing by my adult memories.

Finally, it all stopped, and I found myself standing in a garden full of large trees and climbing vines, creating a cozy alcove. Behind me was a large marble statue of Hades of all people, while another farther along one of the paths seemed to be Zeus. My eyes scrunched in confusion. Where was I? This wasn't one of my memories.

Not seeing anyone around, I followed a path leading through the garden's center. As I walked, I passed hundreds of different plants I had never seen before with a multitude of smells and colors. More statues of Greek gods and goddesses were interspersed throughout the area, and it became a game to figure out who was whom.

Along one path, I came upon a hidden pond and stopped to run my hand through the fish-filled water. One of them came up and swam under my fingers, giving a little wiggle before darting away, bringing a smile to my face.

Standing, I continued to meander through the gardens, periodically stopping to smell or touch a flower but still not seeing anyone. Finally, I came to a plot at the very edge of the garden, half-hidden behind another statue, this one a female. I couldn't place her, though she seemed familiar somehow. After a moment, I realized why. She looked a lot like Hades' Alexandra. But why would an effigy of Alexandra be in this garden? All the rest of the figures had been gods and goddesses.

As I rounded the stone likeness, I came to a stuttering halt. Sitting among the flowers was a beautiful woman in a long, glittering gown.

I ducked behind the statue, hoping she hadn't seen me. Creeping to the side, I peeked around the corner. The woman sat meditatively with her legs crossed, her gown flowing around her, and her eyes...blessedly closed. I breathed out a sigh of relief.

"You don't have to hide, Carolina." I sucked in the breath I had just released, almost choking on it. "Come. Sit with me."

I hesitated but then moved around the statue. The woman still had her eyes shut.

"How did you know who I was?"

She laughed lightly. "I knew who you were the minute you entered my garden. Don't be afraid. Come sit with me." She patted the spot next to her among the flowers, and I carefully lowered myself to the ground.

"Who are you?"

"Do you not remember me?" She laughed softly. "Not surprising, I guess, considering we only met once when you were a very young child."

As she opened her eyes and looked at me, a flicker of a memory went by. A woman surrounded by an ethereal light with glowing amber eyes, standing over me as a child. I had thought she was an Angel. She had touched me and... I blinked the memory away and looked at the woman sitting next to me.

"It was you, wasn't it? Who helped smuggle me away from Hades? That's how my mother and Aiden got around the god's blood bond. That's how my memories were changed. You're a goddess."

A smile spread across her face. "I told them you would remember one day, no matter what I did. It has been foretold, so it shall come to pass."

"What was foretold?"

"Your destiny."

I groaned and swiped a hand over my face. The last time something was foretold about me, things hadn't gone so well. Why did it seem like fate had it in for me?

"You cannot fight your destiny, Blue."

"And just what *is* my destiny? To join the dark side?" My voice dripped with sarcasm.

The woman smiled in amusement. "You're hardly Luke Skywalker. Though I guess your current predicament might be considered similar, given that Hades is trying to recruit you to his side. In our world, he would be the closest thing to the leader of the dark side."

"How did I get so lucky?" I deadpanned.

She shook her head, her smile growing. "Luck has nothing to do with it."

"I know, I know…it's destiny, it has been prophesized. Ooooo." I waved my hands back and forth.

The woman smirked at my dramatics. "Blue, of all people, you know how much truth is in prophecies. Look at yours."

I grunted. A prophecy had been made about me long before I even knew who or what I was. Actually, before I was even born. "According to your prophecy, there would be a great upheaval within the Fae, one that would cause a rift that would spread throughout, resulting in fighting among the clans. People would be divided, and sides would be taken, leaving the clans broken and unprotected and opening them for a dark ruling power to take over.

"During this time of strife, a girl child would be born. One more powerful than any seen before. One who could unite all the Fae once more, but only if she discovered her true self which had been hidden from her. She would have to face many Trials before she could even begin to understand her real power and become who she was truly meant to be."

"Yeah, been there, done that. Still trying to recover."

She chuckled while shaking her head. "You have yet to see things through to the end, my child."

I looked at her in confusion. "What do you mean? I faced the Trials and helped reunite the clans."

She smiled knowingly. "Did you?"

I scowled at her. "The Trials are over. All the Fae have come together to clean up the mess Larkin created. Voila! Neat little bow."

"Hmm."

I didn't like the sound of that. "What do you mean, *hmm?*"

She smiled and shook her head. "That's something you'll need to discover for yourself, I'm afraid."

"Why are you guys always so cryptic when it comes to this kind of stuff? Would it be so hard to just say, '*Hey, so here's what's gonna happen.*'?"

"You know that's not how it works. Everything you do, every decision you make, can change how things turn out."

"Then what is the point of a prophecy?"

"They're more like...guidelines."

"Okay, Captain Barbosa. Any more sage advice?"

She laughed and took my hand. "Pay attention to everything you've seen. Everything you've heard. Even the smallest, seemingly inconsequential details could tell you something."

"How will that help me defeat Hades? How can I stop him from using me to get revenge on his brother?"

"Trust those around you, Carolina. Every single person who was put in your path is there for a reason." With that, she leaned forward and kissed me on the forehead. "If you ever have need of me, you have only to call. I'll do what I can."

"Why do you want to help me?"

"Because nothing is more important to me than my family, and that now includes you."

I looked at her, confused. "Who are you?"

She slowly started to fade out, another smile tugging at her lips. "You can call me Aunt Hera."

I stared at where she had been sitting, my mouth slightly agape. Hera? Holy crap. My mind had just been blown once again. Just when I thought I was getting used to all the god stuff. Shaking my head, I plucked one of the white blooms from the ground beneath me, twirling the stem between my fingers. Looking down at the flower, I realized it was an asphodel. The flower of Hades. I wondered if that was supposed to be a good omen or a bad one.

After my strange dream—which had left me more unsettled than rested—I slipped out of bed to get ready for the evening. Keane had already left, his side of the bed still slightly warm from where he had lain. I knew he hadn't gone far, so I decided to check on Tristan while he was away doing whatever he needed to do.

Knocking on Tristan's door, I peeked around it, only to find Brokk and Nick there. "Oh, sorry. I'll come back later."

Brokk rose with a smile. "No, no. We were just leaving. Tristan, once you're back at Moon Tree Hall, we'll s-set up a meeting to discuss those matters."

On their way out, I stopped Nick briefly. "All good?" I was naturally referring to Iridia being back.

He nodded happily and whispered, "Better than I thought, actually. She's a marvel."

I smiled widely and patted his arm. "I'm so glad."

They left, leaving me alone with Tristan. I turned to find him glowering at me. "What?"

"What the hell were you thinking? Going off on your own like that?" I pursed my lips but didn't say anything. He had every right to be angry with me. When I didn't respond, he let out a sharp breath. "I get that you feel responsible, Blue. I do. But you need to let us help you. We're a team. If something were to happen to you, I...I don't know what I'd do. Nor would any of the others, for that matter. Okay?" I nodded solemnly. "Promise?" I nodded again. "Good, now... What the hell is up with you and Nick? You've done nothing but whisper and meet secretly since we got here. I don't like it."

I sat in the chair next to his bed, smirking. "Why the fuss? You don't see Keane stomping around like a jealous lover, do you?"

"I'm not jealous." I raised a brow in disbelief. "Okay, so maybe I am. A little. Whenever you're around him, I get this warm and fuzzy feeling from our connection."

I shook my head. "I'm only going to tell you this because I'm sick and tired of the glares you've been throwing poor Nick's way. He doesn't deserve it." When he went to protest, I held up a hand. "Nick and I were...each other's firsts."

He shut his mouth and stared at me. "You mean like—?"

I interrupted him before he went into more detail, wanting to avoid discussing the specifics. "Yes, just like that. Enough said. But please, I promised Nick I wouldn't tell Brokk. Can you imagine how awkward it would be to know your partner slept with your stepdaughter?" I shivered dramatically.

Tristan watched me, seeming to be trying to determine if I was telling the truth or not, before he finally nodded. "I won't say anything."

"Good. Now, are you ready to get out of this bed and back into the thick of things?"

Tristan groaned, flopping back against his pillows. "More than ready. I feel like I've been cooped up here for weeks, not just a few days."

I nodded knowingly. "We need to sit everyone down and have a brainstorming session. I'm kind of at a loss for what to do now."

"Are you...are you asking for help?" He gave me a mock shocked look.

"Yeah, yeah, yeah." I stood and lightly punched him in the arm.

"Hey! Recovering patient here."

I laughed and went to the door. "Get dressed. I'll meet you out in the dining area in a few."

I left Tristan's room and went to check on my mom. The door to her bedroom was open, and she was sitting on the edge of her bed, staring into space. Her eyes were swollen and red from crying, and my heart ached for her. I remained in the doorway, not wanting to startle her. "Mom?"

Her head came up, and she gave me a small smile. "Blue. Come in."

I walked over and sat on the bed next to her, taking her hand in mine. "How are you holding up?"

"It's so weird being back here in this theater. In this room. I honestly never thought I'd see it again."

"Have you had a chance to sit and talk to Brokk?"

She nodded, squeezing my hand. "We were up for most of the night together. His partner Nicholas is lovely. I heard you knew him in high school."

"Briefly. I actually dated his younger brother for a bit." There was no way I was telling her the full story. She nodded distractedly. "I'm sorry about... Aiden. It was my fault that he did what he did."

She looked up at me, tears glistening in her eyes. "Your father loved you very much. He just couldn't leave you there with Hades, knowing what he was capable of. Don't you dare feel guilty. He would give his life a hundred times over if it meant you stayed safe."

I pursed my lips and looked down at our joined hands. "Mom, about my father..." I wasn't sure I wanted to burden her more right now, especially with the knowledge that Aiden wasn't actually my father, but I also didn't feel right pretending to be mourning a man as something he wasn't. "Aiden wasn't my father."

"Oh, honey. Just because you didn't know him doesn't mean he wasn't your father..."

"No, Mom. You don't understand." I took a deep breath. "You were pregnant before you even went to rescue Aiden."

Her brows drew together momentarily before smoothing out as she gave me a small, tolerant smile. "I think I'd know if I had a relationship like that with someone else."

"You had him remove your memories of your time together in case Hades discovered your pregnancy."

"Blue, what are you saying?"

I decided to just put it out there. "Poseidon is my real father."

She pulled back from me, her eyes widening in shock. "No, it can't be. I'd never, he'd never... He's a god. Gods and Fae don't mix."

"Actually, they do, more often than you realize." I thought about Hades and Alexandra.

"But..." Though she protested, I could see by the look on her face that she was thinking about it. Probably remembering all the weird abilities

I had as a child and Hades' seemingly obsessive interest in me. "Is that why Hades wants you so badly? Because you're part...god?"

I nodded. "He kidnapped you initially because you have some godly bloodline, as well. Hence why you're so powerful and can travel incorporeally."

She shook her head in astonishment. "I can't believe it."

"Trust me, I had a hard time accepting it, too. It still throws me for a loop sometimes."

She looked at me, her eyes roving my face. "I always wondered why you hadn't gotten any of your fa—Aiden's looks or temperament." She choked a bit on his name. It took her a moment to compose herself again, and I just waited quietly, holding her hand. "H-have you spent time with...Poseidon—I mean your father?"

I nodded with a smile. "Yeah, he's been helping me with, well, a lot of things, actually. He's been really great."

She bit her lip in a gesture reminiscent of my bad habit. "So, you're sure..."

"Without a doubt."

Iridia leaned back against the pillows on her bed. "I just can't believe..."

"Poseidon is actually at Dock Street right now, helping Grandfather with research."

"My father knows?"

I gave a small laugh. "He was thrilled, actually. They are currently trying to research your family tree to see if they can discover where the god's bloodline entered the Grayson line. Not that it matters in the grand scheme of things, but it would be nice to know whose blood the Grayson's carry."

Iridia stared at me, noticeably overwhelmed. "I'm sorry to drop this on you, Mom. I just wanted you to know so you'd understand why I felt like I did."

She took a steadying breath. "Does everyone else here know?"

"Yeah. Even the Elder Council knows at this point, as does all of Vaimpír society." I thought about the rumors Cedric had heard. "I guess it doesn't need to be a secret anymore."

"The Vaimpír…"

I grimaced a bit. "I need to fill you in on a few things."

She sat quietly as I told her all about my introduction into Vaimpír society, Keane's parents, our bond, and even my connection to Tristan. When I was done, she looked thoughtful. "Are you in love with Keane?"

I started. Out of all the things she could have asked after my information dump, that was her first question?

"I think…" I paused and let my emotions run free, feeling Keane's pass through me in return. "No. I *know* I'm irrevocably in love with him."

"Good. I think he's the perfect match for you. And what about Tristan?"

"What about him?"

"Do you still love him, as well?"

"While I love Tristan, I'm not *in love* with him, if that makes sense." Saying that again reminded me of Cora, and I wondered if my mother knew that her sister was still in love with Tristan.

"That's good. While a twin flame is a connection like no other, it's highly volatile. Those in romantic relationships with each other rarely last. They're just not meant to stay together like that."

We were suddenly interrupted by a loud, screeching sound. We covered our ears and looked around. "What on earth is that?"

Iridia looked at me, her eyes wide. "That's the perimeter alarm. Something breached the wards."

Chapter Twenty-Two

We ran into the living area, where everyone else had gathered. Keane gave orders to his men while Tristan and Brokk discussed defenses with a few of Brokk's soldiers. I walked over to Keane.

"What's going on?"

"We're not sure yet. The alarm just means that something that shouldn't be here crossed the first set of wards."

"How did whatever it is get through?"

"No idea."

Just then, Sebastian popped in. His wings were on full display, so I knew it must be serious. We hadn't let Brokk and the others know what he was. Brokk and his men simply gaped, but Sebastian just ignored them and came straight over to Keane and me.

"Bast, what's going on?"

"It's Hades' hellhounds. They've managed to breach the first set of wards. I can't be certain, but I think his army of Demons isn't far behind."

"How? I thought the wards were set up to specifically keep them out?"

Sebastian shrugged. "Seems Hades figured a way around it."

"Shit. Something tells me he's no longer bound to his castle, then."

Sebastian nodded. "That would probably be a good guess."

I turned to Brokk and Iridia, who were standing together. "I assume you have protocols in place to keep your people safe?"

Brokk nodded and gestured to a soldier standing on his left. "My captain is prepared to initiate it should Hades manage to breach the second set of wards."

"How many sets are there?"

"Three."

I looked around the room at all the faces. "You know we could avoid all of this if I just gave myself over to him, right?"

"Not gonna happen." Keane clenched his teeth, his hand going to my arm.

"I don't think he would hurt me, Keane."

"I'm not taking that chance."

"Neither am I." Tristan moved to my other side.

"Don't let your fa—Aiden's sacrifice be in vain, Blue." Iridia gave me a stern look.

Keane raised his brows at her slip, and I shrugged. "I thought she had a right to know." I turned, taking in the room as a whole. "What's our plan of action, then?"

"First, we need to contain the breach. Sebastian, where exactly did they enter?" Keane took charge as usual.

"On the eastern border."

"Anywhere else?"

"Not that I saw."

"Good. Brokk, can your rune specialist divert some power to reinforce the second and third wards on that side? Have a small battalion set up a blockade behind the third set of wards, as well."

Tristan's brow furrowed. "What if it's a trick, and we put all our defenses on one side, only to have him come in on another?"

Keane shook his head. "Strategically speaking, that seems highly unlikely. The only side Hades could send an army from is the eastern border. At least without causing panic in the human population. And I don't think that would be his goal. We'll have small patrols working every border just in case, but I don't think he'll come from another direction. Cullen, Mckile, Ronan, I want you front and center on that blockade."

"Yes, sir!" They saluted as one before donning their gear and loading themselves up with weapons. When they were ready, they bumped fists with Keane, kissed me on the cheek, and strode to the elevator. I fervently hoped nothing happened to any of them.

Keane looked down at me with a crooked grin. "Don't worry, they can handle themselves."

I chewed on my bottom lip. "I know they can, but that doesn't make me worry any less."

Keane turned to Sebastian. "Can I count on you to be our eyes in the sky?"

"As long as they don't start shooting flaming arrows or anything."

"Obviously. Can you see if you can get closer to them? I want to know if Hades is among them."

"Yes, sir!" Sebastian gave him a mocking salute before he popped out.

Brokk stood stock-still, looking pained. "I don't have the fire or manpower to withstand a Demon army." He looked helplessly at Keane and Tristan.

Tristan nodded, his brows drawing together. "I've already called for reinforcements. Though even with my men, I don't like our chances. If it were just the hellhounds, it wouldn't be a problem. But a Demon army?"

Keane looked thoughtful. "We'll definitely need something...extra. Excuse me a moment. I need to make a phone call."

With that, he walked away, a cell to his ear. I watched him go with a feeling of trepidation before turning back to Brokk. "I'm sorry to have brought this down on your home and people, Brokk."

"Nonsense. You came here to rescue Iridia, whom you've brought back to us. Not to wage war. That's on Hades. Besides, you're family. And family protects their own."

I nodded, though I still wasn't convinced. I thought about my dream and wondered if Hera would be willing to help. Shaking my head, I dismissed the thought. Hades was her brother, why would she help me fight him?

As the evening wore on, things got even more tense. I watched from the rooftop with detachment as Tristan's forces came through the portals Keane and his men opened. I hadn't realized his army was so large, but it still felt small compared to what was out there waiting for us.

Though the second set of wards had yet to be breached, it seemed like Hades' forces were gathering just outside of it. And they were a scary bunch. I had watched them through a spying rune Sebastian had managed to set up.

Keeping to the woods so the humans didn't see them, there were all manner of Demons, from tall, human-like ones to stuff made of nightmares that crawled on all fours, their heads bending at odd angles. And there were literally thousands. There seemed to be no end to them. To make matters worse, there still had been no sign of Hades, and I wondered where he was and what he planned.

I was stretched out on one of the couches in Brokk's living quarters, staring up at the ceiling, listening as Keane and Tristan plotted over some maps spread out over the dining room table.

They were deciding on the best places to engage the Demons, when I spoke up, catching their attention. "I don't want the Demons to come into the city. I don't want to see a bunch of innocent humans hurt." I sat up and leaned over the back of the couch to look at the men.

Keane nodded in agreement. "I think we should go on the offensive and open a portal here, here, and here." He pointed at the map. "We'll do it all at once, surrounding the army on all sides."

"That's a bit of a risk," Tristan countered. "What if some of the Demons breach the portal?"

"We'll do it from outside the third wards, so even if they do, it won't put them anywhere near here. And we'll have men on standby, just in case."

I nodded, looking thoughtful. "That sounds like a good plan. Where will we enter?"

Tristan and Keane shared a look before turning to me. I knew I wasn't going to like what they said next. "We want you to stay here."

I jumped to my feet. "Oh, hell no! I'm not just going to sit around hidden behind these walls while people put their lives on the line for me."

"Blue, Hades wants you. If you're out in the open, what's stopping him from taking you while we're all distracted?"

"Who's to say this army isn't all a ruse to do that anyway? If you all go off to fight and leave me here, he could just come and take me."

"He won't be able to breach the third set of wards. And we'll leave men here with you, just in case."

"You didn't think he'd be able to breach the first wards, yet here we are."

Tristan let out a frustrated sigh. "Blue, you're staying here with Iridia, and that's final."

I huffed and crossed my arms. "Like you saying so will keep me put. I'm your greatest weapon."

"And our biggest weakness."

"I can literally stop time."

Keane gave me a stern look. "Who's to say it will work on the Demons? After all, it doesn't work on all the hellhounds or even Sebastian."

"Scythe is different, and you know it." Keane was one of the few who knew I had helped to create the hellhound. "Bast, however? I still don't know why he's immune."

Keane gave me a long-suffering sigh before rolling out the ultimate weapon. Guilt. "Please, Blue? If you're out there, I won't be able to concentrate, and the distraction could get me killed."

I groaned and ran a hand over my face, knowing I didn't have an argument against that. "Fine. But the minute I see or feel something happen—to either of you—I'm not going to just sit by and watch."

Tristan moved to protest, but Keane held up a hand. "And I wouldn't expect anything less."

Just about then, the elevator dinged, and several well-dressed gentlemen stepped out. I looked at them in surprise, recognizing their faces immediately. "Malakai?"

He grinned in my direction. "My dear Blue! It's so good to see you again, though I didn't think it would be this soon." He came over and gave me a kiss on the cheek.

"What are you doing here?"

"My son called and said he needed backup. So, here we are."

I looked behind Malakai to see all six Barons with him. They all bowed in my direction upon catching my eye.

"I...I don't know what to say. I thought the Vaimpír stayed out of Fae politics."

"That was before."

"Before what?"

He took my hand in his. "Before you."

I was shocked, to say the least. "You're here because of me?"

All the Barons looked at each other before shrugging and nodding their heads. "The future Queen of our clan must be protected." Malakai smiled and bowed his head in my direction. Before I could comment, he turned to Keane.

"Son, why don't you fill us in? We have already stationed our men around the area. They are awaiting your orders."

The Barons walked away with Keane, leaving me standing in my befuddled state. Iridia came over to me and took my arm, leading me back to the couch. "What did you think would happen when you bonded with Keane, the Dark Prince himself?"

"I..."

Iridia laughed and patted my arm. "You still have plenty of time to think things through. Malakai and Camille are hardly ready for retirement."

"But for them to come here, to help us? It's unheard of."

"True. The Vaimpír have kept to themselves for centuries when it comes to things like this, never taking sides. But they have never had a Fae-slash-goddess heir, either."

Without warning, another loud keening alarm sounded. I looked at Iridia in panic. Her expression was grim. "The second wards."

Jumping to my feet, I raced to the large mirror Sebastian had placed the spy rune on, connected to the one in the woods with the Demons. Iridia was hot on my heels. "They're not moving," she observed.

She was right. Not a single Demon had stepped a foot over the line. They all stood still as statues, barely moving an inch. "What are they waiting for?"

No sooner had I asked the question than the legion parted, and Hades walked from between them—swaggered, actually. He was dressed impeccably, in all black as usual, his polished persona evidently back in place. He stopped a few yards from his army, clearly within the second wards. His stance was nonchalant, with an unperturbed smile, as if he hadn't a care in the world. "Carolina Blue! If you don't give yourself over to me, I'll be forced to release my Demons on the good people of the Fernsong Clan." His grin turned malevolent. "Humans and Fae alike." He glanced to where the rune was, seeming to look right at me. "You have one hour." With that, he walked back into his throng of Demons and disappeared.

"Dammit!" I slammed my fist into the wall and turned to the men watching me. "We can't let him do that." The Barons all took a nervous step back.

Keane stepped forward and put his hands on my shoulders. "Calm down, Blue. We won't allow him or his Demons to enter the third set of wards. We'll make our move long before the hour is up."

I nodded, my anger deflating as quickly as it had risen. "Sorry," I mumbled to the men staring uncertainly at me.

Keane kissed my forehead before pulling me in for a tight hug. "We're going to take this guy out, Blue. I promise." I took in a deep breath before letting it out. I really wished I had his confidence.

Just before the hour was up, I watched as the men dressed in their fighting gear and leather armor. The Vaimpír strapped long, twin katanas to their backs, while Tristan and Brokk each affixed traditional swords to their sides. I had never seen the Fae or Vaimpír like this.

I was about to go talk to Tristan when a hand shot out of a darkened corner and pulled me into a hidden alcove. I looked up as a strong pair of arms encircled me. Keane pulled me in tightly to his body, his nose immediately dipping into my shoulder to inhale sharply. Lifting his head, he stared into my eyes.

"I don't like leaving you here, *ma moitié*, any more than you want to be left."

"I know." I lifted my face to his, our lips connecting in a fervent kiss. I held on to him tightly, afraid to let go. "You should feed before you go."

"Blue..."

"Please." Not only did I want him to feed so he was at his strongest, but I also wanted that connection one last time before he left. Just in case...no, I wouldn't even consider something happening to him.

With a normal soulbond, if one of the Vaimpír died, it would kill the other. As nothing was *normal* about our bond, we had no idea what would happen. I hoped it would be the same, as I didn't think I could live without him.

I felt the pressure of his teeth just before they broke through my skin. I whimpered quietly as the sensations raced over my body, reveling in our connection and feeling it pulse brighter. Soon, Keane was pressing against the back of my head, and I knew he wanted to feel the same. Quickly manipulating the magic within me, I produced a pair of fangs. With hardly a thought, I leaned into Keane's neck and bit him, as well. He moaned into my throat, the sound vibrating down the entire length of my body, leaving me quaking. Pulling back, Keane cupped my face between his large hands.

"Blue, I..." He paused, seeming to have a hard time continuing.

I stood on my tiptoes, pressing my lips to his. "I love you, too." Keane's mouth parted in surprise. I took advantage and slipped my tongue inside, savoring the taste of him before I broke the kiss and placed my forehead on his, holding his face like he was holding mine. "I love you with all my heart, so you'd damn well better come back to me."

A tear that I had been trying to hold back slipped free. He caught it on the tip of his thumb and looked at it before his eyes met mine again. "I love you, Blue." His voice was quiet, then he repeated it louder. "I love you." I closed my eyes and let the intensity of what he was feeling flow over me, through me, a smile blossoming on my face even as more tears slid down my cheeks.

He kept repeating it, kissing the tears from my face. Finally, he stopped and pulled back slightly. "Nothing will keep me from you—not even death." We stayed hidden for a little while before we knew we couldn't put it off any longer. As I moved to pull away, his grip tightened on my arms. "One last thing. I want to give you something."

"Oh?"

He pulled a long, wooden box from a table behind him. "These were mine when I was young. I figured they would be the perfect size for you." Opening the box almost lovingly, he pulled out two beautifully handcrafted katana swords. I stared at the intricately hand-carved handles. "While I know you love Hiccup, you know as well as I do that it won't do you any good against a Demon should one attack. These, on the other hand, will slice through anything. And much like most supernatural creatures, a Demon cannot live without its head—at least most of them."

I took one of the swords out of his hands and slid the blade from the sheath. It came free with a well-oiled, nearly silent hiss. "They're beautiful."

"It's what all Vaimpír carry when going into battle."

"Are you sure you want me to have these?"

"I'd love nothing more than for you to carry a part of our heritage with you."

Taking off Hiccup's shoulder holster, I let Keane fit the carrying straps for the swords around my shoulders and onto my back before he locked the sheaths into place. I practiced pulling the blades in and out a few times so I wouldn't accidentally slice myself open—which would be just my luck. Keane grinned at my childish glee before turning and pulling out another set of much larger swords, which he strapped to his back. Pulling me to him one last time, he placed a hard kiss on my lips before walking purposefully away without a backward glance.

As soon as Keane left, Tristan came over. "Be safe, Blue, and whatever you do, stay hidden. You can't let Hades get a hold of you, or all of this will be for naught."

I rolled my eyes before pulling him into a tight embrace. "You stay safe, too. No getting killed. If you do, I'll just have a Síofra bring you back as a ghost so I can make your afterlife as miserable as possible."

He chuckled and placed a kiss on my cheek before following the other men into the elevator. I gave them a last wave as the doors shut. Looking over at Iridia and Nick, I saw they were also a little emotional.

We had decided they shouldn't leave much-needed soldiers behind. Between Iridia's and my magic, we could take care of ourselves. And though Nick was human, he was quite a skilled fighter, but, unfortunately, would be no help against Demons. Like me, he was a bit miffed to be left behind, but we both knew it was for the best.

As the minutes ticked down to Hades' allotted time, I watched the mirror without blinking. The Demons all remained completely motionless until the last second. Then, as if someone had fired a starting gun, they moved. I held my breath as three huge portals opened around them, forming a circle, and the Fae and Vaimpír armies poured out.

The fighting was fierce. The Demons were unprepared for the sneak attack and suffered huge casualties until they readjusted. Then, I started to see Fae and Vaimpír go down. I felt each and every one like a stab to the heart. I hoped they weren't dead, but I wasn't so naïve as to think that wouldn't happen. I did, however, see Vaimpír offering their blood to their fallen comrades—Vaimpír and Fae alike—which amazed me. It reminded me of what Hera had told me about not reuniting all the clans yet. She had been right. I hadn't before. Now, they were. Vaimpír and Fae working together after all this time. It was truly a momentous occasion. However, now was not the time to celebrate.

I tried not to follow the imposing figures of Keane and Tristan as they fought side by side. Instead, I continued to scan the crowd of bodies, looking for one in particular. But Hades was nowhere to be found.

333

Chapter Twenty-Three

"Where are you?" I leaned both arms against the wall as if getting closer to the mirror would help me find him.

"Blue, come sit down." Iridia patted the couch next to her.

I shook my head. There was no way I wasn't watching this fight. This was my fault, and I'd take every ounce of pain, every injury and death, and lay it on my soul to answer for when my time came.

Unexpectedly, a flash of white obscured the rune. I sucked in a breath as Sebastian fell from the sky right in front of it. His once beautiful white wings were tattered and soaked in blood. I held in the scream that threatened to push out. I watched as he half-flew, half-crawled over the final ward line before collapsing on the other side. The Demons had yet to breach it, so he was safe from further harm, but I didn't think he would last without help. There weren't any soldiers on that side. All the fighting took place farther down the ward line. Not even stopping to think, I grabbed my leather jacket and swords and dashed for the elevator.

"Blue, no!" Both Iridia and Nick grabbed my arms, trying to pull me back. "You can't go out there."

"I can't leave him to die." I tugged away from their hands.

"No, Blue. You promised. You promised you would stay hidden. Otherwise, what are they fighting for? Why are they giving their lives to keep you safe if you're just going to throw it all away?"

I stopped, taking a deep breath before looking at them. "I have to save him. He has saved me countless times. How could I live with myself if I let him die when I know I can save him?" I held up a hand when they would've argued. "Hear me out. I have an invisibility spell. I can use it to get to Sebastian. No one will see me, and he's behind the third set of wards, which the Demons can't breach. Please, let me save him."

They looked at each other before finally conceding. "But we're coming with you." I started to protest, but Iridia just shook her head. "Someone has to watch your back." I pursed my lips but finally nodded, actually feeling better knowing they would be there with me. Nick grabbed a broadsword held in a scabbard strapped across his back while Iridia grabbed a pair of small, silver daggers that she stuffed into her jacket pockets.

"Ready?" They nodded. Together, we stepped into the elevator.

The ride up was silent, each of us lost in our thoughts and anxieties. As the doors slid open, I carefully peered into the vestibule. There wasn't a soul around. Slipping out, we quietly made our way across the room until we reached the open door that led to the backstage hallways. Moving slowly and carefully, constantly listening, we moved down the hall and onto the stage.

The theater was eerily silent. None of the usual sounds for a Friday night were around as Brokk had closed everything for the weekend, having no idea what might happen. His people had been sent away to hide until the all-clear had been given, so even the staff that normally kept an eye on things was gone.

We stood on the empty stage, debating whether to open the portal right there. I was pretty sure I could get through Brokk's wards. Nick didn't think it was a good idea in case something managed to cross the third set of wards, while Iridia was undecided. I argued that we wouldn't be able to carry Sebastian far, and we didn't want to be stuck outside.

After a few minutes of heated discussion, I finally convinced them. Iridia and Nick kept an eye on things around us as I quickly pulled my invisibility spell over me. Nick started when he turned, and I wasn't there anymore.

"Blue?" His voice was a harsh whisper in the silent theater.

"I'm here."

"Whoa. It actually worked."

"Did you doubt me?"

"Well..."

I laughed. "Never mind."

With a concentrated effort, I envisioned the field where I had seen Sebastian go down. After untangling the wards, the portal flickered but then opened. I quickly slipped through, closing it behind me. I spotted Sebastian right away. He was lying still as death. I couldn't even see his chest moving and was afraid I was too late.

Running in a slight crouch, I continued to look around for any possible Demon attacks. Contrary to what I had told Iridia and Nick, I had no idea if the invisibility spell would work with Demons.

When I was next to Sebastian, I leaned down and, with a shaking hand, checked his pulse. He was still alive, thank the stars! With another glance around, I tried to open a new portal, but it didn't work. My heartbeat sped up as I tried again...still nothing.

Dammit, what was going on?

All of a sudden, I heard a snuffling sound to my right. I quickly crouched next to Sebastian, hoping whatever it was wouldn't be able to see me or be able to cross the wards. I could hear my heart drumming in my ears as whatever it was got closer and closer.

The bush not far from us shook before two glowing red eyes appeared, followed by a scaly black head. It was a hellhound. I froze in horror, knowing my invisibility spell wouldn't fool the hound's sense of smell. I briefly debated pulling my swords and fighting but then reconsidered. Instead, I carefully lay down next to Sebastian and pulled his wing over my body. I hoped the smell of his blood would disguise my scent.

The hellhound seemed to pause just on the other side of the ward next to Sebastian, and I held my breath. The minutes ticked by, agonizingly slow, as it stood there motionless. I was beginning to think I'd need to find a way to take it down when it finally moved on. I shakily let out the breath I had been holding. It must've been searching for a weak spot in the wards.

As soon as the hellhound was out of sight and I couldn't hear it anymore, I carefully moved out from under Sebastian. Pulling extra power from my core, I put my hands out and concentrated on my portal. It flickered in and out but didn't solidify—it must have something to do with the wards.

I let out a muffled curse before dropping my invisibility spell and pushing everything I had at it. Finally, the door solidified, and I sighed in relief. I grabbed Sebastian under the arms and quickly dragged him through the portal and into the theater. Both Iridia and Nick jumped as I fell through, slumping to the floor with Sebastian half on top of me—he was heavier than he looked. The portal disappeared as I lay there panting.

"You okay, Blue?" Nick looked at me in concern.

I nodded, though I was still having a hard time catching my breath. Both from the exertion and the adrenaline dump from my fear earlier. Once I finally felt I could move without passing out, I sat up and, with Nick's help, maneuvered Sebastian onto the pillow and blankets that Iridia had found somewhere. Sebastian looked to be in bad shape, blood soaking every inch of him. Iridia had also found a first-aid kit along with some water and rags. I quickly dunked one of the rags into the water and started cleaning the blood from Sebastian. I was surprised that most of his wounds already appeared healed or were well on their way. He must have accelerated healing like most of the gods.

"Should we see if we can move him downstairs?" The words had barely left Iridia's mouth when Sebastian let out a groan. His eyes slowly blinked open, and he looked around as if trying to get his bearings.

"Bast?" At the sound of my voice, his head swiveled to me, and a slow smile overtook his features. My eyes narrowed. Something wasn't right. Sebastian had *never* smiled like that. I started backing away, grabbing both Iridia and Nick as I did.

"Blue, what's the matt—?"

Nick cut off as Sebastian rose elegantly to his feet as if he hadn't just been lying unconscious.

"Hello, little one."

Fuck. As we watched, Sebastian's visage rolled down and off, leaving Hades standing in his place. Iridia covered the scream that rose to her lips as she tried dragging me behind her. I stood my ground. I had known it would always come down to this. I didn't know why I had tried so hard to avoid it.

With a flick of his wrist, he pushed Iridia and Nick from the room and locked the outside doors of the theater. They pounded on the glass, trying to get back in. I didn't dare take my eyes off him.

"Where's Sebastian?"

Hades shrugged, unconcerned. "I have no idea. Probably still circling the battlefield like some overgrown buzzard." I felt a bit of relief knowing that Sebastian was still alive. "I knew you would come for him, though. And as he was above what the rune could see, you would never know I wasn't him. He was the perfect cover. Now, it's just the two of us. I've been waiting for this moment for years."

"I won't help you." I reached behind me and drew the katanas.

"You wound me, my dear Blue. You're refusing to help your uncle, the man who practically raised you, who taught you everything you know."

"What you want to do isn't right. Imprisoning and hurting Zeus won't give you back the years taken from you. Or Alexandra." I felt the shot of pain that coursed through Hades' emotions at the mention of her. His face hardened.

"You have no idea the pain of losing someone you love, but you will if you refuse to help me." I watched as he drew a flaming rune in the air, keeping my swords at the ready. It started to circle faster and faster until an image appeared. There, on a field full of blood and ash, stood Keane with his men. They were fighting ferociously, their movements so fluid it looked like they had been choreographed. It seemed nothing could touch them as they sliced through Demon after Demon. But as soon as one exploded into flames, another was there to take its place. I knew they couldn't hold out forever, no matter how strong they were. "One flick of my wrist, and I can send hundreds of thousands of Demons at them all at once. Even your precious Vaimpír Prince couldn't handle that."

I sucked in a breath but refused to back down. "If you kill him, you kill me."

"Oh? Do you think the bond you share would sever both your lives?" He tilted his head to the side, a smug smile crossing his lips. "How naïve you are. The bond you hold with Keane is not merely some Vaimpír soulbond. Your tether to him is the bond of a god. Killing him would never kill you."

I shook my head in disbelief. "How can you know that?"

"Did you think you were the first to make such a bond?" His laugh was dark. "I had such a bond with my Alexandra. Oh, yes, even a human can be soulbound to a god. Even when I banished her, we were still connected, though I blocked it." I felt the guilt that lanced through him as he thought of Alexandra and their bond. "Perhaps if I had not, I'd have known she was in trouble..." He looked at me again, his eyes glowing. "You *will* help me." I felt panic welling up. Would he really kill Keane to force me to do his bidding? "Tick Tock, little niece."

I searched my mind for any way out, but there was nothing. No matter how I looked at it, it meant either giving myself up or sacrificing those I loved. Not only them but also innocent people—humans and Fae alike. Why was my life worth more than all the others?

We continued to stare each other down as I waged my internal battle until something out of the corner of my eye caught my attention. Something was happening on the field of battle. I narrowed my eyes and watched as two figures systematically made their way through the Demons. One swung a large broadsword, which flashed brightly in the moonlight as it moved. The other threw out spells and cut Demons down with a pair of throwing daggers that returned as soon as they had found their mark. My head swiveled toward the theater entrance in shock. Nick and Iridia were gone.

Crap.

Noting my distraction, Hades looked the same way. "Well, well. It looks like we have ourselves a pair of heroes." He turned to look at the battle just as the pair reached Keane, and I felt the anger and fear filter through our bond. With a roar of rage, something burst from Keane. I felt it blossom in our connection, causing it to burn hot and bright. I sucked in a breath and watched in awe as a wave of power rippled through the throng of Demons.

With looks of shock, the Demons burst into flames, leaving Keane and his men standing in an empty field. Those who had been fighting froze, looking around in surprise while Keane stood in the middle of a burned-out circle, breathing hard, his shirt gone and blue flames licking over his entire body. As he looked up, I saw flames flickering in his eyes.

"It can't be!" Hades roared as he grabbed me by the arm. Before I even had a chance to react, we disappeared, only to reappear on the battlefield. The abruptness of the move left me feeling sick and disoriented, and I fell to my knees on the ground, trying not to puke up my guts.

When I finally got my stomach under control, I looked up to find Hades a few feet away, standing toe-to-toe with Keane, their eyes boring into each other. All our forces were standing in a loose circle around us, weapons at the ready should they be needed. I shakily got to my feet.

Though I knew Keane was aware of my presence, he didn't look away from Hades. Hades, however, glanced over at me and smiled, his grin dripping with malice before he turned back to Keane. "I should kill you where you stand, Vaimpír. It appears you're the only thing standing in the way of what I want."

"You and I both know you can't."

Hades laughed lowly. "Are you so sure?"

Keane smirked. "Had you asked me that a day ago, I would've said no. However, now that we both know whose blood runs in my veins, yes, I'm sure."

The grin slipped from Hades' face, and he growled. "Fucking Asmodeus."

"You called?" I jumped as a familiar English-accented voice spoke from beside me. Turning my head, I gaped at Sebastian, who now stood casually next to me. His hair and wings were black, and his eyes were glowing red. Unlike his usual casual appearance, he now sported a three-piece black suit, and his whole demeanor was more...proper.

"Bast?" My voice came out as a whisper of disbelief. He turned his head toward me and winked before stepping forward, putting himself between Hades and me.

"Hades, my old friend. How have you been?"

Hades turned furious eyes toward him. "What is the meaning of this, Asmodeus?"

Bast grinned at him. "Whatever do you mean?"

Hades stepped forward, getting into Sebastian's face and baring his teeth. "How dare you create a child without my permission?"

Bast smiled patiently. "We all have our little secrets now, don't we, Hades?" He glanced toward Keane. "Though my grandson should hardly be a surprise. I am one of the seven Princes of Hell, after all—the Prince of Lust, to be exact." Hades growled in response. "Oh, do simmer down, Hades. I'm sure we can come to an understanding. It seems to me that you're in desperate need of something to enact your revenge on a certain lightning god, am I right?" When Hades only continued to glare at him, Bast gave a long-suffering sigh. "What if I were to tell you I hold a vital piece of information that could change everything?"

Hades backed up a step, his expression going from angry to wary. "And what could you possibly know that would change things?"

Bast grinned cheekily. "Ah, well, I don't want to toot my own horn, so to speak, but you do know that I'm a great purveyor of secrets. I know things about humans and gods alike that would shake the very foundation of this world."

"Asmodeus..." I could tell Hades' already short patience was running out.

"Right, of course. But first, a deal. If I give you this information, you'll agree to leave my descendants..."—he gestured toward Keane—"to their own devices. And that includes their affiliated family, as well as... Blue."

Hades' eyebrows drew together. "How do I know your information is worth that much?"

"Oh, trust me. It is." When Hades continued to stare at him, he sighed. "Is one's word worth so little these days?"

"You're a Prince of Hell." Hades' tone was flat.

"That doesn't mean I don't have honor." Bast rolled his eyes. "Fine. If what I have isn't as worthwhile as I say it is, then while you'll still leave my family alone, you may take the girl. I'll make sure no one stops you."

"Like hell he will." Keane's voice was a deep growl, as he took a step toward me. Bast held up his hand to stop him, his eyes begging Keane to trust him. Keane let out a frustrated huff but stepped back with a nod.

Bast turned back to Hades. "Do you agree?"

"Done."

"Excellent! Now, first, I need to call in a favor." Reaching into his vest pocket, he produced a large golden coin. But not just any coin. I recognized it from one of the texts I had studied while preparing for the Trials. It was a coin the gods gave as an IOU of sorts, a rarity in their world. Hades' eyes widened when he saw it. Bast just grinned and rubbed the coin. "Oh, Hera! It's time for you to repay your debt."

With a shimmer of light, the goddess stood before us. She looked around with interest, her eyes landing on me before turning to Bast. "Asmo, what can I do for you?"

"My darling Hera, so good to see you again. I have need of your services for this contract."

She raised her brows but then leaned in when he indicated for her to come closer. While he whispered in her ear, her eyes traveled from Keane to me to Hades, and then she nodded.

"Very good."

"Enough with the theatrics, Asmodeus! Tell me what you know."

A smug smile settled onto his face. "Alexandra is alive."

Chapter Twenty-Four

Hades' face registered shock before disbelief and anger once more poured over his features. "Liar."

Bast retained his superior smirk. "I figured you would say that. Which is where Hera comes in."

"Like I'd believe a word she says. She's Zeus's wife. She would lie to our own mother for him."

"Obviously." Hera gave Bast a disgruntled look, but he just waved her away. "You know it's true, dear Hera. There's no use denying it." He turned back to Hades. "However, her word is not the reason I brought her here. Hera?"

Hera stepped forward with a sigh. "If I must." Raising her hands, she closed her eyes and seemed to draw on her power. A streak of lightning flashed across the sky, followed by a low rumble of thunder. The air around her shimmered until a figure slowly began to appear.

The person who emerged rounded on Hera in anger. "What is the meaning of this?" She tried to step forward but looked to be stopped by an invisible wall. "Hera!"

"Hello, Demeter."

"How dare you take me from my gardens?"

"I do apologize, but I knew if I simply asked, you would have refused."

Demeter looked around at the gathered assemblage. "What is going on here?"

"It's time, Demeter."

Demeter's eyes narrowed on Hera. "Time for what?"

"To tell Hades the truth."

Demeter swung around to face her brother, fear slowly overtaking her features. "No... No! I refuse." Hades watched her in confusion.

"Demeter. You made me a promise. When the time was right, you would reveal her to Hades. That was the only reason I helped you."

Demeter shook her head sharply. "I don't want to. She's mine. I won't give her to him."

"Demeter. You know that's not true."

Hades stepped toward Demeter. "What is going on, sister? What have you been hiding from me?"

She sealed her lips and shook her head, causing Hera to sigh. "Demeter. Don't make me do this the hard way." When Demeter still refused, Hera tsked and raised her hands again.

Demeter fell to her knees, grabbing her head while moaning. "No... No..." Her moans soon turned to screams. We all watched, shifting uncomfortably at the scene before us. Finally, Demeter fell to the ground, panting as Hera lowered her hands.

"You do know I could just take her, Demeter. I figured you would still have a chance to be a part of her life this way."

Demeter lay there quietly and sobbed. "Fine. I'll tell him." She raised her tear-filled eyes to Hades. "Remember when I told you I had an affinity for Alexandra?" Hades nodded, looking suspicious. "I found out quite by chance that a jealous lover of yours was planning to kill her. I tried to get there first to save her, but I was too late. She had been stabbed, and her life was ebbing fast. There was nothing I could do. Just before her death, I...I called Hera and asked her to help me transform Alexandra into a goddess."

Hades stepped back as if he had been punched in the gut. As fantastical as it sounded, she was not the first person I'd heard of being transformed by the gods after their death. Sebastian—well, I guess his name was actually Asmodeus—had once told me about a Princess who was transformed into a Nereid upon her death.

Hades' eyes went from Demeter to Hera. "Is it true? Is my Alexandra alive?" His voice was barely above a whisper.

Hera's eyes shuttered, and she gave a soft warning to Hades. "Yes, and no. She's alive, but she's no longer the Alexandra you remember. Nor does she remember you."

"Why?"

"The transformation from human to goddess isn't an easy one. It's much less stressful to suppress their human memories until they can integrate into our world."

My mind suddenly took me back to Hera's garden and the statue she was sitting behind. That was why Hera had an effigy of Alexandra in her garden. It all made so much more sense now.

"Why have I never seen her?"

Hera looked toward Demeter. "Demeter has taken her on as her daughter, the Goddess of Spring. She has been kept sequestered at Demeter's estates."

Demeter finally spoke up, though she refused to look at anyone. "Her name is now Persephone."

Bast chuckled. "Like in all the myths the humans created so long ago."

Demeter nodded. "I...I thought it fitting since she was already considered my daughter in all those stories."

Hades strode forward, stopping just where the shield that held Demeter started. "I want to see her. Bring her to me."

"Hades, please. She doesn't know who you are. She has a whole new life now. She's happy. Why can't you just leave her alone? You cast her away before."

Hades' face contorted, his voice rising in anger. "Because my brother lied and manipulated me. Not because I didn't want her. You of all people know that. I love her." He turned to Hera. "Can you restore her memories?"

Demeter cried out in distress, but Hera just ignored her. "I can. Though she may not respond well to remembering her human life, considering some of the hardships she endured. She may even hate you."

Hades nodded in resignation. "I'll take that chance. To have my Alexandra back, even if she hates me." He looked toward Bast. "Our bargain is complete. I'll leave your grandson, his family..." He looked toward me a bit sadly. "And even my niece to their own devices from now on."

"Excellent!" Bast turned toward me, where I stood with my hands on my hips. "Ah, well, I should probably be going..."

"Bast..."

"Lots to do, you know..."

As he started to disappear, I grabbed his arm. I was shocked when he solidified again. He looked down at my hand in surprise, as well. "Fascinating."

"That actually worked?" I shook off my astonishment and looked at him through narrowed eyes. "You wanna explain why you've been hiding who you were this whole time?"

"Umm, not really."

"Bast." I faltered for a second. "I mean, Asmodeus."

He smiled crookedly. "Bast works. I rather like it." Then, his smile slipped a little. "I'm sorry for deceiving you, but it was necessary. That part of Keane had yet to awaken, and I couldn't intervene."

"So, Keane really is part Demon?"

Bast nodded and looked toward where Keane was talking to his father and the other Vaimpír. "Yes. His mother is my daughter, though she'll never admit it. Her mother was the most beautiful Vaimpír I had ever seen, and I was immediately smitten. Unfortunately, she didn't survive Camille's birth, and though I tried, I just wasn't what Camille needed. I knew the Cargills had been trying to have a child but were unsuccessful. Since Camille favored her mother and was mostly Vaimpír, I knew they would be able to pass her off as theirs. It couldn't have worked out any better."

"Did they ever tell her who her parents were?"

"I went to her when she came of age and told her everything, but she didn't want to have anything to do with me." He shrugged offhandedly. "I can't blame her. But I wanted her to know what she was getting into if she decided to have children."

"Is that why she ended up with twins, and Rhys has his disability?"

Bast nodded. "While the twins appear mostly Vaimpír, I have a feeling their Demon sides are much more prevalent than they let on."

"They are a bit...odd."

"It seems they inherited my ability to see the future. I have a feeling they'll be seeking me out soon."

"Is there any way to heal Rhys?"

"I was a bit hopeful that the Demon side would help with that as he got older, but only time will tell in that regard."

I deflated a bit in disappointment, causing Bast to chuckle.

"I'll look into it further since you seem so interested."

I smiled widely at him.

Keane walked up and wrapped his arms around me from behind. He leaned down, kissed my cheek, and murmured in my ear. "I thought I told you to stay hidden."

"And I told you that if something happened, I wouldn't stay back."

He laughed and nodded to Bast. "Grandfather."

"I'm curious. How long have you known I was your grandfather?"

"Until today, it was merely a guess. The twins sparked my curiosity as they were so rare among the Vaimpír. However, it has been proven time and time again that twins are often the result of a union between a Vaimpír and a Demon."

"And what led you to me?"

"In my research, I came across an anomaly. It was in an older text describing several accounts where you had a child with you. While nothing said it was *your* child, I began to wonder. Why would the Prince of Lust be toting around a small child if it wasn't his? I couldn't find any more accounts after a few years, which made me curious. I began looking through the Vaimpír histories. Just about the time the child disappeared from your accounts, one appeared in those of Jasper and Lucy Cargill's—who, until that point, had been considered barren. It wasn't too much of a stretch to put the two together."

"Very clever. I thought I had all records of Camille's existence before she was five removed from the histories."

"I do have a question for you, though. Why did my Demon side wait until now to awaken?"

"That question is a bit complicated to answer." He pondered for a moment. "It's been found over the centuries with unions between Demons and Vaimpír, that the first child is basically a pure-blood Vaimpír. Very little of the Demon side is carried over. They don't know why. It's only as more children come along that the Demon side becomes more prevalent.

"With you, however—probably because of who I am—my powers transferred to you, though they lay dormant. It took Blue's unique magic to awaken them. The reason they didn't awaken right away was that you weren't allowing her magic to flow through every part of you. Once you accepted that you loved her, there were no more blocks. You opened every part of yourself to her."

"So, you're saying I now have the powers of one of the Princes of Hell?"

Bast chuckled. "Actually...yes. You'll find that your normal Vaimpír powers are increased exponentially, and you will have a few new ones. Like your command of hellfire. I hoped..." He cleared his throat, looking a bit unsure of himself. "I hoped you would allow me to be a part of your life so I could teach you."

Keane considered it for only a few seconds before he nodded. "I would be honored."

Bast's face brightened before he glanced at Hades. "Brilliant! Now. Not that I don't want to stick around and chat, but I think it best if I make myself scarce for the time being. I'll be along to see you again once you've completed your business here." He looked down at my hand still on his arm. "If you would?"

I started in surprise and looked back at my hand, not realizing I was still holding him. "Oh! Sorry." As soon as I let go, he winked and disappeared.

Taking Keane's hand, I moved closer to where Hades was talking with Hera. Demeter still sat on the ground looking dejected, though it didn't appear that Hera was holding her prisoner anymore. I looked around and only then realized that all the soldiers from the Fae and Vaimpír armies were gone.

Reading my thoughts, Keane looked down at me. "I sent them back to the theater. I didn't think they needed to witness what comes next."

I smiled softly. "Thank you." He lifted my hand and placed a kiss on the back of it before we both turned to the gods arguing before us.

"I want you to bring her to the Underworld."

Hera shook her head at Hades. "That would be much too traumatic."

Hades grumbled. "I don't want to do it here on Fae territory, but I don't want it to be somewhere Demeter has control, either."

Demeter glared at him, but Hera just looked thoughtful. "We need somewhere that's neutral ground."

"Why not your garden, Hera?" Hera turned to me with a smile. "It's somewhere that neither Hades nor Demeter control, and if Persephone is the Goddess of Spring, the flowers would make her feel at home."

"A perfect solution." Hera looked at Hades and then Demeter. "Do you agree?" When they both nodded, she raised her hands, and we found ourselves standing in the middle of Hera's garden.

I was surprised she had brought Keane and me along. Hera turned and took my arm, leading me away from the others and keeping her voice low. "I'm going to need your help with this, Blue."

"My help? What can I possibly do?"

"Once I've broken the enchantment holding Persephone's memories, I want you to freeze time, leaving only the three of us out. Can you do that?"

"Sure. But why?"

"Once I give Persephone her memories back, I want to give her the chance to decide for herself if she wants to keep them without Hades' or Demeter's interference." I nodded solemnly, immediately understanding as she continued. "Can you also talk to your love? Ask him if he would he be willing to step in to help control Hades if Persephone decides not to keep her memories and things go downhill. I believe with his grandfather's abilities and his connection to you, he now has the power to do so."

I chuckled as he answered in my head. "He says you can count on him to do whatever is necessary."

Hera appeared a bit surprised but then laughed softly while shaking her head. "I'd forgotten how closely you two are connected. Okay, are we ready?" At my nod, we walked back to where Hades and Demeter were stuck in a glaring contest. "Demeter, Hades, stop that." Hera's voice snapped their attention to her. "Demeter, are you ready? Please contact Persephone and bring her here."

Demeter seemed as though she were about to argue, but with a warning glare from Hera, she huffed out a breath and closed her eyes. Her eyelids seemed to flutter before Persephone—aka Alexandra—appeared with a shimmer of light. Upon seeing the people standing around her mother, Persephone quickly moved behind Demeter. "It's all right, my darling. There is no need to be afraid." Taking her hand, she pulled Persephone from behind her.

Hades started to step forward, his eyes bright with tears, but Hera put a staying hand on his chest. "Patience, brother."

Demeter laid a hand on Persephone's shoulder as she pointed toward us. "Persephone, there are some people I want you to meet. These are my friends, Blue and Keane." Persephone lowered her head and gave us a small hello. "And I'm sure you remember my sister, Hera."

Hera stepped forward and took one of Persephone's hands in hers. "It's good to see you again." Persephone smiled shyly up at her.

"And this is my brother, Hades." Demeter's voice shook a bit as she introduced him.

Persephone's eyes widened as she took in Hades standing off to the side. He slowly took a step forward as if approaching a skittish animal. Reaching out, he took one of her hands and brought it to his lips. "It's an honor to finally meet you, Alex—" He cleared his throat. "Persephone."

A blush suffused her cheeks while her hand trembled a bit in his. Tilting her head to the side, she regarded him from beneath her long lashes. I thought there was a flash of recognition, but then it was gone. The look of hope on Hades' face slipped to one of disappointment before he cleared his expression and stepped back, turning to Hera expectantly.

Demeter turned toward Persephone, putting her hands on her cheeks. "I want you to know that I love you. You're the daughter I always wanted. The time we have spent together has been the best of my life."

"Mother?" Persephone looked at Demeter in confusion.

With a wave of Hera's hand, Persephone's eyes closed, and she slumped in Demeter's arms. Tears streamed down Demeter's face as she laid her daughter on the ground. Hera signaled for Hades and Demeter to step back before she knelt at Persephone's head. Much like with the *memoria revelare* that had been done on me, she held her hands over Persephone, her fingers spread, and started to chant. I idly wondered if I'd had Hera do this for me if it would've gone better because, in no time at all, Persephone was waking up, her eyes blinking slowly.

As Hades and Demeter dove toward her, I froze time, leaving only the three of us out of the loop.

"Wha...what's going on?"

Hera helped Persephone to a sitting position. "Welcome back."

Persephone shook her head before looking down at her hands, flipping them over, front to back. "How...?"

"Give it a moment. It will take a minute or two for your memories to return."

As she was sitting there processing, she looked around, her gaze landing on me, then Keane frozen next to me, then Demeter, and finally Hades.

"Hades..." Her hand went to her mouth, and tears formed in her eyes. "Is that...is that my Hades?"

Hera helped Persephone to her feet. "Yes, my child. The time has finally come for you to remember everything and make a few choices."

Persephone walked over to Hades, her eyes taking in every feature. Hesitantly, she lifted her fingers to his face, tracing where her eyes had just gone. "How is he frozen like this?"

Hera nodded toward me. "Blue is helping me with that. She's Poseidon's daughter. One of her unique abilities is to freeze time. We wanted to give you a chance to process all your returned memories and make a few choices before they have a chance to influence you." Hera indicated both Hades and Demeter.

Persephone stepped back from both the god and goddess and carefully sat on a nearby stone bench. "Choices? What choices?"

"Do you remember what happened to you? What went on between you and Hades, then what happened in the mortal realm?"

"Yes." Persephone's voice held what had to be remembered pain. "Zeus tricked Hades into thinking I had slept with him, and Hades banished me to the human world without letting me explain. I always thought he would come to his senses and come back for me...but he never did." Her eyes went distant as she recounted the memory.

"Zeus, however, pestered me day and night. He became so obsessed that his other lovers got jealous of his attention on me—even if it wasn't wanted. One night, a Nymph named Minthe came to my house. I thought she was another of Zeus's jealous lovers, but it turned out that she was obsessed with Hades. I didn't know it, but Hades had refused to take another lover after me. Minthe thought he would finally take her to bed if she killed me." Tears leaked from Persephone's eyes.

"All I could think about was that Hades didn't want anyone but me, and how I had to get back to him somehow. In the scuffle, Minthe stabbed me and left me for dead. That's when Demeter appeared and saved me." She choked back a few sobs, trying to gain control of her emotions.

Hera laid a hand on Persephone's shoulder. "I want to give you a choice, my child. You can keep your memories, or I can erase them permanently. I know you've been happy in your new life with Demeter, and it can remain that way—none of your tarnished past to remember, none of the pain Hades inflicted on you, and no memory of your human death. Or you can choose to embrace your past and all you were and are now."

Persephone looked at Hera wide-eyed. "I...I can choose?" She looked over to where Hades stood frozen.

Hera nodded. "If you decide you don't want to keep your memories, we'll deal with Hades if he puts up a fuss. You don't have to worry about your choice other than it being what you want."

Persephone nodded and looked back down at her hands. "While I've enjoyed my life with Demeter very much, I've always felt like something was missing." She peeked again at Hades. "And now I know why. I think...I think I want to keep my memories."

Hera smiled in understanding. "Very well. Let us know when you're ready, and we'll release them."

Persephone took a deep breath. Standing, she turned to face Hades and Demeter. "Okay. I'm ready."

I turned and first placed my hand on Keane. He smiled when he saw Persephone ready to face off with Hades. "I see we've made our decision. If you need my assistance, my lady, you have only to ask." He bowed slightly in her direction. She smiled nervously and nodded.

"Here we go." With a thought, I brought time back into motion.

Hades stumbled forward, catching himself before he fell. Demeter wasn't so lucky and crashed to the ground. Hades' eyes went straight to me in accusation. "Did you just...?"

"Yes. Get over it." I crossed my arms and glared at him, causing Persephone to giggle. His eyes immediately moved to her, softening as they did.

He took a step forward, but Keane let out a low growl. Hades threw him an annoyed look before turning back to Persephone. "Alex—Persephone."

"Hades."

"Do you...do you remember me?"

She nodded softly.

Without warning, Hades dropped to his knees at her feet, bowing his head. "Can you ever forgive me for what I did? I was wrong to not listen to you. You tried to tell me, but in my rage, I refused to hear you. A day hasn't gone by that I don't regret it."

"Why didn't you ever come to get me then?"

He huffed out an ashamed breath. "Pride. Stupidity. Self-torture. You deserve someone better and a better life than I can give you in the Underworld. You love flowers, you love to grow things, you deserve to be in the sun, where you and your plants can flourish."

"Oh, Hades…"

"When I finally came to my senses, it was too late. You were gone." When Persephone didn't respond, Hades reached into the inside pocket of his jacket. "I saved this. I always carry it with me." As he opened his hand. Persephone gasped, her fingers going to her mouth. For on his open palm lay the gold bracelet that had been her mother's.

"Ha…Hades…" She reached out a shaking hand and took the bracelet, turning it over in her fingers. "You saved this?"

He nodded, his head bowing again. "I knew what it meant to you, so I've kept it close to my heart since the day I found…since the day you…" He couldn't seem to bring himself to say it.

Without another word, Persephone threw herself into his arms. Taken by surprise, he almost fell back but managed to maintain his balance and hold on to her at the same time.

"I love you, Hades. I always have and always will. Even when I didn't have my memories, I knew something was missing. And that something was you."

"I love you, too." Hades' voice was choked up as he brought her face to his. "I've never stopped loving you." He leaned down and kissed her deeply.

I smiled and grabbed Keane's arm, pulling him back. Persephone didn't need our help any longer. "I think that's our cue to leave." I turned and started walking toward Hera. Just as I was about to ask her to send us back, a hand landed on my shoulder. I looked up in surprise to find Hades' glowing amber eyes staring into mine. A quick glance over my shoulder found Persephone having a quiet, animated conversation with Demeter.

"Blue. I want to apologize for everything I've done. I know an apology seems highly inadequate considering all I've put you through, and you'll probably never forgive me, but—"

I held up a hand to stop him. "I know what it means to love someone so much that you would do practically anything for them—in life or death." I glanced over at Keane. "And while I'm not ready to hug it out or anything right now, you did threaten to kill the man I love, after all. Maybe someday in the future we can try to rebuild our relationship."

"I would like that." Giving me a small smile, he moved back to Persephone's side, wrapping an arm around her.

I turned to Hera. "For now, I think it's time for us to go back to the Fernsong Clan. I'm sure they're worried."

Hera smiled and opened her arms to me. As I gave her a hug, she whispered in my ear. "You will always have a place here with me should you need it."

Chapter Twenty-Five

In the weeks following everything with Hades, Keane and I stayed at the Fernsong Clan to clean things up and help Iridia get settled while Tristan and the rest went back to Dock Street. By the end of the third week, though, I'd had enough of family bonding and was more than ready to get back to my life.

Deciding it was time, I went in search of Keane. I found him lounging on our bed reading a book, and smiled at the picture he made. "What are you reading?"

Keane looked up at me before glancing at the cover of the book in his hands. "I'm not sure, to tell you the truth. It was sitting on the nightstand. Something called *Night Flower*. It's actually pretty good, though the author's ideas about vampires are quite laughable."

I chuckled and crawled up onto the bed, laying my head on his stomach. His hand immediately started caressing my hair, causing me to sigh in contentment. "Keane?"

"Hmm?"

"As much as I love spending time with my mom and Brokk, do you think we can go home?"

He set the book down with a dramatic flourish. "Thank the gods. I thought you would never ask. We can leave right now if you're ready."

I pinched his side before leaning up to kiss his lips. "Smart-ass. Come on, let's go find everyone and say our goodbyes."

After a few heartfelt entreaties to get us to stay, which we respectfully declined, it was time for us to head out. Thankfully, since we were no longer limited when it came to portaling, we could skip the ten-hour drive and just jump back to Dock Street.

No sooner had we stepped through the portal than Mckile approached Keane. I waved off his apology for stealing Keane away and went to our bedchamber. As I stepped through the door, I came up short. Sitting on the end of the bed was a hellhound.

"Scythe? What are you doing here?" I ran into the room, dropped my bags, and wrapped my arms around his large head, hugging him to me.

"It's good to see you, too, Mistress. I've brought you several gifts from Hades."

"Gifts?" I pulled back as he nodded his head toward the dresser. On it sat my statue, the one with the piece of my soul that Hades had stolen. "My statue!"

"He said it belongs with its true owner, as does his other gift."

I looked around but didn't see anything else. "What other gift?"

"Me."

My eyes widened as I sat back. "You? He has...he gave you to me?"

"I'm no longer bonded to Hades. I'm once again and forevermore your protector."

"Oh, Scythe!" I threw my arms around him again, even happier than before.

"I take it that means we have a dog now. I hope you know how to use glamour, hellhound. Otherwise, it's going to be interesting trying to explain a giant, scaly dog with glowing red eyes that breathes fire to the people at the dog park." I turned to find Keane leaning casually against the doorframe and grinned at him. "What do hellhounds eat anyway?"

Scythe chuffed out a doggie laugh while shaking his head. "*I can take care of myself, Vaimpír, don't you worry about it.*"

Keane grinned, then turned to me. "I need you to come with me. I have something to show you." He held out his hand.

I looked at him curiously, sensing something beneath his tone. "What is it?"

"It's better if I show you."

I stood, and Scythe got up and followed. Keane glanced down at him. "I take it I'm going to have to get used to your protector coming everywhere with you from now on, aren't I?" After I nodded, he sighed. "I guess we could always get him one of those service-dog jackets. You know the ones that say *Do Not Pet?*" I laughed and shook my head. "Hey, don't laugh. You know it only encourages me."

After moving into the elevator, Keane entered the passcode, and we started down. I raised an eyebrow at him, but he just shrugged while leaning casually against the wall, his arms and ankles crossed as always. When the doors opened, we were once again in Dock Street's lower-level dungeon. Wyn stood guard, just as before.

"Hey, Wyn. How's it going?" His face lit up with a smile before he saw the hellhound at my side and did a double-take—his eyes widening slightly. I patted Scythe on the head. "Don't worry, he's harmless. Well, mostly."

"Umm, sure. Okay." I held in a giggle as he backed up a few more steps. "You guys have already been cleared to go through. Just knock on the door when you're ready to leave."

"Got it. Thanks, Wyn." He watched the hellhound cautiously until he was out of sight, and the door shut behind us.

"On a first-name basis with the guards down here already?"

"Jealous?"

"Not yet."

I smiled mischievously, hoping Jackson was still the next guard. Sure enough, as we rounded the corner, I saw Jackson's unmistakable bulky outline at the end of the hall.

"Jackson, my man. Need to pat us down before we head in?"

His head snapped up at the sound of my voice, and I watched as he swallowed loudly while looking at Keane. "Umm, no. We're good today."

Keane raised his brow at me, but I just smiled. Jackson scrambled to open the door behind him and stepped out of the way so we could pass. As Keane was going by, Jackson kept his head down. He was so focused on not looking Keane's way that he ran right into the hellhound. He yelped in surprise as he took in the massive creature.

"What in the world is that?"

I snickered. "This is Scythe, my hellhound."

"Your hell...hellhound?" His jaw hung open as he looked between Scythe and me.

"Is there a problem?"

Jackson snapped to attention and looked at Keane. "No, sir. Of course, not." With that, he went back through the door, sealing it behind him.

Keane looked over at me. "You gonna tell me what that was all about?"

I just grinned. "Not yet."

Keane scowled but led me down the length of cells. Cedric met us about halfway. "His cell has had the proper modifications made. We should be all set now."

"Whose cell?"

I looked between the two of them but neither answered me. Instead, they led me over to a cell that was a few down from Celeste's. It had already been opened, and there, sitting on the bed was someone I hadn't expected to see again.

"Larkin?" He looked up at his name, his expression going weary as soon as he saw me. He looked a lot worse for wear, at least since the last time I had seen him. He had lost weight, his skin practically hung from his bones, and scars were visible on multiple parts of his body—including a nasty slash across one of his eyes. I wasn't sure what had been done to him while the gods had him, but whatever it was had evidently been bad.

I glanced over at Keane. "What's he doing here? And how did he get here, for that matter?"

"He just showed up." I turned an incredulous gaze on Cedric. "I was making my rounds, and when I came back down to check on Celeste, there he sat, already in the cell."

I refocused on Keane, raising my brows, but he just smiled. "Cedric, can you give us a moment alone?"

"Oh, sure thing."

I watched Cedric until he went into the apartment across from Celeste's cell before I turned back to Keane, giving him my best, you'd-better-tell-me-what-the-hell-is-going-on-here stare.

Keane chuckled and moved in closer. "Bast dropped him off early this morning."

"What? Why?"

"I talked to him about your issues with Larkin's powers, and he agreed that you needed to return them to him before they corrupt you. Plus, it's about time Larkin answered for all he's done to the Fae."

"Is it really a good idea for me to give him back his powers, though?"

Keane nodded his head toward the cell. "Everything has been prepped. He won't be able to use his charm talent, and even if he manages to shift, he won't be able to escape. You and I both know it's in your best interests."

I nodded slowly, knowing he was right. "Okay." I hoped I could do this. I'd worked with Keane a few times over the past few weeks on how to take and transfer powers, but it was still touch and go at this point. Reaching into my core, I was surprised to find that I could still feel my magic, unlike the last time I had been down here. Keane must have made sure I had permission to use it.

I quickly sorted out the magic I knew was Larkin's. I was sure it wasn't everything, as my body seemed to have absorbed some of it, but at least his charm talent and his Wolf could be transferred back. As I prepared myself for what I had to do, I felt a nudge on my consciousness. It was Gareth, Larkin's Wolf.

"Well, lass, I guess this is goodbye."

"So it would seem."

"You know, I never thought I'd say this, but I think I'm going to miss hanging out with you."

I laughed softly. *"I'm going to miss you, too. While the shifting part sucked ass, running as a Wolf was a once-in-a-lifetime experience."*

Gareth seemed to look out through my eyes at Larkin. *"Can't say I'm excited to see that louse again, but it's what the moon goddess wants, so who am I to question it? Don't you worry too much about him from now on, though. I'll make sure to keep him in check."*

"I'd appreciate it. And who knows? Maybe I'll take you along for the ride again sometime."

Gareth chuckled. *"I look forward to it."*

With that, Gareth slipped back, and I watched as Keane disabled the cell and opened the door. Scythe went in first and corralled Larkin into a corner.

"What are you doing? And what the hell is that?" He was practically balled up in the corner of his bed, holding his pillow out between Scythe and him as if it would protect him.

"Hello, Larkin. Been enjoying your time with the gods?"

He glanced fearfully at me. "Why am I here?"

"It seems the gods have decided it's time for you to finally answer for your sins here as well as there."

"The Elders are going to find out about you. I'll tell them. You'll no longer have any secrets." His threat fell flat as his voice trembled.

"Oh, don't be too sure about that." I smiled a bit maliciously, not letting him see my nervousness. Keane stepped forward and took Larkin by the arms, holding him still. He tried to struggle, but Scythe growled, and he froze in place.

Like before, I allowed my hand to go incorporeal and turned it over, looking at it. I heard Larkin whimper but ignored him. Reaching forward, I pushed my hand into Larkin's chest. He froze, his eyes going wide, his breath sticking in his throat. I quickly found his empty core, which would have contained his magic if he still had any. Very carefully, I allowed the power I had collected from him to flow back. As Gareth passed over, I thought I felt a caress along my body and smiled. Finally, I pulled my hand from his chest. He gasped in a breath, his body shaking. When he recovered some, his eyes flew to mine in surprise.

"It's back." Keane let go of him, and he started to pat himself. "I can feel it. It's back!" He moved toward me, but both Scythe and Keane growled, and he stopped, dropping to his knees in front of me instead. "Thank you. Thank you so much."

"I didn't do this for you. You hardly deserve it. And know that if I ever find out you're mistreating Gareth, I'll gladly take him away from you for good."

Larkin nodded solemnly, practically sobbing at my feet. "I'll never take it for granted again."

I stepped away in disgust and left the cell. Keane reset all the security and closed the window.

"How do you feel, *ma moitié?*"

"Strangely like I'm missing something."

Keane wrapped an arm around my shoulders. "I guess that's to be expected now that another spirit isn't residing within you."

A sudden racket behind the main door to the cells, drew our attention. A lot of thumping and cursing came from the other side before the door was flung open, banging hard against the wall. Keane quickly thrust me behind him protectively. I watched cautiously from around him as Jackson dragged a scruffy-looking man through the door.

He was putting up quite a fight, giving Jackson—who was no small guy—a run for his money. Cedric came running out of his room at the commotion and it took he and Jackson working together to finally subdue him. Keane moved and opened one of the cells, and they thrust the man through the door, quickly shutting it behind him.

"You all right, Jackson?" Keane looked him over, noting the scratches and blood running from his arms and face.

"I'll survive." He spit a bit of blood on the floor while rubbing his jaw. "Just give me a minute to wash up and I'll be back on duty." I watched as he limped out the door before turning back to the man in the cell, who was slowly getting to his feet. As he turned to face us, I sucked in a breath.

"Hello, poppet." Leaning against the back wall of the cell for support, his face a riot of bruises and cuts, was none other than Fiorian, Larkin's former bounty hunter.

Keane crossed his arms over his chest and moved closer to me. "Well, well, well. Look what the cat dragged in. We've been wondering where you managed to sneak off to."

Fiorian just smirked at Keane. "Aw, did you miss me?"

"You and I have a small score to settle. You managed to slip your guards before I could visit you last time."

"Yes, well, things to do, money to make and all that. Being locked up in a cell wasn't really in my plans."

I scoffed. "No loyalty among thieves, huh? What about all your fellow conspirators? What about Larkin?"

Fiorian turned his attention to me and shrugged. "I'm just a hired gun, sweetheart. A delivery boy, remember? I work with whoever is the highest bidder."

"And who did you get paid to kidnap this time?"

"Who said I kidnapped anyone?" I gave him a deadpan look causing him to grin. "Perhaps I just missed you, poppet." His expression turned calculating as I snorted. "Or perhaps, I just haven't picked up the package yet..."

My eyes narrowed. "Does this have anything to do with, Larkin?"

"Larkin?" Fiorian's brows shot up in genuine surprise. "Last I heard, he was tied up somewhere with the gods."

I bit my lip to keep from saying anything else but as usual my face seemed to say it for me.

"Well, now, that *is* interesting. Perhaps the rumors in the shifter community are true." He chuckled to himself. "Wouldn't be surprised if this started an all-out war."

Keane gave him an unimpressed look. "I don't suppose you would be willing to let us in on some of those rumors."

Fiorian just pushed off the wall and went over to the narrow bed. He flopped down on it and placed his hands behind his head while closing his eyes as if dismissing us. Cedric, who had finished setting up the security on the cell, pressed the button to close it. Just as the door was sliding shut, Fiorian called out. "Any time you're ready, Rutherman, just come see me. I think I'll hang around for a bit. It seems as though things are about to get *very* interesting around here." As the door clamped shut, we heard the start of his soft snores.

I stared at the closed cell door. There was no way it was a coincidence that Larkin and then Fiorian had shown up on our doorstep on the same day, within hours of each other. I looked toward Keane with a grimace. "I guess this means we're hanging around Dock Street for a while longer, huh?"

"Looks like it."

I sighed before pushing the troubling thoughts aside. There was nothing we could do about it right now, after all. I slyly glanced at Keane, who watched me in amusement. "What do you say we sneak off to your place for a little midnight swim while we can? No suits."

A slow grin spread over his face before he scooped me into his arms, causing me to giggle. With little effort, he did what should've been impossible down here in the dungeons—he opened a portal. "Now, how can a man resist a request like that?"

Want to know what happens next?
Be on the lookout for Book 3 in the Blue Series...

Ethereal Mutation Productions, LLC

Acknowledgments

Who knew the writing and publishing process would have so many cogs and wheels? When we started this journey with Carolina Blue, we had no idea what we were getting into. Here we are with book two...and we still have no idea. Okay, so maybe a little bit of an idea, ha-ha. But I can tell you, no two books follow the same path. We've faced new challenges, along with new opportunities this time around and, honestly, it's been a grand adventure. One we can't wait to take again with you as we dive deeper into the world of the Fae with Blue, Keane, Tristan, and all the other characters you've come to love.

As before, the first—and most important—person I need to acknowledge is my husband, Derek. He was with me through every little step in creating Blue Blood, from the brainstorming to the final sentence. I would write a chapter and then record it. He would listen and then ask his questions, give his critiques, and offer his suggestions. It was a give-and-take the entire time. Even when I would get stuck, I would try to explain to him where my brain was and he would do his best to give me ideas. He even wrote a version of the scene in Chapter

Nine after Blue went, as he calls it, *Super Fairy,* to help me with my writer's block. He laughingly tells people, "Yeah, and of the entire page I gave her, she used *one* sentence." Now don't let him fool you, most of that scene was *loosely* based on his ideas, ha-ha. What was the sentence you ask? When Keane says, "*Much...and now your wings?* " One of the most notable moments we had during the whole process though was when we got to the final chapter and he finally got the nerve to tell me—he didn't like the second half of the book. And you know what? Neither did I. I had been feeling for weeks that it just wasn't right, that I had taken a wrong turn somewhere. So, I took the last thirteen chapters or so, moved them to a new file—I learned to never delete anything because you never know when a line or idea might come in handy—and started over. Yup, the story you read is completely different than the first one I wrote. As one of the T-shirts you will often see me wear says, "Write, Re-Write, Re-Re-Write."

And speaking of Re-Re-Writing, I have to give a huge shout-out to my editor, Chelle Olson. Once again she took a good story and made it great, polishing it with a magic that only she possesses. Her ability to understand where my mind is trying to go, even when I don't articulate it quite right is nothing short of amazing. Add to that, her abundant knowledge of history, fantasy, mythology, and lore just blows me away every time. I'll make a vague reference to something, and she'll know just what it is leaving comments or additions. I couldn't ask for a better editor. Thank you, Chelle! <3

To my Betas, you guys are the best. You couldn't wait to get your hands on book two, and you devoured it faster than I thought possible. Once again, your insights and suggestions were invaluable in making the final edits. And yes, you'll have to wait a bit for book three. Though

I had it written, it was another case of *'something's just not right'*. So, I'm in the process of another re-re-re-write, ha-ha.

To our son, our family and friends, our Golden Oak family, and our work families thank you for all of your love and support. You've been absolutely wonderful. Not only have you helped us with your positive comments and encouragements but you've also taken the time to tell your friends, share our posts to get the word out about our books, and leave reviews on Amazon and Goodreads. All of it was noticed and appreciated.

To my Facebook, TikTok, and Instagram followers thank you for putting up with all my crazy social media posts—especially when the platforms were doing everything they could to keep the posts about my books suppressed. Thank you for helping me spread the word, for your awesome reviews on both Amazon and Goodreads and even just taking the chance to read my books based on our interactions on social media.

And finally, a special shout-out to my girls, Hannah Russamano and Liz Parks. My two best friends, and the most supportive women you could ever find. They both stepped up and have gone above and beyond when it comes to helping me from Hannah listening to the audiobook drafts in the super early stages—Fairy porn!—to Liz helping me with book blurbs and off-the-wall ideas in text after text at all hours of the night. Though I don't get to see or talk to either of you as much as I would like, just know that you are so important to me, not only in my writing but in my everyday life. I love you both!

To My Readers,

Thank You

I hope that someday I'll become the author you tell everyone: if she publishes it, I'm reading it.

About the Author

Heather Bartleson lives in sunny Florida with her husband and son. When not writing, you can be sure to find her on some beach searching for shells or sitting with a good book in hand—especially if it's by the clear waters of the Gulf Coast. A voracious reader since childhood, Heather has consumed everything from the classics to the smuttiest of smut and has loved every bit of it. It's not unheard of for her to polish off several books in a day when the mood strikes. In addition to reading and writing, she also enjoys creating art in all its forms. If you haven't already, make sure to check out her series on social media, "Trying to Visualize Book Expressions while Writing..."

Don't forget to visit her website, *heatherbartleson.com* for updates, book blurbs, book inspiration photos, and more!

SOCIAL MEDIA

www.facebook.com/heatherbartleson_author

Instagram @heatherbartleson_author

TikTok @heatherbartleson_author

www.youtube.com/@heatherbartleson_author